About the authors:

Bradley Marcus Paul is a professional writer who's been published in numerous media formats for over 20 years. He's used a variety of names over that time, mostly due his multiple personalities demanding that they get some "ink." He lives just outside St. Louis, Missouri because the rent is cheap and he doesn't know how to love a hockey team that might actually win the Stanley Cup in his lifetime.

Joseph Godstow has used his wit and creativity professionally in marketing and sales for the last 15 years throughout the United States. He was published once, but then sold the newspaper company that published him to a conglomerate in Bermuda... even though he didn't actually own the company. To this day, finance students use that as a case study for their doctorates. He also lives just outside of St. Louis, Missouri, but only because his lawyer says he can't live on the Bermuda property he acquired in that "transaction."

Also by Paul and Godstow:

Ummm....

OK, we haven't written anything else... But you can follow us through our friend Mark P. Bradley's Twitter account:

@MarkPBradley

*Authors' note – Thanks for your help with this, Mark! It only took us **six years** to write, edit, fight, abandon, return, and then publish this travesty of the English language. God only knows how long it would have taken us to set up all that other social media shit. So, yeah, we suck.*

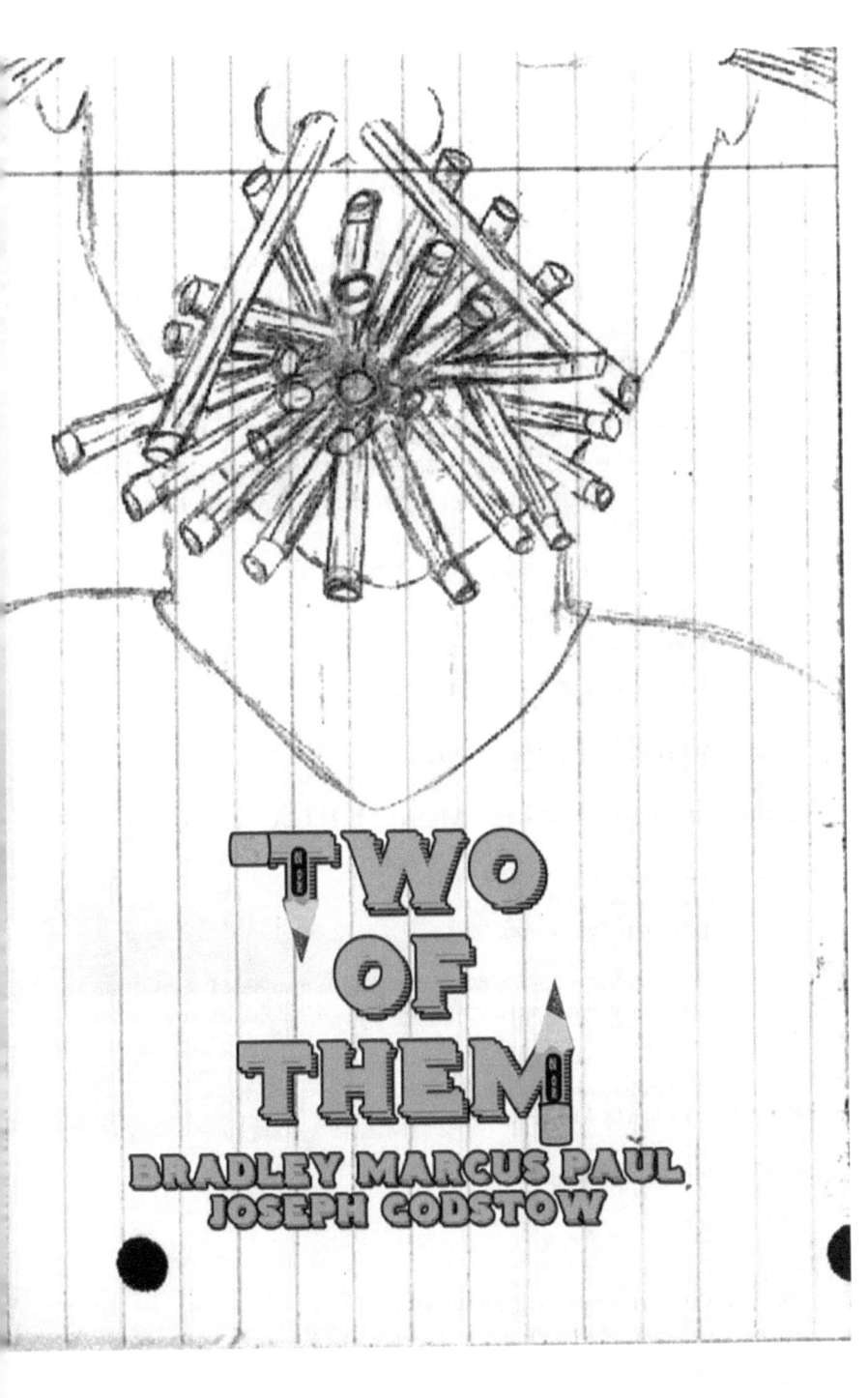

TWO OF THEM

BRADLEY MARCUS PAUL
JOSEPH GODSTOW

FUNKSHUNILYLITERIT WORKS, L.L.C.

This is a work of fiction, and any similarities to anyone else's experiences in life are not only coincidental, they're also, well, pitiful. Everyone, from our fellow readers to anyone directly or otherwise associated with Funkshunilyliterit Works L.L.C., apologizes in advance to anyone who has lived through anything that may resemble anything contained within these pages. If you actually experienced anything similar to any of the nonsense contained in this novel, then… well… *damn*.

Again, if your life has anything at all in common – in *any way* – with the bullshit contained in these pages… the members of Funkshunilyliterit Works L.L.C. recommend that you avoid:

- human interaction
- low-flying planes
- forks, and
- toasters near swimming pools.

Just don't risk it. Thanks in advance!

Funkshunilyliterit Works Mgmt., L.L.C.

Front Cover Illustration by Victoria Touchette
Back Cover Design by Mark P. Bradley

Printed and bound in the United States of America

Third Edition

ISBN-13:
978-0692320426 (Funkshunilyliterit Works, LLC)

ISBN-10:
0692320423

TABLE OF CONTENTS

CHAPTER 1

FIVE THOUSAND HOLES IN
BLACKBERN, BLAH BLAH BLAH

Mitch arrived at his office just as he did most mornings - ten minutes late. He quickly shimmied between the glass doors of the main entrance of Razor Software and scurried through the lobby, hoping that by keeping his head down and avoiding eye contact with everyone, he would somehow render himself invisible to the co-workers he passed.

As he slipped into the dark stairwell and jogged up two flights of stairs, he told himself the daily lie about still being in shape - all the while ignoring the bass drum pounding in his head, courtesy of the ten Anheuser-Busch products he had imbibed just seven hours earlier.

He quickly, yet quietly, opened the heavy steel door to his floor, and the ever present 71.3-degree air bathed his flushed cheeks. The gentle hums of hard drives and fluorescent lights seemed to be a little louder than normal, though.

Keeping his eyes fixed on the grey swirls of industrial carpet beneath his feet, he strode quickly towards his cube. He noticed he was breathing a little heavier than he should be, and glanced at the waistline he referred to as his "*flat spare tire.*" For a moment, he wondered if he still looked as good as he did ten years ago when he'd graduated from college.

As he turned into his cube and collapsed into his ergonomic chair, setting down his satchel and sucking air as quietly as possible, Mitch peeked over his cube wall and confirmed that his boss was nowhere to be seen. He felt momentarily relieved.

Mitch then looked around his office cube – with taped-on decorations of corporate awards and St. Louis Blues hockey paraphernalia - and he sneered a little. He longed for the days when this company had its casual irreverence for anything corporate, and resented the fact that some faceless Board of Governors sacrificed that culture in the name of dividends and stock splits. He'd somehow hoped that since this company was located in St. Louis instead of Silicon Valley, it might have somehow avoided such a corporate takeover. He also hated the fact that he couldn't wear tennis shoes to work anymore.

As Mitch continued pining, he realized that if the building ever went up in flames, the only thing he would try to save would be the Brett Hull bobble head doll nodding away at him from the shelf above his monitor.

Mitch knew that, at this point, his life was nothing more than "corporate sponsorship" of a college kid lifestyle - and that really bothered him, especially because his cube had begun to feel more like a prison cell holding him back from what he really wanted to do. He still dreamt of being a novelist and semi-celebrity, but so far the only *celebrity* status he'd achieved was as a regular at his local bar's happy hour. And even there, he was sure he was a mere "B-list" celeb. He put his face in his hands and felt a little disappointed in himself.

"*I need to finish that book...*" he thought. Then he laughed to himself thinking, "*OK, I need to **start** that book.*"

He looked again at the Brett Hull bobble head, and its relentless nodding appeared to be agreeing with his last thought. Then suddenly, the phone rang.

"Mitch Paulson," he answered.

"Mitch, it's Dave in printing," the voice replied. "We're under the gun on this one, bud. Is the manual for the new Melmo game ready?"

"I don't know," Mitch said uncertainly as he tried to straighten up and act professional, defying the dragging feeling his mini hangover had on him. "Lemme go down to confirm with the testers that we're good to go and I'll get back to you."

"OK, but make it quick," the voice insisted. "If this ain't going today, I've got two other manuals I've gotta get out the door."

"I'll call you right back, Dave. Don't worry."

Mitch darted out of the cube and re-entered the concrete-walled stairwell. The echoes from the door slamming behind him were as pronounced as the odor of mildew he smelled as he ran down the stairs – this time, all the way to the basement.

He kicked open the fire door and entered a small, dimly-lit basement hallway. With half-finished drywall, more stain-proof carpeting, and cardboard boxes stacked on each side, the lone unpainted wooden door at the end - with posters of rock bands, bikini models, and "Warning – Do Not Enter" signs - the entire hallway had more of a dormitory feel than that of a Fortune 100 subsidiary.

As he contorted his way past the boxes, he felt the vibrations and deep rumblings from a barrage of simulated explosions emanating through the walls. Even the boxes around him quivered with each blast.

Mitch cringed as he thought about the sensory assault into which he was about to enter.

Behind this door sat Chance and his fellow video game testers, Jim, Mike, Seth, and Greg.

All five were merely faceless voices in the pitch-black darkness of the room. With their backs to each other in a circle of bean bag chairs, their frantic button-mashing over the latest version of "True Patriots 2: Liberation" was only equaled by the intensity of their stares into their individual flat screen monitors – which were mounted to the walls opposite their bean bags.

This room, with its lightning-fast server, countless sub-processors, cutting-edge 65-inch plasma screens, a THX-enhanced subwoofer sound system, and the soft glow from a Mountain Dew vending machine in the corner... well, the setup would make most NORAD workers jealous. It was probably the most expensive room in the building. Even the new CEO didn't have it this good in his office.

Flashes of artillery explosions cast chaotic flashes across the walls like a myriad of unsynchronized strobe lights, and the reverberations from the surround-sound speakers created a feeling of thunder with each detonation.

Mitch slowly cracked open the door and stuck his head inside the cyber arena.

"Hey Chance!" Mitch called out. "Is the Melmo game...?"

"ON YOUR SIX, Clydesdale!" Chance yelled into his headset while strangling his controller and leaning back in his beanbag. *"ON YOUR SIX!!! Northeast corner! 6th floor! Third window!* TAKE HIM OUT!!!"

"Calling in a fire mission now," Jim calmly responded.

"Cover your ass or grab your ankles, bitches!" smiled Seth. "Here come the Hellfires!"

"*Chance!*" Mitch tried to yell over the blaring sound effects. "*I need to know if...*"

"DOWN! DOWN!" Chance screamed. "EVERYONE DOWN **NOW!!!**"

As the video game's rockets roared through the overhead speakers, the realism overrode Mitch's common sense and he dove into the circle of bean bags like it was a foxhole in Vietnam.

On the video screens, the building that was the focus of their attack suddenly disappeared into concussive splatters of white, yellow, orange, and red pixels, illuminating the room to near-blinding levels. The team lifted up their controllers in triumph and screamed lustfully.

"Now THAT'S how you clear a building!!!" yelled Jim.

"Yeah, fuck that 'room-by-room' shit!" added Mike.

"OK, hit pause, fellas," Chance ordered, aiming a remote control at the wall.

The florescent ceiling lights flickered on as each tester rubbed their eyes from the sudden brightness. Chance turned and smiled widely at the rest of his team.

On Chance's testing team were four young men - all of whom seemed to struggle mightily with the concept of personal appearance. They could be most easily described as the type of guys whose wardrobes consisted of only superhero and wookie t-shirts. They were also apparently not fond of bathing and were likely to get more aroused by anything on PlayStation than in Playboy. Simply put, they were stereotypical in their geek-ness.

Then there was Chance, a man of little ambition and even less concern for anything or anyone other than himself. Chance was one of those people who simply got by on his looks, his charm, and his quick lip. He knew it too, and he was OK with it – even if he'd never admit it.

His good looks and trendy "slacker" fashion stood in stark contrast to the rest of his team. Chance also relished being the Alpha Male in this group of misfits, and he had no trouble pulling rank when it suited him.

Chance was also Mitch's roommate and best friend since college.

"So," Chance asked, "what did you guys think of the explosions?"

"Well, honestly..." Greg said, "I think we need more body parts flying out of them."

"I was thinking the exact same thing," Chance concurred.

"If you're gonna add limbs," said Seth, "they need to be on fire when they're flying out of the building."

"Yeah," they all agreed.

"And add sheets of paper," Chance added.

"Paper?" scoffed Seth.

"Yeah!" Chance insisted. "It's a fuckin' office building! It's not like the enemy would've built *empty useless buildings* just so we'd have something to blow up!"

An argument ensued as Mitch began clawing himself up from the beanbag circle. Just then, Chance noticed Mitch.

"Mitch!" Chance said as he flashed his trademark smile. "Hey bud, what are you doing down here?"

"Um, I'm guessing you guys are done testing the new Melmo game," Mitch said as he got to one knee.

"Wha..." Chance asked as he gave Mitch a look of confusion. "*Melmo game?*"

"Dammit Chance!" Mitch yelled. "Don't tell me..."

"Just kidding, bud," Chance replied with a smile. "Duh – it's done."

"How long did you..."

"Ten minutes," Chance interrupted. "Looks great, the six-to-ten-year-old demographic should love it."

"So, is there anything else I need to add to the manual?"

"Yeah," Chance sniffed. "'Don't play this fucking game.'"

The rest of the testers laughed in agreement.

"OK," Mitch sighed, as he dusted off a knee. "Wait, are you guys wearing headsets?"

"Again, duh..." Chance replied.

"But you're sitting two feet away from each other."

"Hey," Chance said indignantly, "if it's good enough for the SEALS, it's good enough for us."

"We have to test the online communication software," Mike shrugged.

"Whatever," Mitch smiled wryly. "You're practicing for the upcoming online tournament."

"Well, there's *that*, too," Chance admitted.

"Fellas," Mitch laughed, "it's just *another* game we have to get out, OK?"

"*Just a game???!!!*" a growling voice barked through the speakers.

The video game's sergeant's face suddenly appeared on one flat screen and glared directly at Mitch.

"*Boy*," the sergeant seethed, "I'll kick that ass from here back to whatever po-dunk Missouri town you came from, you *pansy-ass writer!*"

Stunned by the face confronting him through the flat screen, Mitch took a step back and then looked around the room.

"Greg," Chance deadpanned to the smallish, pimple-faced geek sitting two beanbags away, "I have no problem telling him that's you."

"Okayyy," Greg said as he flipped a switch on his headset and his real-life squeaky voice whimpered through the speakers. "I was just kidding, Mitch."

Mitch shook his head as he glared at Greg.

"Yeah Mitch, you got us," Chance smiled. "We're practicing *while* we're testing, but that's 'cause this year we're gonna take the title back - especially since we get to practice on the game before it goes to market."

"Chance," Mitch said, "that's, like, *cheating...*"

"Cheating?" Chance sneered. "Lemme tell you about cheating. We tore through every opposing team for the past two years running. Then last year, this super team came out of nowhere. They must've had real military training because they ripped us to shreds. *That's* cheating."

"Oh yeah," Mitch laughed. "That Phlegm team or whatever they called themselves?"

"Phamaliag," Chance corrected with a scowl. "The Phamaliag Cell."

"Yeah, that's it," Mitch replied. "You thought they were eastern European or..."

"Malaysian," Chance interrupted. "Yeah, we thought so until we hijacked their chatter from the last tournament. Now we're sure they're our guys – definitely American, definitely military."

"You hacked into their *chatter*? How did you..."

"I can't really talk about that. But after they kicked our asses, we looked all over the internet trying to find out who these guys are, and found nothing – I mean, they're *freakin' ghosts*. No footprints anywhere. Seth found *one* posting that said they're a bunch of SEALS who've been stuck in Russia for the last four years doing some deep covert thing, and their only R-and-R is to play these online tournaments."

"Yeah," offered Jim. "Some people say they hand-crank a generator every five minutes just to give them enough power to log on."

"And some say they only sleep one hour a night, too," Mike added.

"Mike, that's from Fight Club," Chance dismissed. "Shut up."

He then turned back to Mitch.

"Anyway... this year, we'll be ready for them."

"Especially with all the extra practice time we're getting," added Seth.

"OK, whatever!" Mitch yelled as he threw his hands up. "Look, are we good with the Melmo game or what?"

"Uh, *yeah...*" Chance said, unsure as to why he had to repeat it.

"No changes???" Mitch demanded.

"No changes."

"And I can send this to print???"

"Sure..."

"Thank you!" Mitch proclaimed as he started to walk out.

"Hey," Chance asked.

"WHAT???!!!" Mitch yelled as he spun back around.

"You want me and the boys to lay down some cover fire before you evac?" he smirked while motioning with his controller.

The group snickered and laughed at Mitch.

"Pfft, that'd be the first time most of you fuckers would have ever laid anything," Mitch replied as he glared at the fraternity of misfits.

The gallery lowered their heads as Mitch walked out and slammed the door behind him.

"Your roommate's a dick," Greg said to Chance.

"He was talking about you, palm pilot," Chance replied. "Not me."

As the day wore on, Mitch stared blankly at his monitor. He slouched back into his chair and realized that – at least for today – he was done with composing stupid manuals for stupid little kids and their stupid little video games.

And that's when the words "Hey bud!" came out of nowhere - snapping Mitch out of his cerebral coma.

Startled, Mitch sat upright and swung his head around to see Chance leaning in his cube.

"Dammit, dude!" Mitch whined. "Can't you just walk into my cube like you have *some connection* to corporate America instead of bouncing in here like you're on a three-day coke binge?"

Grabbing a stress-ball toy off the shelf, Chance planted his butt on the corner of Mitch's desk, indifferent to the paperwork he was crumpling.

"Mitch, you really *are* a writer..." he sighed as he made the toy squeal incessantly.

"What's *that* supposed to mean?" Mitch growled as he shoved Chance off his desk and tried to straighten out the damaged papers.

"I mean with all the comparisons, bud!" Chance retorted.

"You mean analogies?"

"Exactly," Chance replied flatly. "Dude, can't you just... you know, *talk*? Do you have to, uh, *anal-gize* everything?"

Mitch just stared at his friend, dumfounded by the comment.

"Hey, you're the one who thought my command of the English language would be a great way to meet women," Mitch replied.

"Yeah, I did. Wow, was I wrong," Chance smiled.

"Thanks," Mitch scowled.

"Hey, stick with me and we'll do just fine, bud," Chance reassured. "C'mon, there's a reason that we're roomies! I'm gonna find a hot chick, and if you're lucky, she's gonna have a beautiful friend and I'll hook you up.

We'll get old and crusty together, getting sloshed every night and watching Blues games while our younger wives cook us dinner."

Mitch simply looked at Chance in disbelief and again thought about who Chance was.

Chance was one of those great-looking "baby of the family" kids who was raised by three older sisters – each of whom unintentionally taught him how to be everything a woman wants. He was also constantly beat up by an older brother, and those thrashings taught him how to be both cynical and fearless towards everything in life.

It was kind of an education by osmosis, but still – it shaped Chance's definition of women, himself, and life in general. And inside, Mitch was jealous that Chance owned that kind of absolutism. Chance embraced a *"Why try when you can just smile it away?"* lifestyle, and the worst part about it was that the rest of the world was letting him get away with being like that.

Then again, pretty people always get that kind of leeway.

And that last sentence was the exact phrase running through Mitch's head as he watched Chance continue his own subtle form of terrorism on his roommate, which he was obviously doing simply for his own amusement.

"Seriously," Chance continued, "it ain't like I'm living with you 'cause I want to see your love handles on a daily basis... or their ability to hold up a bath towel on their own, for that matter. Dude, how do they do that, anyway? That's gotta break at least two laws of physics, don't it?"

"Fuck off, I ain't got love handles," Mitch sneered.

"I know, but I just love giving you shit," Chance smiled. "You take it so well."

Mitch leaned back in his chair, covering his face with his hands and sighing.

"Are you done?" Mitch asked.

"With what, giving you shit? Mitch, I haven't even *begun* to..."

"With *work*, Chance," Mitch pleaded. "Are you done with *work* today?"

"Oh," Chance replied, slightly confused. "Yeah dude, absolutely."

"Good," Mitch said. "I need a drink,"

"Well then, power down so we can drink up!" Chance proclaimed. "Budgie's is a waitin'!!!"

CHAPTER 2

WAIT A MINUTE BABY,
STAY WITH ME AWHILE

"Thursday Night Happy Hour starts NOW!" Chance yelled, trumpeting his own arrival as he shoved open the doors to Budgie's Bar & Grille. Raindrops sailed into the bar as he bounded through the doorway, high-fiving and greeting his fellow drinkers, as the crowd welcomed him with hoots and cheers.

"Compadres, how goes it?" he shouted across the bar.

Catching the door on its rebound, Mitch just stood in the doorway, shook his head, and marveled at Chance's relentless energy and absolute need to be the center of attention.

Mitch never felt that need. He just liked his corner seat at the bar of the corner dive. For Mitch, there had always been something comfortable about Budgie's. It was an old building that was in dire need of upkeep, and it kind of reminded Mitch of himself. Sparsely decorated with random sports team logos and beer posters, very low lighting, and walls that went from old brick to varnished wood and back to brick – no one would ever confuse this place with being a trendy nightclub. It was a pub in every sense of the word. There were no flat screens in the place, just old tube TVs hanging from poles that hung from the ceiling at random points where proprietors believed the roof would support them. Their crowning achievement, though, was an old 60-inch projection television that they'd somehow hoisted 15 feet off the floor and literally braced to the far wall above the pool tables.

At least the 20-foot-high ceiling kept the place from ever getting too smoky.

Mitch actually relished the fact that Budgie's didn't have all the stuff that a lot of the other bars in the area had, because that's not why people came to the place. They weren't there for pool, or shuffleboard, or even music. They were there to get drunk and engage in *mostly* good-spirited verbal warfare.

Basically, it was Mitch and Chance in every way.

Mitch greeted his fellow regulars as he worked his way towards the long, narrow bar that jutted out from the back left wall and into the middle of the room. Renee, the resident bartender, had Mitch's beer waiting for him as he sat down.

"Another day, another dollar, Mitch?" she smiled.

"Another day, another verb, Renee," he replied exhaustedly.

"Really?" she turned excitedly. "Are you talking about the novel?"

"Ugh," he sighed. "No, just user manuals. That's how I get paid, ya know."

"Yeah, but you've been talking about writing this book for over a year now. Have you even started on it?"

"Well, ya see, there's this..."

"I don't wanna hear it, Mitch," Renee glared, raising a palm to his face.

Renee was a beautiful woman - but she was also a "no bullshit" chick. With shoulder-length straight brown hair, sultry eyes, a smile that could dismiss the most eager of suitors, and a glare that could disarm the most willing of combatants, well... everyone knew that even though she didn't own the bar, when she was working, she *owned* the bar. Her ability to take control of any situation made most male patrons outwardly respect her, secretly covet her, and quietly fear her a little, too.

Mitch curled his lip and nodded in agreement.

"No need to bore her with excuses," he thought.

"Well, at least Chance is in his usual form," Renee groaned, turning to watch Chance perform some kind of pro wrestling move on another patron while the impromptu audience of regulars howled their approval. Chance mocked slamming one man's head onto the bar, and then raised his hands gloriously as he bellowed.

"Yeah, he saw that move last night on the wrestling show, and then tried it on me," Mitch replied.

"Really," Renee replied with tepid fascination. "How'd that work out for you?"

Mitch said nothing, but pointed to a red mark above his eyebrow that looked strikingly similar to stitching normally found on the armrest of a couch.

"Ooooh," Renee replied, stifling a chuckle. "Are you two *ever* gonna grow up?"

"Well, you don't see any grey hairs on this head yet, do ya?" Mitch asked. "This lifestyle must be working."

"Hey Mitch!" Chance yelled from across the bar. "Get over here and tell the fellas about how I pounded your head into the armrest last night!"

The group cheered him on and encouraged him to come over.

"Hey Chance!" Mitch mocked. "Why don't I come over there and tell the fellas about how you pounded the neighbor's cat last night?"

The group fell silent and looked at Chance.

"Well..." Chance replied, "Pussy *is* pussy. Am I right, boys???"

The group roared with approval.

Renee rolled her eyes and walked away. Mitch just laughed and shook his head as he leaned on the bar, knowing full well he shouldn't try to outdo Chance's infinite lack of shame.

Happy hour passed into evening, and amid the talk about work, women, sports, *whatever*, Chance abruptly announced, "Alright fellas, gotta drain the main vein."

Smattered comments of "Thanks for sharing" were uttered as Chance headed to the restroom.

As Mitch sat at the bar with his beer, Renee suddenly realized that Chance had been gone for a little too long for her liking.

"OK, where's Chance?" she asked as she turned to Mitch.

"I'm sure he's fine," Mitch said, rolling his eyes.

Renee then saw Chance emerge from the restroom with a taunting smile, and her face became engulfed with rage.

"My phone number had *better **NOT** be* back up on the wall in there!" she yelled at Chance, leaning across the bar and pointing.

Chance pulled his head back in astonishment.

"Renee, I would *never* do that," he explained with a cocked smile.

Renee leaned across the bar to scold Chance about already having to change her number once - which gave Mitch an unobstructed view of the main door.

As his eyes refocused on the entrance, he suddenly perked up as the silhouette of a beautiful woman entered.

Her rain-soaked locks covered just enough of her face to provide the level of mystery that every man loves to stare at long enough to solve. As she swept back her dampened waves to reveal her face, Mitch suddenly felt every ounce of air leave his lungs.

With long one-length blondish-brown hair, wide eyes, a face that bordered on addictive and a smile that would push any man across that border, she made Mitch shake his head and squint to be sure he was seeing what he thought he was seeing. Her small build had curves in all the right places, and her jeans kept very few secrets.

She smiled meekly at the bouncer, feeling like a complete mess from the rain. He responded with a sympathetic smile as he offered her a roll of paper towels. She politely declined as she squeezed the rain from her hair onto the mat.

Mitch sat there staring, utterly amazed. As she approached the bar, he felt a knot of anxiety within his stomach. Mitch was notorious for coming down with some form of paralysis every time he found himself in the presence of any woman he found attractive, but there was something special about this lady. She was just... *magnetic*. He simply *had* to try. As she sat down just a few seats away from him, his fear of rejection was overwhelmed by the need to *at least* talk to her.

"Gotta love the weather this time of year," Mitch said, leaning in on his elbows.

"Yeah," she laughed apologetically while still trying to shake the water out of her hair, "I don't remember them saying it was going to rain today."

"They didn't," Mitch smiled with a calm confidence. "Welcome to fall in St. Louis."

"I know, I know," she laughed. "You'd think after living here most of my life, I'd have an umbrella in my car."

"*Most* of your life?" Mitch asked, fishing for conversation.

"Well, I just moved back a few months ago, but yeah, I grew up here. Apparently, I'm still re-learning about the whole 'rain coming out of nowhere' thing," she sighed as she pointed to her still-wet locks.

"Don't worry, it'll all be snow and ice soon enough. Mitch replied. "Sooooo, where'd ya move back from?"

"Tempe."

"OK, *now* I'm curious," Mitch said. "Why on Earth would you leave Tempe to come back here?"

"Well," she sighed, "my family still lives here, and I just needed to get my life in order. I figured the best place to do that was back at home."

"Good idea," Mitch smiled. "My name's Mitch, by the way," he added, extending his hand.

"Ellie," she replied as she shook Mitch's hand while flagging down the bartender.

"A glass of white wine, please," she said as Renee approached.

Renee nodded and grabbed a wine glass.

"Ellie? Really?" Mitch asked, trying to get her attention back on him. "That's a great name."

"Well thanks. My dad came up with it. My mom always said Dad named me after Elle MacPherson, but I was born way before she became famous."

"Well, your dad must be clairvoyant."

"Uh, no..." Ellie corrected. "His name's Chris."

Mitch's shoulders sank at her response.

"No, I meant..."

"I'm just messing with you, Mitch," Ellie smiled. "That was sweet, though," she said as she rolled her eyes, acknowledging the pick-up line.

"What? I meant it."

"Well, then *you're* sweet," she smiled again, this time accepting the compliment.

She had seen Mitch getting ready to come up and talk to her when she walked in, and was already thinking up excuses to kindly blow him off. But he seemed like a nice enough guy, so she sized him up again out of the corner of her eye.

Ellie then noticed a group of guys all huddled around a table, staring and pointing at her and Mitch.

"I think your friends are talking about us," she said, somewhat amused.

"Friends?" Mitch looked over and glared in their direction. "Uh, sure. I guess you could call them my friends. They're more like my co-drinkers."

"*Co-drinkers?*" Ellie asked.

"Yeah, ya know," Mitch explained. "The people you work with are your co-workers, so I figure the people you drink with are your co-drinkers."

"Interesting," she replied as she took a sip of her wine.

"Well... I just came up with it, actually."

Ellie laughed, guardedly impressed. She then discretely gave Mitch another look-over and thought to herself, "*Yeah, he could stand to lose about ten pounds.*" But Ellie also thought that about herself, so it was forgivable.

"So, what do you do?" Mitch asked.

"Well, right now, I'm a cosmetologist."

"That is sooooo cool!" Mitch replied. "But I gotta ask... how do you handle the weightlessness?"

"What? Uh, no. That's not what I..."

"*Ahhh*, I'm just *messin'* with you," Mitch teased. "Besides, that's just a line from an old movie. I can't take credit for it."

"Okay," Ellie nodded as she smiled a little more widely. "We're even."

"So, how long have you been cutting hair?" Mitch asked.

"Oh, I dunno, a few years, I guess."

"Doesn't sound like you like your job much," Mitch replied.

"No, I like it," Ellie said. "It's just... it's just not what I want to do for the rest of my life."

"OK, I've just gone from interested to intrigued," Mitch replied, leaning a little closer. "Tell me your grand plan."

"Honestly, I want to eventually break onto Broadway," she said tenuously, expecting Mitch to scoff or judge her.

"Then what are you doing back here?"

"Well, I need to get some money together before I head to New York, and I figure I gotta start somewhere," she explained, her eyes widening a little she visualized being on stage. "I have a few auditions next month locally, but..."

"So in your heart, you're really a thespian," Mitch smiled wryly, emphasizing the misnomer.

Ellie just laughed, even though she'd heard the joke before.

Chance suddenly wedged his way between Mitch's backside and another bar patron to grab more longnecks when he overheard Mitch's last comment.

"Whoa, you're into chicks?" Chance interrupted, looking over Mitch's shoulder and staring Ellie dead in the eyes.

Ellie faked a smile as Mitch bit his lip in frustration.

"She's in theater, Chance," Mitch growled, gritting his teeth while keeping his back to him. "Ya know, *Broadway*? You *go away* now."

"Oh, got it," Chance nodded, pretending to understand as he grabbed the beers off the bar. "Pops always said that people in theater were like that," he smiled as he elbowed Mitch in the back and disappeared into the crowd.

"Was he joking?" Ellie asked.

"Probably not," Mitch laughed. "That's my roommate, Chance."

"You have a male roommate and he's making gay jokes?" Ellie teased.

"Hey," Mitch smiled, acting overtly macho. "I'm straight," he bellowed, dropping his voice into baritone and jokingly holding up a flexed bicep. "Chance? Well..." he paused. "OK, seriously though, we've been friends since college and we both work for the same company software, so it just made sense to share a place – you know, save money, try to get ahead and what not."

"Oh, so you're both geeks," she taunted again, curling away with mock horror.

"Hey, Bill Gates is a geek," Mitch countered with a wide smile. "For that kind of cash, label me *all you want...*"

Ellie laughed again – even more impressed with his sure-footed response. And with that laugh, Mitch felt a little more confident.

"Actually, I'm kind of in the same place you are," he continued.

"Really, how's that?"

"I write the user manuals for video games. It pays the bills, but it kind of sucks. It's not what I want to do with my life, either."

"OK, now *I'm* intrigued," Ellie imitated, leaning closer.

"Well, I have this idea for a novel that I've started on. I'd love to eventually be a novelist – at least one who's successful enough to live off the book sales and – dare I say it – even turn a few into movie scripts."

"Wow, another dreamer," Ellie nodded, feeling a kinship with someone comfortable enough to share *their* dream. "Here's to dreamers," she added as she held up her wine glass.

"Amen, sister," Mitch replied as their glasses clinked together. "Long live the dreamers."

"Long live the dreamers," she echoed.

She then thought to herself, *"OK, who is this guy?"* Feeling like it was her turn to say something interesting, Ellie said, "Well, you have me at a disadvantage now, because I don't know a fancy name for your job like you had for mine."

"Let's see," Mitch pondered. "For the user manuals – call me a *Nerd Communicator.*"

Ellie nodded and laughed.

"For the novelist... hmmm," Mitch continued. "How about, Hemingway, or maybe Shakespeare?"

"OK, *Bill,*" Ellie teased.

"Wait," Mitch asked, "is that Gates or Shakespeare?".

"Well, if it's Gates, the *least* you can do is pay for this drink."

"And if it's Shakespeare?"

"Then you're *way* too old for me – but you have to cast me in your next play."

"Renee???" Mitch suddenly yelled across the bar. "Another glass of vino for this lass! And put it on the *'Bill',*" he smiled, pointing to himself.

"Very nice!" Ellie laughed.

Over the next hour or so, Mitch and Ellie found themselves lost in conversation and laughter. As Mitch told her more about his novel, his conviction and passion intensified Ellie's attraction more with every word he spoke.

For Mitch, Ellie could have said she aspired to bathe in bio-hazardous waste, and he would have still wanted her – but the fact that they were both creative and shared similar dreams of fame? Well, that just made her even more amazing to him.

They continued talking and staring into each other's eyes amazedly when Ellie's phone rang.

"Hey!" she answered. "Where *are* you???"

Mitch sat silently as the conversation continued without him.

"No, no, that's fine," Ellie said. "Yeah, well, I guess I'll just have to find *someone else* to hang out with tonight," she somewhat announced while winking at Mitch. "OK, OK, well... wait, she did what? Oh, that bitch. Yeah, you were right. Uh huh, yeah. Oh my God, what a bitch! I know... I know... I don't know how you put up with her... Yeah... OK... Well, look, I'll let you go. We'll talk about this *tomorrow*... What? No! OK, well, maybe. Yes... yes... well, *I* think so..."

Mitch realized Ellie's friend was grilling her about him. Ellie tried to be discrete, even though it was more for show than an actual need to be discreet. Still, Mitch smiled even more confidently.

"Look, we'll talk tomorrow," she continued. "No, I said we'll talk tomorrow... OK, fine, I'll call you when I get home. Yes, when *I get home*... Oh shut up... Alright, talk to you then... Bye."

"So, I'm guessing that was your missing friend?" Mitch asked.

"Yeah, she got tied up at work," Ellie replied. "I have *no idea* what to do with myself now..." she sighed and rolled her eyes, feigning helplessness.

"Well, you can hang with me," Mitch smiled.

"Well," Ellie's eyes switched to feigned scrutiny, "...if you *insist.*"

"Oh, I *do.*"

"OK, but I can't stay too much longer."

"No worries," Mitch smiled with a shrug. "I'm good with as much time as you've got to give."

They continued talking and laughing, feeling an undeniable mutual attraction. Ellie was impressed by Mitch's candor and the way he looked her right in the eye when she spoke – like no one else mattered at all. As they talked about their pasts, their careers, their interests, and their dreams, they each began speaking more softly, forcing each of them to move closer.

Ellie then saw her watch out of the corner of her eye, and was shocked by how late it had gotten.

"Oh wow, Mitch," she exclaimed. "It's really late. I gotta get home."

"OK, well…" Mitch replied, desperate not to lose the moment. "Can I take you out tomorrow night?"

"Um, *where*?" Ellie asked, daring him to impress her one last time.

"A Blues Bar?" he suggested, thinking about the Blues' season opener tomorrow night.

"*Broadway Blues Bar???* I haven't been there in years! Sure! What time?"

One part of Mitch's heart sank, knowing he was likely going to miss the Blues' season opener because of this. But his other side was elated that this beautiful woman was willing to go out with him, and that fact quashed any concerns he had over missing one hockey game.

"*Worth the sacrifice*," he thought to himself.

"How about seven?" he asked.

Ellie grabbed his phone and programmed her number into it.

"OK," she smiled as she looked up, "I'll meet you there."

"I can pick you up, if you want."

"Not on a first date," Ellie countered with a half-smile. "It's a rule of mine. But you *will* be there, right?"

"Count on it," Mitch replied.

"Good, I'll see you then," Ellie smiled again.

Mitch took her hand and kissed the top of it.

"I look forward to tomorrow night."

"Wow," Ellie stammered. "Um… me too."

And with that, she turned and left the bar.

Mitch watched the door close behind her, and then leaned backwards over the bar. He stretched his arms out and let out a heavy sigh as the co-drinkers erupted with cheers. Feeling somewhat silly about all the attention, Mitch sauntered over to his friends, accepted their high-fives, and laughed about all the comments encircling him until he suddenly noticed something.

"Hey, where's Chance?" he asked.

"Cab," they deadpanned in unison.

"What the fuck?" Mitch asked. "OK, which one of you bought the Jager shots?"

They all stared at him blankly, trying not to look guilty.

CHAPTER 3

TORN AWAY FOR THIS BEAUTIFUL CHASE

The plain white walls, the high ceiling, and the solitary ceiling fan gently swaying in the air gave Mitch and Chance's apartment the air of any typical soon-to-be-successful young professional's home. Well, almost.

Interspersed between prints of Monet, Blues memorabilia, and movie posters were the orange stains from last month's hot wings food fight. At least the black pleather sofa and matching loveseat were easy enough to keep clean – or at least, keep the *appearance* of being clean.

In the middle of the far left wall stood a grey stone fireplace with three logs recklessly stacked atop a pile of flattened beer boxes, which were going to maybe be eventually lit up as kindling.

Mitch and Chance's friends – Lawrence, Rich, and Tom – were already there getting ready for the game. Staring at the projection-screen television that sat to the right of the fireplace – and surrounded by enough liquor on top of an old wooden coffee table to make a protestant rethink his faith – Lawrence and Rich were getting settled in.

Lawrence was a large, muscle-bound man. No one was even sure how tall he was – no one had bothered to ask. Even the straightest of men couldn't deny Lawrence had the looks, and the fellas in the group were only too happy that he was their friend, particularly considering how much he worked out.

Large muscles matter in tense situations, after all.

Directly across from the front door was the sliding glass door that opened up to the deck, where the barbeque pit *normally* was.

But as Mitch walked out of his bedroom, he realized that his friends were tailgating in the middle of the living room – complete with Tom manning a suddenly *indoor* barbeque pit.

Tom had been Mitch's friend since grade school, and even though he could be just as obnoxious as Chance when "the guys" were hanging out, he was always a complete gentleman when ladies were present. But tonight was the Blues season opener, so... he was in full-on obnoxious mode.

"DUDE!" Mitch yelled at Tom. "Take the barbeque pit *outside!!!*"

"But..." Tom replied. "*The game...*"

"Turn the fuckin' TV *TOWARDS* YOU!" Mitch commanded. "The damn thing's on wheels for a reason!"

"Mitch, you shouldn't even be leaving," Chance interrupted, appearing suddenly from the kitchen and stepping between them. He crossed his arms after setting his beer on the breakfast bar that ran from the midpoint of the room to the edge of the sliding door.

"We gotta talk – *right now!*" Mitch yelled, half-manic from both the chaos around him and the stress of the impending date with Ellie.

"Totally, bud," Chance agreed, looking at Mitch's shirt. "No way would I wear that shirt to meet her."

"I SAID NO MORE BARBEQUING IN THE APARTMENT – I FUCKIN' MEANT IT! I DON'T CARE HOW MANY FANS YOU'RE GONNA...," he paused, realizing what Chance had just said. "Wait, what's wrong with this shirt?"

"Um," Chance replied, "*seriously?*"

They both looked at Mitch's black t-shirt, which displayed a white stick figure holding up a stick-figure hand and the phrase "Rock On" written in sloppy lettering at the bottom.

"Chance," Mitch said, "this shirt rocks."

"Fine then, why hold back? Go all out, get the mullet wig and make sure you have that Poison CD playing when you pick her up."

"Ugh – look, I gotta go. No more burn marks in the floor, got it?"

"But Mitch, that shirt..."

"Hey, I got this date all worked out. I'm meeting her at the Broadway Blues Bar, where they serve oysters - *aphrodisiacs*..." he winked. "And there are enough TVs in that place to where I can hopefully keep an eye on the game – so don't worry about me. I got the haircut, the shirt, the shoes, the teeth whiteners..."

"*Every rose has its thorn,*" Chance sang mockingly. "Wait, teeth whiteners?"

"Oh yeah," Mitch smiled. "Wan hooked me up with some prototype teeth whitener from his home town."

"His *home town*?" Chance echoed. "You mean, in *China*???"

"Yeah, why?"

"Have you *not* watched the news in the last five years?"

"Yeah," Mitch replied. "My teeth are whiter than ever."

"But there are probably chemicals in that stuff that even the *Chinese* haven't legalized yet... I hope you don't end up having a kid with three dicks just so you can have white teeth."

"Whatever," Mitch sneered. "Besides... as if you wouldn't wanna have three dicks."

"Only if I had four hands."

"Four hands... for...?"

"Never mind," Chance dismissed and then smiled at Mitch. "OK fine, you look great. Get outta here and blow that chick's mind."

"Planning on it..." he replied, opening the door.

"Then maybe *she'll*..." Chance added.

"God willing," Mitch interrupted as he closed the door behind him.

CHAPTER 4

REVVED UP LIKE A DEUCE, ANOTHER RUNNER IN THE NIGHT

Mitch had been using his fake ID to get into Broadway Oyster Bar since he was 17, so he was very familiar with the neon lights, the old and over-varnished woodwork, and the recklessly-plastered 60-year-old concert posters that decorated every inch of available wall space.

As he sat at the bar waiting, the glow of the neon "Grab some Buds" sign above his head reflected off his favorite t-shirt. He sat there looking at his shirt and contemplated what Chance had said about it. Slowly, he began to feel less certain of his choice of clothing.

Realizing that it was too late to do anything about it, he simply listened to the monotonous drone of bar chatter until the sound caused him to drift off in thought.

Almost magically, Ellie suddenly appeared and looked down at his shirt.

"Aw, I love your shirt," she smiled.

Mitch met her eyes and sighed with relief.

"Thanks!" he smiled. "Hey, the only table I could get is over there," he shrugged as he pointed to a dark corner of the restaurant where no view of the televisions.

"Ya know," she asked, "do you mind if we just sit somewhere... um, *close* to a TV?"

"Uh, sure," Mitch replied with anticipation. "No worries."

She took off her coat, revealing a Blues jersey.

"Good. It's the Blues season opener tonight, and I've been waiting four months for this day."

Mitch was awestruck.

"Wow, me too!!!" he exclaimed. "Ya know, there's a TV right here at the bar. Should we just sit here?"

"Really?" she asked excitedly. "You don't mind?"

"Uh, nooo..."

"Ya know," she said as she draped her coat across the back of the bar stool, "the worst thing about Tempe was no Blues hockey, no decent hot wings, and no Budweiser on tap... at least, not as cold as it should be."

"Barkeep!" Mitch yelled with a raised hand while grinning from ear to ear, "Two frosty Buds and a dozen five-alarm wings!!!"

Mitch couldn't believe the depth of his good luck when a muffled voice began calling.

"Mitch... *Mitch???*"

He felt a tapping on his shoulder, which shook off his daydream and dragged him back into reality. He turned to see Ellie wearing a sexy little cocktail dress.

"Um, I hope I'm not overdressed," she stated uncertainly, looking at Mitch's t-shirt and jeans with a raised eyebrow.

"Um, no... no," Mitch stuttered. "Wow, you... you look fantastic! I'm probably undressed."

"Huh?" she asked.

"I mean, under-dressed."

"Oh, OK."

"Hey, our table's ready over there," he said as he pointed to the dark corner.

"Aw, nice!" she said. "Good choice, Mitch! How'd you get such an out-of-the-way table?"

"Because everyone else here wants to watch the game," he muttered.

Over the course of dinner, conversation, a few bottles of wine, and even a couple of oysters he managed to choke down, Mitch was already feeling there was something different about Ellie. The conversation and laughter flowed effortlessly, and he and Ellie seemed to be really clicking.

For a moment, he wondered if it was the oysters and the wine, but he quickly dismissed that thought. Her sense of humor, the way she smiled, the way she tucked her hair behind her ear, her unapologetic willingness to give her opinion... hell, *everything* about her... was special.

Even though Ellie was feeling the same way towards Mitch, she was doing her best to not get too excited about him. Her past boyfriends had taught her that.

As Mitch signed the credit card receipt, Ellie heard the band beginning to play on the outside patio.

"Hey, are you a blues fan?" Ellie asked.

"Oh yeah, do you wanna go see what they're doing?"

"*Absolutely!*" she smiled.

Mitch tossed the receipt across the table and bolted towards the nearest TV, which was surrounded by a crowd of people decked out in various Blues garb. He tried to wedge himself into the best spot to see the television.

"Mitch?" Ellie called after him while standing at the doorway to the patio. "I think the band's out here."

"Wha..." Mitch said as he turned back toward her voice. "Oh, you meant *blues*... not *the* Blues."

"Huh?" Ellie asked.

"Nothing," Mitch dismissed as he walked towards Ellie. "I was just gonna grab us a few drinks, but apparently there's a big crowd watching *something* on TV..."

"Well, don't worry about it," Ellie smiled. "We can get drinks out here. There's no line at this bar."

"No shit..." Mitch mumbled.

Ellie grabbed an open table on the covered patio as the band started playing. Mitch waited at the bar while the bartender made their drinks, but he was staring at Ellie as she settled into her seat. He was so impressed by her that the hockey game was suddenly not so important. He then thought that he should, maybe *just a little*, re-evaluate his priorities and not screw this up over a hockey game.

"There's always the highlights," he thought.

He brought their drinks to the table and scooted his chair closer to her. People were already crowding the dance floor, and thereby shining the stage lights throughout the covered patio area.

After the band finished the third song, they dropped the house lights and started making indiscriminant sounds, trying to build tension. The drummer scattered tings from his cymbals across the darkness as the bassist played one low note as quickly and rhythmically as he could.

"What's going on?" Ellie asked.

"No idea," Mitch said.

The guitarist suddenly made his instrument squeal a high-pitched note and then bent it down to the bowels of human perception. Both Ellie and Mitch smiled as they nodded along to the rhythm that was slowly being revealed.

The singer began to mumble verses in baritone, and, just then, black lights flooded the stage. Every band member was suddenly aglow in bluish-purple as they began playing a heavy groove.

"Oh wow," Ellie smiled.

Mitch simply as well, until he noticed eight very close points of white light moving against the back wall of the stage. As he moved his head, they seemed to be moving with him. He suddenly realized that these points of light were shooting out of his mouth. He quickly closed his lips.

Ellie looked over at him confusedly.

"Where were those little lights coming from?" she asked.

Mitch's eyes widened with panic as he pressed his lips together.

"Mitch?" she persisted.

"I..." he began as he turned his head, but the glints from Mitch's teeth shot out again and hit the bassist across the bridge of his nose, blinding and dropping him like he'd just been shot. The band stopped playing and started looking around for whatever had flattened their bassist, but the black lights continued to glow.

Mitch covered his mouth with both hands and tried to motion to Ellie that they needed to leave immediately.

"Mumpf ffpt mmummph v mrreurr!!!" he muffled with both hands over his face.

"What?" Ellie asked as she glared at him.

"MUMPF FFPT MUMMPH V MRREURR!!!" Mitch repeated, this time more forcefully.

"Mitch, I can't understand you!" she said as she pulled his hands away from him mouth.

Worried that he would blind Ellie by answering her, Mitch turned his head towards the bar and wanted to yell, *"Let's get out of here!"* But as he opened his mouth, another flash escaped – this time, the beams caught the bartender square in the face and drove her backwards into her shelves of bottles. She slid down the back wall and onto the floor as bottles randomly toppled around her.

Ellie suddenly realized what was happening.

"OK then," she said agreeably. *"Time to go?"*

Mitch, with his eyes wide and hands again tightly pressed against his mouth, nodded emphatically.

As they got outside, Mitch hunched over and pointed his face straight at the ground, hoping to limit any additional damage. Thankfully, as he parted his lips, the blinding points of light were no longer there.

"Are you alright, Mitch?" Ellie asked, nearly panic-stricken.

"Um," Mitch said slowly. "Yeah, I think so."

"*Oh...my...God!!!*" Ellie laughed. "What just happened in there???"

"I'm guessing it was the teeth whitener I used tonight," he shrugged in humiliation, while remaining hunched over. "The chemicals apparently don't like black lights."

Ellie leaned over lower than Mitch's head and looked back up into his face. Then, she started laughing hysterically.

"That was *SO FUNNY!!!*" she screamed. "*OH MY GOD!!!*"

Mitch was just relieved that Ellie wasn't angry. He covered his anxiety by laughing along with her.

"Where'd you get that stuff?" Ellie asked between laughs, trying to breathe.

"Don't ask," Mitch moaned with a smile. "Let's just say that I ain't buying anything else from China."

"No kidding," she said as she hugged him. "Well, I don't think we should go into any more bars until you get your teeth fixed."

"Probably not," Mitch agreed.

For the moment, Ellie wasn't sure what to do. The teeth thing would have been horribly humiliating if it weren't so damn funny. And the way Mitch handled it – embarrassed, but not whiney or begging her to forgive him – well, the whole package impressed Ellie, even if she didn't know why.

"Tell ya what," Ellie offered. "Walk me to my car, and we'll get together again really soon."

A part of Mitch was upset with himself because his vanity had caused an early end to a great date. But the other side of him was elated that she wanted to go out with him again.

So, he nodded in agreement.

They started walking through the Soulard area – an historic part of St. Louis with the kind of interconnected masonry walls that are a staple of all old river towns. What was once a series of factories, stores, and flat-roofed shotgun homes had been converted to one of the trendiest areas in the city. Built before the invention of zoning ordinances, this old neighborhood of rotting brick shells was now a neighborhood of bar after bar after bar, mixed in with a few novelty shops, some *very* expensive homes, and then, more bars.

As Mitch walked Ellie to her car, they weaved through the socialites that crowded the brick sidewalks and cobblestone streets.

"So, you write the user manuals for video games," Ellie said, taking his arm after another group passed between them. "It must be nice to do something with your talent. Not too many people can say that these days. You must be happy."

"Not really," Mitch shrugged.

"But you're getting paid to write," she countered.

"Yeah, but I want to write something that matters," he explained with a tinge of disgust in his voice. "Right now, I'm writing manuals for gamers."

"Oh, I'm sorry."

"No reason to be," Mitch smiled. "Look, I don't like it, but I see it for what it is. The job allows me to have an apartment and buy things, ya know? It's kind of a necessary symbiotic relationship."

"Symbiotic? What, are you are a sci-fi geek too?" she teased.

"Aren't you?" Mitch countered.

"Well, kind of," Ellie smiled. "I know a few people who are really into all that stuff, but you still didn't answer my question."

As they passed another series of bars, Mitch noticed the myriad of colors from the dance floor's lights shooting through the windows and decorating Ellie's face as they passed.

"OK," Mitch admitted. "Look, you'll never catch me at any of those conventions or anything, but there's something so appealing about the whole genre."

"What?"

"Well, it's the freedom to have anything - *anything you want* - be possible. And because of that, you can get your point across by telling a story in a unique way. I think that most of the time, a science fiction story is the most effective way to affect people. You don't have to hold to a timeline, be historically accuracy, or even recognize the laws of physics. You just need the human condition."

"What *human* condition?" Ellie laughed. "Especially if they're aliens?"

"Hey, we wouldn't be able to relate to any of it if there wasn't a human condition within the story."

"I never thought of it like that," Ellie replied.

"Yeah, because *anything* is possible with science fiction," he continued. "Alien races, utopian worlds, sufferings and triumphs that would normally be totally unbelievable? In science fiction, it's *all* plausible. Anything's possible, but it would all be meaningless without the human condition. Without that..."

"I get it," Ellie nodded and lightly tugged on his arm as she reflected on what he'd just said. "If only my dad could have explained it that way."

"Well, maybe your dad's not as verbal as I am," Mitch replied, almost proudly. "It's what I do for a living."

"Wow, so now you *are* a writer!" Ellie mocked.

"OK, look," Mitch stated to reinforce his point. "Have you ever read a book or saw a movie that altered the way you looked at something?"

"Sure...I guess."

"That's it right there. That 'paradigm shift', that *moment* - I want to have that effect, but on a whole lot of people... if only just once. I want to shift the world. All that *'If I only affect one person, then I'm happy'* crap? I mean, *seriously*? I don't want to affect 'just one person' like so many of those so-called *artists* claim. Talk about setting the bar pretty low," he scoffed.

"Everything I wrote in college impressed my mom – does that make me a success?

"*If I only affect one person*," he continued mocking, "God, then I'm a failure. How bad must my work suck if only one person is moved? Shakespeare didn't change one person, Orwell didn't affect one person. Those guys broke hearts, changed minds... altered the whole world's perceptions. Like, do you know what the name of the first space shuttle was?"

"Enterprise, right?"

"Yep. Guess where they got the name from."

"No idea."

"Think Captain Kirk."

"No way."

"Oh yeah. And what about those old flip phones? Ever seen anything like that before?" he asked as he feigned flipping one open, "Beam me up, Scottie," he said in a bad Shatner impression while looking right at Ellie.

"C'mon... are you serious?"

"OK then, how about your tablets? An MRI? These inventions were all modeled after a little TV show."

"A *little* TV show?" Ellie corrected. "Star Trek was HUGE. I mean..."

"*HUGE?*" Mitch interrupted. "The *original* Star Trek?"

"Yeah."

"Do you know how many seasons it was on the air?"

"At least ten or fifteen, right?"

"Try *three.*"

Ellie looked at him in disbelief.

"Yep, 'CSI' has them beat them by at least fifteen years."

Ellie looked at the brick sidewalk in silence, feeling both impressed and a little humbled.

"I want to *affect* people," he repeated for emphasis. "Affect them *like that.*"

"Wow, Mitch," Ellie smiled. "You've just affected me. Put me down as your first."

"Awesome," Mitch smiled. "One down, the rest of the world to go."

Ellie looked at Mitch and softly smiled. She suddenly pulled him close and gave him the kiss that he had been waiting for his entire life.

In the middle of the kiss, Mitch thought to himself, "*HOLY SHIT! IS THIS ACTUALLY HAPPENING?*" As he pressed his lips to hers for a moment longer, hoping to prolong it, she slowly pulled her lips away and looked directly into his eyes, almost inquisitively.

He only smiled back, took her hands, and gently pressed his forehead against hers as he returned her blissful smile.

He then continued leading her towards her car. As they walked hand-in-hand across the brick-laden sidewalk, Mitch was lost in the moment. He basked in how easily they communicated, how perfectly they seemed to fit. Nothing about this was contrived. And he didn't even *know* this woman yet. And even more incredibly, she liked him too.

"I hope you become a great writer," she said as they continued walking, placing her head on his shoulder.

"I already am," he shrugged, almost apologetically. "I just need to finish the novel."

"Well then," Ellie replied, charmed by his confidence, "that should be a walk in the park."

"After tonight," Mitch added as he leaned his head on hers, "I'm thinking anything is possible."

She pulled him to her and kissed him again. Mitch ran his fingers through her hair and kissed her back, keeping her close while also waiting again for her to pull her lips away – not wanting to shortchange himself of one second of the kiss.

As Ellie pulled her lips back - this time with a smug smile - Mitch smiled back. But he didn't stop.

"Seriously, it's no different for you," Mitch half-whispered. "I mean, you're an actress, right?"

"Ac-TOR," she corrected.

"OK, fine... so, you're an actor."

"Yes," she replied. "But right now, I'm a *struggling* actor."

"Nah, struggling is a state of mind," Mitch smiled. "I mean, you're already a great actor, right?"

"I think so, yeah."

"OK, then, like me, you're just on one part of the journey, too. It just hasn't started paying off for you yet, either. You're already a work of art – you're just a work of art 'in progress' right now."

"You really think so?"

"Look at the business world - all those guys who started with nothing in their garages and are now multibillionaires. In their hearts, they knew they had a great product that everybody was going to want. You just have to look at yourself in the same way. You just have to *know* you're a great actor that, eventually, is gonna be what everybody wants. *They* just don't know it yet, because you're still 'in progress.'"

"But you've never even seen me act."

"But I will," he replied with certainty and a smile. "And besides, I don't need to. I'm a great spotter of talent."

"OK," Ellie laughed. "Well maybe one day you'll be a great writer and I'll get to play the lead when they turn your book into a movie."

"Hey, ya know, if that ever does happen, I might insist on being involved in casting... heck, maybe I'll require it in my contract."

"Wow, wouldn't that be great?" she smiled as she looked up at the stars. "You'd get rich and famous from your book, then I'd have the inside track on the lead role."

"Well, maybe," Mitch half-smiled. "Depends on if you play your cards right..."

"OK, you jerk," she smiled and smacked his chest. "You're gonna pay for that one."

"Now, or when I hire you for the movie?"

"Oh, not now," she shook her head in false arrogance. "I'll have to see how the movie does first. Then, once it's a huge success, I'll make my killing on the sequel – when you'll *need* me to reprise my *Oscar-winning* role. That's when it'll cost ya... if you wanna keep me, that is."

"I hope we get to the point where you rake me over the coals," he said, staring intently as he pulled her close and kissed her deeply.

She returned the kiss with equal eagerness, and - as she caught her breath - said, "It's a date."

Just then, Ellie's phone rang with an unusual tone.

"What kind of ring tone is that?" Mitch teased, looking at her purse.

"My text alert," Ellie replied. "It's Danni - my friend who didn't show last night. She's just letting me know that the Blues won in shootouts – whatever that means."

"Um, *what?*" Mitch asked with wide eyes, trying to comprehend what Ellie just said.

"Yeah Mitch, I knew about the game," Ellie said with a naughty smile. "It was the first game of the season, right? You wouldn't shut up about that team when we were talking last night, but you still kept our date. By the way - was it so hard to miss a game and spend the evening with me instead?"

"Uh," Mitch choked for a second. "Nooo," he finally said with a smile.

"Good, because that's what really impressed me about you – you were willing to skip the game for me. It's funny because, as I was leaving to meet you tonight, Danni told me she was gonna have a few beers and watch the game. Yet, even though I knew how big of a hockey fan you are, you were still coming to have dinner with me instead. And that felt really good."

"Wait a minute," he paused, stopping his gait and realizing the circumstances. "When you asked if I was a Blues fan, you knew *exactly* what you were doing, didn't you."

"Well, we *did* have two bottles of wine," she shrugged. "And... yeah, I was feeling a little mischievous. But I was having so much fun with you and didn't want to lose you to a hockey game. So, I hope you're not mad."

Mitch stared at her for second with a look of both disbelief and amusement.

"Well, I *did* want to see the game," he admitted, "But I don't regret choosing you over the game. I've had a blast tonight."

"Tell ya what," Ellie offered. "I'll make it up to you."

"*Really?*" he smiled with implied eagerness.

"Get that thought outta your head right now, mister," she laughed.

"Wait, what are you talking...." Mitch replied, sarcastically pretending to be oblivious to what she meant. "Oh, wow – you thought I was thinking... hey, I'm not that kind of guy, missy, sooooo..."

"Just... shut up," she smiled widely, fully amused by Mitch's attempt to turn the teasing around on her. "Just take me to a hockey game."

"You want to go to a hockey game?"

"Yeah... with *you*."

"So, I guess this means there's gonna be a second date here?"

"Well, silly, if the kisses weren't enough of a clue for you..." Ellie giggled. "And I'm assuming the Blues will be playing a game in town sometime soon, right?"

"Uh, yeah," Mitch raised an eyebrow. "That kinda happens a lot around here during hockey season."

"OK then, I look forward to it," she smiled. "Here's my car." She then turned, kissed him one last time, climbed into her car and said "call me" as she pulled away.

Mitch stood there dumbfounded as she drove off.

He then let out a huge "YYYYEEEEESSSSSS!!!" and jumped in the air. Briefly channeling Muhammad Ali, he shadow-boxed a few punches and then lifted his fists in the air triumphantly and bounced around like a victorious prize fighter. And as he walked back to his own car, he settled into a confident strut with a smile almost wider than his face could hold.

CHAPTER 5

ME AND MY, ME AND MY,
ME AND MY, ME AND MY FRIENDS

The next morning, Mitch walked out of his bedroom and into the maelstrom that was his living room. Countless empty cans and bottles, crumpled chips, scattered popcorn buds, and half-consumed everythings were strewn everywhere.

Unfazed from years of waking up to this kind of disaster, Mitch indifferently picked up a paper plate with a nub of bratwurst and a dried mustard puddle from the couch and placed it atop the conglomerate of empty beer cans on the coffee table, like miniature grain silos. He then ran his hand under the various bits of trash lying on the couch until he found the remote and turned on SportsCenter.

As the TV droned on, he assessed the disaster around him. Noticing an open bag of Red Man chewing tobacco on the table, Mitch thought back to the black light incident from the night before.

"*Maybe this will take that crap off my teeth,*" he thought.

He picked up the bag and grabbed a handful of the tobacco. Cringing at both the appearance and the odor of the large hellish wad of brown leaves, he closed his eyes and shoved it into his mouth.

As he slowly became aware of the actual *taste* of chewing tobacco, he began fighting his gag reflex as tears ran down his cheeks. He leapt into the kitchen and spat the wad into the already-overfilled trash can.

He then poured a cup of coffee and swished it in his mouth – hoping to both stain his teeth *and* remove the horrid taste at the same time.

Still, Mitch was in the thralls of a minor panic attack over his teeth.

"*What if this is permanent?*" he thought.

He looked around the kitchen with newfound resolve. Carrying his cup of coffee, he grabbed an ashtray with a half smoked cigarette in it, and planted himself back on the couch.

"*Let's just get this over with,*" he thought.

He put a smaller wad of tobacco in his mouth and again attempted to chew. With the tobacco still in his mouth, he took a drink of his coffee, swished it, and swallowed the coffee. Then he lit the remainder of the cigarette and tried to take a drag off it while widening his lips to expose as many teeth to the smoke as possible– which ended up making a flat hissing sound.

As he sat there, he methodically alternated between the four staining agents – chew, swish, drink, drag...chew, swish, drink, drag.

Mitch suddenly no longer felt nauseated so much as he did dizzy, but he remained determined. He then noticed the tube of teeth whitener on the floor underneath the coffee table. In a fit of anger, he slung it into the still-smoldering fireplace. As Mitch clenched his jaw with the satisfaction of destroying the stuff that nearly ruined his date, he suddenly became aware of odd wick-like hissing sounds emanating from the fireplace.

Suddenly, like the afterburners from a fighter jet, a blue hue blasted out from the fireplace, singeing the coffee table and lightly toasting Mitch's eyebrows.

Mitch looked down at the cigarette that was still in his lips, and realized that it had been smoked down to the filter, resembling a spent 4th of July 'snake'. He spat the filter into an empty beer can as the table's edges continued to smolder.

Just then, Chance walked out of his bedroom wearing boxer shorts, a cowboy hat, a Blues jersey, about 20 plastic Mardi Gras beads, and work boots. He rubbed his eyes and then saw Mitch. He stood there and just stared, silent and confused.

Mitch saw what Chance was wearing and stared back at him, equally silent and confused.

"Rough night?" they asked in unison.

"What the fuck are you wearing?" Mitch asked, undaunted by the symmetry.

Chance then looked at the table with its edges still smoldering, and, thinking that last night's partying had done something to cause it, he cringed.

"Um, I can explain," he pleaded as he pointed to the table. After several seconds of trying to remember, he confessed, "OK... I can't. But before you start yelling at me like a little bitch, I'll pay for it, OK?"

Mitch had planned to tell Chance that the table's current state had nothing to do with him... until the "little bitch" comment.

"Tell ya what," Mitch grimaced, "we'll split the cost, OK?"

"Deal!" Chance proclaimed, leaping at the offer. "And I'll get the beers tonight!"

"Fair enough," Mitch smiled, amused by the fast one he just pulled on Chance.

"Dude, I don't know what the table's made of," Chance added, "but it smells really *minty*."

"I know, right?" Mitch agreed a little too quickly, "That *is* weird... Oh, by the way, the date went awesome."

"Cool!" Chance smiled. "Didja get laid?

"What? No, I..."

"Don't care then," Chance dismissed, completely uninterested. "OK, check this out. After the game, we went all Mardi Gras-ey. We tried to get some chicks walkin' by to show us their tits...one thing led to another... and, oh by the way, Tom says he knows this killer carpenter that can get those burn marks outta the deck."

Mitch, suddenly solely focused on Chance's last comment, stood up and yelled, "What *burn marks???*"

But as he stood up from the couch to look at the deck, he felt a sudden massive head rush from the tobacco and caffeine overdose – and collapsed to the floor.

"Should I go get you some nicotine patches?" Chance asked uncertainly, standing over Mitch.

"What? " Mitch said as he clawed his way back onto the couch. "No... I..." he said, stopping his sentence long enough to scoop the chaw from his lip and put it in a random empty beer can.

He then got to feet, fully intending to launch into a tirade at Chance, when his cell phone rang. When he saw "Ellie" on his Caller ID, Mitch leashed his rage as best he could as he forcefully pointed at Chance, mouthing, "You-Me... we're gonna talk."

He then pressed Talk and said, "Hello?"

"Hey, what's going on?" Ellie answered.

"Ellie, hey!" Mitch replied, trying to hide the anger for Chance and the dizziness from caffeine and tobacco. "Can you hold on a sec?"

"Sure."

Mitch covered the phone and pointed at Chance.

"I am *NOT* helping you pay for the deck, too!" he scolded in a loud whisper. He then returned the phone to his ear and tried to put a smile in his voice. "So, have your eyes stopped dilating yet?"

"Yeah, they're fine," Ellie laughed. "Did you get rid of that teeth whitener stuff yet?"

"Um, you could say that..." Mitch commented, looking again at the smoldering furniture. "So, what's going on?"

"Oh, nothing," Ellie answered. "I had a great time last night."

"Me too," Mitch smiled as he sat back down on the sofa. "We'll have to see that band again sometime."

"Heh heh, yeah - when the bassist gets his eye sight back," she teased. "Hey listen, the reason I called was just that I was wondering what you were doing tonight."

"Really?" Mitch asked. "Uh, nothing. What do you have ... OH CRAP," he realized in mid-sentence. "I promised Chance we'd go out for a few beers tonight."

"Well, where are you going?" Ellie continued. "Maybe I can meet up with you."

Mitch hesitated while looking at Chance, who was now sitting right next to him and picking his nose with the eraser end of a pencil. Mitch then cringed at the thought of Ellie hanging out with Chance.

"Uh, no," he replied. "I don't think that'd be a good idea."

"Why not?" Ellie asked.

"Well, I, um..." he stammered. "I just wouldn't want either of you to feel like a third wheel. What about Tuesday?"

"No, Tuesday's no good," she answered. "Hey, maybe I can bring a friend for Chance."

Mitch again looked at Chance, who, at that point, had a pencil dangling from each nostril and was lifting his chin, trying really hard to see the tips of the pencils.

"Wow," Mitch accidentally said aloud while looking at Chance. "Look," Mitch explained into the phone, "I don't know what this girlfriend ever did to you, but trust me, it wasn't bad enough to subject her to Chance."

"Did I hear my name?" Chance asked, turning to look at Mitch and wildly swinging the pencil ends.

Mitch tried to wave him away from his conversation, but Chance kept staring at him.

Mitch then covered the phone and said, "Chance, I have a box of pencils in my room, if you're interested."

"Sweet!" Chance smiled as he got up and started to jog out of the room. "I'm gonna try to get five in each nostr..."

But in the middle of his sentence, he stumbled into the wall face-first and began screaming.

Mitch, envisioning the pencils skewering Chance's cerebral cortex, turned towards him in a wide-eyed panic.

As Chance turned to face him with his hands covering his face, he removed his hands, smiled, and said, "*Just kiddin'...*"

"*Asshole!*" Mitch thought to himself as he scrunched his lips. He grabbed the bratwurst nub off the paper plate and slung it at Chance.

Chance dodged the sausage and caught it rebounding off the wall. He briefly surveyed the sausage, looked at Mitch, and popped it in his mouth.

"Thanks bud!" he said while chewing and walking out of the room.

"What, is something wrong with him?" Ellie asked through the phone.

"Depends," Mitch answered, still staring at where Chance had been standing. "How long does Salmonella take to set in?"

"What?"

"Nevermind."

"C'mon, *you* live with him. He can't be *that* bad," Ellie reasoned.

"Um..." Mitch paused.

Chance walked back in the room with pencils gripped in each hand.

"Hey Mitch," he whispered.

Mitch tried to motion him out of the room, looking at the floor and trying to avoid eye contact.

Chance ignored his gyrations. "Five bucks says I can get twenty pencils in my head."

Mitch frantically shook his head "NO".

"Is he good-looking?" Ellie continued.

"OK, *twenty* dollars," Chance countered.

Mitch, desperate to get Chance out of the room, nodded frantically in agreement and waved him out.

"Sweet," Chance smiled.

"Wait," Mitch tried to continue with Ellie. "What'd you just say?"

"Tell me about him," Ellie said. "Is he good looking? Does he have a job? Is he a pig?"

"Well, first," Mitch started, "don't know, don't care. Second, Yes – remember, you saw him for a when we met? And third, well... his nickname in college was 'Chance - The Other White Meat.'"

"Oh yeah," Ellie laughed, "I remember him. The friend of yours who thought I was a lesbian, right?"

"More like 'hoped', but yeah."

"Oh, this'll be perfect!" Ellie laughed. "My friend Danni is just the person to keep a guy like him in line."

"Danni?" Mitch asked.

"Yeah, it's short for Danielle, but she goes by Danni. Ya know, Mitch, she's a former Miss Texas, a sportscaster, and the only thing she likes more than chauvinistic men is hot women."

"Um, *what?*" Mitch choked, trying to clear his throat.

"Yeah, we were college roommates," she added, "and we did *everything* together."

"Really..." Mitch spat. "*Everything?*"

He then paused, contemplating how to respond.

"Hey, how's about I just cancel with Chance and you, me, and Danni go out?"

"Mitch," Ellie scoffed, "I'm kidding. Sounds like Chance isn't the only pig in that pen."

"Wha... oh, well, um..." Mitch scrambled, "*So was I, Ellie.* I was just playing along. You know that."

"OK, so look, mister," Ellie directed. "Danni can handle herself. She can put any guy in his place. The moment he acts up, you and I will have a good time watching her tear him apart, trust me. So you need not worry about Chance."

"You have no idea what you're asking for," Mitch cautioned.

"Just realize that I'm giving you an opportunity to take me out a second time," Ellie continued. "Not many men get this opportunity, but I happen to find you a little cute, somewhat nice - if not a little adolescent - and sweet. Now, are you going to take advantage of this or should I open an e-harmony account?"

"If you do open one, let me know," Mitch replied sarcastically. "I get $50 every time I refer someone."

"See?" her voice smiled, "That's the Mitch that I want to see tonight."

Mitch's heart raced at what she said. Her words, for that moment, made him feel like a god. Then, his eyes widened with panic when he thought of Chance coming along. His stomach began twisting into knots as he weighed whether or not to risk Chance screwing this up this soon.

And that was when Chance walked back in with a pencil in each nostril and each ear

"Dude, I couldn't get two in each nostril, but does this count?" he asked as he pointed to a pencil in each ear.

Mitch's face sunk as he ordered Chance away with one commanding thrust of his finger. Chance walked back out of the room, sneering.

"Look, how about just you and I go somewhere," Mitch negotiated. "If you want to invite Danni to meet up with us, that's cool."

"It's just that Danni is very protective," Ellie replied, almost apologetically. "And I'm afraid she will embarrass me, or worse... *you*. With the way she picks people apart, I don't think that'd be a good idea."

"Picks apart?" Mitch asked, suddenly concerned.

In that moment, it made a heck of a lot more sense to bring Chance along for the vetting process, if not for mere comparison's sake. Mitch figured he'd look positively golden to Ellie and Danni if Chance was standing next to him being, well, *being Chance.*

Chance walked back into the room with a mouthful of pencils. "I winub. Bay ub," he warbled, holding his hand out for his $20.

Mitch gazed in horror upon Chance. He had pencils in each ear hole, one in each nostril, and the rest simply jutting from his mouth. Chance's entire head now resembled a Spartan phalanx.

Temporarily dumbfounded, Mitch then smiled as the question torturing his gut was inadvertently answered by Chance's "Chance-ness."

"Hold on a sec, Ellie," Mitch said, temporarily ignoring the glaring distraction of Chance's graphite arrangement. "Hey bud," he said to Chance, "I know I said we'd go out and have a few tonight, but Ellie's on the phone and she wants to meet up."

Chance spat out the pencils in disgust.

"*Are you shittin' me???!!!*" he raged, ripping the pencils out of both nostrils at once, which – in the process – took every one of his nose hairs with them. "Do you.... *AAARRRRGH!!!*" he wailed as he collapsed to the floor.

Mitch jumped up and stared as Chance got to his knees with tears streaming down his cheek.

"Dude, are you OK?" Mitch asked with more annoyance than concern.

"FUCK NO, I'M NOT OK!!!" he screamed as he rattled his head, trying to shake off the pain. "I JUST GAVE MY NOSE A *BRAZILLIAN!!! FUUUCK!!!*"

After huffing twice to cope with the pain, he returned to his rant.

"Are you telling me after one lousy date where you didn't even get *laid*, you're just gonna dump on all of us???"

"*All* of us?" Mitch asked.

"*Yeah!*" Chance continued. "Everyone's meeting us at that new place with the stripper waitresses, remember??? And the fuckin' game is on! Against the fuckin' *Blackhawks*! Even *Joe's* comin'! That's fuckin' great, how quickly you'll dump on your friends for a piece of ass, you pussy!!!"

"Um, okaaay," Mitch replied calmly. "What I was *going to* say is Ellie has a friend," then, covering the receiver, he mouthed, "she's hot," and, uncovering the receiver, continued, "she wants to know if you wanna double."

Chance looked at his roommate and, without blinking, stood up and replied, "OK."

"Wha..." Mitch asked. "Are you *sure*? What about *the guys?*"

"Who?" Chance asked, confused.

"Ya know," Mitch repeated, "*everybody? Joe?*"

"Ahh, fuck 'em, they'll be fine," Chance replied. "They were all just here last night anyway."

Confused, but ignoring Chance's 180-degree turn, Mitch returned to the phone.

"OK Ellie, we're in," he replied into his phone.

"Wait," Chance interrupted. "Does she have big tits?"

Mitch tried to cover the mouthpiece in time, but Ellie heard him anyway and began laughing.

Mitch simultaneously cringed and sighed.

"Sorry about that," he said. "Let's meet at Budgie's at seven."

"What?" she asked, jokingly stunned. "You're not going to pick us up?"

"Well, um..." he stammered. "I *can*, but I thought you had this rule..."

"For the *first* date," she corrected. "This is the second date. These are entirely new rules now."

"OK then," Mitch replied, trying to catch up. "At any point am I going to see these rules?"

"It's on a need-to-know-basis," she replied. "So... no."

"Can I at least get the Cliff Notes?"

"No."

"Dammit... alright." Mitch conceded. "Gimme directions..." he sighed as he reached for a ripped up envelope from an unpaid bill. As he scribbled down her instructions, he said, "Alright, we'll be there."

"Great!" Ellie answered. "I'll see you about 6:45!"

"You're gonna *love* Chance," Mitch sighed.

"Not as much as you're gonna *love* Danni," she replied with a smile. "Alright, see you then. Oh, and by the way, tell your roomie to take a shower and not wear anything stupid."

Mitch looked at Chance and suddenly wondered if Ellie was somehow seeing inside their apartment. He pulled back the blinds from a nearby window, looked up and down the street.

"Uh, no..." he replied tentatively. "He wouldn't do anything like that," he answered as he continued to look around. "Um, see you tonight."

"Bye..." Ellie replied, her voice trailing off anticipatorily.

As Mitch hung up, Chance clomped towards the front door still wearing his boxer shorts, boots, Blues jersey and Mardi Gras beads.

"Hey, I'm heading to the mailbox," he said. "Ya need anything mailed?"

"Chance," Mitch pleaded as he looked at Chance's outfit, "it's Saturday."

"*Yeaaaah*," Chance replied. "Mail *comes* on Saturday, dumbass."

Mitch wanted to protest Chance's walking through their apartment complex in that outfit, but he just acquiesced.

"No, dude," he said as he shook his head in resignation. "Go ahead."

CHAPTER 6

AND THE GIRLS LIKE THE BOYS
LIKE THE BOYS LIKE THE GIRLS

As Chance finished getting ready, Mitch ran down the stairs and shoved open the scarred, heavy wooden door that enclosed the stairwell to the apartment complex. He skipped down the small grass hill and caught himself on the hood of his old junker - a faded royal blue 1992 four-door Toyota Corolla.

His car could have been considered more of an eye sore than a vehicle. Besides the numerous spots where rust was winning the war for territory, the front left fender was still in its black-primer color from the day Mitch replaced it himself - and every time Mitch looked at that fender, he remembered that night in college.

He was just grateful that he'd happened to be near his car when one of Chance's college 'girlfriends' first grabbed the tire iron. Luckily, she'd only had enough time to pummel and scrape that fender before Mitch was forced to tackle her. Even back then, Mitch knew you couldn't discuss anything with a woman who was sobbing *that* pitifully - especially when she's holding a tire iron over your car.

It was only made worse because, *for some reason*, she believed the car was owned by her *supposed* boyfriend, Chance (yeah, he kind of lied about that). And while her *supposed* boyfriend (yeah, Chance, uh, kind of lied about that, too) was still upstairs kicking one of her sorority sisters out of their dorm room, she was performing impromptu body work on Mitch's car.

With all those factors coalescing at that one critical moment, well... tackling her was simply the only way to save the car. At least, that's what Mitch *told himself* to minimize the lingering guilt he felt about the NFL-quality tackle he laid on her. To this day, he blamed Chance for lying to her about owning the car, but he never brought it up, because... it was Chance.

Mitch stopped his reminiscing as he opened the car door. Surveying the back seat filled with crumpled fast food bags, a myriad of paper cups, and countless straw and candy bar wrappers – he curled his lip.

"This ain't gonna work," he thought.

With only ten minutes remaining before they needed to leave, Mitch improvised. He popped the trunk and began frantically moving all the trash from his back seat to the trunk.

"There's that Tool CD," he muttered as he pulled another handful of trash from under the seat. He grabbed an empty McDonald's bag and quickly began stuffing scattered french fries and straw wrappers from his floorboard into the bag. He then brushed his hand over the back seats, trying to herd the crumbs over the crest of the seat and into that same bag.

As Mitch nearly finished cleaning, Chance came walking out.

"Um, wow," Chance said, noticing Mitch's trunk load of trash. "Ever hear of those big metal square things? I think they're called *dumpsters.*"

Mitch looked up and glared.

"No time," he dismissed. "Ya know, half of this garbage is yours, anyway."

"Eh," Chance shrugged, "still, you really should try cleaning your car out more than once a millennia."

"How about you *buy a car* before criticizing mine?" Mitch suggested.

"Are you kidding?" Chance replied in amazement as he looked the vehicle over. "Do you know how expensive these things can get?" He then leaned against the car to watch Mitch shaking out the floor mats.

Mitch noticed Chance's complete inaction.

"Li'l help?" he asked.

"No thanks," Chance replied.

"You wanna meet Danni, or do you wanna stay here?"

Chance huffed in defeat. He reached in back and pulled the little square floor mat out and began shaking it up and down as if he were salting a steak.

Mitch noticed Chance's indifferent effort.

"Fuckin' forget it," he said in disgust. "Just get in."

As they pulled down Ellie's street, they counted the house numbers down until they got to Ellie's house. Ellie and Danni were talking on her front porch as Mitch and Chance pulled up.

Mitch realized he'd found the house, but paused uncertainly in the middle of the street. Ellie noticed him and waved. Mitch and Chance waved back, then Mitch suddenly pulled forward quickly and drove past her driveway.

Ellie slowly lowered her hand as a look of utter confusion crossed her face.

"Where's he going?" Danni asked.

"No idea," Ellie replied.

Mitch had planned to park in the street, but there were a line of cars parked along the front of her house.

"What are you *doing*?" Chance asked angrily.

"First impressions, dude," Mitch replied as he turned the car around in the middle of the next intersection. "I don't want to look like the cocky guy who just thinks he can park in the driveway."

"Ya know, I've always wondered what a date with *no-chance-of-sex-at-the-end* looked like," Chance deadpanned. "Now, I know.

Mitch again passed her house while smiling and waving.

"Yes, ladies, we're both dorks," Chance muttered as he smiled and waved to the girls as they passed by again.

The girls both stared blankly and half-waved back as Mitch's car again drove past their line of sight.

"OK, park here!" Chance ordered.

"Hold on," Mitch argued as he wrestled with his steering wheel. He pulled all the way back down to the end of Ellie's street, turned around again, and parallel parked between a beat-up 70's Buick and their friend Lawrence's brand new Hummer. Lawrence, coincidentally, happened to live across the street from Ellie, but Mitch and Chance were more concerned with saving face than they were about why Lawrence never mentioned the beauty that lived across the street... at least, not at that point.

"Ya know," Chance added, growing more frustrated with Mitch's indecisive driving. "This is why you never get the quality chicks. This *first impression*, dude? Wow, just wow."

"Fuck off," Mitch sneered as he rocked his car back and forth into the parking space.

From Ellie's vantage point, the nose of his car seemed to appear then disappear behind the large shrubs at the edge of her property. The girls silently looked on with amused fascination. Danni stifled a laugh, unsure of how to react.

"OK, OK!" Chance growled, growing impatient. "STOP!"

Just then, Mitch felt his bumper hit Lawrence's Hummer. Chance and Mitch looked at each other in horrified silence, fully aware of how much their large friend loved his Hummer.

Chance hopped out as Mitch pulled forward a few inches and got out as well. He looked at Chance for the damage report.

Chance looked back at him in horror. Mitch's heart sank.

"You are so..." Chance started, "LUCKY!" he excitedly whispered. "Just a scratch, he'll probably never even notice."

Mitch sighed heavily as he walked back. But when he got there, he saw a four inch indentation with a little of his car's faded blue paint embedded in the chrome.

"*Never notice???*" Mitch nearly squealed. He then sighed and looked at Chance. "Should we tell him?"

"Yeah, Mitch, that's a good idea." Chance replied sarcastically. "There's Lawrence's house over there. Why don't you go knock on his door and tell him?"

"I shouldn't leave my car here, should I...?" Mitch asked, almost rhetorically.

"What do you fuckin' think?"

Mitch's car suddenly pulled into Ellie's driveway and the boys emerged to greet the ladies.

"Mitch, what was all that?" Ellie asked as the boys got out of the car.

"What?" Mitch shrugged like a little boy. "Just checking out the neighborhood. Besides, it's not like you two had to wait outside for us," Mitch said as he got closer.

"You're a dork," Ellie teased.

"That's what I said!" Chance announced.

As they walked up Ellie's driveway, Mitch was impressed with Ellie's home. Unlike the surrounding homes, which were more cheaply-built wooden homes with bargain-priced siding and stilted wooden porches, Ellie's house sat a little further off the road, giving her a larger front yard. And it was modest enough - a single story, two bedroom brick home from the 1940's, complete with aluminum awnings and that decorative circle thing found in the center of all the screen doors from that era. Her concrete driveway was on the far left edge of the property and ran along the side the house to the backyard. Although it was definitely an older house, the flower beds and shrubs were all well cared for, the windows were clean, and the brick was recently power-washed. She was obviously a landlord's dream tenant.

"Danni just got here," Ellie explained. "Her job does this to her all the time."

"Hi, I'm Danni," she said, introducing herself to Mitch with a scrutinizing smile that let Mitch know he was being sized up right then and there.

Danni was shorter than Ellie, but probably just as pretty. With brown-to-reddish shoulder length wavy hair, a confident smile, and an air of accomplishment that only enhanced her attractiveness, she appeared to be everything Ellie had said about her.

"Ah, the mystery friend!" Mitch exclaimed as he shook her hand, trying to ignore the pang of intimidation he felt from her scrutiny. "I'm Mitch, and this is Chance."

Chance walked up and shook Danni's hand.

"Hi, love the shoes!" Chance complimented.

"Thanks," Danni said uncertainly.

Danni was a little unsure of how to take Chance, but Chance sized her up immediately and shot Mitch a quick nod of approval. Mitch smiled back and shook his head. He knew exactly the phrase running through Chance's mind.

"Proportionally disproportionate - I know," Mitch thought to himself.

"And Chance," Mitch continued, "this is Ellie. You may remember her from..."

"Oh yeah, you're the actress who likes chicks, right?" Chance said with a teasing smile.

"Um, yeah, that'd be me," Ellie laughed.

"Knock it off," Mitch scolded.

"I'm kidding," Chance smiled.

"Oh, I know," Ellie replied. "Mitch has told me *all* about you."

"Really," Chance said as he turned and glared at Mitch. "What's he said?"

"I didn't lie about anything, bud," Mitch replied.

"You didn't answer the question, either," Chance insisted.

"Let's get going," Mitch announced, trying to change the subject. "The game will be starting soon."

Chance and Danni climbed into the back seats. Ellie sat up front and watched Mitch insert his key as the car began to ding. Mitch then turned the key and the ding faded away, but the car didn't start.

They all looked at Mitch.

"No-no, not now," Mitch muttered. He ran a gentle hand across the dashboard. "Come on, baby," he whispered into the speedometer. "Don't be jealous of her. Just work with me here."

He turned the key again and the engine started up. Mitch let out a sigh of relief.

"You talk to your car?" Ellie asked.

"Hey, this car got me back and forth between home and college for the full six years," Mitch explained. "She can be..."

"*She?*" Ellie teased.

"Oh yeah," Mitch replied. "Most cars are female; any guy will tell you that. Only a few are definitely dudes. Dragsters, for instance..."

"And Monster trucks," Chance chimed in from the back seat.

"Exactly," Mitch concurred. "Anyway, *she* can be a little temperamental sometimes, but she's reliable. She's always been good to me, so I've stuck with her."

Taken aback for a minute, Ellie began wondering if he was this loyal with everything in his life.

"I told Mitch he needs to trade her in for a newer model," Chance wisecracked as Mitch backed the car out of Ellie's driveway.

"Wow, Ellie told me you were a real romantic," Danni commented with dreamy sarcasm. "I can so totally see that about you right now," she added, not meaning a word of it.

"Keep it up Chance, and we'll all be walking home," Mitch cautioned. He then stroked the dashboard lightly again, put the car in drive, and whispered, "He didn't mean it baby... you know that's just Chance."

Ellie stared at Mitch again, still wondering if he was serious.

Mitch looked at Ellie and smiled widely.

"I'm just kidding," he laughed.

Ellie then sat back and laughed, relieved that Mitch wasn't actually crazy.

"Sort of..." Mitch mumbled as he put the car in drive.

CHAPTER 7

SHE'S THE BLADE
AND HE'S JUST PAPER

As they entered Budgie's, Mitch grabbed one of those tall, semi-sturdy bar tables and surrounded it with nearby stools as Chance asked the ladies what they wanted to drink.

"Chablis for me," Ellie said.

"Bud Select," Danni answered.

Chance suddenly smiled at Danni.

"I like you already," he said.

As Mitch and the ladies got comfortable, Chance delivered everyone's drinks.

"So Danni, what do you do for a living," Chance asked, "I mean, besides work out and look hot?"

Mitch and Ellie both rolled their eyes at the same time.

Danni just laughed. "Awww, that's so sweet. Do you steal all your lines from the internet?"

"Got my own twitter feed," Chance replied.

"I'm a *lobbyist*," Danni answered, ignoring Chance's response.

"A power broker?" Mitch asked. "Who do you lobby for?"

"Well, right now, the Sierra Club and Greenpeace," Danni explained. "We're trying to get the oil company to clean up that spill off Galveston."

"Alright!" Mitch commended, lifting his bottle. "A girl with a cause, trying to change the world."

"Wait," Ellie interrupted, "I thought you were working *for* the oil company last month."

"I was," Danni said. "A few weeks ago, my contract ran out."

"So now you're working for the other side?" Ellie asked.

"Well, the environmentalists needed an authority," Danni explained. "Who knows more about the situation than me?"

"Aw, I LOVE IT!" Chance exclaimed.

"Wait, so... I'm confused," Mitch pursued. "What *do* you believe in?"

"*A paycheck*?" Danni replied sarcastically, annoyed that she had to state the obvious.

"Me too," Chance agreed, smiling even more widely. "All companies just jerk us off while making millions off our talents."

"So, Chance, you work with Mitch, right?" Danni asked. "Are you a writer, too?"

"No way," Chance's nose curled at the suggestion. "Screw that."

"Yeah, that'd take too much work," Mitch shot back.

"OK, then what do you do?" Danni continued.

"I'm a Lead Quality Assurance Analyst," Chance announced proudly.

"*Whatever*," Mitch whispered to Ellie. "That's the first time he's *ever even stated* his job title."

"I make sure games like True Patriots perform to their specifications," Chance continued, ignoring Mitch's mumblings.

"*No kidding?*" Danni asked excitedly. "My girlfriends and I play True Patriots all the time!"

"So do me and my underlings!" Chance replied. "Maybe we've run into each other on the battlefield before! What's the name of your team?"

"The Phamaliag Cell," Danni said with a smile.

"The... *what?*" Chance stammered as his face sank.

"Phamaliag Cell," Danni continued, energized by being able to discuss cyber-battlefield stories. "Yeah, when I'm online with my girlfriends, we tear all those little boys up - they never knew what hit them."

Mitch's eyes widened with shock as Chance shifted in his seat uncomfortably.

"But..." Chance started stammering, "I heard... you guys were... like SEALS or something."

"Yeah," Danni smiled. "My friend Rita put that out on an internet chat board as a joke. It was too funny. But *no*," she sighed as she looked up to the ceiling and batted her eyes innocently. *"It's just us girls..."*

Chance sat motionless.

"So, what's the name of *your* team?" Danni asked Chance.

"Um, Alpha... Warface... Killers."

Ellie snorted hard as she tried to stifle a laugh. Mitch just chuckled, enjoying watching Chance struggle with being incredibly conflicted over trying to charm his very nemesis.

"From the Gateway Challenge semifinals last year!" Danni bounced with excitement. "Yeah, I remember you guys! Ooooh, you guys were good... up until the point where you left your entire left flank completely naked. We just pretty much walked right in like a buzz saw and ripped through your entire unit in about a minute and a half. I'm guessing you never saw us coming over that hill, did you?"

"Uh, no," Chance dismissed. "We didn't."

Ellie stared at Chance with a silent, wide smile, thoroughly enjoying how much Chance was simmering under the surface.

"Wait..." Mitch suddenly said as the realization hit him. "Phamaliag... Phamali... fema .... *OH MY GOD!*" Mitch yelled as he doubled over with laughter, nearly falling off his stool. "*THAT'S SO AWESOME!*" he howled, trying to breathe between fits of laughter.

"What?" Chance snapped at Mitch.

"You... AHAHA!!!" Mitch screamed. "You 'tester' geeks... you... *their... AHAHAHAHAAAA!!!*"

"*WHAT???!!!*" Chance yelled so loudly that the other patrons of Budgie's turned to look at him. But since he was now fully annoyed by not being in on the joke, he really didn't care what anyone else thought.

"You... gamer...*heroes*... HA HA HA!!! You... *Alpha Warface Killers*... ha ha HA!!!" Mitch gasped between laughs, "Y'all were destroyed by... the *FEMALE EGG CELL???!!!*" he bellowed. "***THAT'S FUCKIN' PRICELESS!!!***"

"OH MY GOD, DANNI!!!" Ellie screamed with laughter as she suddenly hugged her friend over Mitch's discovery. "YOU GIRLS ARE SO KICK ASS!!!"

Danni hugged Ellie back, then looked down and humbly chuckled to herself.

"Wait 'til I tell the fellas at work on Monday!" Mitch spat as quickly as he could between fits of laughter.

"Look!" Chance barked as he pointed at Mitch with a stare that threatened his very life. "That team... they... they *took the Gateway title, OK???!!!* They went to the FUCKIN' *Nationals!*"

"And barely lost in the finals," Danni shrugged humbly.

"YEAH!" Chance quickly yelled in agreement. "IN THE *FINALS!!!*"

"Aw, Chance," Danni said, lightly rubbing Chance's back. "Look at it this way, big guy - Fort Bragg went down quicker than you guys did."

Chance, sensing a moment to change the subject, just smiled.

"Hey, nobody goes down quicker than me," he smiled.

"Oh my God, you *are* a pig," Danni sighed in disbelief. "C'mon, let's go do a shot. I'm gonna need it if I have to deal with you all night."

"*All* night?" Chance asked.

"Ugh," Danni groaned as she threw her head back. "Look, if you behave, I'll give you some exploits we found in your game, OK?"

Feeling like he'd just regained his swagger, Chance simply smiled at Mitch and Ellie as Danni walked up to the bar.

"*Come on!*" Danni yelled at Chance.

"See ya guys," Chance said with a quick flick of an eyebrow.

"Oh my God, that was so great!" Mitch sighed as he caught his breath.

"I know!" Ellie replied, also regaining her composure. "I didn't know anything about that, either!"

"So, you're not a member of the Phamaliag Cell?" Mitch smirked.

"I'm not into video games at all," Ellie said. "But Danni says it's how she relieves stress. She says it's really cathartic."

"It can be," Mitch agreed. "I'm just not into that team-based, multi-player stuff. I'd rather play hockey video games."

"Why's that?"

"I dunno, there's just nothing quite like delivering a really solid body check."

"Speaking of which," Ellie added, pointing to the 15-feet-off-the-ground projection TV. "The game's about to start, isn't it?"

"Yeah," Mitch said. "Let's get those two... *holy crap*," Mitch said, pointing to Chance and Danni, who had just briefly kissed.

"What?" Ellie asked.

"Chance and Danni," Mitch continued. "I never thought God would create Chance's equal... but, they're kissing – *already*."

"Nuh-uh," Ellie said as she spun around just quickly enough to see the kiss.

"Dear God, there's two of them," Mitch suddenly realized. "Call Homeland Security."

"Oh, relax," Ellie replied, cuddling a little closer to Mitch. "Maybe she just has a use for him."

"Yeah, yeah, I know," Mitch complained. "The bigger the asshole they are, the more you ladies like them."

"Hey, not all women are suckers for guys like Chance," she said, somewhat bothered by Mitch's presumption. "We all wanna have sex, too – and some of us, well... maybe she's had a hard week and just wants to have a little fun. It may not be love, but it may be just what she needs."

"Sooooo," Mitch turned and smiled, "are *you* just looking to have fun, too?"

"*Hell no*," Ellie snapped, feigning insult while taking a drink. "I'm not easy, and you'd better not be, either," she said as she put down her newly emptied wine glass. "I'm wanting a little more than just that."

"No problem," Mitch laughed. "Renee?" he called out. "Another vino here!"

"I get it," Ellie smiled as she scooted closer still to Mitch. "Trying to get me drunk?"

"Nah," Mitch replied. "I want a little more than that, too. But I'm also open to compromise..." he smiled with a shrug.

Ellie laughed and shook her head.

"Cute. Now, which color are we?" she said, pointing to the game on TV.

"Well, we're called the Blues, sooooo...."

"Oh *look, honey,*" she said mockingly while pointing to Chance and Danni. "Chance just got another kiss. He must be being *nice* to his date."

"OK, babe... sorry," Mitch apologized. "Just kidding with ya. We're the team in red."

"Really?"

"What? *No!*" he replied incredulously with scrunched eyebrows. "C'mon, we're the *Blues*, for crissake!"

"Oh," she replied as she stared down her nose. "You're gonna pay for that."

"I bet Danni knows what color the Blues are," Mitch mumbled to himself.

"WHAT?" Ellie asked.

"Renee?" Mitch called out. "Where's that drink?"

CHAPTER 8

WE'LL DO SOME DRINKIN',
MAYBE HURT OURSELVES REAL BAD

Mitch never understood when his friends would bash the women they dated or married. Outside of the obvious burden of having to listen to complaints about *whatever*, he always remembered that whenever he'd been in a relationship, he was – for the most part – happy. Mitch mostly wrote off his friends' complaints as "dude bravado," especially when he'd quietly snicker to himself while watching his friends fold and accommodate their women every time the protests became unmanageable.

The same was true this time around for Mitch. He and Ellie had been dating for about three weeks now and things were going incredibly well, as most relationships do early on. And he, for the most part, was ecstatic. Ellie seemed to be everything he'd ever wanted in a woman... well, other than wishing she'd be a little more liberal with her sexuality. But still, he had no complaints - even simply talking to her on the phone made him smile.

Although, Mitch was more than a little envious at how quickly Chance and Danni's relationship had progressed on a physical level. He told himself that Chance and Danni's thing was superficial and short-term - and being aware of that fact should have satiated his envy. But Chance was getting laid nearly every day... at least that's what Chance was telling everyone. So, telling himself how superficial Chance and Danni's relationship was, well... it didn't help – not one bit.

He was just grateful that Chance and Danni weren't doing their *"writing the sequel to the Kama Sutra"* when he was home. But seeing Danni bounce past him on her way out of the apartment with her post-coital energy, then seeing Chance lie motionless on the couch in his post-coital coma... well, Mitch just kept reminding himself that he and Ellie had something more going.

So this evening was something Mitch really needed - another Blues game was on TV, all the fellas were getting together at Budgie's, and it was time to get rowdy and have a few beers... or more. Mitch told himself that he, at the very least, deserved that much.

The boys were huddled around the bar watching the game and just talking about the usual – women, sports, and work – as the game started. Then Rich stormed into the bar.

"OK! OK!" Rich huffed as he pulled his coat off with the bar doors swinging back into their frame behind him, "what'd I miss, girls?"

Not one person in the group moved their eyes from the TV.

"Nothing... yet," they groaned in unison.

Chance shot Rich a look after he'd referred to the group as "girls." That kind of bravado was not normal for Rich, and Chance momentarily wondered where it came from.

"Has it started snowing yet?" Chance then asked, dismissing his initial thoughts.

"Oh yeah," Rich answered.

"What can I get you, Rich?" Renee asked.

"Gimme a hiney."

"A *Heineken*?" Renee asked.

"No, I want a *hiney*," Rich smiled wickedly, emphasizing the double entendre.

Chance pulled his head back, even more shocked at Rich.

"You ain't gettin' this hiney, Rich," Renee replied flatly. "What do you want to drink?"

"Bud Light's fine."

"So, how bad are the roads?" Chance asked with a squint, investigating Rich a little more closely.

"Slicker than cum on a gold tooth," Rich announced with a giddy smile.

Right as he'd said that, and the group slowly turned and stared at him.

"*Awwww!*" they all yelled in disgusted approval.

Renee was reaching for his beer when she heard what he'd just said. She shuddered simply closed the cooler without getting his beer.

"Renee, um?" Rich asked.

"After that comment," Renee said, "you're gonna wait. There *are* ladies in the room."

Chance snorted, mocking Renee's suggestion.

"Planning on celebrating sober tonight, Chance?" Renee asked.

"Noooo," Chance shook his head emphatically while making his eyes as wide and innocent as possible. "I was just thinking how insensitive that comment was to any fine young lady who's needed to have bridge work done," he said, all the while knuckle-knocking with Rich under the bar.

Even though he tried to give her the innocent, puppy dog eyes, his "I'm so full of shit" smile was still bleeding through.

"The first period just started," Mitch announced, even though he was equally baffled by Rich's cocky behavior.

"Whew, good," Rich replied.

"Rich," Chance turned and shot an annoyed glare, "you know the game's on the radio too, right?

"Yeah, but I haven't figured out how to switch to AM on my new car yet."

Mitch, slouching against the bar, put his face in one hand/

"Again with the car..." Mitch mumbled.

"You've owned that car for, what, four months now?" Chance asked.

"Yeah."

"It's not a new car anymore," Chance replied flatly. "Get over it."

The group laughed in agreement.

"That's cute, Chance," Rich replied. "Why don't you get a car so you don't have to envy mine so much?"

"I will," Chance agreed. "Right after you get a penis so you won't have to envy mine so much."

The boys burst out laughing and the regular light-hearted shoving ensued.

"Oh, I know I got a penis. And the wife is REALLY sure of it after last night."

"Wow," Tom mocked, "what kind of proof were you able to come up with?"

"Hey boys, knock it off!" Mitch announced. "The game's back on."

The group stared intently at the game. They leaned and motioned with the players' every moves and strides while yelling and cheering like maniacs – until another commercial came on.

"Ya know," Tom said over the break, "speaking of new cars, has anyone ridden in Lawrence's Hummer yet?"

"No," Chance complained. "That asshole won't even let me go on beer runs with him. He said he's afraid I'll take it for a joyride while he's in the store. Can you believe that shit?"

"Hey," Mitch realized, "where *is* Lawrence?"

"Right here, fellas," boomed a voice as Lawrence emerged through the front door.

"Lawrence!" everyone yelled.

"How's it goin', boys?" he replied with a smile, then simply pointed at Chance, letting him know that he'd heard Chance's comment.

Chance merely nodded and looked directly at the floor.

Lawrence then worked his way up to the bar where Mitch's gaze was firmly fixed on the TV.

"Hey Mitch, what's up?"

"Lawrence, how you doin', bud?" Mitch said while not moving his eyes from the screen.

"Hey, did I see your car again last night across the street from my house?"

"Yeah, probably – I was dropping off Ellie."

"*You?*" Lawrence scoffed. "*You* took *that* Ellie out last night? *She's* the Ellie you've been talking about nonstop?"

"Yeah," Mitch again replied in monotone, "one in the same."

"Dude, shut up!" Lawrence smiled as he slapped Mitch's shoulder.

Mitch finally looked away from the game and flashed Lawrence a confused smile.

"What?" he asked.

"Mitch, Ellie is a total hottie! Dude, I've seen her in the front lawn in a sun dress... Sweet mother of God, if my wife knew I was lookin' at Ellie like that..."

"No worries, Lawrence," Mitch said, taking another swig of his beer and turning back to the TV. "Your secret is safe with me."

"Oh, I ain't worried," Lawrence smiled confidently as he put his enormous hand on Mitch's shoulder and lightly shook him. "If you ever *did* say anything to my wife, I'd just kill you."

Mitch's smile quickly faded as he tried to maintain his balance, but the strength in Lawrence's arm made Mitch's head wobble like a rag doll. His eyes slowly moved back to look at Lawrence, who was staring him dead in the eye and grinning widely. Mitch flashed an uncertain smile and slowly returned his now-completely-widened eyes back to the screen - all the while trying to ignore that sudden twinge of fear he felt in his gut.

"Hey wait a second," Mitch said as he turned again toward Lawrence, "you've lived next to her for, like, four months now, and you never thought to set me up?"

Lawrence merely chuckled at the suggestion.

"Honestly Mitch?" he said, "I never thought you'd ever have a chance with a woman like her."

Chance bellied-up to the bar behind Mitch and was taking a big swig of his beer as the conversation continued.

"Oh, *really*?" Mitch squinted, now insulted. "Well maybe Ellie wasn't quite as immune to the ol' Mitch charm as you thought there, bud."

Chance spewed his beer across the bar and doubled over in laughter, pounding the bar in hysterics. Lawrence stood there and laughed with Chance.

"Chance!" Renee scolded him from behind the bar. "Knock it off!"

Once the first period ended, Lawrence sat up.

"Hey fellas," he announced, "come outside for a second. You boys are gonna *love* this."

The group followed him outside as he extended his arms towards his Hummer.

"Lawrence, we've already seen your car," Mitch complained. "Yeah, it's fuckin' *beautiful*, OK?"

"Of course it is," Lawrence stated proudly as he pointed his keychain at the vehicle. "But I know you guys. You probably wanna get a look *up close*."

"Finally!" Chance complained.

"Go ahead, Chance," Lawrence offered with a taunting smile. "Get in."

As Chance pulled on the door handle, a siren erupted and multi-colored flashing lights – the kind normally found on emergency vehicles – beamed in every direction. All at once, the boys crouched down and looked around like spooked deer.

"AHAHAHAHA!" Lawrence laughed as he turned off the alarm with his keychain.

"Dude!" Chance whined. "NOT COOL!"

"That's why I just had it installed," Lawrence shrugged. "Like I said, I *know* you guys."

"What's that supposed to mean?" Rich asked.

"Well, consider this my warning to any of you," Lawrence replied, as he looked directly at Chance. "Just in case any of you ever think about takin' my baby for a spin without askin'... I'LL KNOW. If anything even touches this car ever again - like whoever that blue-car-driving mother fucker who scarred up my bumper a few weeks ago was – I'LL KNOW..."

Mitch laughed as his and Lawrence's hands clasped mid-air.

"I love it," Mitch complimented, then shot a look of horror at Chance as Lawrence was looking the other way.

Chance looked back at Mitch with primal fear in his eyes.

"NEVER SAY A WORD," Chance mouthed to Mitch.

"OK," Chance said, resuming a normal speaking tone, "now open her up for real."

As the game went on, the boys continued tearing through beers and carrying on about work, women, the home teams, and giving Renee a hard time at every turn. And despite their best efforts, the Blues lost the game.

Mitch was more bothered than the rest of his crew. For some reason, he always took a Blues loss personally. He downed two Jager shots, stumbled back towards his friends, and straight into Chance's braggadocio.

"So anyway, fellas," Chance declared, "Lemme tell ya, we ALL should live like I did today."

"Really," Rich asked.

"Yeah, first, I called in sick this morning so I could sit around all day and play the video games that *I* wanted to play. Then I ordered a pizza for lunch and popped my first beer as soon as the hottie delivery girl dropped off the pie. I ate the whole thing and played a few more rounds on the PlayStation when Danni showed up. I nailed her like drywall for about an hour, kicked her out, took a nap, got up, popped another brew, and then headed up here to hang out with you losers. Now *that's* a king's day..."

"Wow, Chance," Tom said. "You've been getting a lot of action from this Danni chick. How long do you think this'll last?"

"As long – and as *often* – as I want it to," Chance nodded with half-smiled arrogance.

Mitch just rolled his eyes, both from disgust and envy. The alcohol in his system, coupled with the Blues loss, was helping him feel a little angry, too.

"In fact, I think I'm gonna call Danni here in a minute and see if she's up for round three... or *four*, depending on who's counting," Chance smiled. "Hey Mitch?" he asked as he grabbed his phone, "Do you mind dropping me off at Danni's?"

"Hey, how do you know I'm not heading over to Ellie's for my own booty call?" Mitch sneered.

Snorts and giggles of laughter emanated from the group.

"What?!" Mitch demanded.

"Mitch," Chance said, "Don't take this personally, but you've got a few more months of basic training before she's gonna let you fire off any rounds."

The group winced and howled.

"Hey, fucker," Mitch growled through his slurring. "I'm ready to... fire... as soon as... um... uh... OK, *fuck you! Walk to Danni's!*"

"No problem," Chance shrugged, enjoying both the buzz he had as well as the antagonizing he was putting Mitch through. "I'd walk the whole way from here because I know that when I get there, I'm gonna *at least* get a mouth hug. I'll bet you wouldn't walk all the way to Ellie's from here."

"Why not?" Mitch mocked. "Because I own a fucking car?"

"Did you say you're fucking your car?" Chance countered. "Because you're sure-as-shit not fucking *Ellie*."

"Look, fucker – I could hit that right now if I wanted to."

"HA!" Chance taunted, "OK then, $20 says you're still rubbing out knuckle children by this time next week."

"Make it $100," Mitch countered.

"Like I'm gonna take your word for it with Prudence over there," Chance laughed.

"*Prudell, you fuck!*" Mitch yelled, now fully pissed off. "Her name is Ellie *Prudell*. Stop calling her 'Prudence'! Ellie hates when you two call her that!"

"Awww," Chance replied pitifully. "If only she'd take care of you the way you take care of her, you chump."

"Oh really," Mitch insisted with buzzed bravado. "I'll call her right now and tell her to get that little ass over to my place."

A few of the fellas encouraged him with grunts and cheers as he continued his rant.

"I'll show you..." Mitch continued. "I'll call her right now and say, 'It's time ta *give it up*, woman!'"

The rest of the men at the bar – even guys he didn't know – cheered even more loudly, and he felt braver than ever.

Mitch blearily glared at Chance as the two engaged in an old-fashioned stare-down.

"Check this out," Mitch slurred as he reached for his phone. He then noticed that his phone wasn't in his pocket. Undeterred, he looked around some more.

"Where's my phone???!!!" he yelled.

Lawrence picked Mitch's phone off the bar and hung it in front of Mitch's face.

"Is this it?" he asked.

"Yeah," Mitch slurred a little. "Thanksh, bud."

As Mitch reached for the phone, Lawrence turned and slung it across the bar like a major league pitcher. The phone exploded into a million shards upon impact with the brick wall.

Everyone fell deafly silent and all eyes grew large.

Mitch, unable to process what he just witnessed, simply let his jaw widen as big as his eyes.

"DUDE!!!!" Mitch yelled. *"WHAT THE FUCK???!!!"*

Lawrence stood silently as he glared at Mitch until Mitch could feel Lawrence's stare minimizing his rage – and also somehow sobering him up pretty quickly.

"Look Mitch, I like you," Lawrence said. "I think you and Ellie - hell, you two might be good for each other. If I didn't think so, I wouldn't even be talking to you about this right now. I'd just let you fuck this up so we could all destroy you about it later. But listen up - I've been Ellie's neighbor for about four months now, and that there is one good woman – beautiful, smart, funny, and kind. She deserves a good man, not an idiot. And I *know* you're not the idiot that was talking all that stupid shit a minute ago and about to make that stupid ass phone call."

"But my *phone*!!!" Mitch pleaded incredulously.

Rich began chuckling to himself.

"What are you laughing at, fucker?" Mitch asked.

"Nothing," he smiled widely. "I got to bang my wife all day for our anniversary... and *I still have my phone...*"

"Fuckin' great," Mitch sighed in frustration.

"Oh yeah," Rich replied, just to rub it in. "And I speared the starfish... *twice*."

"Nice," Chance muttered quietly as he again knuckle-knocked with Rich.

Mitch just glared at both of them.

"Look Mitch," Lawrence continued, trying to get Mitch to re-focus. "I just did you a favor. Imagine if I'd let you make that phone call. Not only would you have lost that bet, you'd have lost that woman."

Mitch suddenly felt a mix of humility, shame, and even a little gratitude.

"Hey," Lawrence insisted, "if you never hear another word I tell you, hear this. There are very few women who come along in a man's life that deserve to be treated differently. I'm pretty sure she's one of them. Don't let Chance, a stupid bet, or anything else screw this up for you."

Mitch silently mulled over Lawrence's words, somewhat motionless. At least, as motionless as any drunk can be.

CHAPTER 9

YOU LOOKED BEHIND YOU
TO SMILE BACK AT ME

The next day, Mitch walked into his apartment and pulled his new phone out of the bag. He looked at it for a minute and shuddered. The thought of what could have happened last night if he'd let Chance and the boys goad him into calling Ellie in his drunken state, it was... well, it was something he didn't ever want to think about again. Relieved that he'd dodged that moment of idiocy, he called Ellie.

"Hi, Mitch!" Ellie answered with a smile.

"Ellie, hey," Mitch chuckled. "How's it going?"

"Pretty good," she said, with her voice beaming through the phone.

"Good to hear, babe," he smiled back. "It was just another day at work for me. How was the haircutting today?"

"Well, you know," Ellie confided, "just another day of listening to a bunch of old women gossip. Oh my God, sweetie, you have no idea what's going on in that nursing home. Did you know they have a 'swap meet' after bingo?"

"Whoa whoa whoa!" Mitch begged. "Spare me the details."

"I *have to* spare you the details," Ellie replied, feigning a serious tone. "It's like with lawyers, one of those stylist/client privilege things."

"So, whatcha got goin' on tonight?"

"Well, I need to get to the grocery store, but I'm thinking about putting it off."

"Why?"

"It's just always such an ordeal," Ellie complained. "I mean, I need to gather a few things first, and then..."

"Ordeal?" Mitch asked. "Um, do you want me to come along to ease the burden?"

"You want to go shopping with me?" Ellie smiled.

"Well, I need to get some things too," Mitch replied, "and if it's gonna be *that* traumatic, maybe I can help make it less painful."

"Um, okaaay," Ellie agreed, "but I have to go home first and get some things."

"To go *shopping*?" Mitch asked.

The automated doors of the supermarket opened as Mitch and Ellie walked in. The antiseptic hue and the semi-sonic hum of halogen lights greeted them, but Ellie's nose was already buried in an expandable folder better suited for legal briefs than the coupon sorter for which she was using it.

Mitch just stared at her in disbelief as they entered.

"Are you auditioning for a Law & Order episode that I don't know about?" Mitch asked.

"Ha ha, very funny," Ellie dismissed. "My coupon organizer needs to be this big if I'm going to get maximum benefit."

Mitch stared blankly at the overflow of clippings that appeared to be in the middle of executing a jailbreak from Ellie's coupon prison.

"What, *exactly*, about that mess is organized?" he asked.

"Look, mister, there's a method to this madness," Ellie reassured. "I don't see you with any coupons. I guess *someone* gets to pay full price..."

"I don't believe in coupons," Mitch countered.

"What, like you *don't* believe in Santa Claus?" Ellie questioned. "Look, here, in my hands. They really *do exist*, OK?"

"No, I mean I just don't believe in the concept."

Ellie rolled her eyes as they each grabbed a shopping cart.

"Oh, please enlighten me," she teased.

"OK, how much do you make an hour?"

"It depends on the number of clients I get... but, still, that's none of your business."

"I'm just trying to make a point," Mitch replied. "Let's just say, hypothetically, that you make $15 an hour. Would you say that you have at least one hour's worth of work invested in that monstrosity?"

"Easily," Ellie scoffed.

"OK, but are your coupons gonna save you $15 today?"

"Just you watch," Ellie reassured.

"Great, you're gonna save $15 in 20-cent increments. I guess we won't be using the express lane," Mitch grumbled. "Still, I'm still pretty sure you can't save $15."

"I bet I can."

"OK, whatever," Mitch conceded. "My point is, my time is worth more than the time it takes to clip those coupons. Instead, I just contemplate whether or not I'm willing to eat whatever is on sale."

"Oh boy, here comes another one of Mitch's *philosophies*," Ellie droned.

"It comes in different levels," Mitch continued, undaunted by Ellie's comment. "Meat on sale, for instance, is usually not a good call. But then again, that depends on the type of meat. Chicken or pork? No way. Kielbasa? Absolutely. Salami? Definitely.

"Mitch, salami has a longer shelf life than Twinkies," Ellie said. "And is probably just as healthy..."

"My point *exactly*," Mitch said as they turned down another aisle. "Whoa, canned ravioli!!! Ten cans for $10??? Somebody call UNICEF – we're gonna eat like *KINGS!!!*" he proclaimed as he swept an armful of cans into his cart.

He paused for a second, looking at the mound of cans in his cart, and then turned to Ellie and asked, "Does that look like ten cans to you?"

"Oh my God," Ellie stared in horror. "Have you read the back of that can?"

"What? The Hot Wheels deal?" Mitch replied "Yeah, they already sent us the five Hot Wheels this month. Can you believe those bastards actually check addresses and limit the number of cars you can get?"

Ellie stared at Mitch in disbelief.

"Hold on, you guys...?"

"Hey," Mitch interrupted, "do you mind if we send some of the cars to your house this month?"

"What?" she asked. "I meant..."

"Those pricks probably check the names, too," Mitch contemplated. "I'll have to put the cars in your name as well, if that's OK."

"Mitch!" Ellie insisted. "Answer me!"

"No, I don't play with them," Mitch paused. "Chance does. And, we don't actually play with the cars, we, um... blow them up with firecrackers."

"*What?* No, I...," Ellie replied, now completely frazzled. "I'm not talking about the damned toy car offer, Mitch! I was talking about the nutritional information! Have you ever even looked at it?"

"Why would I do that?" Mitch answered. "To confuse me into not eating it? Hey, this is a good value. Ten meals for ten dollars - perfect."

"You can't just eat crap like that all the time," Ellie protested.

"Oh, I don't," Mitch replied. "Take chicken. Chicken's good for you. I eat that all the time."

"Oh yeah, as in, 'chicken wings and five pitchers of beer.'" Ellie mocked. "That's *real* healthy."

"You didn't seem to mind 'em on Saturday," Mitch said.

"Well, yeah, but I was at the gym for two hours working it off on Sunday," Ellie replied.

"As did I," Mitch agreed. "We played wiffle ball for *three hours* on Sunday."

"Wiffle ball is not exercise, Mitch! And besides, you played it *while drinking and barbequing more wings!*"

"Well..." Mitch replied, considering her point, "yeah."

"Hey, I'm not trying to give you a hard time," she continued.

"Too late."

"Look," Ellie smirked, "I loved college, too. I just eventually graduated and became an adult."

"OHH!" Mitch yelled, over-dramatically grabbing his chest. "I must need some *vegetables* too!," he said sarcastically as he began throwing random cans of vegetables into his cart.

"It's probably a heart attack," Ellie smiled.

"I know, I know, I should treat my body like a temple," Mitch admitted sarcastically.

"And less like a frat house," Ellie added.

"Frat house!" Mitch laughed. "That's a great analogy! Especially when you think of all the beer, all the pizza, all the late-night video gaming... Oh wait, what am I going to tell the *sorority girls*?" he continued, feigning wide-eyed terror and rattling his head.

"You're going to tell them that you're a 'one-girl' party zone now," Ellie smiled as she pulled him close to her as they stood nose-to-nose in the middle of the aisle/

"*Oh really...*" Mitch whispered.

"Really," Ellie confirmed.

"Cool," Mitch smiled. "So are you going to help me pick out that one lucky sorority girl?"

Ellie tried to shove him away, but Mitch grabbed her wrists and pulled her close again. She lightly slapped his chest.

"That wasn't nice," Ellie pouted, with her lower lip fully extended.

"I'm sorry," Mitch replied as he tickled her cheek with his nose. "Tell ya what... as long as you're in my life, I'll start treating my body more like a temple."

"Good," she smiled and gave his nose a quick peck.

"And as the first order of business in the new 'Temple of Mitch', I will sacrifice... this cow."

He grabbed a large rump roast with a big bright red "Sale!" tag on it and lugged it into his cart. He turned to Ellie and smiled.

"Only four days old," he shrugged, "so it's safe."

"Oh, how selfless of you to sacrifice that *cow*," Ellie said as she rolled her eyes.

"Well, technically, it's already been sacrificed," Mitch agreed as he scrunched his lips. "Soooo, if you want something tangible, I will sacrifice..." he paused as he looked around and then quickly disappeared down another aisle, reappearing with a 30-pack of beer in his hands. "... my own liver."

Ellie shook her head and laughed.

"I must be the luckiest woman on the planet," she sighed.

"Damn right you are," Mitch replied, not missing a stride. "Now c'mon."

"Hey, I've got to buy stuff, too!" Ellie called after him, opening her coupon folder.

Mitch stopped, turned around, and stared at Ellie.

With her nose in the folder, Ellie suddenly pulled out a handful of coupons and waved them at Mitch.

"Aisle one," she ordered.

"You mean we have to *start over*?" Mitch cringed.

"Come on..."

They retraced their steps, only this time it was Mitch following Ellie. And this time, they plodded through each section – stopping sporadically for Ellie to grab two different cans of the same type of food, look at her coupon, then begin reading the back of each can for nutritional information.

At each stop, Mitch did something different to annoy Ellie when she began to take too long. One time he bumped her butt with his cart over and over again until she turned and glared at him. Another time he commented that he finally understood why she considered shopping an "ordeal." Still another time he started "shooting" bags of marshmallows into her cart like it was a basketball hoop. As she removed one bag and turned her back, he shot another bag into her cart.

At one point, Mitch took one of the cans Ellie was reading out of her hand, put it back on the shelf and put the other can in her cart. When she protested, he threw random cans into her cart until she started yelling at him. He turned and ran down the aisle with his cart, looking back at her and laughing like a little boy. Ellie gave chase, laughing as well and threatening to run him over with her cart.

After they finally checked out their groceries and walked to his car, Mitch began to put their bags in his back seat.

"Let's just put them in the trunk," Ellie offered.

"Um," Mitch paused. "The trunk latch broke yesterday," he shrugged, even though Mitch still hadn't cleaned out the trash-filled trunk from their second date – not that he was going to let Ellie see that.

After loading the bags into the car, Ellie eagerly pulled out her grocery receipt and quietly reviewed it as Mitch pulled out of the parking lot.

"Do you know how cool this night's become?" Mitch asked while driving and eating a Slim Jim. "You *never* see freakin' Slim Jims on sale!"

"Hey, be respectful," Ellie cautioned. "That thing might be one of your elders."

"Did you see where I put my Yoo-Hoo?" Mitch half-turned, ignoring Ellie's comment.

"Look," she replied, equally ignoring Mitch's question and shoving her receipt in Mitch's face. "I saved $18.00. So I was right."

"Yeah, but we spent two hours in there, so you're saying your time is worth $9 an hour. So, technically, I was right."

"I just saved $18."

"Great! Can I get a $9 haircut from you?"

"Looks like you already have one," Ellie replied.

"Nice," Mitch smiled. "I just don't think that file folder mess is worth $18."

"You don't care about $18."

"No."

"Mitch, seriously! Do you even care about anything?" Ellie snipped, getting frustrated with Mitch's indifference and unwillingness to admit he was wrong.

"Yeah," Mitch said. "I care about my legacy, what I'm gonna leave behind. I mean, you care about your performances, right?"

"Obviously, yeah."

"That reminds me," he paused. "I meant to ask you about the audition last night. How'd that go?"

"Well, my agent said that the director said no one read better than me, but that they were looking for a woman with more curves."

"For *'The Sound of Music'*?" Mitch scoffed.

"I know, can you believe it?" Ellie agreed. "Apparently, they want someone with bigger tits. My agent and I have talked about it, and I think I'm going to do it."

"Do what?" Mitch asked.

"Get implants," Ellie replied.

"Are you kidding?" Mitch sneered.

Ellie looked at him in silence, waiting for him to continue his thought.

"God, Chance would punch me in the nuts if he heard me say this..." Mitch continued with dread. "It's just, you shouldn't sell out just so you can have the *opportunity* to get a part."

Ellie curled her lip in disgust.

"Well, maybe if you ever get in the 'business', you'll understand."

"And by *'in the business'*, you mean getting a gig in the spring series at the municipal theater?"

"Mitch, quit belittling the theater here! Just because it's not Broadway doesn't mean it sucks, OK?"

"OK, OK."

"Look," Ellie continued, "all I'm saying is, if you have an opportunity in front of you, and the people who *can* give you that opportunity want you to make a small compromise before they'll give you the chance, you have to at least consider it."

"Elective surgery is a not a small compromise, Ellie!" Mitch countered. "You have to sign a waiver to not sue the doctor if he *kills* you, for crissake! Just for *bigger tits*???!!!!"

"Mitch, that's a little over-dramatic, don't you think?"

"No," Mitch shook his head. "Big tits are not worth your life."

"I'm *not* risking my life, Mitch! OK, put it this way. Let's say you get an offer on your novel for $1 million, but they tell you that they want to make a few 'little changes' here or there – just tweak it a little after they buy it from you. They basically say, 'Here's $1 million dollars to sell us your book and walk away.' What would you do?"

"I'd walk," Mitch answered.

"See? Exactly."

"No, I'd walk out," Mitch corrected.

"Oh bullshit!" Ellie snapped.

"Ellie, I'm not writing this thing just to start a thought for somebody else to finish. When I finish my novel, I want to be able to stand by every word. If somebody doesn't like it, I can live with that. But I don't need some college intern to come in, take what I've written and screw it up just to make it more 'grammatically correct', and *then* leave me to take a beating from critics about something that wasn't even mine."

"But what if they make it better?"

"Holy shit, that'd be even worse! How could I ever write again? Knowing that what I wrote wasn't good enough? Right now, I write freakin' instructions for a living, and I try to do a good job. But if one of my manuals suck, no big deal. My 'readers' are only a bunch of gamers who really only care about the game, and will hit internet blogs for the cheat codes, anyway. If they tell me to change something, I'll do it - no biggie. Maybe five people actually see my work before it goes to production for thousands to read. But you know, those teenagers don't care about how well the manual was written. To them, it's just a tool. It's not art.

"When we express our art – you with your acting and me with my writing – we put ourselves out there for the whole world to judge. It's a *'this is what I've created, whaddaya think?'* situation. People will look at what we've created and judge us on it. So, I just want to make sure that when I do write something and put my name to it, it's truly my work."

Ellie just looked at Mitch and smiled. She always felt closest to him when he'd talk passionately about her acting and his writing. She placed a hand on his knee because, in that moment, she began to feel like she'd finally found someone who related to her on a level that she never thought anyone else would understand.

She put her head on his shoulder and smiled as the streetlights flashed across the dashboard.

Mitch smiled warmly and offered her a bite of his Slim Jim.

Ellie would normally never eat one of those things, but in that moment, it sort of felt like a further act of bonding - so she rolled her eyes, sighed, smiled, and chomped off a bite. She then reached behind her seat, cracked open Mitch's bottle of Yoo-Hoo, took a drink, and handed Mitch the bottle.

"Long live the dreamers," she smiled as she handed it to him.

"Amen, sister," he smiled back, taking a drink.

He briefly wondered if she'd known all along where the bottle was, but even that wasn't really important at that moment. He was just happy that he had found a woman who understood him when he did launch into one of his rants. Sharing a Slim Jim and a bottle of Yoo-Hoo with her only made it more perfect.

CHAPTER 10

PARADISE BY THE HALF-BOARD LIGHTS

"Oh my God," Ellie whined as she drove like a maniac towards Mitch and Chance's apartment. "Mitch is going to be so pissed off!"

"And Chance is going to just be a joy to deal with," Danni added. "Ugh, I'm not looking forward to this now."

"You know what fanatics they are about hockey," Ellie continued as she took a hard right turn and cut off another driver entering the intersection. "And this is our first *official game!*"

"Well, honey," Danni reasoned, "They're just going to have to understand. We all have to work, ya know."

"I know."

"Did you call Mitch?"

"Yeah, and he sounded pissed. He didn't even react when I told him we were running late. He kind of growled and said, '*Just get here,*'" she said in as low of a voice as she could muster while hunching her shoulders, as if imitating a Neanderthal.

Danni suddenly giggled.

"What?" asked Ellie.

"Did you ever notice how whenever we repeat what a man says to us, we make him sound like grunting, no-brained ape?"

Ellie thought for a minute and started laughing.

"Yeah, we do. But then again, when you hear them repeat what we say, they shake their head and get all high-pitched like we're whiny, no-brained cheerleaders."

"Good point," Danni agreed.

"Hold on," Ellie said as she took another hard right turn.

Danni grabbed the "oh shit" handle above her door and nearly swung into Ellie's seat from the hard turn.

"Hey," Danni asked impatiently, "what are you so worried about, anyway?"

"I really like this guy, Danni," Ellie replied. "He's been so sweet to me, and I know this game is important to him. I should have just taken the day off."

"*Unt-uh!*" Danni scolded. "The minute you start accommodating them is the minute they start expecting you to accommodate them. You need to treat him like the dog he is and make him wait by the door for you. Just occasionally reassure him that mommy will be there at some point."

"Danni, Mitch isn't like that," Ellie countered. "He's not like the other guys. He respects what's important to me. I want to show him that I respect what's important to him, too."

"Don't tell me you're falling for him," Danni asked cautiously.

"Well, let's just say '*so far, so good*'."

"Oh God," Danni sighed.

"Wait a second, what about you and Chance?" Ellie said.

"What about *us*?"

"Well, according to Mitch, you two are going at it like the world's going to end any second."

"Well, there's no denying he's hot," Danni giggled. "And that bod of his – *wow*. He's one of those types who apparently never have to work out, ya know?"

"Makes me sick," Ellie added.

"I know," Danni agreed. "Still, he's just a toy. I know it, and he'd better know it. He's never been serious about anything in his life – other than drinking and trying to manipulate everyone around him. I'd be a fool to think he'd take any relationship seriously."

"So, what are you going to do?"

"Fuck him."

They both sat silent for a moment as Danni's crass comment hung in the air like a foul odor - until they both started giggling.

"*Fuck him 'til he can't fuck no more!*" Danni proclaimed as Ellie again took another hard right turn.

Ellie and Danni knocked twice on the boys' apartment door and walked in – with both of them apologizing at the same time while simultaneously explaining why. The result, though, was indistinguishable rabble.

Chance was standing over the simmering BBQ pit on the deck, with a beer in one hand at a pair of tongs in the other. He merely turned and smiled at them, shaking his head in amusement.

Both ladies suddenly fell silent from Chance's lack of urgency. They then heard the radio broadcasting a hockey game in its typically tinny AM-band sound quality.

"Oh my God!" Ellie asked in a near panic. "The game's already started????

Chance just laughed.

"Naw," he yelled from the deck. "We knew you two would be late, so we built that into the schedule."

"You did *what*?" Danni asked.

"Well, I told you the game was at six, right?" Chance answered.

They both stood there motionless, waiting for Chance to complete his explanation.

"It doesn't start until 7:30," Chance continued. "But since we knew you'd be late, we built that in to the time we told you to be here – just to make sure you'd be here."

They both continued to stand there, now silently enraged.

"Bratwurst?" he offered.

"You lied about what time the game was?" Danni sneered as she stomped towards Chance. "I left a meeting early and didn't even have time to take a shower!!! Then we rushed our asses over here and ..."

"...you were still late," Chance interrupted. "Now that I know your lateness-factor a little better, I'll adjust all the future 'times' that I lie to you about."

"You're an asshole," Ellie sneered. "We're only 20 minutes late."

"Twenty minutes is the end of the first period," Mitch said as he appeared from his bedroom wearing his replica Blues jersey and carrying an open beer in one hand and an older version of a Blues jersey in the other. "Here," he said as he tossed the jersey at her. "Put that on."

"But I bought this shirt just for tonight," Ellie protested as she pointed to her new top.

"No girl of mine is going to a Blues game in anything but a Blues sweater," Mitch replied.

"But Mitch, this shirt..." she repeated, "I bought this especially for tonight."

"And it looks great, but *this sweater* is mandatory wardrobe for any game," Mitch replied, pointing at the jersey in her hand.

"Sooooo," Ellie said teasingly, as if daring Mitch, "if I were to strip naked right now, you'd still make me put this on?"

Mitch's eyes widened, imagining her proposed scenario, then smiled as if in blissful heaven.

"Oh abso-fuckin-LUTLY!" he stated emphatically. "In... a... heartbeat..."

Ellie tilted her head sideways in an attempt to comprehend what Mitch meant.

"Oh my," Danni giggled. "Ellie, I think you just stumbled on his kink. You'd better get *really* comfortable with wearing that jersey."

"Dammit, why didn't I think of that one???" Chance yelled from the deck as he flipped a bratwurst.

"Please," Mitch chuckled and asked softly, "please just put it on, and wear it with pride."

Ellie sighed, dropped her purse where she stood, and slipped the jersey over her head.

"Happy?" she asked, raising her arms to model the uniform.

Mitch just smiled more widely.

"Yes," he nodded, "you've never looked more beautiful. Now, please... grab a beer and a brat."

"Um, no thanks," Ellie declined. "Do you even know what's in a bratwurst?"

"My guess?" Chance called out. "Flavor and calories."

"Yes, but that's not all..." Ellie tried to explain.

"Ya know, I've heard a lot of things on the sausage question," Chance waxed, "but I prefer the 'don't ask, don't tell' philosophy with things like this."

"Kinda like Mitch and his canned ravioli?" Ellie asked.

"Speaking of which, did you get my Hot Wheels yet?" Chance volleyed back as he pointed the tongs at her.

"I'll take a bratwurst," Danni interrupted, "with sauerkraut, onions, peppers, mustard, two beers, and somebody's keys."

"We have mustard and wheat bread," Chance replied. "Those are your options. And you know where the cooler is."

Danni, frustrated by Chance's response, grabbed a beer from the cooler on the floor and then turned to Ellie.

"Lemme see your keys, there Prudence," she ordered.

As Ellie handed her the keys, Danni selected the longest key and promptly stabbed the bottom of the beer can. Then, balancing the can carefully to minimize any spillage, she quickly said, "Here," as she tossed Ellie's keys back to her.

Danni wrapped her lips around the newly created hole, tilted the can upright, and blindly opened the top of the can. In three gulps, the beer can was empty. Danni let out a small burp and slung the empty can somewhat towards their trash can. Missing her target, the aluminum shell bounced around the floor.

Ellie and Mitch stared at Danni in disbelief.

"I need to catch up with these two," Danni reasoned, wiping her lips with her forearm.

"You're not getting my keys again for the rest of the night," Ellie said. "Cops don't like it when your car keys smell like beer, Danni."

She then turned to Mitch.

"Mitch, if the game hasn't started yet, what is that on the radio?"

"Yeah," Danni asked, "what are we listening to?"

"It's on the VCR, babe," Mitch answered. "And it's the 'The Monday Night Miracle.' Chance and I relive it before every game."

"What's the Monday Night Miracle?" Ellie asked.

Freezing in place from abject shock, Chance suddenly dropped the tongs, and Mitch - without breaking his glare at Ellie - reached over and hit pause on the old VCR.

"*What is the Monday Night Miracle*???" Mitch mocked.

Danni had found Chance's keys and, after puncturing another can, shotgunned another beer and slung the empty can against the nearest wall. She then tossed Chance's keys indifferently through the open sliding glass door and right into his range of grasp. He swiped them out of mid-air with cool indifference.

"Thanks babe," Danni said, again wiping her mouth with her forearm.

"You're not getting my keys the rest of the night, either," Chance stated.

"Hey Mitch, I know about the Miracle!" Danni laughed, ignoring Chance's lack of reaction and energized by her sudden buzz. "Come on, Ellie, you know about that one... 1980 Olympics? U.S. v. Soviets? Lake *Flaccid*? *DUH*..."

Danni swayed a little as she flashed an "I'm with ya, fellas" smile while elbowing Mitch in the ribs. She then looked Mitch in the eyes and held out her hand, waiting for his keys.

Mitch just shook his head as he handed his keys to her.

"Just wash the beer off when you're done, OK?"

"Uh, no," she smirked defiantly as she took them.

"Wow, Chance," Mitch announced, reverting back to Ellie's earlier comment. "We've got some ed-ju-ma-catin' to do here."

"No shit," Chance agreed as he put the lid on the BBQ pit and then carried the remaining bratwursts in on a plate.

They gathered around the TV as Chance fast-forwarded through an old grainy video. While Chance was doing that, Mitch gave the ladies a crash course on the Monday Night Miracle – a title created by St. Louisans for the night when the Blues were losing five to two at home with 12 minutes remaining in the third period of an elimination playoff game back in 1986.

"OK, here it is," Chance interrupted and quickly sat on the couch next to Danni.

The girls listened intently as Mitch and Chance, with eyes nearly closed, orchestrated the comeback with ridiculous motions through the air. The announcer then blared that Greg Paslawski had just scored, making the score 5-4, and the boys threw hands in the air.

The girls were beginning to feel the tension that the boys were, responding to the sound of the crowd's maniacal cheers emanating through Mitch's television.

As the old recorded crowd whipped itself into a frenzy, the announcer yelled that the Blues stole the puck and, in the blink of an eye, the player spun around and buried the puck, tying the game.

Mitch and Chance stood up, yelled, and high-fived as the announcer detailed the play gleefully. Ellie and Danni half-smirked, but continued to play along.

Then, as the tape continued to play, Mitch and Chance both leaned forward and stared at the faded picture as if they were seeing this game for the very first time.

Ellie looked at Danni and shrugged, then both leaned in as well, even though neither knew why.

They all stared at the old, almost blurry, image of the Blues skating down the ice. The play developed as the announcer's voice heightened with excitement.

"Here's Ramage, for Federko too far, Federko steals the puck from Reinheart, over to Hunter who shoots, blocked, Wickenheiser scores! *Doug Wick-en-heis-er*! The Blues pull it off and it's *unbelievable!!!*"

Chance and Mitch jumped up and hugged.

Ellie and Danni just stared at each other and smirked again.

"*THIS* is the cup that we all got to keep for one day," Mitch explained. "*That game*."

"They won the championship-cup thingy with that game?" Ellie asked.

"It's called the Ryder Cup, blondie," Danni corrected.

Mitch scowled and cringed.

"Uh, no," Chance said. "They lost the next night and were eliminated from the *Stanley* Cup playoffs," he said, correcting them both with one sentence.

Ellie and Danni just shook their heads, now thoroughly confused as to the significance of the game.

"Sooooo..." Danni began to ask.

"OK, it was just a really good comeback, alright?" Chance groaned.

"Oh, OK," Ellie and Danni said, still trying to understand.

"So," Ellie asked, "is Wiggihousen playing tonight?"

"That game was in 1986, babe," Mitch stated.

"So?"

"Um, time to go," Mitch said, deciding not to explain why no one from a 1986 NHL team could still be playing hockey today.

The four of them approached the entrance gate of the arena as Danni slammed the remainder of her beer.

"Folks, you cannot bring any containers into the building," the usher at the gate announced. "Please dispose *your* receptacles into *our* receptacles."

"OK, girls," Chance said. "Time to chug."

Mitch and Ellie tilted their heads back as Danni slam-dunked her empty can into the nearest trash bin. "Ya better catch up, ya ninnies," she announced while slurring a little.

"Whoa, I love it!" Chance proclaimed, reveling in Danni's aggressive drinking. "We've got a pro here, Mitch. Let's see if she runs sprints or marathons."

"I run Farrakkans, you *wusses*," she swayed with each step, hinting that she was fighting the very rotation of the Earth itself. "*Woo hoo!!!*" she howled as she walked through the turnstiles. "*Go Ba-looz!*"

"So," Ellie asked as she walked through gate, "who are we playing tonight?"

"Cal-*GARY*," Mitch pronounced, talking as if he'd been raised in a barn on the Canadian plains.

"OK," Ellie continued, "so why does Cal Gary have two first names, and what team does he play for?"

"Cal-*GARY* is *not* a person, it's a city," Chance corrected, "in Canada."

"Ohhhhh..." Ellie asked, now mocking Chance. "Is that near *Calgary*?"

"Hey, you're in a hockey rink right now," Chance scolded. "You're at 'the pond'. You need to learn the lingo *and* the dialect."

"Wow," Ellie smirked, "I had no idea that hockey, *or you* for that matter, were so, um, *multi-cultural*." She then turned her back to Chance and followed Mitch.

As she turned away, Chance leaned towards Ellie and gestured like he was about to slap her into next week. Danni stood there and muffled a laugh at how annoyed Chance had gotten.

"OK, a couple of basics, and you'll be fine," Mitch said as they walked to their seats. "First of all, there is no such thing as a short 'i' in hockey. It's not an organization, it's an organ-*eye*-zation. And the puck is not always the puck. Sometimes, it's the biscuit. And the idea is to put the biscuit in the basket, which is also known as the goal. Got it?"

"Um, yeah. I got it, Mitch. This ain't exactly quantum physics."

"Alsooo," Mitch continued, ignoring the sarcasm, "almost all the players don't go by their real names.

Usually, it's just the first half of their first or last names, followed by e-y. Unless they just use their initials. Other than that, just call them 'boys' collectively – as in, *'skate boys, skate!'*"

"Got it," Ellie nodded.

They entered the arena and began walking down to their seats just as the first puck dropped.

"You guys take this WAY too seriously," Danni said, just a step behind them. "Where's the beer guy?"

"Too seriously?" Chance asked. "You need to realize that this is a war that's fought every night."

"Um, isn't 'war' a little over-dramatic?" she asked as she stared down at the steps.

As they arrived at their seats, just four rows from the ice, a Calgary player checked a Blues player into the Plexiglas so hard that it shattered the pane, causing Ellie and Danni to scream and clutch their respective dates with the kind of terror usually reserved for horror movies.

As a huge brawl broke out in front of them, Chance and Mitch began shouting out advice like a pugilist's corner men. Finally, order was restored, and Chance wryly smiled at the girls, who were both still in shock and fiercely clutching their men's shirts.

"Well," Chance paused, "kind of like war. You know, just *not as violent.*"

As they took their seats, the other regular season ticket holders around them greeted them by giving them the typical grief. To the girls, it seemed like just another night at Budgie's, but at the hockey game - same shit, different people.

At the first intermission, the four of them weaved their way through the masses of people trying to go every which way in the halls of the arena. Mitch led, holding Ellie's hand, and Chance - right behind Ellie - was holding

Danni's. At one point, a person wearing a Calgary jersey walked past them.

"Asshole," Mitch deadpanned.

"*Asshole,*" Chance echoed a split second afterwards, in a higher pitch.

"Do you know that guy?" Ellie asked.

"Huh? Who?" Mitch asked, completely oblivious.

"Uh," she replied, now even more confused by his response, "forget it."

Danni, now very buzzed, just tilted her head, also trying to figure out what they were talking about.

A second later, another Calgary-clad fan moved right past them in the crowd, and, as they passed, Mitch and Chance repeated their "Asshole – *Asshole*" response in the same intonations as before.

"OK, is this another one of those 'hockey culture' things?" Ellie asked.

"Uh," Mitch smiled. "It's just something Chance and I..."

"OH, I get it!" Danni yelled, now feeling euphoric from the beers. She spotted an exceptionally large man in a Calgary jersey, bounced into a small open space in the crowd.

"*ASSHOLE!!! AHAHAHAHA!!!*" she yelled as she pointed her finger in his face and laughed wickedly.

Everyone within a ten foot radius stopped and stared in shock.

"C'mon!" Danni yelled at Ellie. "We're in a hockey rink! What are you waiting for?"

Ellie, taking her cue from Danni's lead, jumped into the same void.

"ASSHOLE!" she too yelled as she pointed at the large man's equally large friend, who was also wearing a Calgary jersey.

Chance stood slack-jawed as Mitch looked down, pinched the bridge of his nose, and sighed.

The first Calgary fan, now fully insulted, glared at Danni.

"Who the fuck are *you, bitch*?" he shouted.

"Hey!" Ellie barked back. "This is one of your hockey culture thingies! So... um, you can't talk to her like that in *our* pond! Right *boys*?" she smiled, looking back at Mitch.

"You *boys* better get a grip on your women," the second Calgary fan growled.

Mitch and Chance looked at each other and knew they were now going to have to defend their women. Inside, their hearts began racing in anticipation of the potential fight.

Chance took a step forward, glaring maniacally and trying to channel Pacino's unhinged stare from Scarface. He then took a deep breath and said...

"Ahhh, they're drunk," he suddenly smiled and shrugged indifferently. "Don't mind them."

"But I'm not drunk!" Ellie protested in confusion.

"See?" Chance said, pointing at Ellie while looking at the large Calgary fan. "See what we have to put up with? Now, how about we buy you boys a beer and forget about this whole thing?"

"Hey *fuck you*, buddy!" the second Calgary fan said.

As Chance continued to negotiate with the angry men, Ellie walked up to Mitch.

"Did we do it wrong?" she asked.

Mitch looked around nervously because he knew that the two large men were now looking for a fight – or, at the very least, a heavy dose of humiliation from Chance and him. He then saw his season-ticket friends from his section walking towards them. At that moment, a thought occurred to him.

"No sweetie," Mitch answered as he turned to watch the large men poking Chance while Chance continued to try to smile his way out of the situation. "You did fine, ya just gotta put a little more emphasis behind it. Watch."

"Yeah, you're damn right you're gonna buy us beers, fucker," the first Calgary fan sneered while shoving Chance. Chance kept his head down and spoke as quickly as he could, all the while smiling, shrugging, and goofily laughing off the pokes. It was all eerily similar to the speech pattern of any smaller schoolboy who found himself alone in the lavatory with his class bullies.

As Mitch's friends approached, Mitch walked up to the large man pushing Chance around as he smiled with a "dare ya" look in his eyes.

"Look, *ASSHOLE*..." Mitch challenged, with a voice that was clearly intended to be loud enough for his season ticket friends to hear. "Why don't you and your *ASSHOLE* friend buy me and all my *friends*..." he paused, looking over his shoulder to confirm his friends were now gathering around him, "why don't you buy all of us beers for putting up with you ASSHOLES for showing up in *OUR* pond."

"YEAH!" all of Mitch's friends said like a crazed mob as they gathered behind him.

"So get out your Visa," Mitch sneered bravely, "*or just get outta here.*"

The first large Calgary fan bit his lower lip and slowly shook his head, resisting the urge to pummel Mitch while realizing he and his friend were now severely outnumbered. He then tapped his friend on the arm.

"Let's go," he muttered.

As they left, Ellie ran up to Mitch.

"Whoa, where did *that* come from???" she asked

"The first rule of warfare, babe... Numbers always win."

"Well, that's not exactly Sun Tsu," Ellie smirked. "But regardless, I'm impressed."

Danni turned to Chance and poked him in the chest, imitating the large Calgary fans.

"Now I think you're gonna buy *me* a beer, fucker," she mocked with a slur.

Chance, still in shock from everything that had just transpired, stared blankly at Danni.

"My hero," Danni sighed with over-dramatic disappointment. "Look Chance, it's OK. We can't all be built for war... *virtual or otherwise*."

Mitch pulled up to the curb outside Ellie's house after dropping Chance and Danni off at Danni's condo.

"So, your *first* Blues game," Mitch said as he set the parking brake. "What did you think?"

"I had a great time, Mitch," Ellie smiled. "I totally see why you love that game."

"So, you'll go to another one?"

"Oh, anytime," she replied. "Hey, do you have a few minutes?"

"Sure, what's up?" Mitch asked.

"I really gotta get to bed soon," she began. "But if you can spare a few minutes..."

"I'm good with as much time as you've got to give," Mitch replied.

"I think I've heard that somewhere before," Ellie smiled slyly, remembering the night she met him.

"Have ya?" Mitch smiled, feigning ignorance. "Well, I meant it then, too."

"Good," she said, "Then, come on in."

They entered Ellie's kitchen through the side door to her house. As she dropped her keys on the countertop, she walked through to the living room and turned on the TV.

"I'm gonna get out of these clothes real quick," she said, as she headed to her bedroom. "Turn on whatever you want, I'll be right back."

"Uh, okay," Mitch said as he plopped himself on her couch and grabbed the remote. "Aw man, who's your cable provider?" he asked as he flipped through the channels.

"I dunno," Ellie called from her bedroom. "Why?"

"You apparently don't have any sports channels," Mitch said. He then mumbled to himself, "What, does cable sell a 'chick package' now? I see you got the damn Lifetime channel."

"I think I have ESPN," she called out again.

"Yep," Mitch answered as he suddenly smiled. "Found it."

"Mitch, I gotta tell you," she continued from the bedroom, "that was great the way you handled those big guys."

"Yeah, that was pretty cool," Mitch agreed. "But what about that goal with one minute left in the game? Oh my God, that was awesome!"

"Yeah, it was great to see them win. I had a great time."

Mitch sat silently watching the TV when suddenly the lights in the living room went out. Startled, he looked around and saw that the TV was still on, so he knew it wasn't a power failure. He turned to the bedroom door and lost his breath, not believing what he was seeing.

Standing in her doorway – bathed in flickering television light – stood Ellie, apparently wearing only the Blues jersey he'd lent her earlier that night.

Her hair was pulled down in her face as she smiled innocently and leaned gently into the room with her hands straining against the top of her bedroom doorway. She gave Mitch a longing look as she strained against the frame, with her craned torso lifting the Blues jersey *just enough* to give Mitch a peek at the bottom of her white panties.

Mitch sat there completely paralyzed. He stared at her deeply and sat up as she slowly sauntered towards him. Mitch quickly, *yet still awkwardly*, scooted over to give her enough room to sit down.

She sat next to him and, without saying a word, grabbed his hair and pulled him to her, kissing him with everything she had.

"Um," Mitch said between kisses, "hockey really does it for you, eh?"

"Well," Ellie said as they continued to kiss and struggle with removing Mitch's own jersey, "it's more about you than hockey."

"Huh?" he replied – not that anything she said would have dissuaded him at that point.

"It's not just what you *did*, sweetie," she breathed as she kissed him again. "It's just everything about us. I have so much fun when we're together, and the way you handle everything, the way you just *are*... well, let's just say that I saw something tonight that I've been looking for – for a while now."

"Wow," Mitch whispered with surprise between kisses of equal passion. "So, I'm what you've been looking for?"

Ellie pulled away and looked at Mitch.

"I'm pretty certain now," she lowered her eyes as if in a confessional as Mitch kissed her neck. She then lifted her eyes. "You think like I think, you feel like I feel, you dream like I dream... *and* you're willing to protect me. So, yeah, I feel safe with you."

Mitch stopped kissing her neck as she uttered those last words and looked her dead in the eye. The flickering of the TV traced her features like a gentle strobe light, but he wanted to see that comfort - that certainty - in her eyes before he went any further. He had to know - especially since he'd waited this long - that she was sure she wanted him, that she wanted this, and that wanted it was for the right reasons.

She never broke his stare, and even smiled with a hint of bliss. She kissed him again, and he pulled her close only to lean her back onto the sofa.

CHAPTER 11

I'VE GROWN STUPID,
HAPPENED OVERNIGHT

Sleeping in on Saturday mornings was the closest thing to a Utopian existence for Mitch. As his digital clock flipped over to 9:02am, his phone rang. Since Ellie was the only one he knew who might think it'd be OK to call him this early, he answered his phone.

"What?" he complained as he answered the phone.

"Hello?" a strange man's voice said. "Is this Mitch?"

"Mmmphhh, yes" Mitch replied.

"Mitch Paulson?" the voice insisted.

"I SAID *YES*," Mitch barked into the phone with his face still buried in his pillow.

"I apologize, sir," the voice replied, "but for quality control purposes, here at Sweepstakes Headquarters, we will only speak to the finalist."

"Sweepstakes?" Mitch asked with a heightened pitch, his voice muffled from still lying face-first in his pillow.

"Yes sir, you are Mitch Paulson, right?"

"I said yes," Mitch growled as he sat up. "This is Mitch Paulson. I swear."

"Thank you Mr. Paulson. Could you please verify your address?"

"Um, 1640 Rosary Lane, why?"

"And your mother's maiden name?"

"Um, Clemens... wh..." Mitch tried to ask.

"Please hold," the voice interrupted. As the telemarketer hit the mute button on his console, he yelled out, "We got a live one here, boys! Check this moron out!"

The telemarketer's cube quickly filled with his fellow telemarketers, all wearing ties and headsets. As they all crowded into the cube, smatterings of "Shh! Shh!" emanated from the group. The telemarketer depressed the mute button and continued.

"Mr. Paulson, I need to send you to our verification department," he said. "Please hold." He then quickly pressed mute again.

One of the other telemarketers then elbowed the one talking to Mitch. "Hey," he said. "Do the Cheech voice."

"NO!" yelled another. "Do Nicholson!"

The telemarketer nodded in agreement, then took a deep breath and depressed the mute button.

"Hi, is this Mitch Paulllssson?" the telemarketer said in his Nicholson cadence.

"We've been through this..." Mitch complained. "Yes, I am Mitch Paulson."

"Sorry about that, Mr. Paulson," the voice resonated. "We take our jobs very seriously here at Sweepstakes HQ. Can you please verify your place of employment, for security reasons?"

"Razor software, why?" Mitch asked. "What's going on? Did I win something?"

"We'll get to that," the telemarketer continued, still steeped in the impersonation. "One last question, Mr. Paulson. Can I please have the name of the high school from which you graduated?

"De Smet," Mitch replied. "Are you gonna tell me what's going on???"

"Awww, you're a Catholic. Good for you, son! I never got the whole '*Catholic*' thing, with the Pope and the hats and the robes and stuff... it all seemed a little – oh, I don't know – *pecyoolier* to me. But hey, to each his own."

Mitch pulled the phone away from his ear and squinted at it.

The group of telemarketers, however, choked on their laughs and snickers as their cohort continued.

"Mr. Paulson, my name is Alan Probe, and let me be the first one to congratulate you."

"Alan Probe! I LOVE IT!" cried one of his co-workers as three others immediately smacked him with their clipboards to shut him up.

"*Congratulate* me?" Mitch asked. "Why?"

"Well, sir, it seems that you have won our sweepstakes, and you are a finalist to win the grand prize."

"*Are you serious?*" Mitch asked excitedly as he crawled out of bed and began walking around the apartment. "I've never won anything! This is so cool! But I don't remember entering any..."

"Mr. Paulson, I appreciate your honesty, maybe we have the wrong person here," the telemarketer baited. "I'm sorry for bothering you."

"Wait wait wait..." Mitch replied quickly, afraid to lose his prize. "Maybe I *did* enter. Where did you have registrations?"

"Well Mr. Paulson, I was about to get to that. We need to validate where you signed up for our sweepstakes. Now, we did have a few registration boxes at a few events in your city over the past year."

"Ahhh, that must be it," Mitch said, thinking he could bluff his way through this. "I probably just forgot. Where were they?"

As Mitch waited for the list to be re-read to him, the other telemarketers wheeled a giant dry-erase board behind their co-worker's desk with a grid that looked eerily similar to a bookie's chalkboard.

"Well Mr. Paulson," he telemarketer continued, "we had one at the Knights of the Klu Klux Klan Outreach Convention, one at the Four-Gender Rights Now Convention, one at the Genital Warts Survival Network, one at the St. Louis GLAAD Mardi Gras Parade, one at the NAMBLA Political Action Committee Meeting, one at the Catholicism WOW convention, one at the Jihad Rehabilitation Wheelchair Drive, and one at Customized Auto Parts and Barbeque Show."

Mitch, horrified by each option up to that point, pounced on the last option.

"OH YEAH!" he exclaimed, "The Auto Parts Show! Yeah yeah, I go to that every year! I probably just forgot about signing up when I was there."

"Oh well that's fantastic, Mr. Paulson," the telemarketer replied, stifling a snicker. "When you registered there, they gave you a 24k gold-plated keychain with four digits on it – a great gift worth over $500 by itself. I simply need those digits so I can get you registered to receive your prize, so please just read those numbers to me... whenever you're ready."

Mitch's eyes widened in horror as he covered the receiver.

"*Fuck Fuck Fuck Fuck Fuck Fuck Fuck!!!*" he whispered to himself.

The telemarketers overheard Mitch's frantic cursing and doubled over with laughter. One of the young men in a tie picked up a marker, put on a cheap bookie's hat, and began booking bets on which event Mitch would eventually admit to attending. Bets were flying everywhere behind the telemarketer as he continued.

"Wait, what's the grand prize again?" Mitch asked, trying to stall.

"A brand new Aston Martin," he replied. "How do you think you would look behind the wheel of that, sir?"

"Ya know," Mitch said apologetically, "I seem to have misplaced my keychain. Is there any way I can still register without it?"

"Well, here's the deal," the telemarketer replied, now overplaying the Nicholson accent. "The only event where there was a registration number was the Auto Parts convention."

The rest of his co-workers continued laughing again as they knew he had Mitch dangling in the wind.

"If you've lost that key, we can't continue - *unless...*" the telemarketer offered, "are you sure you didn't, *maybe*, attend one of the other events?"

"Aw, come on," Mitch pleaded.

"Sir, we have strict federal laws here to which we must adhere," the telemarketer said as authoritatively as Nicholson ever could. "I'm not even supposed to be doing this, but I'm trying to help *you* out here, son. If you want to claim your prize, you need to *tell me* that you attended one of the *other* conventions, if you catch my drift."

Mitch sighed in defeat. "What were the other conventions again?" he asked, cringing.

The telemarketers rolled with laughter. "OK, Mr. Paulson, we have the Knights of the Klu Klux Klan-Outreach Convention, the Four-Gender Rights Now Convention, the Genital Warts Survival Network, the St.

Louis GLAAD Mardi Gras Parade, the NAMBLA Political Action Committee Meeting, the Catholicism WOW convention, and the Jihad Rehabilitation Wheelchair Drive."

"Well wait, what's NAMBLA again?" Mitch asked.

"The North American Man Boy Love Association," the telemarketer answered. "Do you love young boys, son?"

"What? NO!!!!"

One telemarketer began bouncing around the floor from laughing so hard.

"My apologies, sir," the telemarketer continued. "But, you *are* Catholic, so, depending on your priest..." he shrugged.

"Look, what about the GLAAD Mardi Gras parade?" I'm not sure, GLAAD is...?"

"Gay and Lesbian Anti-defamation Alliance, sir. Maybe you were on one of the floats..." the telemarketer suggested.

"NO, DUDE!" Mitch yelled.

"Yes sir, no means no," he replied indifferently. "Look Mr. Paulson, it's no big deal. If you just pick one, we can get you what you've already won and get you registered for the Aston Martin."

"Look," Mitch pleaded, "just pick one for me, OK?"

"Due to Federal Regulations, I can't legally do that Mr. Paulson. You need to pick one."

"Ugh, OK," Mitch shook his head, breathed deeply, and readied himself to claim one of these organizations. "OK, maybe we were downtown during a football game or a military air show, and maybe I accidentally signed up at a booth while I was drunk with my two stripper girlfriends," he added quickly, trying to save face. "So, I'm guessing it's probably the..."

The telemarketers all crouched around the telemarketer with money in their hands, anticipating Mitch's decision.

Mitch grumbled to himself at the choice he had to make. But his sense of shame was no match for the chance to win the Aston Martin.

"It had to be... the... GLAAD Mardi Gras parade."

The group of telemarketers erupted with screams of both "NOOOO!" and "YESSS!"

"Mitch, I like you, son," the telemarketer continued as money changed hands behind his head. "So here's what I'm gonna do for you. Since we didn't have confirmation numbers, I'm just gonna take your word that you attended."

Mitch curled a lip with disdain as he squatted against the wall by his bedroom door.

"I still need you to claim your winnings," the telemarketer added. "So I'll need a recording of this."

"What?" Mitch asked in disbelief.

"Federal Regulations, sir. You *are* willing to let us record this, right, son?"

"I guess," Mitch shook his head as his shoulders sank.

"Great son, please hold. I'll transfer you so one of our verification professionals can get this recorded," he said, again overemphasizing the impersonation.

Mitch squatted against his wall listening to the musak blaring through his phone and feeling like he'd just been in a fight.

"Wow, Christian Slater must have really fallen on hard times..." Mitch mumbled to himself.

The telemarketers began to clear out of the cubicle, taking the white board with them as the one who registered Mitch looked at his watch, counting the seconds before he'd again depress the mute button.

One telemarketer then leaned back into the cube and said, "Do Connery this time."

"No," the telemarketer replied. "I wanna see if this moron will even recognize my voice again after everything we've put him through."

The telemarketer then depressed the mute button.

"Is this Mitch Paulson?" he asked.

"Yes, why do you keep asking this?"

"We're recording this, sir. It's all part of protocol. Now is this Mitch Paulson?"

"Yes."

"And you are at least 21 years old?"

"Yes."

"And currently employed at...what is this, Raisin software? What kind of name is that for a software company???""

"It's RAZOR, not RAISIN!" Mitch yelled. "RAZOR SOFTWARE!!!"

"Oh, I see. My mistake. And you make over $60k a year?"

"Uuuuhhh, yeah," Mitch muttered as quietly as possible. "Sure."

"Great, Mr. Paulson," he continued. "You and your wife will only need to attend a 90-minute presentation so we can tell you all about our wonderful resort and all of its amenities. You'll also hear about all the wonderful benefits of vacation ownership. And, at the end of the presentation, you will receive your prize, which could be one of the following – a new Aston Martin, a 14-day all inclusive cruise to all southern Caribbean ports of call, a year's membership to the jelly of the month club, a $100 gas card from Bene petroleum, a $50 coupon book redeemable on Branson's main street, or a top-of-the-line "green" energy efficient boom box.."

"Uh... *wife*?" Mitch clarified.

"Yes, you both need to attend in order to claim your prize. Is that a going to be a problem?"

"Didn't I just talk to you earlier?" Mitch asked.

"Sir, you are in the final stages of qualification. I assure you that we have not spoken until this point."

"OK, OK," Mitch dismissed. "Not a problem."

"Great," the telemarketer smiled. "You'll need to bring two forms of ID for security reasons – one of which needs to be a credit card or a check."

"Uh, OK... wait, where's this presentation?"

"Ah yes, this is the best part. The preliminary grand prize, which you've already won, is an all-expense-paid trip to our Parador Seis resort on the strip in Cancun, Mexico."

"Mexico??? *Really???*"

"Yes, Mr. Paulson. And since you've been so patient with me, I'd like to let you know that you can double the odds of winning by bringing another couple. Do you know anyone else that would like a free trip to Mexico?"

"I can *double my odds? Really?*"

"Absolutely."

"I know just the couple to bring!"

"Great! I'll certainly give that perk to you. Just bring them. Goodbye."

The telemarketer quickly hung up as the few other telemarketers who remained could no longer keep their laughter quiet. As soon as he'd taken the headset off, he began laughing outrageously and joking with the rest of them.

"He *let* me double his odds of winning!" he screamed. *"What a tool!"*

Then, a few cubes down, another voice boomed.

"I GOT A LIVE ONE!"

The telemarketers smirked at each other, then jumped up and sprinted out of the cube like it was a fire drill.

"I've got $20 on NAMBLA for this one!" the telemarketer yelled as he unplugged his headset.

CHAPTER 12

MEXICAN HAIR DISPOSAL

Danni paced throughout her condominium while talking to Chance on the phone, explaining that she was coloring her hair for the vacation. From her neck down, she was wrapped in beach towel underneath a plastic smock, with thick paste in her hair and enough tin foil wraps in her hair to help SETI search for ET.

"Um, honey, you sure you wanna do this the night before we go on vacation?" Chance asked. "You're cuttin' it kinda close, aren't ya?"

"Chance, it's not like I'm getting a new haircut," Danni explained. "All I'm doing is putting some auburn highlights in it... it'll be fun."

"Hey, how about going totally red?"

"What?"

"And make sure the carpet matches the drapes," Chance reminded.

"What the..."

"Wait, I forgot. You have linoleum in the basement - never mind."

Danni held the cell phone away from her head and stared at it in disgust. She simply pressed End.

As she traversed the luxury furniture filling her fully-furnished, high-end condo, Ellie sat at the kitchen table reading the latest People magazine.

Danni stopped about ten feet away from her and shot her a concerned glare, waiting for Ellie to notice. When Ellie remained unresponsive, Danni cleared her throat.

Ellie looked up from her magazine.

"What?"

"Are you sure we're not leaving this in too long?" Danni asked.

"Danni," Ellie sneered, "I know what I'm doing."

"But you didn't set a timer," Danni almost whined. "I feel like you're just kind of winging it, and I want it to look really good for our vacation."

"What do you want me to do, Danni?" Ellie asked, raising her voice. "Use the timer on your two thousand dollar microwave? I wouldn't even begin to know how to work that damn thing."

"Well," Danni offered, "if you think that would help. I can show you how to..."

"Dammit, Danni," Ellie whined back. "People pay me $80 to do this every day!"

"But..."

"I checked the time when we started. You have about two more minutes, OK?

"Um, OK," Danni replied, obviously still uncomfortable.

"FINE," she steamed, frustrated by being forced into the doting hairdresser role she always had to play at work. "Here," she said as she slung a magazine towards Danni. "Read this while I get the water warm."

As Ellie stomped over towards the sink, Danni walked up to the chair vacated by Ellie and sat down with unsteady legs. She nervously paged through the magazine in a vain attempt to distract herself from the minor panic attack she was experiencing. She was also trying to work up enough courage to address Ellie's sudden Linda Blair cameo.

Normally, Danni wouldn't take this kind of abuse from anyone, but in this instance she decided to be a little more diplomatic – mostly because she was fully aware that yelling at the woman who was in full control of the future of her hair might be a bad move for her locks.

She looked up from the magazine and drew a breath.

"Hey Ellie," she asked delicately, "is something wrong?"

Ellie, leaning on her hands over the fancy sink, sighed and slunk her shoulders.

"I'm sorry, Danni," she said as she turned to face her friend. "I'm just really nervous because this is the first time Mitch and I are going to be together nonstop for three days. I'm just stressed out because I really want this to go well. I think I really like this guy."

"Uh oh," Danni smiled teasingly. "You *are* falling in love with him, aren't you?"

"What? No."

"Yes, yes you *are*," Danni insisted.

Ellie just sighed, knowing that any denial she'd try would be quickly disarmed by her expert lobbyist friend.

"Look, this is a great opportunity for you two," Danni continued. "This is the time when you get to find out whether or not he's a serial killer."

"What?" she asked.

"Oh, you know – his bad habits and all."

"He's not a serial killer."

"Yeah, but what if he leaves the seat up?"

"Oh God," Ellie envisioned with a smirk. "Let's hope he's *only* a serial killer."

"Ellie, it's going to be fine," Danni reassured. "This vacation is a great chance to see if you two work well together in close quarters. You'll get to find out just how much work you'll need to do on him, or if he's even worth the effort."

Ellie leaned back against the sink and laughed.

"Heck, look at this like a 'starter marriage' with a 3-day no-fault return policy" Danni continued. "If after these three days you like what you see, you'll know better if you wanna keep him. If not, you can walk."

Ellie laughed.

"OK," she nodded, "you're right."

"Of *course* I am. Now just relax, we're gonna have a great time."

"*Oh shit!*" Ellie realized. "*Time!* Get over here!"

Danni slung the magazine across the room and darted to the sink, as Ellie quickly started the water. Danni and Ellie frantically pulled the foil wraps off Danni's head.

"Where's your sprayer?" Ellie asked confusedly.

"The faucet head *is* the sprayer," Danni answered while still feeling around her own head for any stray foil wraps. "Just pull it out."

Ellie grabbed a handful of Danni's hair and forcefully shoved her head down into the sink.

"What, did Chance teach you this technique?" she asked as her chin narrowly missed the rim of the sink.

Ellie looked around as she milked the paste from Danni's hair. Danni stood as still as possible as Ellie continued to squish and pull on her locks, many of which were now dangling into the sink drain itself. Ellie suddenly let out a frustrated sigh.

"What?" Danni asked.

"I can't see a damn thing here, Danni," she huffed. "I need more light."

Maintaining a firm grip on the back of Danni's head, she noticed the light switch.

"Hey, is this a..." she asked as she flipped the switch.

Suddenly Danni's head began bouncing rhythmically on the bottom of the sink as her hair got caught in the garbage disposal. Her head pounded the basin, resonating like a bass drum with each thump, accompanied by a high-pitched yelp with each impact.

Ellie's eyes widened with horror as she flipped the switch back to the off position.

"Oh my God!" Ellie cried.

Danni remained standing motionless for a second.

"So..." she finally said indifferently, "how much do you charge people for *this* treatment?"

"I can fix this, I can *fix* this, I *can* fix this," Ellie desperately reassured Danni, while to convince herself at the same time.

"Here, lift up," she instructed while lifting Danni's head by her chin.

Suddenly Danni's hair went taut, and they both realized her hair was caught in the disposal.

"*Ellie!*" Danni yelled angrily.

"OK, I know a plumber," Ellie offered.

"You are not calling a *fucking plumber!*" she snapped.

"But..."

"Get me the fuck outta here!"

"OK, hold on," Ellie surrendered as she went to the kitchen table and pulled out her scissors. "I'll save as much as I can," she said as she began snipping away at Danni's hair, staying as close to the drain as possible.

Once her head was free, Danni slowly stood up and glared at Ellie, her hair hanging in a wedge shape and sticking out in so many frazzled directions that she appeared to have recently been electrocuted.

"Listen, Danni," Ellie explained. "I can..."

"MIRROR," Danni commanded, holding out her hand.

"But..."

"*MIR-ROR*," Danni enunciated with force.

Ellie sheepishly handed Danni the mirror.

Danni stared blankly into her reflection and wanted to cry, but she was too pissed off. Her rage and panic was so overwhelming that she instead fell into indifference, because it was the only reaction she could employ that didn't involve Ellie's immediate dismemberment. Resigned to the mess, she let out a giant sigh and glared.

Ellie, terrified that Danni was about to have a meltdown, never lifted her eyes from the floor.

"Ellie," Danni seethed. "Look at me."

Ellie's eyes slowly rose to meet Danni's.

"I sincerely hope that acting thing works out for you," Danni scolded, "because you *suck* as a stylist."

She then held up the mirror again, ran her fingers through the disaster on her head and her eyes widened even more.

"You didn't even get the fucking color right!" she yelled in frustration.

"Yeah, I saw that too," Ellie confessed, "I just didn't want to say anything...ya know, *in case you liked it.*"

Danni put the mirror to her side and glared again at Ellie – quivering with anger, but not saying a word.

"What do you think about going jet black?" Ellie offered.

CHAPTER 13

IT'S A LITTLE TOO LITTLE,
IT'S A LITTLE TOO LATE

Mitch and Chance were engaged in another battle of NHL ETERNAL on their PlayStation while they waited for Ellie and Danni to arrive for their vacation. Chance, wearing a sombrero, was already in full fiesta mode for Mexico.

"I swear, if I have to test another Nora The Navigator game," Chance droned while working the controller, "I'm gonna start climbin' the trees to try to find a smiley-faced dildo and stab her pet chimp in the eye with it."

"Dude, it's in level nine," Mitch deadpanned, equally engrossed in the game.

"Nuh-uh," Chance smiled. "Is there really one hidden in the game?"

"Oh *yeah*," Mitch laughed, his eyes still not moving from the TV. "I told them not to hire Jack after he got fired from Superstar Software for all the porn he hid in his Mega Auto Theft game, but hey, what do I know?"

"Oh my God, that is so *cool*," Chance smiled, his eyes still not leaving the screen, either. "So, level nine, eh?"

"Yeah," Mitch explained, "instead of leaping over Pedro on your way past Nora's cabin, just leap on his lap and give him your backpack. He'll whip it out of the backpack and start workin' Nora over BIG TIME."

Chance just smiled and shook his head in disbelief while continuing to play the game.

"Man, for the first time in my life, I can't wait to get back into work on Monday," he sighed.

"And to get extra points, you can tune in the Bat channel using Nora's ankles," Mitch added. "It's one of those cross-promotional thingies for the new Bat movie."

"Wow," Chance shook his head again, eyes still fixed on the game, "See dude, this is why video games totally rock."

"And we get paid for them, too," Mitch added. "Talk about Zen..."

"I think I'm turning Buddhist as we speak..."

"I underst... aup - goal."

"Yeah, fuck you," Chance sniffed.

"Hey, put your newfound God in goal if ya don't like it," Mitch suggested. "Buddha can cover the whole damn net without having to flinch."

"It's early, bitch," Chance warned. "Corral yer horses."

As usual for their entrances, the girls knocked twice and then walked through the door. Dragging their luggage with them, they entered the room in mid-argument.

"Look, I used to have that same haircut!" Ellie justified.

"Yeah, back when Pat Benatar was relevant," Danni retorted, walking in revealing a now jet black hairdo cut to the length of her chin.

"Hey!" Mitch interrupted their argument without looking away from the screen. "Pat Benatar is still relevant!"

"Dude, I have no idea why Ellie even gets in a car with you," Chance belittled, not moving his eyes from the screen either.

Danni and Ellie just stood there, nervously waiting for the boys to notice Danni's haircut - but the boys were completely engrossed in their video battle. As the girls realized that Mitch and Chance weren't going to take their eyes off the game, they both sighed, walked into the kitchen, and began making margaritas.

"Dude," Mitch continued while still playing, "Pat Benatar was a total hottie back then."

"WHAT?" Chance asked, still not seeing Danni. "Hey, I'll give you that she had an awesome voice and a great ass, but I just couldn't get past the haircut... made me think of a little boy - *every* time."

Danni's eyes widened with panic as she overheard Chance's comment. As Ellie was pouring the tequila into the blender, Danni grabbed the bottle out of Ellie's hand in mid-pour and took a huge swig straight from it.

The digital hockey players continued to skate across the screen as time began to wind down on their match.

"Just admit defeat, dude," Mitch reasoned. "I'm up 13-9 with five minutes to go. You're not going to catch me."

"Hold on," Chance said confidently as he hit pause.

He then executed a series of weird button and joystick combinations, and suddenly his roster was transformed.

"OK, ready," Chance said as he resumed the game.

"Wait, no..." Mitch stated as he tried to read Chance's new roster.

"You said you could beat me with my team," Chance reminded him.

"Dude!!!" Mitch yelled, "Who is that? *Edmonton* Gretzky???"

"Yep," Chance laughed, "bonus feature. Oops, goal."

"Who was that who passed it to Wayne? Wait, *Mark Messier*? Are you *kidding me???*"

"Nope, that's him," Chance replied. "I signed him mid-season with the Wayner," he teased.

Mitch now appeared to be in a full-on wrestling match with his controller as he struggled frantically to get the puck back.

"Wait, um, HEY – what? Is that...?" Mitch whined.

"Goal," Chance announced.

"*Ovechkin???!!!*" Mitch yelled, becoming more furious. "*C'MON!!!*"

"Oh, you wuss," Chance mocked. "AGAIN, you said you could beat me with my team," he continued as he rattled his controller. "This is my team."

"Yeah," Mitch tried to reason over his own gyrations, "but..."

"Goal."

"WHAT THE *FUCK!!!*" Mitch screamed, sounding more and more like a sailor with each passing minute.

"C'mon Mitch..." Chance sneered as the puck was immediately dropped again. "Quit your bitchin' – you still got a... wait, aup – goal," he smiled. "We're tied."

Mitch suddenly stood up and screamed at the television.

"FUCKIN' *STOP IT!!!* THAT GUY HASN'T EVEN BEEN DRAFTED YET!!!"

"We're tied, *c'mon*!" Chance ordered, commanding Mitch to continue playing. "Puck's dropping!"

"You fuck," Mitch gritted his teeth with near insanity. "I'm gonna..."

As they both struggled against each other and their handheld controllers, a voice from the game yelled, "The clock is winding down... 4, 3, 2... Shot by MacInnis! GOAL!"

Mitch stood up violently and slung the controller across the room.

"MacInnis IS A *BLUE, YOU FUCK!!!*" Mitch screamed maniacally. "HE'D NEVER BEAT *HIS OWN TEAM!!!*"

"Um, easy there Mitch," Chance replied calmly, pretending to be fully ashamed of Mitch's tantrum - even though on the inside he was loving every minute of it. "It's *just* a game..."

Mitch knew Chance was thoroughly enjoying this, which made him even angrier. He then turned to see Ellie and Danni just standing there glaring at Mitch, equally uncomfortable by Mitch's behavior. Mitch then noticed Danni and, for a split second, his eyes widened with horror at the sight of her haircut. But, in that same moment, he saw an opportunity.

"Sooooo... seriously Chance, c'mon..." Mitch asked, acting as if he was calming down. "You didn't think Pat Benatar was even a little bit hot?"

"No."

"And you would've never banged her?" he persisted.

"No, dude!" Chance complained as he stood up. "I-would-never-fuck-Pat-Benatar," he enunciated. "If you want to fuck that little boy, knock yourself out."

He then stood and turned for the kitchen... where his eyes met Danni's.

"Oh shit," he muttered.

Mitch then lifted his arms to the heavens and whispered, "He scores!"

Danni stomped up to him and slammed her purse against Chance's head, knocking him to the floor.

"Wow," Mitch said, "love really *is* a battlefield."

"Say another word, and I'll kick your ass, too," Danni seethed at Mitch.

Chance, still lying on the floor with his hands up defensively, just stared unresponsive for a second.

"Did you just hit me with your best shot?" he asked without flinching.

Danni stepped up to him and whacked him again with her purse. She stood over him silently and simply glared, daring him to say something else.

"Hey, Danni," Mitch said, trying to smooth things over, "honestly, it looks great."

"Don't you pity-fuck me," she scowled.

"No honestly," Mitch said. "It's just... well, it's a big change, ya know? A little 'heads up' would've been nice. Anyway, you two need to finish those drinks. The limo will be here soon."

"Honey," Chance explained to Danni as he got to his feet, "Hey, that 'look'... it... it just didn't work for Pat back then, that's all," Chance began backpedaling. "But, it's totally hot on you... *now*."

"We'll talk about it later," Danni threatened. "Ellie, let's chug these so I don't kill any of you."

"Are you gonna need my car keys again?" Ellie teased.

"Oh yeah, after all you've done already...go ahead and join in, you Beauty School Dropout."

"Danni, I said I was sorry," Ellie pleaded. "Besides, I'm going for the part of Sandy, not, um, Frenchie... " her voice trailed off as she slowly realized how unnecessary it was to point out that fact at that particular moment.

"Holy shit," Mitch realized. "*You* did that to her?"

Ellie shot Mitch the most evil glare she could muster.

"I mean," Mitch corrected, realizing his misstep, "Hey, you got an audition?"

Ellie just glared emotionlessly. "This spring," she said coldly as she sipped her margarita.

Chance tried again to change the subject.

"Um, hey Mitch, put on those sissy cargos shorts so we can stuff them full of beers."

"Dude, the limo's stocked," Mitch said. "This ain't a Blues game."

"Oh, I know," Chance agreed. "We'll need them to smuggle a few authentic Coronas back for the ride home."

"Oh yeah," Mitch nodded. "Good thinkin'."

CHAPTER 14

JIHAD ME AT HELLO

Inside the limo, everyone's mood had gone from edgy to celebratory. The radio blared, the liquor flowed, and the laughter and yelling reinforced the feeling that this vacation was going to simply kick ass from here on out. Even their limo driver was mixing martinis for them as he drove them to the airport. To them, if that wasn't a sign of upcoming good times, nothing was.

As they pulled up to the Departures gate, they all, for lack of a better term, tumbled out of the limo.

"I'll take care of the limo driver," Mitch said as he regained his footing. "Grab my bag and I'm right behind you, OK?"

"Got it," Chance said.

As Mitch was tipping the limo driver, a flatbed truck drove by on its way to the new runway construction site. The truck hit the speed bump a little too fast, causing debris to fall from the truck and onto the ground nearby. Mitch quickly reached back in the limo, grabbed his carry-on backpack, and entered the airport with a happy buzz, completely oblivious to the truck's spilled contents.

Chance was already at the security checkpoint that Ellie and Danni had passed through. He smiled as he noticed the attractive, young TSA associate manning the gate.

"Wanna get 'blown' instead?" she smiled, gesturing towards their new bomb-making detector machine.

Chance looked to see that Ellie and Danni were well outside of earshot.

"If you're doing the blowing, sure," he smiled. He passed through the checkpoint, grabbed his bags, and turned back to smile at the TSA worker.

"We gotta do this again sometime," he whispered seductively.

The TSA worker smiled back, mildly amused.

"You're gonna miss your flight, sir," she smiled back, "but it was nice blowing you."

Sensing the rejection, Chance nodded in defeat and walked away, picking up his pace to catch the girls.

Just a few steps behind Chance, Mitch approached the same checkpoint.

"Wanna get 'blown' instead?" the TSA agent asked.

Stunned by the proposition and still a little unsteady from his buzz, Mitch rolled his eyes in feigned disbelief.

"Shuuure," he slurred.

Mitch stepped into what looked like an oversized, high tech phone booth. As he positioned his feet on the stenciled patterns on the floor directing him where to stand, a series of mini air cannons began hit his body zone by zone. When the air jets shushed upon his shoes, instantaneously, alarms began blaring and red lights blinked maniacally.

"Wow," Mitch asked confusedly, "is that a good thing?"

"Is an alarm *ever* a good thing?" the TSA agent scowled with a raised brow.

Before Mitch could un-smile, two linebacker-sized TSA agents pounced on him like lions on a baby gazelle and began pounding him into oblivion.

Mitch's eyes came back into focus as he found himself in a concrete-walled room, complete with a steel table, a closed circuit camera, and a two-way mirror. As he reached up to rub his aching head, he realized his wrist was handcuffed to his chair. Yet, as confused as he was, the only thing Mitch could think about was his overextended bladder.

Mitch growled and moaned as he fought with the handcuffs. He then turned to the mirror.

"My cousin is the assistant regional manager of the TSA in Spokane, you fucks!" he screamed defiantly. "You're all gonna pay for this!"

At that moment, the door opened and in walked a TSA agent. For a moment, Mitch wondered if she moonlighted as a Hooters calendar girl. She gently approached Mitch, smiled and placed a folder in front of him. She pulled her chair around to his side of the table and sat next to him.

Mitch suddenly lost all his angst, his lips sliding from rage-mode to charm-mode. He then briefly wondered if the TSA was hiring.

"Hi, Mr. Paulson," she greeted with a voice was even sweeter than a mother reading a bedtime story. "My name is Carrie. I'm here to help straighten things out..." she said, leaning close enough to let her perfume waft across his nose.

The double entendre made Mitch's smile widen like a frat boy on his first visit to a strip club.

"Hi!" he replied, nearly stumbling through the word.

"I'm sure this is all just a misunderstanding," she reassured. "Oh, I almost forgot. I have to tell you, for legal reasons, my name is Agent Carrie Anderson. Here's my ID badge."

She pointed towards her badge – which happened to be resting upon one of her healthy-sized breasts – and pushed it closer to his face.

Mitch took note of how desperately her buttons were straining against her uniform.

"Oh, no problem,' he smiled agreeably. "You have a job to do."

"I knew you would understand," she smiled as her gaze deepened. "You have very understanding eyes."

Mitch began to wonder if this was going to turn into one of Chance's "doesn't count" moments he'd always talked about. In the past, Chance's ability to call one of these "moral mulligans" – like a quarterback calling an audible when he recognizes an opportunity to leverage – were the basis of most of his best stories. Even if it was just for the night – or the hour – Chance never saw a problem with it.

"No know, no foul," he'd always say.

And in the past, Mitch lost a little respect for Chance every time he did it. But now, faced with the same possible opportunity, Mitch suddenly understood Chance's reasoning for his "doesn't count" mulligans. In fact, at that moment, it made perfect sense.

He then leaned into Carrie.

"I know you can't let dangerous people on these planes," he began. "And even though I may look *dangerous*" he emphasized as he feigned a hostile glare, "I'm just an author."

She tilted her head like a confused puppy.

"I write novels..." he explained slowly, trying to give her another clue.

She squinted uncertainly.

"I write... *books*?" he asked, as if playing Password.

"OH, I LOVE books," she replied giddily. "You're a *writer*?"

"Well," Mitch corrected her with assertion. "A novelist, if you wanna get specific."

She tilted her head, once again oblivious.

"Yes, I write books." he corrected himself in defeat.

"So, tell me something you've written."

"Well, have you heard of 'Nora and Pedro in The Magical Castle'?"

"No, but it sounds *fascinating*...

"Well, the New York Times said it was a little incendiary," he replied in an aloof tone, "but *what do they know?*"

Her eyes widened with awe.

Taking note of the lack-of-intellect of his immediate audience, Mitch continued.

"I then followed that up with a smaller book called 'The Grapes of Wrath.' Have you heard of that one?"

"WOW," she melted. "Yeah, I saw the movie! That's so cool! OK, well, lemme get back to work here for a minute. So, you're going to Mexico for vacation?"

"Yep, and hopefully to get a car," Mitch added.

"Don't tell me..." she smiled, "It's an El Camino, right?"

"Uh, a what?"

"You know, one of those Mexican cars."

"Um..."

"Well, come on, if you're getting the car from Mexico... right? I mean, *duh*."

"Actually," Mitch continued, trying to ignore her comment, "it'll be an Aston Martin if I get it."

"Oooh, nice," she smiled, then she squinted again in confusion, "But, if you're going to get a car, why didn't you just drive down to get it?"

Mitch shook his head trying to figure out a way to explain to her that he couldn't drive down to pick up another car because then the car he originally drove down would be...

"*Eh, never mind,*" he thought to himself.

"I'm just kidding," she laughed as she slapped his shoulder. "I'm not *that* stupid. I know you can't drive across the ocean."

Mitch's eyes widened even more this time, and he again shook his head trying to remove the malfunction of his brain trying to comprehend what she just said.

At that moment, Carrie's walkie-talkie blared from her shoulder harness.

"Carrie, we need you in Room 2."

Carrie shrugged at Mitch and smiled.

"Well, duty calls," she said. "I'll be right back."

Mitch contorted a smile back. Then the phrase "duty calls" reminded him of his full bladder.

"Hey," he called after her, "wait, can you let me..."

"I'll be right back, sweetie," she interrupted. "Just relax."

Mitch sunk back into his chair and sighed in frustration.

Not thirty seconds later, the door flung open and the agent stormed in, this time with her hair in a ponytail. She yanked the draw cord on the blinds, and the blinds slammed down with authority. She paused, glared at Mitch, and swiped the cable off the back of the closed-circuit camera.

"Whoa, all RIGHT!" Mitch said enthusiastically as he was already telling himself this was exactly one of those 'doesn't count' moments Chance had always bragged about.

"Hey," Mitch smiled widely. "I really like your hair up like that!"

She circled Mitch as if assessing the best angle of attack, stopping directly behind him.

Mitch turned his head frantically from side to side, trying to see where she was. Still, he attempted to act coy.

"*Sooooo*," he asked broodingly, "are you gonna uncuff me for this or do you think I'm *too dangerous*?"

She stopped cold and glared incredulously.

"What the *fuck* did you just say to me?" she growled, daring him to repeat it. She then stomped around to the front. "You don't fuckin' *know me!*" she sneered, leaning into his face.

Confused, yet even more turned on, Mitch tried to regain his confidence by continuing to smile wryly.

"But, your hair," he persisted. "I said like it like that... It fits you better. Are you gonna play bad cop this time? Maybe *smack me around a little*?" he leered wickedly.

She stomped up to him and, with a homerun-type swing, smacked him across his face with her clipboard.

His face felt as though it was about to come off his skull. Undaunted and desperately trying to show that he was "man enough" for her, he turned his head back towards her and smiled.

"Hey, before we do this," he asked with less certainty, "aren't we supposed to establish a 'safe word' or something?"

"WHAT???!!!" she barked.

"Well," he explained, "I always thought I'd use '*Anaconda*.'"

She planted her feet right at his ankles and then climbed up onto the chair, straddling him. With her one free hand, she grabbed the neck of his t-shirt and leaned on him, unintentionally pressing on his bladder.

Mitch tried to ignore the strain by looking directly at her tits and smiled.

"*This is a once-in-a-lifetime 'doesn't count' thing,*" he thought. "*I can ignore my bladder for now.*"

She shoved the clipboard under his chin, forcing his eyes to meet hers.

"What the FUCK were you looking at?" she scolded. "Did you just stare at my tits? *What kind of pig are you?*"

"Any-kind-of-pig-you-want..." he replied rhythmically as he nodded back-and-forth to his words, all the while smiling.

She just hovered over him in silence, with disbelief and rage written all over her face.

"Wait," Mitch asked, sensing her displeasure, "do you want me to call you something else?"

"BOY," she screamed in a maniacal rant, "You can call me GOD, because that's EXACTLY what I AM to you right now!!! I will put you in a place where your ass will be up for auction every day!!! Don't you EVER look me anywhere but in the eyes!!! I will FUCK your world up so bad that you'll NEVER WANT TO see the light of day again!!! I'm gonna destroy *you*, your *cell*, your *family*, AND your *FUCKIN' FAITH!!!* By the time I'm done with you, you'll be beggin' for a conjugal visit from *JACK FUCKIN' BAUER!!!* "

"Um," Mitch quivered as he turned his head slightly with eyes widening from sudden fear and the slow realization that this was NOT going to be one of Chance's 'doesn't count' moments.

"'*Anaconda*'?" he offered with uncertainty.

Still straddling him, she grabbed two handfuls of Mitch's shirt and began bouncing on him while nearly pulling him out of his chair.

"Tell me RIGHT NOW where the fucking bombs are!!!" she screamed.

Mitch's eyes nearly popped out.

"*Bombs?*" he whined like a helpless puppy.

At that moment, the door opened and in walked Carrie. Her eyes widened as she saw the woman still straddling Mitch.

"Terri!" Carrie yelled. "I thought you were on vacation!"

"I was," Terri growled, her gaze never breaking from his face, "until this asshole thought he could blow up my airport."

Mitch looked over in shock to see Carrie standing in the doorway. He then quickly looked up at the woman in his lap, and then did a double take with both of them, realizing that he had no idea what the fuck was happening.

"But, he's a writer, Sis!" she pleaded. "He's not a terrorist!"

"*Sis?*" Mitch whimpered. "You're *sisters?*"

"Try 'twins' you fuckin' moron," Terri belittled. "You obviously weren't the mastermind of this attack."

"See, this is what sucks about you being my older sister," Carrie complained calmly, obviously rehashing an old argument. "You never listen to me. He's NOT a terrorist. He's just a writer!"

"Yeah, he's the fuckin' writer all right," she seethed. "He probably wrote the Al Qaeda for Dummies manifesto."

"Nooo, he wrote the Wrath of Khan, dammit!" Carrie yelled. "Remember? *Mr. Roarke?*"

Mitch wanted to correct her, but at that moment he was a little too preoccupied by the psychotic twin straddling him in the chair.

"He's got enough TNT on his shoes to blow up your IQ, sis!" Terri yelled.

Carrie looked confused again

"Huh?" Carrie asked. "I told you to stop using those monograms I don't know!"

"Monograms?" Mitch asked in near-delirium.

"OK, fine!" Carrie admitted. "I meant mammograms."

Terri and Mitch both turned and looked at her bewilderedly.

"You know, *mammograms*?" Carrie insisted. "Like 'BFF' and all?"

As Mitch's jaw nearly dropped into his lap, he looked at Carrie with his most sincere "are you fuckin' serious?" stare.

"Great," Mitch then mumbled to himself, "*she's* the good cop."

Terri, undaunted, returned her focus to Mitch. Realizing the pounding was about to resume, Mitch simply moaned for mercy.

"This fucker's got designs to level this place," Terri continued, "and I'm gonna get it outta him if I have to water board him until he shits a river!"

"*What?*" Mitch cried.

"Wait!" Carrie pleaded to Terri.

"NO!" she screamed at Mitch. "YOU INTERRUPTED MY VACATION, FUCKER!" she yelled, now fully enraged and pouncing on Mitch's bladder harder, and yet rhythmically to every word. "WHERE'S–THE– FUCKING–BOMB???"

"*TERRI!*" Carrie screamed. "THERE IS *NO BOMB!!!*"

"How do *you* know, Sherlock?" Terri turned as she climbed off of the chair.

"Oh no," Mitch suddenly shuddered.

"Because we've had eight positive detections in three minutes," Carrie rebuked. "One is an 82-year-old grandma from Texas. Another was an eight-year-old from Des Moines whose daddy is a Homeland Security agent!"

"What?" Terri asked, suddenly intrigued as she took the file from Carrie's hands.

"We just found an explosives spill outside," Carrie explained as Terri rapidly paged through the file folder. "It must have come from the runway construction site. Everyone's been walking through it and setting off the alarms – *that's* how I know he's not a terrorist, OK?"

Terri then glared at Carrie.

"Why didn't you tell me this sooner?" she demanded.

Carrie stuttered incoherently, not really saying anything. Terri ignored her sister's ramblings and turned to Mitch.

"Sir, I apologize for the misunderstanding," Terri said in a professional tone as she straightened her torso. "I hope you understand that it is our duty to protect everyone on these flights and we have to take our jobs seriously."

Mitch, broken and slinking over in the chair, shrugged.

"Sure, no worries," he said as he tried to wave off her apology - until the handcuffs caught his hand in midair and knocked his arm back down.

"We always have to look for dangerous people," Terri continued. "Still, this was a misunderstanding and I want to make it up to you. Is there anything I can get you?"

"Um, yeah," Mitch confessed, his head still hanging to one side. "I need my backpack 'cause I kinda pissed myself."

They both looked at the floor beneath Mitch's chair and saw the puddle.

"Ewww!" Terri cringed.

"Awww," Carrie said as she tilted her head sympathetically.

Mitch's mind tried to calm his heart, which was still trying to leap from its rib cage. But the thought of being forever labeled a terrorist, the disappointment from the loss of the 'doesn't count', and the embarrassment of the puddle at his feet – it was all a little, um, too much to process right at that moment.

CHAPTER 15

TERMINAL AIRFARE,
CROSSING THE RED LINE

Mitch, fresh in his cargo shorts, slung his backpack over his shoulder and darted out the door of the Security Area. He quickly shoved his way through the masses as he looked at his watch. He quickly realized that if he didn't find his gate in the next two minutes, he'd miss his plane. And, no, Chance wouldn't ask anyone to wait for him. Chance was more likely to close the plane door himself.

As he hopped over a suitcase and side-stepped an elderly couple, he jumped onto the people mover. His eyes frantically scanned both sides of the terminal as he tried to locate his gate.

"MITCH!" Ellie suddenly yelled from the gate counter as she saw Mitch passing by.

"There he is," Danni said to the stewardess as she, Ellie, Chance, and the gate attendant all stared at Mitch.

Mitch waved, then looked down and realized that the people-mover was going to overshoot his gate. He leapt the rail of the people mover and onto the belt of the people mover going the other way. But his momentum, coupled with the speed at which the other belt moving in the opposite direction, leveled him like a bowling pin.

The resulting loud THUD resonated loudly throughout the terminal. Ellie covered her face in shame. Chance laughed out loud. Danni stood slack-jawed. The gate attendant quickly looked down at her desk, pretending to not have seen it.

Mitch pulled himself up on the people mover that was mindlessly pulling him the other way and again leapt the railing. With a few quick steps, he staggered to a stop, and then ran up to the gate and handed the stewardess his ticket, while still a little woozy.

"What happened to you???" Ellie demanded. "When did you change your shorts?"

"Not now," Mitch replied as he smiled at the stewardess.

"MITCH!" Ellie insisted.

"NOT NOW!" Mitch snapped back with a glare, then again turned to the gate attendant with an over-reassuring smile.

The gate attendant stared at Mitch coldly, handed him his ticket back, and simply said, "Go."

The four of them jogged down the finger to the plane just as another stewardess was getting ready to close the door.

After they got settled into their seats, Mitch relayed his story to Ellie. Chance and Danni, sitting in the row behind them, leaned in and listened. After completing the story, Ellie just stared at him resentfully.

"You were detained," Ellie repeated for clarification.

"Yeah." Mitch replied.

"By the TSA."

"Yeah."

"By female TSA *twins*."

"Yeah."

For a moment, Ellie moved her eyes around as if making mental notes of everything Mitch had just said.

"Look Mitch," Ellie finally said with a sneer, "if you're gonna lie to me, at least make it believable. Chance, switch seats with me."

"Ellie, I..."

"Shut up. I don't want to look at you right now," she said as she took Chance's seat and Chance climbed over Mitch.

"So, dude," Chance whispered as he settled into Ellie's seat, "what *really* happened? Did you hook up with that TSA hottie with the blow machine or what?"

"Wha – NO!" Mitch yelled. "I'M NOT..."

"Shhh Shhh," Chance said, trying to quiet him down.

"I'm not lying," Mitch restated more calmly. "It all happened."

"Mitch, that story is so awesome!" Chance quietly laughed. "So, were the twins totally hot?"

Mitch simply snickered. Chance snickered back in acknowledgement as they knuckle-knocked.

Suddenly a hand appeared above Mitch and smacked him on top of his head.

"HEY!" Mitch cringed. "What was *that* for?"

"For noticing they were hot," Ellie's muffled voice said from behind his seat.

"Look, babe, I..."

"I'm still mad at you," Ellie grumbled, "even if you *are* telling the truth."

Chance elbowed Mitch and mouthed the words, "She'll get over it."

CHAPTER 16

THIS MUST BE JUST
LIKE LIVIN' IN PARADISE

As the plane came to a stop on the tarmac, the hatch to the fuselage opened and passengers began moving down the open stairwell into the Mexican sun. Mitch, Ellie, Chance, and Danni emerged from the plane, paused, looked around, and walked down to the tarmac.

All around them was warm bright sunlight, palm trees that swayed in the ocean breeze, and lush green foliage growing on every spot of land that hadn't been paved.

They all breathed in the warm salty air briefly as they crossed the tarmac.

They emerged from the airport into a concentration of cab drivers all jockeying to grab their next fare. As the four approached the melee, Mitch suddenly saw a man selling jewelry from a folding table.

"Ellie," he called as he turned towards the table. "Come here."

Ellie followed him over to the table as Mitch perused the seller's wares. He then saw a ring that resembled a diamond wedding ring.

"What are you doing?" Ellie asked.

"If you're gonna be my wife on this vacation, you're gonna need a ring," Mitch replied. "Can I see that one?" he asked the man behind the table.

As he handed Mitch the ring, Mitch turned to Ellie.

"What do you think?" he smiled.

"Is that the best you can do for me?" Ellie sarcastically snapped.

"Yep," Mitch replied. "I don't want us to get disqualified for any reason, so..." He then turned to the man. "How much?"

"Twenty American," the man replied in a thick Mexican accent.

"Well, if that's three months' salary for you, I'm thinkin' I'll have to keep my job at the salon."

"Save it, babe," Mitch teased. "It'll do for now."

Ellie's eyebrows lifted in surprise.

"For now?" she asked.

"Yes, beautiful," he smiled as he paid the man and took the ring. He then gently took her hand and slowly slid the ring on her finger.

Ellie's eyes widened and her heart raced a little.

As he slid the ring onto her finger, he said softly, "With this ring, I... hope I win an Aston Martin," he quickly finished.

Ellie suddenly shoved him away.

"You really know how to ruin a moment, don't you," she sneered.

"What?" Mitch asked bewilderedly. "It's a *toy* ring!"

Ellie stormed past Danni and Chance, who were standing alongside watching the whole thing. Danni squinted angrily at Mitch, shook her head, and chased after Ellie.

"WHAT?" Mitch asked again, as if expecting to get an answer if he asked it a second time.

Chance looked down and began to laugh.

"You gonna get one for Danni?" Mitch asked.

"Noooo-ho-ho," Chance continued laughing. "I don't want *any* of your problems."

Mitch ran up next to Ellie and tried to ask her what was wrong, but Ellie simply had one lip curled and was shaking her head, ignoring his questions. Mitch began to persist until he noticed a man standing expressionless amongst the overly-eager cab drivers. As Mitch looked more closely at the man, he realized he was holding a sign that read "Paulson"

"Hi," Mitch smiled. "We're the Paulson party."

The man suddenly perked up.

"Oh, si, si," the man replied. "Please senor – come with me."

As he signaled them to come to the cab, the four of them pushed through the crowd of people and a got a full view of the driver's taxi, which was essentially being held together by rust and bungee cords.

"Oh dear God," Ellie groaned, realizing that this was the group's transportation to their hotel.

The driver walked around and loosened the bungee cord holding down his trunk.

"Help you with your bag, senor?" he asked.

"Mitch," Chance called uncertainly. "This isn't our ride, is it?"

"Hey," Mitch reasoned. "We'll be fine. Besides, it's free."

"It ain't gonna be free if it costs us our lives," Danni replied with terror.

"Ellie?" Mitch asked. "Please tell her we'll be alright."

"Why?" Ellie replied. "Maybe you're baiting her into something, too."

"What the fuck is going on with you two?" Mitch asked. "OK, fine. Danni, if we wreck, you can harvest all of my body parts, OK?"

"You're gonna owe me for this..." Danni pointed at Ellie.

"Don't look at me," Ellie replied.

They loaded their bags into the trunk and crawled into the cab. As the car pulled away, the bungee cord strained against the bouncing trunk lid, briefly exposing their luggage with every bump.

As they approached the resort area, all four stared amazedly at each ostentatious property that they passed. The imminent luxury that was apparently awaiting the end of this cab ride suddenly altered Ellie's mood. She was more understanding, if not feeling some comfort from Danni's "dog" analogy that she told her early on in this courtship.

"Wow, Mitch!" Ellie exclaimed. "Look at that place! Is that where we're staying?"

"I don't think so," Mitch replied from the front seat, as he stared with the same wide-eyed amazement. "I don't speak Spanish at all. I can't remember the name of the place, but I'll recognize it when I see it."

Chance, Danni, and Ellie kept sliding from one side to the other to see each resort they passed, each time squashing each other like children straining to catch a glimpse of their own personal idol.

"Oh Mitch! Mitch!" Ellie yelled, slapping his shoulder. "Tell me we're staying THERE."

"Wait, wait," Mitch replied with anticipation. "Aw, no," he then answered. "But that is where we're going to pick up my prize."

"Mitch, about this presentation..." Chance began.

"Not now, Chance," Mitch dismissed. "Let's get to our place first."

"Do you even know the name of the place we're staying at?" Chance insisted.

"Hold on," Mitch said as he dug a piece of paper out of his front pocket. "OK, here it is. The name of our resort is 'Parador Seis.'"

"Si," the cab driver replied. "We go to Parador Seis."

"Awesome," Mitch replied. "I can't wait to see that one."

"Wait, Mitch," Chance cautioned as he thought, "that's... what the fuck? That's Motel Six!!!"

"Huh?"

"That means Motel Six in Spanish, you dumbass!!!" Chance scolded.

"No it doesn't!"

"Yes Mitch!" Chance growled. "Remember high school Spanish?   UNO-DOS-TRES-CUATRO-CINCO-fuckin'-Motel-SEIS!"

"Are you sure?" Mitch asked in disbelief.

At that moment, the taxi pulled into the parking lot of the only cracked, crumbling, and stained structure on the strip. Everyone's jaws dropped as the driver put the car in park. The four of them slowly got out and, with horror, tried to absorb the fact that this was their hotel.

One of the three hookers standing in front of the stairwell raised a hand at the cab.

"Hey babbeee," she called out. "You wanna be mi pappy?"

"This has got to be wrong," Mitch said.

"No senor," the driver replied. "Thees es Parador Seis. Thee sign right there sayes so."

Mitch looked at the old road sign with an arrow of mostly shattered light bulbs across the top. The sign below had so many broken and missing letters that it actually looked like it read "Orar Si".

"OK, Antonio Banderas." Mitch sarcastically asked Chance. "What's that say in Spanish?"

"Pray yes," Chance replied. "It says 'Pray yes.'"

"Are you telling me this is the resort???" Ellie asked.

"No no, senora," the driver said. "Thees es the hotel you stay at while you see the resort. Hotel es where you stay, resort es where you visit."

Danni, thoroughly disgusted, turned to Chance.

"OK, honey," she said. "Lemme see your wallet."

"What, why?"

"Wallet" she reiterated while holding out her hand.

Chance sighed as he dug his wallet out of his back pocket.

"OK, since we *are* married, these..." she said as extracted his credit cards, "are *ours*." She smiled and nearly gave the wallet back when she noticed an O-shaped ring on the back of his wallet. 'Whoa whoa whoa - wait a second. What *is* this?"

"Hey!!!" Chance protested as Danni pulled out Chance's condom.

"Haha, seriously?" Danni mocked. "Magnum? Are you kidding? What responsible pharmacist sold you this?"

Chance's head sank as she smirked.

"I'll hold on to this," she said gleefully as she dropped it in her purse.

Chance started to protest, but Danni was having none of it.

"Hey, the only time you're going to use it is when I'm around anyway, *right?*" Danni glared. "So, there shouldn't be a problem, should there?"

Chance just stood there and grumbled, unable to think of anything to say. No, he didn't plan on cheating on Danni while he was on vacation, but...

"*Hey, you never know,*" he thought to himself.

As Danni and Ellie turned and headed towards the strip of outlet stores, Chance suddenly thought of a response.

"Hey, if we're married, then we won't NEED that!"

Danni and Ellie kept walking, ignoring Chance.

"And IF we're married," he continued yelling to Danni, "does that mean you're at least going to give me a ..."

"Unt-uh," Danni sang. "*Mar-ried...*" she wagged a finger back at him as she continued walking with Ellie.

As soon as they were out of earshot, Chance elbowed Mitch.

"We'll see how married she is after four pitchers of margaritas," Chance scoffed.

CHAPTER 17

YOU CAN CHECK OUT
ANY TIME YOU LIKE

Chance and Mitch hauled the bags up the stairs to the hotel office and dropped them in front of an old wood and stucco desk. The old hound dog resting lazily in front of the desk didn't even flinch, nor did he feel the need to move out of Mitch's way.

Mitch took one step over the dog and was basically straddling him as he rang the silver bell atop the desk. Chance merely chuckled as Mitch stared at the dog, amazed by his unwillingness to get out of the way.

An old Mexican man, possibly even older than the desk, appeared in a wife-beater tank top and baseball cap from the back room.

"Can I help you, senores?" he asked as he waddled out from the back room.

"Yes," Mitch said, still straddling the dog, "I need to check in. Paulson, party of four."

"Oh, si," the old man replied. He grabbed a three-ring binder and placed it in front of Mitch. He flipped through the papers, found Mitch's name, and had him sign in.

Mitch signed the book and looked up to find Chance had gone back outside to flirt with the hookers.

"Chance!" Mitch yelled.

Chance, without flinching or turning to look at Mitch, continued talking with the ladies while holding up a "one minute" hand signal.

"Uh, senor?" the old man interrupted.

"Yes?" Mitch said, turning his head back to the man.

"I need to know which day you will go to the presentation," he replied. "Today or manana."

"Manana," Mitch replied. He then turned his head back and yelled, "CHANCE!"

Chance nodded to each of the ladies and shook their hands. He then turned and headed back towards Mitch.

"Morning or Afternoon?" the old man continued.

"What?" Mitch asked, thinking he was done registering. "Uh, morning's fine."

"Very good, senor," he replied. He then turned, grabbed a key off of a hook, placed it on the desk, and began waddling back into his office without saying a word.

"Um, sir?" Mitch called.

The old man turned and looked at him.

"When can we go see the resort?"

"Anytime, senor," he replied as he turned and waddled back to the back room.

Chance bounded into the office like a newborn puppy.

"Alright, plan B has been negotiated if we need it," he smiled.

Mitch just sneered and slung a bag at his head.

"Let's just get this shit to the room, OK?"

They opened the door and entered a room sparsely decorated with torn upholstery, peeling paint, cracked window panes, and bed sheets that were too old and stained to know if pale yellow was their original color. They looked around the room, uncertain of how the girls were going to react to their accommodations.

"Dude, there is NO WAY the girls are gonna stay here tonight," Chance said. "What are we gonna do?"

"Um, let's check out the resort down the way," Mitch answered. "Maybe they'll let us stay there."

"OK, but what about the bags?" Chance asked.

"Just toss them in there for now," Mitch cringed. "We need to find the girls and then get some answers at the resort."

After bringing Ellie and Danni back to the room and surviving a heated conversation about the condition of the place, Ellie and Danni finally agreed to head to the resort to resolve the problem.

They walked down the road to the resort, with Ellie and Danni being a good 200 feet ahead of Mitch and Chance. As the ladies got to the point of the street across from the entrance, they paused and marveled at the ornate beauty of the white stucco gates and gentle fountains flowing in front of the sign that read "Arenas Celestiales". They both smiled and looked at each other with nervous hope that they would be staying in this resort instead of that hole of a hotel. They hurriedly crossed the street and walked in through the white stucco gates. Once across, they looked back at Mitch and Chance – and made big sweeping motions with their arms, telling them to hurry up.

As the boys reached the point on the street to cross as well, they looked side-to-side and tried to decide when they would attempt to cross the road.

At that moment, a car pulled up in front of them, blocking their path. Two teenage boys inside the car looked at Mitch and Chance and smiled widely.

"Hey, touristas, si?" asked the teenager riding shotgun. "You want some ganja?""

Mitch and Chance stared at each other for a second, then slowly looked around to see if anyone else was watching.

Ellie and Danni suddenly realized that the boys were just now crossing the street as the mysterious car pulled away.

"What was that?" Ellie asked Mitch as they got closer.

Mitch's eyes got wide with fear.

"Um, directions," he smiled. "They needed directions..."

"Two local boys were asking *you two* for directions?" Danni countered.

"Hey," Chance scoffed, "we told them we weren't from around here."

The girls stared blankly at them without saying a word. They knew they were lying, even if they weren't sure what they were lying about. They then turned and walked into the main lobby.

The four of them entered a grand room in the main entrance. The open-air lobby had tall white archways, shiny ornate tiled floors, and woodwork that glistened as if it had just been polished.

Mitch was temporarily awestruck by the beauty of the room, but as soon as he saw the main desk, he put his head down and walked deliberately towards the hotel clerk.

"Can I help you, senor?" the man smiled.

"Yes," Mitch complained. "I'm Mitch Paulson, I won your sweepstakes. But the hotel you have us in is unacceptable – it's disgusting. I need you to get us a room here for the weekend.

The clerk looked down at his computer.

"You said 'Paulson'?" he asked.

"Yes."

"Si, senor, we have you in the computer. But our resort is booked for this weekend, I'm not sure there's anything we can do for you."

"Then I need to speak with a manager," Mitch insisted.

"Si, senor," he nodded. He picked up the phone and briefly spoke in Spanish and then hung up the phone.

"My manager will be out here shortly," he said.

"Thank you," Mitch replied.

No more than a minute later, a strikingly handsome, well-dressed Latin-American man appeared from the office behind the desk.

"Welcome to Arenas Celestiales," he said as approached. "My name is Raoul, and I am the manager. How can I help you?"

"Well," Mitch explained, "I won the sweepstakes you guys had, but the hotel you've put us in, it's, um..."

"Is there something wrong with it?" Raoul asked.

"Find something right with it," Danni interrupted. "I dare you."

"Entonces tengo que llamar a mi gerente para arreglar esto ahora?" Raoul replied, testing their ability to speak Spanish.

The four of them stared blankly, completely baffled by what he'd just said.

"Oh, I'm sorry," Raoul smiled, "I did not realize that none of you spoke Spanish. I apologize. What I said was, 'So, I should call my boss and take care of this right now?'"

"I think so, yes," Mitch insisted.

"Un momento," Raoul replied. He then turned and yelled, "JUAAAN!"

Instantly, a young bellboy ran up to Raoul and stood at attention beside him like a soldier.

Raoul began screaming at him in Spanish, and all four of them believed he was chewing the boy out, although none of them bothered to wonder what the bellboy had to do with the apparent mix up.

Unfortunately for the four of them, what he'd actually just said was, "Can you believe every one of these American assholes expect the best accommodations even when they get their room for free???!!! Tell your boss he did a fantastic job of finding that '*SHIT HOLE!!!*' And what do you think of the tits on this blonde over here, eh???"

Juan briefly looked at Ellie and smiled

"Oh yes, yes, senor Raoul," Juan replied. "Si."

But Raoul was not finished. He continued screaming at the bellboy, but due to the group's inability to speak fluent Spanish, none of them knew that Raoul had merely told Juan, "Now, nod like you agree with everything I've said and tell me everything will be fixed – *in English* – OR ELSE!"

"No problema, senor," Juan replied dutifully. "Si, si, everything will be fixed."

Raoul then lifted his arms and turned back to the four of them.

"I apologize for the misunderstanding, senor Paulson. We will find more suitable accommodations, and I will try to have a room for the four of you here. You know, this will probably work better for us because we want you to see all the amenities we offer anyway, and also we can get the presentation out of the way first thing tomorrow morning. Is this acceptable for you?

"Wow, yes!" Mitch replied. "Thank you!"

"Bueno!" Raoul smiled. "OK, my boss will contact me shortly and we will resolve these problemas as soon as we can."

"Ya know," Ellie smiled, "I've heard that Mexico is quite accommodating. I guess they were right."

Raoul then stepped between Mitch and Ellie and gently took Ellie's hand.

"You have no idea, senora," he replied in a soft, low voice.

Ellie suddenly felt a little flush and slightly dizzy as Raoul stared deeply into her eyes.

"In the meantime, ladies," Raoul suddenly said again in a normal tone, "please enjoy our pool while your husbands take a look at our list of activities that are going on today and tomorrow."

Ellie giggled and blushed a little.

"Um, Okaaay," Ellie said. "C'mon Danni, let's see the pool."

Mitch just squinted, not sure how to react. He wondered if Raoul was actually trying to move in on Ellie right in front of him, but as Mitch was about to say something to Raoul, Chance slapped Mitch's shoulder.

"Come on, bud," Chance bounced. "Let's see what they got!"

Mitch looked at Chance, then turned back to say something to Raoul, but Raoul was nowhere to be seen. Mitch sighed as he watched Ellie and Danni walk through another large archway into the pool area. He then begrudgingly followed Chance to the Activities board, which hung on a heavy wooden door in the same pool area.

Chance eagerly read through the list. Mitch just stood next to him and watched Ellie strip down to her bikini. As she got into the pool, she saw Mitch staring at her the whole time. She smiled at him and waved.

Mitch, slightly embarrassed from being caught staring, goofily waved back. He then turned to read the list with Chance.

"Hey," Mitch suggested as he began reading, "You think the girls would like the horseback riding thing tomorrow?"

"Dude!" Chance exclaimed, as he suddenly slapped Mitch's shoulder again. "We could totally go international!"

"What?"

"Bring our game to Latin America!" Chance nearly squealed as he began to bounce and point at the list like an excited puppy. "This is the chance we've been waiting for!!!"

"What are you talking about?" Mitch asked in total confusion.

"We can get the team back together!" Chance announced as he pointed to the two-on-two sand volleyball competition.

Mitch's face sank with horror.

"Oh no," he thought. *"Not again."*

"What?" Chance asked, confused by Mitch's complete silence.

"Dude, um," Mitch began, "Look, we're here to spend time with the girls. And you know how these tournaments are... we'll be out there all day."

"So?" Chance insisted. "Dude, we were undefeated at Budgie's! We never even lost a set! And we'll blow the girls' minds when we win!"

"Chance, my back's been kinda iffy lately..." Mitch whined as he reached for his back.

"Fuck off," Chance sneered. "Your back's fine. Look, we're in Mexico, we can play volleyball for a real crowd, on *real* sand, and now you wanna suddenly go all Jose Wuss-vo on me?"

"Dude," Mitch pleaded, "it's just..."

"C'mon man, gimme a break," Chance interrupted, "Ever since they cancelled the second year of that tourney, I've been *dying* to get back out there. Dude, we were the *sultans of sand*!"

"Chance," Mitch explained, "there's a reason they cancelled the tourney."

"I know, I know," Chance agreed, "they said the tournament was 'uncomfortable for some patrons', whatever the fuck that means."

"Chance, look." Mitch pleaded.

"No, dude, I'm not letting this go," Chance replied defiantly.

Mitch stared at Chance for a second, then, realizing that Chance was not going to even try to listen, simply began walking towards the pool.

"Where are you going?" Chance called out. "You're not going to bail on me!"

Mitch ignored Chance's calls as he dove into the pool with the girls.

As he surfaced, Mitch only heard *"...annon ballllll"* as Chance landed two feet away. The ladies sheltered themselves from his huge splash and shot him evil looks as Mitch wiped the water from his face.

"C'mon Mitch," Chance continued as soon as he resurfaced. "We're on *vacation*, we never get a chance to do this, and we finally have another opportunity to showcase our talents."

"Drop it, Chance," Mitch sneered.

"What are you guys talking about?" Ellie asked.

"Nothing," Mitch insisted.

"*Nothing*?" Chance questioned in disgust. "NOTHING? We are the reigning champions of Budgie's two-man sand volleyball tournament!!! And yet *Mitch* here refuses to enter the resort tourney!"

Mitch rolled his eyes.

"Come ON!" Chance continued. "The tournament starts at four, and I've still got to sign us up – let's go!"

Mitch sat there, still unresponsive.

"Ellie, tell your boyfriend to quit bein' such pussy," Chance ordered.

"Mitch," Ellie smiled, taking full advantage of the opportunity, "quit bein' such a pussy."

"What," Danni asked, "are you guys good or something?"

"Oh yeah," Chance began bragging. "My mom was a Division I All American at UCLA in the 70's. She took home four straight NCAA championships as captain and later coached them for five more years before she fell in love with my dad. She's taught me everything she knew about volleyball since I've been old enough to walk."

"Chance, that's awesome!" Ellie said elatedly. "Mitch, you guys should play!"

"Ellie," Mitch cautioned, "we really shouldn't..."

"Why not?" Danni insisted.

"Well my back's been..."

"Aw, I'm sorry," Ellie mocked. "Was I too rough on you last night?"

"Well, position 64 was a little tricky," Mitch smirked up with fake pride.

"Ellie?" Danni asked, "you two got to Position 64?"

"NO," Ellie responded indignantly, "he's joking... we're still working on getting him past Position two..."

"Hey, enough about Mitch's short fuse already," Chance interrupted. "Look Mitch, we're lifelong friends, right? If you asked me to do something for you, I'd do it. I'm asking you to do this one thing for me."

"Really?" Mitch asked. "You'll do any favor I ask?"

"Outside of sexual favors..." Chance paused, "...yes."

"Alright then," Mitch smiled, "kill me before 4pm today."

"MITCH!!!" Ellie and Danni screamed.

"Ha ha, whatever dude," Chance dismissed. "I'm going to go stretch out and we'll see you down here at 3:30." he ordered as he walked off. "Be ready."

"You SAID you'd do whatever I ask!!!" Mitch yelled after Chance. "I expect to be dead by 3:55, you coward!!!"

Chance walked off completely uninterested in Mitch's bellowing.

Mitch stood in the pool, fully realizing what was about to happen. He started writhing, splashing, and slapping the pool water in a furious rage

"*Fuck! Fuck! Fuck! Fuck! Fuck!*" he yelled.

Ellie and Danni stared wide-eyed as Mitch temporarily lost his mind, then looked at each other in bewilderment

Once his tantrum had subsided, he asked Ellie if she'd brought the video camera.

"Yeah," she responded cautiously, more worried that he might blow up again than why he was so upset. "Why?"

"I need you to record this."

"Record what?" Ellie asked.

"JUST record the whole tournament while we're in it," Mitch insisted. "I REALLY need you to do this. You can't leave until we're out of the tourney, OK?"

"Wow," Ellie smirked, "a little vain, aren't we?"

"No," Mitch glared as he pulled himself out the pool, not bothering to explain it to her. "This is an intervention."

CHAPTER 18

NO CONTACT VOLLEYBALL

The sun seemed to still hang at the midpoint of the sky as a small crowd began to gather around the court. With the ocean lapping just a stone's throw away from the nylon-tape-defined borders of the sand volleyball court, Mitch and Chance's opposition took to the sand.

Mitch stood alone in the middle of his side of the court shirtless with knee-length swim trunks, and cringing at the mere presence of the spectators who'd shown up. He sized up the net that lightly waved in the ocean air, and then nervously looked around for Chance. On the inside, though, he was hoping that Chance had gotten drunk and was passed out somewhere.

Just then, the back of the crowd began to part and heads began turning as someone pushed through the group. As the person got to the front of the crowd, Mitch realized it was his teammate, Chance, who emerged wearing a tight, horizontal rainbow-striped sleeveless t-shirt and *short* spandex shorts.

"Oh, come on," Mitch groaned as he pointed at Chance's shirt. "Are you *fucking* kidding me? Is that all you had to wear?"

"It's a hundred degrees out here and this is the only sleeveless shirt I got," Chance answered.

"Go shirtless then!" Mitch barked.

"No dude," he replied. "You know how sensitive my nipples are."

Upon overhearing Chance's phrasing, two men in the crowd perked up like prairie dogs and smiled at both of them. Mitch noticed the two men leering and just shook his head as he and Chance took their positions on the court. As Mitch continued to examine the crowd, he realized that several men wearing banana hammocks were checking him and Chance out – yes, in *that* way.

"I had to wear something if we're gonna be diving in the sand," Chance continued as he took his position on the court. "Hey, are you gonna parade around all day without a shirt?"

"Chance!" Mitch scolded. "Don't even *mention* the word 'parade' right now."

"What? Why?" Chance asked as the whistle blew and their opponents served the ball to them, starting the match.

Chance bumped the serve to Mitch, who gave Chance a perfect set one foot off the net. Chance leapt into the air and spiked it down the line for their first point.

The crowd stirred, as if impressed by the play.

"Alright!" Chance yelled as he slapped Mitch on the ass. "Let's get this going!"

Mortified by Chance's slap, Mitch stood upright.

"DON'T smack my ass like that, fucker! Let's just get this over with."

"C'mon Mitch," Chance complained. "Show some *pride*!"

A few of the men in the audience cheered Chance's comments to Mitch.

Chance turned and looked at the men confusedly, baffled why they cheered so late after the play was over.

Mitch again simply shook his head.

"You're freakin' killing me," he said in disgust as he got in position for the next play.

Chance, preparing to serve the ball, stopped and looked at Mitch.

"What is *wrong* with you?" he asked.

After they won the first game, Chance ran up and again slapped Mitch on his ass so hard that the smacking sound reverberated off the spectators.

The crowd erupted.

As Mitch looked around, he realized that the crowd was becoming decidedly more male. Ellie and Danni were just about the only women around – and they were cowering by the bar, trying to make themselves as small as possible. Still, Ellie faithfully continued recording.

As the day wore on, Chance and Mitch tore through the competition just as Chance had predicted. Mitch followed every point with overly-manly grunts and shoving Chance aggressively. Chance countered by smacking Mitch on the ass. With every win, and seemingly every ass slap, the crowd had apparently adopted them as the home team.

"Chance, quit slapping my ass!" Mitch ordered after another winning point.

"C'mon, Mitch," Chance pleaded. "This is our signature move. Check it out, the crowd *loves* it!" he pointed to the now healthy crowd of men.

As Mitch looked at the throngs, Chance smacked his ass again and the crowd erupted.

"See?"

"*Fuckin' knock it off!*" Mitch spun around.

"What's your problem?"

"OK, look – if we're going to have a signature move," Mitch sneered, "then I get to pick it. We either do the 'Top Gun high-five/low-five' thing, or the 'Sammy Sosa double-chest-thump-peace-sign' thing."

Chance, annoyed by Mitch's protests, acquiesced.

"OK, fine," Chance said. "We'll do the high-five thing from Top Gun."

"Thank you!" Mitch snapped.

The final round started as the sun began to set across the distant mountain ridge, creating an element of serenity everywhere – except on the court. The crowd, the cheering, and the tension of the championship match that was about to start all stood in stark contrast to the elongating shadows and hues of orange and pink in the sky.

Even though the sun was setting, the crowd had grown – even if Mitch was the only one who was fully aware that there were almost no women left in the audience.

Just as they'd done from the beginning of the tournament, Chance accepted the opponent's serve and bumped it to Mitch, who once again gave Chance a perfect set. And once again, Chance leapt into the air and spiked it cross-court for a winner. The crowd erupted.

Mitch turned to Chance to do the Top Gun move. Their hands met for the high portion of the move, but as their hands went down for the low-five part, Chance side-stepped Mitch and smacked him on the ass harder than he had all day.

The crowd went crazy as Chance held his hands up, gloriously soaking in the crowd's adoration.

Mitch turned and gritted his teeth as he watched Chance play to the crowd.

"Teamwork's about compromise, bud," Chance shrugged. "I'm giving them what they want."

Mitch just glared emotionlessly at Chance and then went back to playing.

After numerous exchanges, volleys, rallies, and digs, Chance and Mitch found themselves holding the Championship trophy. Chance was grinning from ear to ear, but Mitch was decidedly uncomfortable by all the men suddenly surrounding him. He didn't even smile for the Championship picture.

Chance suddenly became confused as he looked around.

"Man, where's all the chicks?" he asked Mitch. "Chicks *love* volleyball..."

Ignoring Chance, Mitch walked out of the crowd and towards Ellie and Danni.

"Hey!" Chance insisted. "Where you goin'?"

"To hang out with *Ellie*," Mitch announced as loudly as could, spinning around to look at Chance. "I'm going to get my *girlfriend drunk!* And then we're going back to the room to have *wild straight SEX*!"

Some of the men in the crowd looked at Mitch confusedly, while others looked at him in disgust. Ellie's eyes widened with horror, but she also couldn't help smiling a little from Mitch's proclamation and bravado. Mitch just shook his head as he turned and resumed walking towards Ellie and Danni.

But Chance was in hot pursuit of Mitch, insisting that Mitch listen to him.

"Mitch! Wait up!" he called, dragging the trophy with him. "Hey, check it out, bud! Think about this! Instead of 50 people watching us, we could have 50 million!"

Mitch stopped dead in his tracks and shuddered, then continued walking. As he got to the bar, he looked at Ellie.

"You recorded the whole thing, right?" he asked.

"Uh, yeah," Ellie replied, handing the camera to Mitch as if it was now somehow 'unclean'.

"Mitch, look dude," Chance rambled with eyes full of dreams as he caught up to them. "I'm thinkin' we should do this on the pro tour."

"We gotta watch this first," Mitch deadpanned.

"You're damn right we do!" Chance smiled eagerly. "C'mon ladies, let's go check out the footage!"

"Uh, we've already seen all we need to see," Danni explained uncomfortably as she quickly sucked a mouthful of Margarita into her mouth. "You two, um, *enjoy*," she said as she swallowed hard. "This is something that should probably only be shared between two *men*."

Ellie slapped Danni's arm. Danni looked at her with a 'what was I supposed to say?' shrug.

"Whatever..." Chance sniffed. "C'mon, Mitch. We got game tape to analyze."

"Hey, Raoul got us a room here," Ellie added. "So, grab our bags and bring them back here, will ya, sweetie?"

As Mitch and Chance walked back to the dingy motel, Chance re-told every play from their glorious day. And, for once, Mitch noticed that he was actually bragging about both of them. But Mitch simply nodded the entire time, never saying a word.

Once they got to the room, Chance iced a bucket of beers and changed into a regular t-shirt.

"No sense in rushing back," Chance complained, "especially since the girls apparently don't want to celebrate our triumph."

"It's probably best if we watch this here, anyway," Mitch muttered.

He tried to hook up the camera to the television, but despite examining every part of the TV, there was no place to connect it to the camera. He scanned the room like MacGyver looking for anything he could use - finally noticing the wires tied to the rabbit ears antenna.

"Fuck it, this has to be done," Mitch mumbled to himself as he began stripping and splicing the wires to the back of the video camera itself.

Chance handed Mitch a beer as Mitch finished his impromptu wiring. Chance held up a high five as Mitch approached the couch.

Mitch cautiously held up a hand, then paused.

"Touch my ass, and this beer is going up yours."

"Don't worry," Chance laughed. "There's no crowd here. But hey, before we start watching this, I have an idea. Ya know, maybe we should send this footage to Gatorade or Gillette, or even Budweiser, you know – to kind of get our foot in the door."

Mitch choked on his own scoff.

"Um, Chance," he pleaded, "let's just watch this first, then we'll talk."

"No dude," Chance insisted, "hear me out."

"Not until after we watch this!" Mitch said even more defiantly.

"Oh... okay, GOT IT!" Chance realized, "You're totally right, dude. That's what all the pros do. I think we should've won that third game at least five points sooner, anyway. *Roll the war footage!!!*"

As Mitch pressed Play on the camera, the images on the screen became slightly disturbing to Chance. Mitch just sat there, silently relieved that this issue would never be a problem again.

Chance saw his own serve, and suddenly tilted his head like a confused puppy. Without moving his eyes from the screen, Chance became silent.

"Wait," Chance asked, "who'd they tape?"

As the images continued to show Chance's volleyball acumen, they also exposed Chance's technique, which was, unfortunately, *incredibly* feminine.

As the TV displayed another of Chance's very girlish serves, he slowly came to the realization that not only did he play like a girl, he played like a girl from 50 years ago.

Thanks to his mother's training, everything about his game was *ultra*-feminine – to the point that only a girl from his mother's generation would be proud of such technique. And his horizontal rainbow-striped t-shirt and tight shorts, well... it truly iced the proverbial cake.

"OH... MY... *GOD*," Chance said in utter shock.

Mitch sighed as he sucked down a big drink from his beer.

"Yup," he deadpanned.

"OH MY *FUCKING* GOD!" Chance reiterated, yelling as he turned to Mitch. "Why didn't you ever fucking *tell me???!!!*" he demanded as he pointed to the TV.

"Too painful," Mitch said as he took another drink and swallowed hard.

Chance turned back to the TV and the long silent pause only emphasized how uncomfortable they'd both become from the recording.

"Maybe you should send the tape to NAMBLA..." Mitch suggested dryly as he gulped his drink again.

"Who?" Chance asked, not actually listening to a word Mitch was saying.

"Nothin'," Mitch laughed to himself.

As the footage rolled on mercilessly, Chance slowly slouched back into the couch. He finally pointed to the screen and, with all the sincerity he could muster, said, "DELETE... THAT... FILE."

"But what about Gillette? Gatorade?"" Mitch mocked.

"I will *fucking kill you* if ANYONE ever sees this!" Chance yelled.

"OK, sooooo..." Mitch offered. "No more volleyball tournaments. Deal?"

"Deal."

They sat there silently for another few seconds as Chance became somewhat despondent over what he was seeing.

"Um," Mitch suggested, "I think it's time we fired that thing up. Whaddaya say?"

"...ere..." Chance choked as he passed the roll of foliage to Mitch, already one step ahead of him.

CHAPTER 19

YOU BETTER COME WITH
YOUR BEST IF YOU TEST HIM

The next morning, Ellie and Danni chided the boys as they walked through the lobby.

"What the hell was wrong with you guys last night? Danni demanded. "Mariachi bands don't have to know Pink Floyd!"

Mitch and Chance just stumbled along absorbing the abuse in dark glasses and un-kept hair.

"I don't care what kind of band it is," Chance replied. "If you're a guitarist, you should know *every song* on 'Dark Side of the Moon'."

"I swear, we drank as much as you did," Ellie continued. "I thought all the food you two ate would offset the alcohol, but you two were out of control! And what the fuck is up with ordering a pizza at 2am? I mean, we'd just had a four-course dinner!"

Chance just looked at Mitch.

"She said 'weed,'" he snickered.

Mitch turned and punched Chance in the chest.

"It was probably from being out in the sun all day playing volleyball," Mitch reasoned. "We probably got dehydrated."

"Did you just say hydro?" Chance laughed again.

Mitch shot Chance a glare that dared him to say another word.

Chance looked down in submission while Mitch changed the subject.

"Alright guys," Mitch announced as they gathered in front of the reception desk. "All we have to do is walk through this presentation, then I'll draw for my prize, and then we can all hit the beach."

"You mean after they try to sell us a timeshare," Chance countered as he rubbed his aching skull.

"What?" Mitch asked.

"A timeshare," Chance griped. "I've been trying to tell you about this ever since we left. They're going to try to sell us..." he paused, "wait, scratch that. They *are going to* sell *you* a timeshare."

"What are you talking about?" Mitch dismissed.

"Mitch, this is a timeshare presentation."

"We're not here for a timeshare presentation," Mitch insisted. "We're here because I won a contest."

"Yeah, the contest was 'Who's the most gullible person on Earth?'" Chance chuckled. "Congratulations, you're a finalist along with thirty other chumps."

"Whatever, Chance," Mitch replied, tired of Chance's banter. "I'm not *that* gullible."

"Dude, don't use words that aren't in the dictionary! You're a *writer*, for Christ's sake."

"Huh?" Mitch asked. "Gullible's not in the dictionary?"

Chance stared blankly at Mitch.

"Wow," he scoffed. "You are so fucked right now."

"You asshole," Mitch growled, suddenly realizing the joke. "OK, so what are we gonna do, then?"

"The same thing you do when offered drugs," Chance said confidently. "Just say no."

Mitch turned his head sideways, looking both at Chance and then the girls, considering the hypocrisy of Chance's advice.

"Ugh," Mitch finally snorted. "OK, Just Say No. I can do that."

"Heh heh, whatever," Chance chuckled, unable to believe that Mitch had the resolve to follow through. "I hope you enjoy your new timeshare for years to come."

Raoul suddenly appeared in front of the group.

"Good morning!" he said joyously. "Are you ready to get started?"

Mitch quickly straightened up as he turned to face Raoul.

"Uh, yes," he smiled. "Who is going to give us the presentation?"

"Well, senor," Raoul replied. "Considering the circumstances under which we met yesterday, I thought I would personally *give it to you*."

Mitch felt an immediate level of comfort, believing that Raoul had already helped them out.

"That'd be perfect," Mitch agreed.

Chance just rolled his eyes.

"Great!" Raoul replied. "Come this way."

Raoul brought the four of them into a large projection room filled with the other "sweepstakes winners" and their friends. Raoul pulled out the chairs for both Ellie and Danni, and then proceeded to sit with the four of them as the lights dimmed and they watched a brief video about the resort.

As the lights in the room returned to normal levels, Raoul escorted them through the resort's many features, suggesting the value of each facet.

Raoul then turned to the group.

"So, Chance," he asked, "do you like what you see? Would you not like to become an owner at our resort?"

"OH YEAH," Chance replied emphatically. "I just wish you'd caught me before I'd bought my 18th timeshare last year."

Mitch shot a stunned glare at Chance.

"I'm sorry," Chance continued, "but me and the old lady here pretty much spend every non-working day in luxurious timeshares on a beach in some remote part of the planet. It's been eighteen of the best investments we've ever made," he smiled as he wrapped his arm around Danni.

Raoul's face sunk at Chance's response.

Mitch continued to be as wide-eyed as he'd been since Chance began this lie.

"Well Chance, it seems that your vacation needs have already been met," Raoul suddenly smiled. "Why don't we let you and your wife go draw for your prize now and I won't waste any more of your time."

"Are you sure?" Chance feigned apology. "I mean, I don't..."

"No no no, es no problema," Raoul insisted. "I'm here to ensure everyone has a muy bonita vacation."

"Well, thanks Raoul," Chance smiled. "If we ever get in the market for number 19, we'll know who to call."

Chance then turned to Mitch and Ellie.

"We'll see you shortly at the swim up bar, OK?"

"Sure, OK bud..." Mitch replied as he rubbed an extended middle finger back and forth across the bridge of his nose at Chance.

Ellie grimaced, knowing Chance had just extricated himself and Danni from this charade.

Raoul continued with his sales pitch, bringing Mitch and Ellie to a table by a second pool area, which was filled with happy families and children laughing, splashing, and playing with their parents.

"So Mitch," Raoul continued, "what do you think of the resort here? Do you think this might make sense, you know, you becoming an owner here?"

"Ehhh, ya know, Mitch hedged. "It's a beautiful resort. I'm just not sure that... ya know, being an owner... I'd uh... have to think about that... for a while."

"Think about *what*, Mitch?" Raoul insisted. "You love to vacation, no?"

"Well, *yeah.*"

"And the resort is muy beautiful, no?"

"Sure it is," Mitch nodded.

"See Mitch, for only $25,000, you can have access to this resort for the rest of your life. Isn't that worth a lifetime of vacations and memories with your *beautiful wife*," he said – leaning in and completely eye-fucking Ellie – then returning back to Mitch, "and your future family?"

Ellie sighed, then backhanded Mitch's shoulder.

"Yeah Mitch," she sneered sarcastically. "Aren't I and *our future kids* worth it?"

"*Of course you are*," Mitch reasserted himself. "I just... well... this is the first timeshare I've ever seen. I want to shop around a bit before committing... you know, be a smart investor."

"So, you *are* going to buy one," Raoul pursued. "So then what you're saying is if I can show you that this is the most beautiful resort with the best amenities at the fairest price, then you'd be willing to become an owner today, si?"

"Wha... I, I didn't... say that," Mitch stuttered.

Raoul then leaned back in his chair.

"Well, that's OK, Mitch," he sighed, starting to tear up a little bit. "Senor Mitch, I have to apologize to you. I don't mean to be pushy. It's just that... I wish I would have had someone to guide me ten years ago when I took everything for granted. You see, I didn't want to say this earlier, but I was married for ten years," he sighed, pausing for dramatic effect.

"And I never took my wife on a vacation. Year after year, she would, ask me, no – *beg me* – to get away from work and take her somewhere to renew that love, that romance that was dying from the day-to-day grind of our vida. We would wave as we passed each other on our way out the door – never appreciating the important things en vida, only concerned about that paycheck that we'd both get at the end of the week. And then, suddenly, it was over. That was it."

"Don't tell me..." Mitch sighed, sensing he was getting scammed. "She left you."

"No, she was kidnapped by Columbian rebels."

Ellie's jaw dropped.

"Tortured for two years, eventually she died," Raoul continued. "The only thing I have left are the emails she sent me when her captors were asleep. All she kept asking me was why I never took her on that vacation I promised her. I think back, if only... we had been... somewhere else... maybe... maybe... she'd still be here with me," he stammered, choking on his tears.

"*My God. This poor man,*" Mitch began thinking.

Ellie simply squinted in disgust at Raoul.

"Wow, dude, I'm so sorry," Mitch apologized. "That's absolutely horrible."

"Si, it is senor," Raoul replied as he wiped away a tear. "And today, es - Dios mio - our anniversary."

Mitch looked up at the sky and felt horrible for Raoul.

Ellie just groaned and rolled eyes.

Raoul smiled knowingly at Ellie with that same seductive look.

Ellie was unable to maintain her glare through his piercing eyes. She simply blushed and looked down.

"Tonight," Raoul sighed, "I take our eight children to her mother's house for dinner. I would love to take them to beautiful dinner, but we can't afford it now. Business has been slow, it has been a muy bad month for me."

"Aww," Ellie said, wanting to see how far Raoul would go with this. "What are their names?"

"Juan, Julia, Cesar, Alejandro, Julia, Manuel, Julia, and Raoulito," Raoul said counting the names on his fingers.

"Wait," Ellie interrupted, "didn't you just say 'Julia' three times?"

"Si," Raoul replied quickly, "I named all of my daughters after my wife, in her honor."

"But, how could you..." Ellie tried to clarify. "I mean, she couldn't have been dead yet if..."

"Let us speak of this no more," Raoul announced as he slapped the table. "Let us talk about *you*, and your future."

"Mitch, honey," Ellie leaned in to Mitch's ear. "Can we talk alone for a second – just you and me?"

Mitch's head was spinning from the tragic tale he'd been told. He felt like he *had* to believe Raoul, because Mitch couldn't imagine someone would be so brazen as to make up a story like *that*. And he was also a little embarrassed by Ellie's rudeness towards this poor man.

"Honey, you know our rules," he chided. "You'll take care of our future kids at home, and I'll take care of our finances."

Ellie's head nearly exploded.

"*EXCUSE ME???*" she scowled as she stood up and recoiled from Mitch.

"Babe, we've talked about this over and over again," Mitch sighed, "don't try to change it now."

He then shrugged as he turned back to Raoul and simply rolled his eyes.

"Women," he droned.

Ellie suddenly felt total paralysis as she tried to figure out what the fuck Mitch had just said to her. In an instant, she felt betrayed, and it was only made worse by the fact that she was simply trying to save Mitch from himself.

Then she had another thought.

"*Mitch must be baiting me into a fight so we can get out of this sales pitch.*"

She smiled briefly at Mitch's genius, then played along.

"Oh, you're right honey," she seethed, defiantly tilting her head to one side. "I got an idea, you bastard. Maybe you wanna take Rebecca on vacation instead of me."

Mitch's eyes nearly leapt from their sockets.

"Who?" he asked.

"Don't patronize me, you asshole! I'm not an idiot!" Ellie yelled, trying to create as uncomfortable of a scene as possible. "I know you hired that slut after you had lunch with your old friend Tom at Hooters three months ago. She's no secretary, she's your *SUCKRETARY!!!* How long did you think you could get away with it before I'd find out???"

"What the fuck are you talking about?" Mitch pleaded, scrambling to save his face – as well as his Aston Martin.

"That's *IT*!" Ellie declared. "Screw this 'family pool', screw this 'resort lifestyle'... screw this, this... *MARRIAGE!!!* I'm not going to be a baby factory for the Mitch franchise, no matter *how much* you're making!!!"

Mitch sat there frozen, only able to manage a forced smile toward Raoul.

"I need a drink," Ellie sighed as she swept her hair back. "Good luck with your secretarial conquests, you son-of-a-bitch! I'm done."

She then took the ring Mitch gave her, slung it across the pool area, and stormed off to the main pool to find Danni and Chance.

Mitch had no idea what had just happened, but his heart was in a full-on panic.

Raoul ran around the pool to retrieve the ring. As he placed the ring on the table next to Mitch's hand, he picked up his cell phone.

"Hold on, I must take this call – it's little Raoulito."

Mitch just sat there trying to understand why Ellie would make up such a story. He wondered if, by trying to stop Ellie from being rude, he'd just lost her. And in that moment, the car completely lost its value to Mitch. Well, *a lot* of its value, at least.

While Mitch hyper-analyzed the circumstances – all the while with his back to the pool - Raoul and the resort staff frantically pulled kids out of the pool and shooed the women away. As Raoul pulled the last child out using a lifeguard's hook, he gave the child some money and shoved him away. Then, he pointed at the bartender, who flipped a switch as the mariachi music suddenly became techno.

At that moment, each man at the pool instantly ripped off their long swim trunks like they were NBA sweatpants to reveal thongs and began oiling each other down.

Mitch was oblivious to it all as he couldn't breathe over the thought that he'd insulted Ellie.

Raoul gathered himself, took a deep breath, and calmly sat back down next to Mitch as he pretended to hang up the phone.

"OK, problema solved," he smiled. "Mitch, let's take a walk by the pool and stretch our legs. I want to tell you about our happy hour. I'm thirsty, are you thirsty? You look like you need a drink, I know I do.

"Sounds good," Mitch sighed.

They walked to the poolside bar, but Mitch was completely dejected. All he could think about was making things right with Ellie. He was also completely oblivious to the suddenly all-guy environment.

"Dos margaritas, por favor," Raoul ordered as they got to the bar.

"Si, you big machismo," smiled the now very feminine male bartender.

Mitch then noticed the bartender, but shrugged as he downed the shot. As he turned around to look at the pool area, he then also realized his surroundings.

"Look, Mitch, es OK," Raoul confided. "I know that you are not married to Ellie."

"What? Huh?" Mitch denied. "Yes we..."

"Don't worry, es OK," Raoul reassured. "Your secret es safe with me."

"But... how did you know?"

"Well, number one, you bought her ring from mi hijo, Fernando. He sells them at the airport for $10 each."

"TEN???" Mitch asked.

"But that es not the main reason," Raoul dismissed. "I can see the way you two act together. You know, I was married once, too."

"So you don't think we could've been married?" Mitch asked with disappointment.

"Her?" Raoul asked. "Mitch, I was talking about you and Chance."

"What?" Mitch asked.

"I saw you two win the volleyball competition yesterday," Raoul explained.

Mitch just began to shake his head.

"That mother fucker..." he mumbled. "Look, Raoul, I AM NOT GAY."

"Do not worry, Mitch," Raoul continued. "Es OK. Just look around you. We are a very... '*progressive*' resort."

Mitch just quivered with rage.

"LOOK, DAMMIT! I AM NOT FUCKING GAY, OK?"

Raoul shook his head in shock.

"Are you serious?" he asked.

"Do I not I look serious, senor *dumbass*???!!!" he yelled.

Raoul's face sank again.

"Oh, hold on a second," he explained as he reached for his cell phone again. "Raoulito es calling me again."

Mitch watched as Raoul started walking onto the dance floor yelling "CHICAS! CHICAS! CHICAS!" into his phone.

Mitch then saw the "supposed" other vacationers scrambling as Raoul yelled. He decided to put a stop to this.

"Raoul, STOP!!!" he yelled. Mitch then turned to the bartender and said, "Gimme another tequila."

As Raoul approached him, he downed the shot.

"Dude," Mitch looked at Raoul, "are you about to do another cast change-out here?"

"Uh..."

"Stop, just stop," Mitch pleaded. "Just go get the paperwork. I'm tired, I'm done. I'll buy the fuckin' thing, OK?"

"Um, OK..." Raoul smiled. He turned to the crowd and raised a calming hand as they all sighed in relief. As the crowd dispersed, Raoul leaned up against the bar next to Mitch.

"Wow, so you are really not gay?" he asked again.

"NOOOO!" Mitch insisted.

"OK, OK," Raoul surrendered. "But, Chance es, no?"

Mitch thought for a second before responding.

"Oh yeah, *flaming*," he smiled.

"Wow, that *is* gay," Raoul said. "But then, what about Danni?"

"Well, the name *is* Danni, right?" Mitch explained.

"Si."

"You didn't notice the Adam's apple?"

"No FUCKING way," Raoul droned.

"Oh yeah, Danni? He's Chance's brother," Mitch smiled as he again looked at the now-role-less bartender. "Shot please."

"So, she – I mean – he... *es Transformer*?" Raoul asked.

Mitch laughed. "Yep. *Post*-Optimus Prime, baby."

"Dios Mio," Raoul sighed as he pulled his hair back. "Shot, por favor," he asked the bartender.

As Raoul downed his shot, he turned back to Mitch.

"You know, senor, I just thought she really liked Pat Benatar."

CHAPTER 20

FRISCO PARASAILING

Mitch trudged into the main pool area with a bottle of champagne in one hand and a big timeshare binder in the other.

Ellie, half-drunk and struggling to stay on her raft, pointed at Mitch as he emerged from the main building.

"What took you so long? Haven't you ever 'dined and dashed' before?!" she laughed as she rolled off the raft.

Chance turned to see Mitch loaded down with his parting gifts and muttered,

"Oh God, please tell me that's the owner's manual for the Aston Martin."

"Uh, no," Mitch replied. "An Aston Martin will depreciate over time – this is recreational real estate, it's an *investment*," he smiled widely, holding up the bottle.

"Holy shit, are you kidding me?" Chance laughed. "You totally drank the Kool-Aid, didn't ya, you pussy."

"If you think investing in prime recreational real estate makes me a pussy, then just call me Mufasa. Raoul told me they're about to raise the prices on these units next week."

"HA!," Chance mocked, "You're not one of the thirty biggest chumps on the planet – you won. Congrats, *you* are the biggest pussy!"

"I'm not a pussy," Mitch replied. "I thought about it, and a timeshare makes pretty good sense for me."

"You're broke," Chance continued. "You never vacation! You don't play golf, you don't like the beach, you don't play tennis, you don't like the spa, you don't even like having strangers touch you – *I'll never understand that* – and, again, you're broke. How does THAT make sense?"

"This could make me do those things," Mitch replied.

"How the fuck is this gonna force you to *not be broke?* And, by the way, where's your Aston Martin, big guy?"

Mitch's head sunk a little as he reached in his pocket and pulled out a Hot Wheels Aston Martin.

"Cool!" Chance replied with enthusiasm. "I can't *wait* to blow the shit outta that in the backyard!"

"Great! You can add that to the list of all the things you've blown," Mitch glared. "What'd *you* win?"

Chance held up a transistor radio that was in the shape of a miniature boom box.

"I guess AA batteries are what make this thing environmentally friendly," Chance shrugged. "OK, so you bought the thing... how far did you talk him down?"

"Dude, they were about to raise the price next week to $40,000. I was lucky to steal it at $25,000 because Raoul made a phone call and found a foreclosure for me," Mitch explained. "I mean, what are the chances of that?"

"Zero, Mitch." Chance groaned as he shook his head in disgust of Mitch's idiocy. "Absolute zero, you chump."

"Oh really," Mitch stood up a little taller. "Ya know what, I'm sick of talking about the 'me' who's *supposedly* fucking my *supposed* secretary behind my *supposed* wife's back. I'm sick of talking about the 'me' who *supposedly* has a best friend that *supposedly* owns 18 *supposed* timeshares! So, fuck it - let's talk about you."

"Me?" Chance asked.

"Yeah, you," Mitch snarled. "You, the big pussy."

"I've been called a lot of things," Chance replied. "But being called a big pussy is a first."

"Really?" Mitch probed. "When was the last time you went up in the Arch?"

"Huh?" Chance deflected.

"The Arch," Mitch restated. "Ya know? The big silver thing downtown? It's only 630 feet tall, for fuck's sake. You have *seen* it, right?"

"I know what the Arch is," Chance said. "What about it?"

"Ever been up in it?"

"Gimme a break," Chance dismissed.

"Really? NEV-ER?" Mitch taunted. "Lived your whole life in St. Louis and *never* went up?"

"Nope."

"OK then," Mitch conceded, "let's scale it down. When was the last time you sat in the upper section of a Blues game?"

"You know you can't see the action from those seats," Chance sneered.

"How about a high dive?" Mitch persisted.

"What?"

"How about a low dive?"

"Well, yeah... duh," Chance scoffed. "I've gone off low dives before."

"Cool, there's one right there," Mitch offered. "Go jump off it."

"Dude," Chance explained, acting as if tiring from the questioning, "I'm just chillin', drinkin', and enjoying myself."

"That's what I thought," Mitch laughed. "Pussy."

"You think I'm afraid to go off that thing?" Chance challenged.

"Yeah, I think you are," Mitch asserted. "You're terrified of heights and you know it. You don't even like being as tall as you are."

"Whatever, man," Chance sneered.

"OK, prove it!"

"Alright, you want me to go off the high dive right now?"

"No."

"Good, because you know I'd do it," Chance countered.

"Actually, I'm going parasailing in an hour," Mitch smiled wickedly. "And you're going with me."

Chance's lips fell still and his skin instantly turned a little gray as he processed what Mitch had just said.

"Bullshit dude," Chance shrugged, trying to hide the anxiety that suddenly had a stranglehold on his gut. "I ain't doin' that."

"That's what I thought..." Mitch mocked. "What was that shit you said yesterday about '*you'd do anything I asked you to*'? You backin' out of that now, too?

"Mitch, fuck off," Chance reasoned. "I'm not scared. It's just that... well, it's expensive, and I'm not about to spend $120 just to prove you wrong."

"Actually, you don't have to spend anything. It's the other prize I won. So... *my treat*," Mitch smiled. "So are you gonna follow through on your word for once, or are you going to live up to your newfound 'pussy' reputation?"

"Look," Chance breathed, feeling a little more desperate, "those guys that drive the boat don't even speak English down there. You could get killed!"

"Correction, *we* could get killed." Mitch agreed. "But since you said you'd do anything I asked you to, we're going up at 4 pm. *Waaay* up."

Chance swallowed hard.

"We'll see who the pussy is," Mitch gloated. "And don't worry, I expect you to find a way to back out... *pussy.*"

There was a long pause as the girls looked at Chance for a response. Chance mulled over his words for a moment, then finally realized he'd run out of responses.

"FINE, I'll go," he sneered, trying to convince himself more so than anyone else. "I ain't chicken."

Chance walked up to the bar and immediately lined up three tequila shots. He slammed each of them – one right after the other – and exhaled heavily as he wiped his mouth and looked around the pool area with sheer dread.

Chance then decided to drink himself a backbone.

As four o'clock arrived, Mitch and Chance began walking down to the parasailing dock. However, Mitch was doing most of the walking for both of them since Chance had succeeded in getting himself fully plastered. Mitch had one arm around Chance as Chance held on to his neck and wobbled down the stairs.

As they walked across the dock, Chance began rambling to everyone they passed.

"I love thish man," he slurred. "Thish iz why I do craaazeee shtuff with him. I nevr evun cunsiderd doin' the thingsh we're doing... not before *thish man* talked me into it. And uh... WOWA."

The parasail operators, hearing every word, looked up and suddenly recognized them.

"Ah, si, the volleyball couple!" the one operator welcomed.

Mitch shuddered and rolled his eyes.

Chance laughed, then turned and hugged Mitch in the middle of the dock.

"I wanchu to know dat I'm happ... happy you an me ir soo closhe," Chance hugged tightly. "I love yu, man."

As they got closer to the parachute, Chance literally began turning white with fear.

The operator noticed Chance's complexion and handed Mitch his sunscreen.

"Here senor, use lotion. Put it on your man."

"*My* man?" Mitch protested, pulling away from Chance. "You put it on him."

The operator turned to his friend on the boat. "Uh, how you say? 'Fo coo'?"

"No no," his friend corrected, "es 'fukayoo'."

The operator turned back to Mitch.

"Fuck you," he smiled. "Si?"

Mitch sighed loudly and began smearing sunscreen all over his wobbling friend.

Within a few minutes Mitch and Chance were shooting hundreds of feet into the air. Mitch screamed lustfully, having the time of his life. Chance clutched the straps with a death grip and squinted his eyes shut, not saying a word.

"Come on, Chance!" Mitch screamed. "Open your eyes! The view is *incredible!!!*"

Chance cracked open one eye, then the other. Still horrified, he managed a fake smile and a nod at Mitch.

As the boat below bounced on the incoming waves, the tether jolted and shook the boys in their harnesses.

Then, one particularly large wave hit the boat, causing them to bounce extremely hard. Chance, who was fully greased with sun block, landed *awkwardly* on the strap running between his legs, pinning his balls under the weight of his body.

"AAAAAARRRGGGGHHH!!!" Chance screamed as he kicked his legs frantically, trying to free himself from the pain. "MY BALLS!!! MY *FUCKING* BALLS!!!"

Mitch hesitated for a second as he evaluated the situation. In that brief moment, he had a myriad of thoughts running through his head. What could he do? How could he help? Did "helping" mean he'd have to put his hand in Chance's crotch? The possible ramifications if he accidentally did touch something down there, well... it was all expressed in a simple sneer of his lip.

"AARRRRGGGGHHHH!!!" Chance continued to scream and squirm, snapping Mitch out of his moment of analysis paralysis.

Mitch took a deep breath, squinted his eyes in disgust, and shoved his hand into Chance's crotch as if he were noodling for catfish. He tried to release the strap, but couldn't find it.

"MIIIITCH!" Chance continued to scream painfully, as the overly-applied suntan lotion ensured that Chance grip on his surrounding tethers was rendered useless. "OH GOD!" he bellowed. "PLEASE!!!"

Chance suddenly grabbed a handful of Mitch's hair from the back of Mitch's head and, using it for leverage, repeatedly tried to lift himself up off the strap.

The boat operators heard Chance and looked up. Chance's gyrations and forceful thrustings of Mitch's head into his crotch (not to mention the animalistic screams Chance was making at the same time) made it appear as if they were engaging in an unnatural act one hundred feet in the air.

"See?" the boat operator said as he turned to his friend and pointed to the aerial display. "*That's* gay. Pay up."

Mitch finally released the strap separating Chance's balls and slowly lifted his head back up. They both hung there momentarily without saying a word.

"Um," Mitch confessed, "Ya know, I think I accidentally touched your junk."

"I know," Chance agreed without looking at Mitch, "you did."

"With my nose."

"Yeah," Chance stated as indifferently as he could. "I know."

They continued to hang there silently in the Caribbean Sea air for another awkward moment.

"Hey," Mitch offered, "at least you ain't afraid of heights anymore!"

Chance suddenly smiled at the realization.

"Hey yeah! I guess I'm not!"

"Alright, dude!" Mitch yelled. "High five!"

"Yeah!" Chance agreed as he held up his hand.

But as Chance held up his hand, the tether suddenly bounced again and Chance shot out of his harness like a blow dart.

"YOU MOTHERFUUUU!!!" he screamed all the way down until the loud splash of the sea silenced his bellow.

Chance emerged from the surf, stumbling and tripping his way to the shore. Luckily for him, the only evidence of his one hundred foot freefall was the transformation of his knee-length Bermuda shorts into a something resembling a scrunched-up pillow thong – or a wedgie that must have come from one of the lower circles of Hell.

Chance turned and looked up at Mitch, still floating high in the air. He then turned to walk back towards the resort, but instead merely collapsed face-first onto the beach.

"Fruckin' Mitsh," he slurred through the sand in his mouth.

CHAPTER 21

I'M LEAVING LOS MEXICOS

The next morning, the foursome made their way through the lobby to catch a taxi back to the airport.

Raoul stood by the main entrance, waiting to see them off.

"Ah, Senor Mitch," he began, "We are so sorry to see you go."

"Eh, thanks," Mitch smiled. "We're just heading down to the taxi. Back to the cold weather, ya know."

"Si, about that..." Raoul explained. "I heard about your experience with the taxi coming here, so I took the liberty of getting a limousine for you."

All four suddenly smiled widely and thanked Raoul. As they stood there talking amongst themselves, Raoul kept looking at Danni's neck from different angles, with different squints, even turning his head sideways and staring from a profile angle... all in the hopes of seeing any semblance of an Adam's apple.

Danni tried to ignore Raoul's stares until she couldn't take it anymore.

"Look," she scolded Raoul. "Is there something on my neck?"

"Amazingly, no, senor... uh, I mean... senora."

Mitch, suddenly aware of what Raoul was doing, hurried the group out the doorway.

"Um, I think I hear the limo," he said. "You guys take my bag. I got a few more questions to ask Raoul before we leave. I'll catch up."

As they walked through the archway, Raoul stepped next to Mitch and focused on Danni's ass.

"Wow," Raoul pined, "That's amazing, there's no *trace* of her, uh, *his* Adam's apple."

"I know," Mitch smiled. "Surgery in the U.S.? Awesome."

"I guess so," Raoul replied. "Is all surgery that good up there?"

"Well, you tell me," Mitch replied with an extended hand that encouraged Raoul to continue looking at Danni's ass.

"Do you think, everything..." he pointed to his own crotch, "*everything*... about the surgery went that well?"

"I don't know," Mitch shrugged. "Maybe you should see that for yourself."

Raoul's eyes widened as much as his smile. He then turned to Mitch and handed him his business card.

"You come back soon," Raoul offered, "si?"

CHAPTER 22

ONE STEP,
I MAKE AN IMPRINT

A mid-December ice and snow storm once again hit the area, and Mitch was helping Ellie shovel her driveway. As they both shoveled, Ellie stopped intermittently to watch Mitch lose his footing every time he tried to lift too much snow in a scoop.

As he nearly slipped once again, Ellie laughed and then looked at him affectionately.

"Hey, what are you doing for Christmas?" she asked. "I know your family isn't in town anymore."

Mitch stopped for a second and sighed.

"Well," he began, "me and Chance do have this bit of a Christmas tradition. It's kind of starts as a competition to see who wakes up first. But anyway, whoever does has to go jump on the other one's bed to wake him up. Then, although it almost kills us, we don't open presents yet... we have to have breakfast – I think it's my turn to cook this year – and, oh yeah, we discuss what we're truly thankful for."

Ellie stood there stunned.

"Then – FINALLY – after we've cleaned up the kitchen, we look in our stockings. After that, we take turns opening up one present at a time until we're done, usually by 11-ish. Why do you ask?"

"Uh, well, um," she stuttered, "well, maybe, uh, later, I was..."

"You not buying any of that crap I just told you, are you?" Mitch asked. "Because if you are, I've got some premium swamp land for sale that..."

"Wait, what?"

"I was kidding, Ellie," Mitch smiled. "Chance and I exchanged gifts last week. What's up?"

"What? Oh, forget it now."

"What? No, c'mon. I was *just playin'*," Mitch insisted as he lifted another scoopful of snow. "Do you want to come over for Christmas dinner? I can order a pre-cooked ham and we can see what bowl games are on."

"I was *going* to see if you wanted to come and have Christmas dinner with me and my family," Ellie offered.

Mitch raised both eyebrows with surprise.

"Wow," he commented, "this is a big step."

"By the way," she continued, "I got Danni a spice rack from Bed Bath and Beyond. What'd you get Chance?"

"Spice rack? I guess that falls in the 'Beyond' part of the store," he observed. "Uh, Chance and I got each other the same thing... you really want me to meet your family?"

"Why wouldn't I? Wait, what do you mean by 'it's a big step'? And tell me what you two got each other!"

"Shots."

"Glamour shots?" she teased.

"Nice one," he sneered. "I got a shot of JD and he got a shot of Cuervo. Easy shopping – everybody loved their gift, no worrying about receipts."

Ellie tilted her head in disbelief.

"Okaaay," she continued, "but what do you mean that this is a big step?"

"I'm just wondering who you're shopping here - me or your family?"

"What?"

"Hey, I'm honored that you asked. I'll go, absolutely. But you're either seeing if they can tolerate me, or if I can deal with them."

"That is just a bunch of cynical crap," Ellie sneered. "I can't believe that I'm trying to include you in my life, spend time with you on Christmas, and you think that there's some ulterior motive."

"Sweetie, you know how families are – you can pick your friends and pick your nose, but you can't pick your family. So, either I am the show horse, or they are. And honestly, I don't care which it is because – regardless, you amaze me, and yes – I would love to meet your family."

Ellie, quietly stewing over Mitch's previous comments, suddenly smiled.

"Just answer me one thing," Mitch added as he scooped another shovel full of snow. "Most families have at least one person that is totally fucked up. Ya know, a family member that everyone talks about and are quietly afraid of? Who is it in your family?"

Ellie was utterly dumbfounded by this tangent.

"I just want a little fair warning," Mitch shrugged.

"What are you talking about???!!!" Ellie began yelling. "My family is *not* crazy! Everyone in my family is a normal, well-adjusted member of society. *We're all just fine, OK?*"

Mitch's face suddenly dropped.

"Oh shit," he muttered.

"WHAT?"

"Well, if – as you just said - everyone in your family is well-adjusted and a good member of society, and - as I have stated - every family has at least one crazy person," Mitch mulled, "then that means, by default – it has to be you. You must be the whack job of the family."

Ellie's jaw dropped open as she tried to say something, *anything* to Mitch.

"Ya know," he added with a shrug, "they're probably a little afraid of you, too."

Ellie's eyes seemed to be pushing their way out of their sockets.

"Just fuckin' with you, beautiful," Mitch suddenly smiled. "That's for the Glamour Shots comment. *Now* we're even."

Completely frazzled, Ellie stared at him and quietly contemplated locations where she could hide Mitch's body. Then, she remembered that her dad owned a wood chipper and curled her lip as she evaluated that option.

"I'd love to go," Mitch continued as if nothing had happened. "What are we having for dinner?"

Ellie glared at Mitch as he overloaded his shovel again and balanced the load, preparing to heave it. She walked up behind him, took her shovel, and shoved it under his feet.

Mitch's feet shot up into the air along with his load of snow. He landed flat on his back, and his shovel-load of snow plopped on top of him.

"No, NOW we're even, asshole!" she playfully yelled and smiled at herself, until she realized Mitch hadn't moved.

"Hey, Mitch?" she asked. "Are you OK?"

CHAPTER 23

AND SHE'S DADDY'S LITTLE GIRL

Mitch was feeling a mixture of excitement and apprehension as made his way to Ellie's to pick her up for dinner with her family on Christmas Day. He thanked God, and even himself, for having the nerve to even talk to Ellie. He also felt like it might be OK to begin to imagine the possibility of bigger things.

Yes, Mitch had teased Ellie about this Christmas dinner being a "big thing," but there was some sincerity in his teasing. This was a big deal for Mitch – for the first time in his life, he honestly could see himself getting married. And also for the first time in his life, the prospect of marriage didn't cause a twinge of panic in his gut.

He pulled up Ellie's driveway and jogged inside to meet her, but she was rushing out the door at the same time and they nearly knocked each other over.

"Whoa!" Mitch yelled. "Babe, I was coming in to get you."

"It's snowing sweetie," she laughed. "I didn't want you to have to get out in the snow."

They both laughed and stood there holding each other in her doorway. Mitch then kissed her deeply.

"It's freezing out here! Where's your coat – wow, you look fantastic," Mitch suddenly smiled.

Ellie was wearing a bright red dress with white trim and black shoes.

"Very Mrs. Claus," Mitch thought, "if Mrs. Claus were a Sports Illustrated swimsuit model."

"Thanks! You look really nice, too," Ellie cooed as she admired Mitch's khaki pants and dark green dress shirt.

"I thought about wearing a tie..." Mitch began.

"No," Ellie said as she kissed him again. "That's not the Mitch I know and like. You be you today."

She grabbed her coat and started to close the door when Mitch grabbed her and kissed her again.

"Should we just stay in?" he smiled as he snuggled closely.

"Mitch, come on," she strained against him as she closed her door. "Mom's waiting."

"Aw c'mon," Mitch suggested. "I'll be quick."

"Oh yeah," Ellie laughed. "That's what every woman is dying to hear."

As they drove down the highway, just talking about nothing, Ellie suddenly perked up.

"OH LOOK!" she nearly squealed as she pointed to a huge billboard.

"What?" Mitch asked, looking at the same huge billboard with a beautiful middle-aged realtor's picture on it.

"Mom's new billboard is up! Wow, doesn't she look great!"

Ellie's mom was sort of a local celebrity, due entirely to the numerous billboards that displayed her 30-foot-tall face dominating nearly fifty percent of each sign she put up.

Mitch often wondered how effective billboards like those really were and how much of it was mere hubris. He'd even joked to himself that he was amazed she could find room for her phone number on those ads.

"Wow," Mitch smiled. "So I finally get to meet the real estate empress. I'll have to compliment her on the new sign."

"Yeah, vanity *is* kind of her sin," Ellie laughed. "Funny how opposites attract."

Mitch wasn't sure what she meant by that, but he wasn't curious enough to ask.

As they pulled into her parents' subdivision, Mitch stopped and noticed the guard house.

"Um..." he said as he turned to Ellie, "just how rich *are* your parents?"

The guard walked up to Mitch's window and motioned for him to roll down his window.

"Can I help you, sir?" the guard asked as Mitch was still cranking the window down.

"Hi Eddie!" Ellie yelled as she leaned across Mitch. "Did everyone in your family make it in for Christmas?"

"Oh, hello, Ms. Prudell!" the guard replied with pleasant surprise. "Yes, they all did. Big dinner tonight at six!"

"That's great!"

"Your sister's already been through. You don't want to keep you mom waiting!"

"OK, better go then. Well, see ya later! Merry Christmas!"

"Merry Christmas to you, Ms. Prudell!"

"So," Mitch asked, now a little intimidated as he pulled past the gate. "You said opposites attract. Is your dad really *that* different from your mom?"

"Well, I told you Dad was an engineer," Ellie explained. "But once the money really started rolling in, he retired. Now, he just dabbles in writing."

"Wow, I hope you become a famous actor someday so I can sit at home and *dabble*," Mitch muttered. "Wait, IS THAT THEIR HOUSE?"

"Yeah, it is," Ellie said, a little embarrassed.

Ellie's parents' home was the type of house that, as you approached it, you just knew it was worth serious cash. A building that was styled as a turn-of-the-20th-century-mansion, it had sandy white brick, tall stone columns that supported the roof above the second floor, and large windows that were jam-packed with wreaths, tinsel, and Christmas lights. The home sat atop a gentle hill that rose up in the middle of at least five acres. Mitch guessed that there had to be at least six bedrooms in this house.

"Listen Mitch," Ellie said as they pulled up the hill, "dad knows you're a writer, and he's probably going to want to talk to you about it, so..."

"Um, no problem," Mitch answered, but only half-listening as he was still awestruck by the size of the house. "I'd love to talk with him about, um, writing. Maybe we can bounce some ideas off each other... hey babe, how many houses did your mom sell to get this?" he asked as he began to park.

"Uh, Mitch?" Ellie smiled as she pointed twenty yards down the driveway, "the front door is over there."

As they walked through the front door of the Prudell estate, the usual overly-joyous hugs and squeals from a close family reuniting were the only sounds initially heard. As Ellie frantically hugged her mom and then her sister,

Mitch dutifully stood by waiting for them to finish fawning over each other.

Ellie's mom was a woman in her late 50's who wore a little too much makeup, which unintentionally made it painfully obvious that her billboard photos were airbrushed, if not spackled. She was wearing a silk lavender gown that glistened in the light of chandelier overhead.

Mitch smiled as he instantly thought, *"You only find something like that at Saks."*

Her mom also apparently had never found a piece of jewelry that she didn't like. It was almost as if she was competing with the ornate Christmas tree itself for shimmer factor. Yes, she was over-the-top with her fashion, but she seemed to have a big heart and was warm and genuine.

Before Ellie could introduce Mitch, Ellie's mom stepped up and extended her hand.

"You must be Mitch," she smiled.

"Yes, ma'am." Mitch nodded.

"Ellie's told us so many good things about you," she said. "I'm Marianne, and this is Ellie's sister, Claire."

"Nice to finally meet both of you," Mitch said.

Claire meekly waved and smiled at Mitch. Mitch, sensing her shyness, simply smiled and nodded back. For everything that Mrs. Prudell was, Claire was the exact opposite. Shy and unassuming, she was a waif of a young lady in her mid-twenties with a simple white lace dress, very little makeup, and even less jewelry.

"And this is her fiancé, Jack," Mrs. Prudell continued.

"Jack," Mitch smiled and shook his hand warmly. "Well, apparently congratulations are in order."

"Well, thanks," the young man in a jacket and tie said. "I'm definitely lucky that she'll have me," he laughed.

"Yes, I'm sure any of us would be," Mitch agreed.

"So come on in, Mitch," Mrs. Prudell insisted. "No reason to be nervous. We removed all the black lights when we heard you were coming."

Mitch stopped and gave Ellie a betrayed look.

"You told them about that?" he whined.

"Aw c'mon Mitch," Ellie laughed. "It was our first date. Of course Mom and Claire were going to hear about it."

Mitch sighed and then began laughing and shaking his head in amused disbelief.

"Mom, where's dad?" Ellie asked.

"Oh, probably in his study," Mrs. Prudell replied. "I'll call him."

"No need," her father replied as he stepped out of a dim hallway and into the room. "How's my precious little angel?" he asked as he kissed Ellie.

"Fine daddy," she said as she kissed him. "Merry Christmas."

Mitch looked at Ellie's father and instantly thought of Chance's coworkers 30 years from now. He had a hint of being a little too self-aware and geeky, but his age had given him the skills to handle those feelings with a casual deftness. He was warm, had a calming smile, and was decked out in a short-sleeved dress shirt – complete with a chest pocket shoved full with a pocket-protector, pens, and a small notepad.

"*Daaad*, it's Christmas," Ellie complained. "Can you please put the pocket protector away? It's so nerdy!"

"Hey," he smiled. "I never know when I'm going to have an idea. And at my age, I can't always remember them...I gotta write 'em down immediately."

"Ugh, OK," Ellie acquiesced. "Come here Daddy, I want you to meet Mitch."

"Ah yes," Mr. Prudell extended his hand. "Nice to meet you, Mitch."

"Merry Christmas, sir," Mitch said as he shook his hand. "And that's a great idea... any writer needs to have pen and paper handy. You never know when inspiration's going to strike."

"Oh yes, that's right," he laughed kindly. "Ellie told me you're a writer, too."

"Well," Mitch feigned humility, "it's a living."

"Ya know," Mr. Prudell explained, "I do a little writing myself."

"Yeah, Ellie told me," Mitch smiled. "I'd love to talk shop with you if you have the time."

"I love talking with other writers," he agreed. "Honey, do I have enough time to show him my study before dinner?"

"I guess," Mrs. Prudell sighed. "But make it quick."

Mr. Prudell then escorted Mitch down a dark hallway and into the dimly lit, redwood study. Mitch smiled as he began examining Mr. Prudell's collection.

"Are all these books yours?" Mitch asked.

"Well, I get asked to read A LOT of books nowadays," Mr. Prudell confessed. "These are mostly all promotional copies."

"That's great!" Mitch praised as he wondered what exactly this man did with all these books and all his free time.

"So Mitch, how long have you been a writer?"

"Professionally? Since college, really."

"Really?"

"Yeah, I wrote for the campus newspaper, then for some trade magazines, ya know, and currently I'm a... hey! You have the entire Double Eclipse series!"

"Yeah, of course."

"Hey, wait a sec...," Mitch pointed, "I've never seen this one before."

"Yeah, it's the latest book," Mr. Prudell shrugged. "It won't be released to the public for another couple of months. You can have that copy if you want."

"Wow, YEAH!" Mitch accepted gladly as he took it off the shelf. "Are you sure I can have this?"

"Oh yeah," Mr. Prudell scoffed. "I've got a few more copies lying around here somewhere."

Mitch quietly envied the Prudells and the connections they obviously had. He held the book with the reverence usually shown to religious artifacts.

"Do you want it signed?" Mr. Prudell asked.

Mitch slowly turned with bewilderment. As he looked at Mr. Prudell, the man smiled with a humble shrug.

"You *know* Elliot Alexander?" Mitch asked.

"Oh God," Mr. Prudell suddenly replied with humility. "Ellie didn't tell you?"

"Tell me what?"

"Yes Mitch, I know him. He's me. Elliot Alexander is my pen name."

The dim light from the solitary lamp only enunciated how far Mitch's face had sunk from the revelation. He stood motionless as a mannequin in the dim light, unsure of what to say next.

"Ahem," Mitch cleared his throat as he snapped out of his trance. "Yes sir, I'd be honored."

"Don't mention it," Mr. Prudell laughed as he took the book from Mitch's hand. "Maybe one day if you want to sell this thing, it might be worth a few more bucks... or maybe less. The public is so fickle, ya know?"

"But you inspire so many..."

"Me?" Mr. Prudell shrugged with a bashful smile. "Well, thanks, but honestly, I just tell a story - something that interests me," he explained as he signed the book. "I've found that a true author doesn't write to be rich, or famous, or to have people love him. A true author writes about something he thinks will entertain – and hopefully enlighten – others. But inspire? That's way beyond my control. Every reader will take something different from it, anyway. I'm flattered if you think my stories inspire others to try to write something themselves, but that's not my goal when I'm writing. I just try to write a good story.

"I never imagined it would become my vocation, much less..." he paused, shooting his eyes around the room, "...all of this. A small house on a couple acres and a laptop would've been fine with me.

"Well, that and my Bentley. Gotta have that." Mr. Prudell joked.

As he handed back the signed book, Mitch suddenly felt unsteady on his feet. He tried to understand everything Mr. Prudell had said, but it was too huge for him to take in just yet.

"Um, thank you, sir – I mean, Mr. Prudell."

"And call me Chris, by the way," Mr. Prudell laughed.

"OK, thanks, Chris," Mitch smiled, thrilled that one of his biggest influences wasn't a narcissistic egomaniac.

"DINNER'S READY!" Mrs. Prudell's voice echoed down the hall and into the den.

"Well, I guess we should join the ladies, eh?" Mr. Prudell smiled.

"Yeah, definitely," Mitch smiled. "Hey, by the way..."

"Yeah?"

"Just out of curiosity, everything you write goes into your books, right? I mean, you don't let anyone else edit your work, what with you being a successful author and all..."

"AHAHAHA!" Mr. Prudell laughed out loud. "Well, Mitch, lemme tell ya. Between the editors, interns, publishers, and focus groups, I'm happy if 80% of my work survives what goes to press."

"What?" Mitch asked.

"Mitch, we all have to answer to someone. My publisher's a nightmare about deadlines, and the arguments I've gotten into with editors? Holy Christ," he sighed as he looked to the ceiling. "Heck, that's why I'm semi-retired now."

Mitch pursed his lips to one side and nodded.

"We can talk about this more after dinner," Mr. Prudell assured. "If Ellie's anything like her mom, you know better than to keep her waiting."

Throughout dinner, they all laughed and shared stories about each other. Mitch learned that Jack was a low-level stock broker who also claimed to play a mean set of drums. Claire was about as innocent as they came, a pre-school teacher with wide eyes and a heart as big as the moon. Mrs. Prudell was ostentatious, but still very down to Earth. And Mr. Prudell, er, Chris, was everything Mitch hoped to be. Humble, passionate, and still wildly successful.

Ellie's family got a good laugh out of Mitch's career path and how he ended up where he currently was working. Comments about "delayed maturity" and "the perfect job for you" were bandied about, and Mitch took it all in stride. Heck, for the most part, he agreed with them.

After dinner, the boys retreated to Mr. Prudell's den to hang out while the ladies did their normal bonding rituals.

"OK, Chris," Mitch asked. "You said you used to be an engineer. How in God's name did you become Elliot Alexander?"

"Actually, it's really funny," Mr. Prudell laughed. "It all started when the girls were little. I started making up stories for them at bedtime, and it was just a cute little bedtime ritual that the girls and I had. But at one point, Ellie just became tenacious about these two characters that I'd made up one night. I mean, simple enough, right? A hero and a princess, and it was just a short 'beat the monster, save the princess' tale. Both Ellie and Claire seemed to really like it - and I couldn't even tell you what I said to them that night - but the next night, Ellie wanted another story about those two characters again. She simply wouldn't let it go."

Mitch laughed and nodded, recognizing the trait was still present in Ellie.

"She'd keep asking about Prince Alex and his bride-to-be, Rachel. *Every night*, she'd ask for another story about those two. So, I had to get creative every night, and it... well, it got so bad with Ellie that I actually started complaining about it to my co-workers. When they asked about the stories, I told them what I'd made up *just so Ellie would go to bed*. But even they loved the stories I'd retold to them, and one of my co-workers then suggested that I write this stuff down and try to get published. And, ya know, there was something about that suggestion that just made sense to me.

"So, even though I was working fifty hours a week as an engineer, I'd still come home every night and 'clock in' again, this time just to work on the story. I started going in to work at five AM just so I could be home by five PM. I would grab a few pieces of Marianne's dinner and head to the basement and start typing. By nine, the kids were ready for bed, so I would go upstairs and read the piece of the story I'd written to Ellie and Claire. My girls became my first focus group for Alex and Rachel. They were my sounding board for the first Double Eclipse novel.

"About a year later, I'd finished my first draft, but I had no idea what to do with it. It wasn't easy back then to get noticed, especially since there was no such thing as the internet or email. I got the novel copyrighted, and - by blind luck - found an agent that would work for next to nothing. We sent out like a bazillion copies all over the place and got rejection letter after rejection letter. Honestly,

I was about ready to give up. I'd gotten to the point where I was just happy that I'd written down a story that Ellie and Claire might one day be able to read to their kids."

"And?" Mitch asked.

"And then one day, the phone rang." Mr. Prudell replied.

"*And?*" Mitch demanded.

Mr. Prudell just looked around.

"And the rest, as they say..." he sighed as if at a loss for an explanation, "...is history."

"Mr., I mean, Chris," Mitch stuttered, "I'm not trying to kiss your ass, but, seriously, you have the career I want."

"Well, thanks Mitch," Mr. Prudell nodded humbly. "If you want, I can look at what you've got and give you some tips... at least, help you avoid some of the mistakes I made, and show you some of the things I've learned from dealing with publishers."

"That'd be great!" Mitch replied as he nearly launched himself to his feet. "I just need to... um... finish enough of it for it to even be 'looked at.'"

"Well," Mr. Prudell shrugged, "if you ever want to really get serious, you know, get to the point where you're actually going to pursue the dream and put the time in like you would any other career, you know where to find me."

Mitch and Ellie said their goodbyes, as Mitch thanked Ellie's parents for their hospitality.

He sat in his car as Ellie slid in and looked over at him.

"He fucking *dabbles* at writing?" Mitch scoffed as he hunted for his car key. "Are you *fucking* kidding me?"

"Babe, listen," Ellie explained with apologetic eyes. "I just... look – they were just *stories* he told us when we were kids."

"That's great," Mitch dismissed, feigning frustration as he pulled his seat belt across his chest.

"Mitch, please," Ellie continued as she did the same. "The first night I met you, I really liked you. Then when you told me about your dream, the first thing I thought was that if I told you about my dad, I'd never know if you actually liked *me*, or if you were just going to use me to get my dad to help you with your dream."

Mitch was about to start the car as Ellie completed the last part of that sentence - then stopped dead in motion. He then turned to her and squinted.

"Have I ever done anything to make you think I was using you, for *anything*?"

"NO," she replied. "But I didn't know you then. I had to protect myself, Mitch. I really thought you liked me, and I didn't want to get it all messed up by telling you who my father was, and then have to wonder if you really liked *me* or not.

Mitch just continued to stare at Ellie, but he could no longer fight the smile creeping up the side of his lip.

"I know, I'm rambling," Ellie continued as she ran out of words while looking into his eyes with a glimmer of hope. "I just hope you can understand," she added softly.

Mitch suddenly realized that she felt both vulnerable and guilty. Inside, he knew that he could easily break her heart by simply launching into a rage about lying, hiding, manipulating, selfishness, – *whatever*. It could have been open season on her. Mitch also knew that Chance would have pounced on this opportunity. But Mitch was flattered that he mattered enough to her that she had to take this kind of precaution just to protect herself. It told him – without her saying a word – that she cared, she really cared... enough to be vulnerable. And suddenly, Mitch fell a little bit farther in love with her.

And as she looked deeply and hopefully into his eyes, his smile won the battle for his face. He then grabbed her and kissed her so softly and passionately that he felt dizzy. He then turned and started his car.

"Which entrance are we leaving from, *Princess Rachel*?" he replied with a hint of disgusted tolerance. "The north entrance or the south?"

"Ha ha, very funny," Ellie smiled. "Just drive straight."

"*Just a bunch of stories*," he continued to mock. "Yep, that proves it."

"What?"

"You *are* the crazy one."

CHAPTER 24

OH WON'T YOU PLEASE,
PLEASE PICK UP THE PHONE

A parking lot of faded pavement arced over the crest of the hill which housed St. Louis' own Municipal Theater. Surrounded by trees that were displaying the small leaves of a new springtime, Ellie's old Chevy strained a little as it dragged itself up the slope and into a parking spot.

Ellie hurriedly grabbed her purse, nearly forgetting to put the car in park, and ran into the narrowly opened wrought iron gates that guarded the entrance.

Ellie waited patiently in the front row with about 100 other actresses from the area. Finally, her name was called. She walked across the stage, exuding confidence in every step, convinced that she should get this role.

"And you are?" asked the casting director.

"Ellie Prudell."

"And you're reading for the part of Sandy Olssen?"

"Yes."

"OK, which song do want to perform?"

"Pick one, I know them all" she smiled. "I've played Sandy in grade school, high school, and at Arizona State."

"OK, then," he turned to orchestra leader, "Start with 'Hopelessly Devoted to You'."

But before the orchestra could start, a dark figure's voice boomed "Wait" from a back row.

Everyone in the auditorium looked back.

"I'm not seeing her as a true 'Sandy'", the voice continued. "Her figure doesn't say 'High School' anymore. Ask her if she'd be interested in a different role."

"Would you like to try out for a different role?" the casting director echoed.

"Sure," Ellie replied, suddenly shaking a little with false confidence. "I, um, know this play inside and out. Do you want me to try for Frenchie, Rizzo...?"

"I'm thinking," the dark voice paused, "Principal McGee."

Ellie shuddered even more on the inside.

"Yes, um," the casting director said as delicately as possible, "we're thinking you'd be better suited as faculty. Do you want to read for Principal McGee?"

"Uh, sure!" Ellie responded, burying her urge to simply break down into tears.

As she began to read her lines in exchange with the casting director, the director's voice again boomed from the back.

"Thank you," said the voice.

"We'll call your agent," the casting director added with a smile.

"Wait," Ellie asked with a hint of desperation, "was there something wrong?"

"Well," the casting director replied, "we think you might be a shade too young for Principal McGee.

"*A shade?*" Ellie thought to herself indignantly. "*Are you fucking kidding me?*"

She then swallowed hard.

"OK, thank you for your time," she smiled as best she could. "I'll look forward to hearing from you."

She grabbed her things quickly, yet as dignifiedly as she possibly could, holding her hand to her lips as she counted her paces to the exit.

She got to the gates and jogged to her car, wrestling with her keys and mumbling diatribes to herself as she finally opened the door. As she slid into her seat, she sat there for a second and looked over at her purse riding shotgun. She then buried her face in her hands and began sobbing openly.

Mitch sat in the darkness of his living room, frantically trying to complete the user manual by tomorrow's deadline. The light from his laptop and his TV were the only sources of light, other than the waning twilight of sunset sneaking through the blinds and scattering across the ceiling. He played a little of the game for the manual, hit pause, switched to his laptop, typed a little, then reached for the controller to resume the game.

That's when his cell phone rang.

Annoyed by the interruption, he sighed and reached for his phone. As his caller ID revealed it was Ellie, he smiled.

"Hey babe," he greeted. "How'd the audition go?"

All he could hear was the sniffles of a woman unable to fully speak over the tears she was choking down.

"Hey, hey," he insisted, trying to both soothe and take control of the situation.

"I," she choked, "I really need to see you right now. Are you busy?"

Mitch's eyes shot between the TV, his laptop, and the clock on the wall. For a split second, he tried to calculate how much he could get done before Ellie got there.

"Uh," he replied uncertainly. "Nothing that I can't come back to."

"I know that I shouldn't have called because of your deadline, but," she sniffed, "I really need to see you."

"It's OK," he said with the same uncertainty as before, while quickly examining his apartment for any stray trash lying around. "I got a lot to do yet, but come on by," he answered, thinking that he had enough time to wrap up what he was working on before she got there.

"You sound busy," she forced through her tears, "I'll let you go."

Mitch suddenly felt a huge hole grow in his stomach.

"ELLIE!" he ordered, "Dammit, don't you do that to me! I said I'm here for you and I meant it! Now, come over RIGHT NOW so we can talk."

"Are you *sure*?" the voice asked weakly.

"YES!" Mitch insisted. "How soon will you be here?"

"Well," Ellie answered, "um..."

A gentle knock suddenly called from Mitch's front door. Mitch turned to the door, rolled his eyes, and hung up the phone.

He opened the door to find a mascara-stained face with eyes that reminded Mitch of a wounded puppy.

"Oh babe," Mitch sighed with sympathy, immediately wrapping an arm around her head.

Ellie buried her head in his chest and began weeping uncontrollably. Mitch helped her to his couch as she struggled to simply inhale. He held her as she tried to relay the tale of her day. But while she spoke, Mitch tried to gently lean her back just a little so he could reach his laptop to save his work.

"And he didn't even let me finish *Mrs. McGee's* lines," she spoke through her tears as Mitch gently nudged her back. "It was the most humili..." she paused and looked to where Mitch was reaching, then shoved him away. "Are you even *listening to me???*"

"Of course I am, babe," Mitch shook his head in frustration. "I just wanted to save my work so I could give you my full attention."

"I knew I shouldn't have come to you for this, you selfish son of a bitch!" she yelled, standing up angrily.

But, in the course of her rage, the wire powering his laptop got caught under her foot, and her stomp sent the plug soaring through the air, landing on the keyboard – which caused the screen to summarily blink twice and go black.

As Mitch strained towards the laptop, the screen dropped to prismed dot. His work was lost. He started to quiver at the horror of all his lost work, reaching toward his screen in helplessness.

"Oh no," Ellie's eyes widening in horror as she suddenly realized what she'd done. "I'm, um, I'm gonna go," she choked, beginning to cry again. "You deserve a better girlfriend, someone who doesn't fuck everything up like I do."

She quickly turned and ran towards the door, but Mitch was quicker. As she cracked open the door to leave, Mitch planted an open hand on the middle of the door and slammed it shut.

Ellie's eyes slowly rose to Mitch's face.

Mitch, now huffing, just glared.

"Look," he growled, "I told you to come over because I wanted you here."

Ellie stood there silent.

"Now, I just lost about two hours' worth of work *because* I wanted to be here for you. And I'll be damned if you're not going to let me be here for you now."

Ellie turned her head uncertainly until Mitch shot her a reassured smile. She threw her arms around him and re-planted her face in the same tear-stained spot on his shirt, resuming her cry without missing a beat.

Mitch wrapped her in his arms, but gently shook his head in disbelief. He looked to God with a "you owe me one" glare on his face.

As the evening wore on, Ellie alternated between describing her day and the occasional return to tears. Mitch listened patiently, trying to help her cope as best he could.

"Hey, Danni and Chance are going camping this weekend," she commented as she wiped her nose. "We should go with them."

"Huh?" Mitch asked incredulously. "Babe, I don't camp."

"Why not?"

"I'm allergic to the outdoors."

"*What?* Shut up!" she mocked between sniffles, almost laughing.

"Look, my idea of 'roughing it' is no room service, OK? If I have to get my ass off the bed and walk to a vending machine, I'm pissed off. I don't camp."

Ellie looked at him amazedly.

"Ya know, every once in a while, it's good to get away from the daily grind," she replied. "Camping is great! We can bring our own drinks, barbeque, hang out around a campfire..."

"Ward off bears, raccoons, mosquitoes," Mitch mockingly continued her thought for her. "Oh yeah – sounds like a blast. Hey, we're going to *need* a campfire... did anyone tell you it's still March? It's gonna be thirty degrees at night!"

"Hey, it's *late* March. It's supposed to be in the 60's this weekend, and even if it does turn cold, we'll just have to find *some way* to stay warm at night," she rolled her eyes suggestively and smiled.

Mitch, suddenly interested, acquiesced.

"Well," he surrendered, "if you *really* wanna go."

"I just wanna pretend that everything about life doesn't exist," she continued, "at least for a *few* days. Screw the auditions, screw the salon, screw all the career plans, screw all the ambitions."

"Screw Mitch?" he offered.

"... let's just get out of this town," she begged.

Mitch merely smiled because, while he hated sleeping outside, the thought of doing something romantic for Ellie overwhelmed his concerns.

"OK," he said, "but, just so you know, I don't even know how to pitch a tent," he warned.

"Oh yeah you do," Ellie continued with her innuendo. "And if you forget, I'll help."

CHAPTER 25

I NEED THAT

"Chance, you here?" Mitch yelled as he entered the apartment. Chance had been at Danni's the night before and in a conference all day, so Mitch had yet to tell him about his and Ellie's plans to go camping with them.

"Back here," he called from his bedroom.

Mitch walked back and found Chance packing his gear for the trip.

"Hey, Ellie just decided that we should join you and Danni camping" he said. "So, do I need any equipment, or do you guys have everything?"

Chance just stopped and stared at Mitch.

"She *what*?"

"Yeah, it'll be great," Mitch continued. "Danni's probably gonna be calling you any minute now."

Just then, Chance's cell phone rang and he saw that it was Danni.

"Hi honey," he answered. "Yeah... uh huh... um... yeah but... yeah but... OK... sure. No, it's OK. Yeah, you're right... it'll be more fun... can't wait. Yeah, Ellie sure is smart, honey. OK, talk to you later. Bye."

He threw his phone onto his bed and stepped towards Mitch angrily.

"Ya know," Mitch continued, oblivious to Chance's sudden mood swing, "I'm really kind of pumped about this now. How big is your tent, anyway?"

"You mother fucker," Chance glared.

"Huh? What?"

"First of all, you're gonna need your *own* fuckin' tent..." Chance growled. "We ain't *'sharing'* here. I have a lot of things I'm going to be trying on Danni, and I'm going to need every bit of square footage I can get... and most of the headroom, too."

"I don't even want to know," Mitch replied

"Yeah?" Chance challenged. "Check this out."

He grabbed a suitcase from under the bed, flopped in onto the bed, and opened it.

"Whoa," Mitch said in amazement. "Is that... is that a *power cord*? I didn't think those things were legal anymore – what, after that incident in Maryland."

"I don't know if it's legal to own, but I know you can't *buy* it in Missouri."

"Gotta love the internet," Mitch smiled.

"Amen, my brotha," Chance smiled. "See, *this* is why you'll need *your own tent*, and probably earplugs. And that's why I need a gas-powered generator, come to think of it."

"OK..." Mitch agreed, "but I don't even have a tent, so I guess I'm off to Wal-Mart. You need anything?"

"*Wal-Mart*?" Chance chided. "Mitch, we need to hit Bass Pro Shop."

"Dude, is there even one close by?"

"Sure, in Columbia."

"That's like an hour away!"

"So, we'll pack a cooler. You'll love this place – they've got guns, knives, and every other cool thing on Earth."

"We need to go there?"

"Yep."

Mitch thought about Chance's insistence for a second.

"Six-pack or twelve?" he then asked.

Chance just gave him a "duh" glare.

The Corolla chugged into a parking spot right next to a brand new convertible Corvette. Chance opened the door as a beer can fell to the ground.

"Nice car," Chance commented.

"Somebody's mid-life crisis," Mitch sniffed as he walked by indifferently.

They walked to the entrance and the automatic doors flung open. For a moment, Mitch swore he heard angels singing. His eyes could not believe what they were seeing.

This store was every outdoorsman's – heck, nearly every *man's* – heaven. It was complete with rock-climbing walls, rows of fishing rods, a shooting gallery, countless guns, hundreds of knives, and 400 horsepower bass boats.

"Get yer own," Chance said as he grabbed a shopping cart. "I'll be in the gun department."

"Right behind you," Mitch smiled as if entering Disneyland. He slowly looked around in awe. As he gawked, he walked to the middle of the store where, displayed like a crown jewel, stood the world's largest freshwater fish tank. And within the tank swam Carl, the world's largest catfish in captivity - and local celebrity. He stood in amazement of both the creature's massive size and the crowd the fish attracted. He then turned to find Chance.

As he arrived in the gun department, Chance was already in full conversation with the rifle salesman.

"Yeah, but you guys *do* have ammo, right?" Chance asked as he examined the barrel of the 44 Magnum.

"For the last time, sir," the salesman explained. "We can't let you load the guns in the store."

"How about blanks?"

"In a hunting store???" the salesman countered.

"Well... yeah, for snipe hunts – *duh*."

The salesman rolled his eyes.

"C'mon man," Chance whined, "can't we shoot anything around here?"

"The shooting gallery is just to your right, sir."

Chance just smiled and looked back at Mitch.

"Let's go."

He took three steps in and realized that the gallery was coin operated. He returned to the counter and held out a $10 bill.

"Change please," Chance said

"*Ten dollars' worth* of quarters?"

Chance's eyes looked to the side to consider the question, then returned his stare.

"Probably, yeah."

Mitch and Chance pumped quarters into the anchored bb guns nearly as fast as they could pull the trigger. They took turns outscoring each other until Chance tried to turn the BB gun on Mitch, only to find its range of motion prevented him from fully turning it at Mitch. He fired in his direction anyway.

"Hey you fuck!" Mitch growled as he tried to turn his gun back at Chance.

They stood there for a moment blasting the BBs into the partition that separated them – until a 16-year-old female attendant kicked them out.

"But I've still got three credits left!" Chance protested.

The attendant reached in her pocket and chucked three quarters at Chance.

"GET... OUT."

"It's alright, Chance," Mitch replied while watching Chance pick up each quarter. "We've got shopping to do, anyway."

"Which way are the tents?" Chance growled.

"Aisle FIVE," the girl snapped.

They made their way back through the store, as this trip to buy a tent quickly became a man's version of power shopping. Their carts were already overflowing with camouflage gear, fishing hats, lures, rods, miner lights, bb guns, boots, and a remote controlled four-wheeler cooler, as they entered the knife department.

Mitch walked past a knife vest display complete with every conceivable type of blade. The sign above the display read "As Seen in the Movie 'Desperado'!"

Mitch's eyes widened.

"Whoa..." he muttered.

At the other end of the aisle, Chance admired the display of large machetes and other huge blades. The sign above the display read "As Seen in the Movie 'Rambo!'"

"Whoa..." he muttered.

They reunited in the next aisle, their carts overflowing with merchandise.

"What did we originally come here for again?" Chance asked.

"Um..." Mitch replied as they entered a spacious region of the store. Suddenly a large disc zipped past Mitch's head, narrowly missing him and landing about 15 feet away. As it hit the ground, it instantly expanded into a full-sized tent.

"Whoa!" Mitch smiled gleefully. "I need THAT!"

"My thoughts exactly, sir," the salesman replied as he walked up. "It's called the 'auto-pitch' and anyone can do it. Look at it this way sir - no more messing with tent poles, directions, frustration... just a flick of the wrist and you're campsite is ready 'like that'. It's the best innovation in pitching a tent since..."

"The internet?" Chance asked.

"My thought's exactly, sir," the salesman agreed. "And it's just as easy to put away when you're done. Here, watch." The salesman walked over and in an instant had the full tent reduced back to its disc form.

"Yeah, but, what's the trick to opening it?" Mitch asked.

"No trick," the salesman replied, "let me show you." He grabbed an eight-year-old boy who was standing nearby, minding his own business. "Hey little boy! Come here," he said as he handed the disc to the boy. "Now, just throw it over there."

The boy did as he was told and the disc exploded into a tent again.

"Holy crap!" Mitch exclaimed.

"Once you've tossed this puppy, all you do is grab a beer, a hammer, drop four spikes in the ground, and bam – you're done! Go get another beer."

"Let me try," Chance asked.

The salesman re-compacted the tent and handed it to Chance, who slung it into the open area and the tent reappeared. Chance and Mitch looked at each other with sheer joy.

"OK, but how much is it?" Mitch asked.

"Well, sir, we have a special that's ending today, so you can get your own right now for $50 off the normal price at only $299.00."

"Um, I don't know. That's pretty pricey."

"Pfft!" Chance snickered. "And a timeshare's not? Mitch, you couldn't even put together our street hockey goal. And that thing only had SIX FUCKIN POLES! I think you should go with this."

"Well, let me try it once, at least."

"No problem, sir." The salesman rolled the tent up and handed it to Mitch. "Once you're done, just let me know what color you want."

"And all I have to do is throw it out there? Like a Frisbee?"

"Absolutely."

"Does it matter if I throw it left-handed?"

The salesman looked confused for a second. "Well, I can't imagine..."

"OK, here goes."

Mitch slung it out into the open with a wide smile. But in mid-air, the disc instead bulged like a Jiffy Pop pan and numerous rods instantly shot in every direction throughout the store.

People dived for cover and children began crying. One rod pierced a can of Deer pheromone, dousing a man nearby. Everywhere around them, stray rods quivered in the walls, shelves, and mannequins.

Suddenly, one of the clerks screamed and pointed to the fish tank. The resident catfish, Carl, was floating upside down in the tank with a tent rod sticking through his belly.

Just then, the little boy who originally threw the disc ran up to the salesman

"Daddy, are you OK?" he asked.

Mitch quickly pulled the salesman up.

"Blue," he whispered. "I'll take one in blue."

As Chance and Mitch lugged their piles of merchandise to the checkout counters, Chance turned to Mitch.

"Dude, that was the funniest thing I've seen in my life!" he laughed out loud.

"Just keep moving," Mitch insisted, not smiling at all.

When Chance got in line, he wrinkled his nose looked around.

"Dear God, what is *that smell*?" he asked, not realizing he was in line behind the man that had gotten the impromptu deer pheromone bath.

Mitch was already checking out in the other aisle when he took a whiff.

"Wow, what *is* that???" he said

The man just looked around nervously,

"Uh, what?" he asked. "I... I don't smell anything," he shrugged as he grabbed his bag and quickly walked out of the store.

As the clerk rang up Chance's fishing hat, she looked at Chance.

"Would you like to wear this out of the store?"

Chance's eyes widened.

"We can *wear these out of here*?" he smiled.

The doors to Bass Pro Shop slid apart gloriously Chance and Mitch emerged from the store strutting like they owned the planet, wearing and carrying every item they'd just purchased.

Just then, the man who'd been sprayed by the pheromone ran past them, looking behind himself.

"Oh no, NO!" he screamed. "GET AWAY FROM ME!!! *SOMEBODY HELP!!!*"

Mitch and Chance watched him run past them, then looked back from where he came – and quickly took a step back to avoid the 12-point buck in amorous pursuit of the doused man.

"No, *that's* the funniest thing you've ever seen," Mitch said as the buck galloped past them.

As they got to the car, Chance noticed one remaining tent rod sticking through the rag top of the Corvette, gently quivering in the wind.

"Mitch," Chance said, pointing to the rod.

"Let's go," Mitch cringed.

CHAPTER 26

OUT UNDER THE SKY

The afternoon sun was slowly sliding down the sky as old Corolla pulled up to a camp site beside a lake in a southwestern Missouri park. As Mitch stopped the car at the first campsite, Chance and Danni pulled themselves out of the back seat and popped the trunk.

"You two sure you're going to be OK tonight?" Chance asked as he walked to the driver's side window.

"Oh yeah," Mitch dismissed. "We'll be fine."

"I've been camping for years, Chance," Ellie reassured, leaning across Mitch. "We'll be OK."

"Alright," Chance answered. "Look, if there are any problems, you'll just be up the road about a hundred yards or so. Just come get us if you need anything."

"And I'll have my cell phone if you need to call," Danni added.

"We'll be good," Mitch smiled.

Chance and Danni pulled their gear out of the trunk and set it aside when Chance returned to Mitch's window and signaled Mitch closer.

"Hey, comeer," he half-whispered.

Mitch leaned halfway out the window.

"You remember how to open the tent disc thing, right?" Chance asked.

"NO, Rambo," Ellie sneered while shooting him a glare from the passenger seat. "We're doing this right. You Yuppie-know-nothings are not going to ruin my camping weekend with your pre-fab tents and Ginsu collection."

Chance's eyes widened with horror as he looked at Mitch.

"You mean, you're gonna..." he paused, scoffing at Mitch. "... actually *assemble* a tent?"

Mitch opened his mouth, beginning to explain.

"LOOK," Ellie interrupted, lifting the sleeve that contained the tent and rods, "my dad has been taking me camping since I was a little girl."

Chance smiled wryly and considered making an age joke – especially after what Ellie had gone through at the audition. But Mitch knew exactly what Chance was about to say and just pointed right at him with his standard "Say it and I'll kill you" glare. Chance just nodded and remained silent.

"Wait," Chance suddenly paused, "she didn't let you bring the knives?"

"She let me bring one," Mitch answered, holding up a small boning knife.

Chance just looked at him dejectedly.

"Well, I guess you'll be safe... if any rabid *chipmunks* attack," he mocked, "Man, I can't believe you let her talk you out of..."

"Don't tell me you brought all those knives after I told you not to," Danni yelled from behind the car.

Chance looked back, smiled, and then rolled his eyes.

"No, dear," he replied dutifully.

Mitch just smiled smugly, enjoying another moment when Chance was getting equally emasculated.

"Alright then, call me if you need anything," Chance sighed as Danni closed the hatchback.

"We'll be fine, Survivorman," Ellie mocked.

Chance simply held up a hand to wave goodbye as Mitch spun out the rear tires, bouncing bits of mulch off Chance's chest.

"There aren't really any rabid chipmunks out here, are there?" Mitch asked.

Ellie just rolled her eyes as they continued driving down the bark-laden path.

"Pull up over there," she said.

Mitch stopped in the parking spot beside their campsite and they began unloading the car. Mitch carried the cooler directly to the picnic bench, set it down, and headed back to the car.

Ellie dropped her duffle bag beside the picnic table and opened the cooler. She grabbed a blue plastic glass and quickly mixed a Margarita for herself. After taking a deep swig, she smiled.

"Alright," she sighed to herself as she looked around at the lake and majesty of all the nature around her. "Tonight is all about us."

She then turned to Mitch.

"So, are you still sorry that we went camping?"

"No," Mitch confessed with a smile. "But, ya know, I'm hoping you've done this whole 'tent' thing before," he said as he carried the tent sleeve from the car.

"Don't worry, babe." Ellie laughed. "My dad taught me well. We'll have that tent up in no time. Can we just enjoy the sunset first?"

"Oh yeah," Mitch agreed, "Absolutely."

"Well, I'm glad we're here," she smiled.

"Me too," Mitch agreed as he wrapped her in his arms. "So, you and your dad did this a lot?"

"Oh yeah," Ellie said. "At least twice a summer."

"And you were OK with sleeping on the ground? No A/C, no mattress?"

Ellie laughed again as she sucked down more of her margarita.

"Well, we had an inflatable mattress, but sometimes it would leak - so we'd end up having to sleep on the ground anyway. But regardless, it made me appreciate my bed and my family even more when I got home. It was sort of like imagining what it'd be like if I didn't have a safe place to run to, ya know?"

"Yeah," Mitch smiled with a newfound understanding. "That actually sounds kind of cool to have had that."

"I think so, too," Ellie said with the same smile.

Mitch then released his grasp around her waist and ventured into the woods, returning with an armful of random sticks and a couple of larger pieces that were going to have to serve as the logs. With considerable assistance from Ellie, they got the fire started and, as it slowly got darker and a little colder, they sat on the ground and snuggled near the fire – leaning against the picnic table that held their drinks.

They spent the next hour talking, teasing, laughing, and drinking a little more steadily. They snuggled closer as the lake gently lapped against the nearby shore with the moonlight shimmying off its waves. Ellie nuzzled into Mitch's neck.

Mitch just smiled and then kissed her deeply.

Ellie returned the kiss with equal eagerness. As the kisses became more intense, Ellie tried to speak between the kisses.

"Hey hero, we don't... have... the tent... set up yet... oh my..." she stammered.

"OK," Mitch replied as he continued incessantly kissing her neck with more intensity. "How fast can we set this thing up?"

"Ummm," Ellie breathed. "Not fast enough."

"Well," Mitch continued, kissing every inch of her neck relentlessly, "I think... we've got a problem," he snickered as he let the hand that wasn't holding his drink wander across her body.

"Hey, Mitch" she half-heartedly protested, "what are... oh wow... now that's not fair."

Mitch, undaunted, continued his seduction.

"OK!" she demanded, grabbing a handful of Mitch's hair. "You win."

Mitch, pulling against his own hair like a leashed dog, shot her a confused look.

"WHAT?" he smiled demandingly.

"Baby," she muttered as she kissed him. "The tent..."

"What tent?" Mitch dismissed as he slung his drink into the darkness and re-focused on her neck.

"OK," she sighed as she leaned back, dragging them both on to the sand.

She pulled him on top of her as she embraced both sides of his jaw and kissed him with everything she had.

Mitch, while continuing to kiss her, now used his one free hand to frantically search the top of the picnic table for the blanket that he was sure was folded up near the corner. As Ellie kissed him aggressively, a stray finger grazed the blanket, and the rest of his hand pounced on the recognized fabric like a hungry spider. He pulled it down so quickly that Ellie's plastic margarita glass went flying in the other direction, drenching the top of the picnic table so that it slowly dripped tequila... and that, along with the ripples of the lake in the moonlight, seemed to be the only markers in existence keeping any semblance of time.

After the moon had risen higher in the night sky, Ellie got up. Chilled, she frantically looked for her jeans.

"Damn it's cold," she shivered.

Mitch, leaning on an elbow and feeling pretty good about himself, just watched her 'dance' in the chilled air for a moment. As she found her jeans and quickly slipped them back on, he half-smiled.

Ellie noticed his expression in the firelight.

"What?" she asked, somewhat bothered.

"Eh," Mitch explained, "there's nothing that breaks my heart more than having to watch you put your clothes back on."

"You're sweet," Ellie conceded, although still determined. "But I'm freezing, so deal with it." Ellie was still feeling the effects of the tequila, and had become noticeably clumsy.

Mitch reached across the sand and pulled his sweatshirt back on while Ellie scurried back under their blanket.

"Hold me," she said in playful desperation.

Mitch obliged without reservation as he wrapped her up with his arms and legs.

"Ah, here lies the mighty camper," he mocked.

"Cute," she dismissed as she snuggled into him and sighed. "Hey, don't you ever wonder?" Ellie asked as her voice trailed off.

"Wonder what?"

"How we survived before we invented all this stuff?" she pondered. "I mean, we're obviously not built to survive these temperatures without clothes and stuff. Whenever I go camping, I always wonder how we did it."

"I'm guessing it was necessity," Mitch replied as he struggled with his own jeans while still under the blanket.

"What do you mean?"

"I mean, there were probably some people in the tribe who hated a few other people for whatever reason, and they forced them to head into lands where no one else was," Mitch said with a shrug. "I figure those lands just had to totally suck - otherwise other people would have already been there. But because the ones that got kicked out couldn't go back, they had to figure out how to survive there."

"Interesting," she confessed.

"It's just a guess."

"But," she asked as she adjusted the blanket, "if that's true, then why are us modern people still inventing stuff?"

"Honestly?" Mitch asked.

"Yeah."

"Sex," he replied, now fully dressed. He removed himself from the blanket and bunched it against Ellie's body to keep her warm.

"WHAT?"

"Think about it," Mitch explained. "Back during our early days, the 'best' man got to have sex with the 'best' woman. But say you're not the 'best' man physically, yet you're in love with the 'best' woman. What do you do?"

Ellie lay there listening intently as Mitch continued.

"We humans have never been good with 'no'. We solve problems, we overcome obstacles. So, say the strongest male has the biggest, *'bestest'* cave. You're the weaker male, so you're not about to take the 'best' cave from the bigger male. And you're not about to impress the best woman with a crappy cave especially because every woman wants to have a man, and a cave for that matter, that they're proud of.

"So, being the weaker man, you think and think until you create something *better* than a cave. Then you invent a hut. But now everyone else in the tribe wants a hut. And that's your ticket 'in' because *only you* know how to make one. So, you build other huts for the other members of your tribe, just not as nice as your hut, obviously. "

"And when the strongest male takes your hut from you?" Ellie countered.

"Then you build yourself another one, hell, a better one!" he answered. "Regardless of strength, force, or even numbers, you get the woman you want. And you have children with her, children that have your 'smarter' genes. You teach them how to build huts, and now your entire family becomes the most important family in the tribe. And it carried on from there - the smartest ones, the most innovative ones, thrived and reproduced. The ones who loved to think and solve problems had the most resources, so they could have the most kids. It's the opposite of a vicious cycle... kind of a 'perfect cycle', more or less."

"But that's kind of cynical, isn't it?" Ellie asked. "I mean, you're suggesting that everything we've achieved as a species is due to the urge to have sex."

"I bet it is!" Mitch laughed. "Seriously, look at air conditioning. I mean, the dude who invented A/C probably had a wife who was always turning him down for sex because she'd always whine about how 'It's too *hot*...' That guy probably said to himself, 'How can I fix this?' and the next day he invented central air."

"Christ, Mitch," Ellie pleaded dejectedly. "Does 'love' even factor into your theory?"

"C'mon!" Mitch scoffed. "You know that sex and love are different, even if they're not separate. I mean, think about how many guys put out any real effort for a woman that they merely want to sleep with? Now, for the woman a guy *loves*, she's different. For her, he'll try to figure out how to stop a sunrise if he has to."

Ellie suddenly smiled.

"*Miiiitch*," Ellie called out. "I want this night to last forever."

"Oh no," Mitch deadpanned, realizing what was coming.

"Can you stop the sunrise for me?" she asked like a daughter asking to borrow her father's car.

"Dammit," Mitch smiled. "See, *this* is why guys don't talk to their women..."

"Awww," Ellie laughed, mocking pity.

"Leave me alone," Mitch teased as he squatted over the fire and threw another branch into it. "I have to figure out how to stop the Earth dead on its axis before sunrise."

"Ya know," Ellie offered, watching him from under the covers and feeling her buzz get a little stronger, "you got a cute butt."

Mitch looked back at her over his shoulder and smiled. He grabbed her plastic margarita glass and made another drink for her.

Ellie smiled as she took another drink and rolled over on her back. She quietly stared into the countless stars above them.

"So," she finally asked as she momentarily felt dizzy, "do you think we're alone?"

"Other than Chance and Danni? Yeah, I think so."

"No, I mean in the universe. Do you think we're the only planet with life?"

Mitch stopped working the fire, looked up at the stars, and then walked back to Ellie and laid next to her.

"God, I hope not," Mitch sighed as he snuggled. "I'd look pretty stupid writing a science fiction novel if we ever find out for sure that we are alone," he said as he kissed her neck.

"Speaking of which," Ellie countered, feeling a little more brazen. "When are you going to start on that thing?"

Mitch continued kissing her neck as he answered her.

"I already started, babe. You know that."

"OK," Ellie insisted as she gently pushed him off her neck, "when are you going to *continue* starting on it?"

Mitch stopped straining to kiss her and instead looked her dead in the eye.

"When the time is right," he answered irritably.

"Ha," she scoffed. "With that attitude, you'll never get it finished."

Mitch got back up and walked back to the fire.

"Remember, we were leaving the world behind?" he grumbled. "Can we not talk about this tonight?

"Why not?" Ellie volleyed back as she propped herself up on her elbows. "I mean, are you even serious about it? You sure used it to impress me. What, was that just one of Mitch's pick-up lines?"

"NO," Mitch scorned as he spun around. "I have a few chapters written, *sort of...* and I have the story line mapped out."

"And how much have you worked on it since we met?" Ellie insisted in a way that seemed oddly similar to Chance's behavior patterns.

"We're not talking about this now," Mitch dismissed, equally annoyed by her sudden Chance-like inquisition.

"Look Mitch, you keep saying that we're both artists. I'm a wanna-be actress and you're a wanna-be author. But the difference between us is that you don't need someone to give you an opportunity to express your art. I need someone's permission to act on stage. You just have to sit in your house and write."

"So, you're saying I have it easier?"

"No, I'm saying that I'm jealous!" she railed. "And I'm pissed off that you have this awesome talent and you do nothing with it, especially when you don't need anyone else's help to express your art!"

"Whatever," Mitch dismissed. "These things take time, you wouldn't understand."

"Mitch, I understand you better than you think I do," Ellie scolded.

Mitch looked back at her disconcertedly, but that didn't stop her.

"You're not working on it because you're scared to fail," she continued undaunted. "You talk about it like you're fully engrossed in it, but all you do is stare at your idea and never do anything with it. I get it, you're scared."

"No, I'm not *scared*," Mitch sneered.

"Then *what else is there?*" Ellie yelled.

"Nothing else, at least for tonight," Mitch snipped as he re-focused on the fire while trying to avoid the impending argument, even though he was now fully disgusted with her indirectly calling him a coward.

"Except how to put this tent up," he suddenly added. "How about you get your Sandra-Dee-wanna-be ass up and help me?"

Ellie's eyes widened with rage, pain, and disbelief of her own ears.

"What did you just say to me?"

Mitch pulled the tent bundle from its sleeve and the fabric and poles collapsed into a heap at his feet.

"DAMMIT!" he yelled, now nearly stark-raving mad from both the tent and the conversation.

Ellie still didn't move, awaiting his response. Maybe the tequila was clouding her judgment a little, but now she was more than a little annoyed with Mitch.

Mitch then saw that Ellie had not moved, and he became even more angered by Ellie's lack of assistance.

"Oh, *that's* right," he seethed. "A few years ago, I could have asked your Sandra Dee ass for help, now I should be asking your Principal McGee ass to get up here, *right???!!!*"

Ellie just laid there expressionless with shock – even though a tear escaped her eye and streaked down her cheek. That last comment hurt, and Ellie was no longer sober enough to put that pain away and use it against him at a later date. She suddenly stood up, walked up to Mitch and slapped him across his face with everything she had.

Mitch, not expecting the slap, collapsed into the sand and laid on his side for a second, trying to figure out what just happened.

Ellie stormed towards his car, not looking back.

"Ellie!" Mitch called after her as he got to his feet. "Dammit, I'm sorry – I was pissed, OK? I just lost it for a second! I didn't mean it!"

Ellie stopped at Mitch's car, then turned back.

"Fuck you and your sex-starved mind!!!" she screamed. "Tell ya what, go invent a time machine - because you're gonna have to prevent the last five minutes from happening before I ever let you touch me again!!!"

She slung open his car door and, in one motion, threw herself in the car and slammed it shut. She then proceeded to quickly slap down the locks to all four doors.

Mitch, hearing the doors lock one by one, muttered, "Oh no."

He ran up to the car and slapped at the window.

"Ellie, I'm sorry," he pleaded. "You pissed me off and I lost it. Please babe, I take it all back!!!"

Ellie violently dropped the bucket seat into the fully reclined position, then just glared at him through her tears.

"I was trying to encourage you!" she screamed with a voice muffled through the windows. "Inspire you, you... you bastard!" She then flipped to her side, turning her back on Mitch.

"You chose *now* to try to inspire me???" Mitch countered incredulously. "*Right now*? When I have *no* laptop, hell – *NO ELECTRICITY*??? Are you *completely fuckin' nuts*???!!!"

"No," the muffled voice replied with a calm indifference. "Apparently, I'm just old."

"Ellie, don't do this to me," Mitch pleaded. "Don't lock me out here!"

Ellie suddenly sat up and slammed two extended middle fingers against the glass and shook them at him like baby rattles. She then lay back down and turned her back to him, curling up in fetal position and remaining motionless.

Mitch rolled his eyes and, in a panic, ran back to the pile of fabric and poles and tried to assemble the tent using the campfire light and a bic lighter. .

"AAARRRRRRGGGGGHHHHHH!!!" he screamed maniacally into the sky after burning his fingers a couple of times on the lighter flame. He threw down the heap of poles and nylon and set off for Chance's campsite.

Mitch followed the lake shore towards Chance and Danni's tent. In the blackness, he spotted a weak source of light muted by tent fabric. He quickened his pace as he approached.

"Oh wow, babe," Chance cooed. "Wait, you brought that? Oh, that's so sweet."

Mitch cringed, knowing he was interrupting the couple.

"Yeah," Danni replied. "But it's not for me."

"Aw, HELL NO," Chance said. "This man is only equipped with a one-way door, missy."

Mitch paused, eyes widening. He then doubled his pace to avoid hearing anything more.

"Aw, come on you, coward," Danni belittled. "You might like it."

"ALRIGHT – STOP!" Mitch yelled.

"Mitch?" Chance called out.

"Yeah, I don't wanna hear anymore!"

Chance's silhouette quickly wrapped itself in blankets and he emerged from the tent as Mitch stood at its entrance.

"Mitch, bud," Chance scrambled, nearly stumbling on the blankets around his waist as he exited the tent. "What's wrong?"

"Ellie's fucking pissed," he sighed. "We never set up the fucking tent, we got in a fight and now she's locked me out of the damn car. She locked me the *fuck out*, dude!"

Danni did a horrible job of stifling a laugh.

"Thanks," Mitch sneered, looking at the tent.

"Sorry..." the voice trailed off from beneath the nylon.

"Dude," Chance said almost apologetically, "Look, I told you to bring the disc tent."

"That's not doing me *any fucking good right now, is it*?" Mitch retorted quickly. "Dude, I got nowhere to sleep!"

"Well," Chance explained with a shrug, "let this be a life lesson for you. Next time, you'll listen to your ol' buddy Chance here."

Mitch looked at him incredulously.

Chance leaned in to whisper to Mitch.

"I'm sorry bud, but don't cock-block me here, please?"

He then stood up and resumed a more-normal volume.

"You're a smart guy," Chance continued. "Figure the tent out. You can do it."

"It's really not that tricky, Mitch," Danni added.

"See?" Chance pointed back at the tent in justification.

Mitch was suddenly torn between feeling betrayed by his best friend and feeling guilty that he was interfering with the night his friend was having - especially since Chance was having the night that Mitch had envisioned having with Ellie.

"Fine!" he growled, "Sorry to bother you two. Enjoy that dildo, bud. I'll *try* not to tell the fellas."

"What...dildo..." Chance replied nervously. "I don't know what you're talking about."

As Mitch walked away, Chance yelled "Come back if you can't get it set up!" while frantically shaking his head "no" and wildly waving him away.

As Mitch returned to the bundle of fabric and the poles, he sighed. Inside, he knew that he wasn't going to be able to assemble this thing. He cleared off the picnic table with an angry swipe of his arm, grabbed the giant wad of fabric and poles, and took one last look at his car parked 100 feet away. One side of him had a broken heart longing for a chance to make things right with the woman in the car, but the other side of him completely hated that very same woman for hijacking his vehicle and leaving him to sleep out in the open wilderness, defenseless.

He wrapped himself wrapped himself up as best he could in the nylon and planted himself atop the picnic bench, the sewn-in poles jutting out and quivering in the night air. He curled into fetal position and went to sleep with a heart full of both worry and anger.

A few drops of morning dew ran down the car window as Ellie awoke and opened the car door. The thick mist and fog that hovered off the ground created an eerie feeling around her, and that feeling was only accentuated by the guilt that Ellie was already beginning to feel as she slowly remembered everything that had happened the night before.

For a moment, she felt a twinge of panic as she wondered where Mitch was and if he was alright. As she frantically looked around, she saw something that resembled an oversized pin cushion crumpled up on the picnic table near the lake, and the hint of a human form within it told her that it was Mitch.

She sighed, relieved that he was both close and alright. She slowly walked up to Mitch, taking her time to make sure she had her justifications ready as she tried to remember everything that was said. As she got to nylon cocoon, she again sighed heavily and gently shook him.

"Mitch, honey," she said apologetically, "hey, wake up."

Mitch mumbled incoherently and repositioned himself.

"Honey," Ellie explained, "I'm sorry. I was drunk, and I was angry, and..."

"And a bitch?" Mitch asked, with his back still turned towards her.

"Yeah," Ellie conceded, suddenly discarding all the excuses she'd prepared in her head. "And a bitch. I deserve that. C'mon, get up. We can talk about..."

Mitch rolled over and sat up.

"OH MY GOD!" Ellie almost yelled.

"What?" Mitch asked, struggling to open his eyes.

"OH MY GOD," Ellie repeated. "Can you breathe?"

"Yeah, I can breathe fine," Mitch snapped. "I think I got something in my eyes last night, but... what's wrong?"

"Um, Mitch..." Ellie tried to remain calm while looking at him, "um, your face..."

"What about my face? What's wrong?"

Chance drove Mitch's car back into town with Danni by his side, and Ellie and Mitch in back.

Somehow last night, something had happened that caused Mitch's face to become so swollen that it had the topography of a beach ball. Every feature was erased by skin that seemed to be straining just to keep everything under his face.

Ellie stared at Mitch's face in disbelief, not sure whether to laugh or pity him.

Danni and Chance, however, did not feel nearly as compassionate.

"Hey Mitch," Chance asked. "I know you sometimes get a little full of yourself, but don't you think you've gone a little overboard this time?" Chance asked.

"What are you talking about?" Mitch mumbled.

"You just kind of got a huge head - *overnight*."

Chance and Danni burst into laughter. Ellie tried to remain quiet due to the guilt of feeling responsible, but she suddenly succumbed to the urge and laughed as well. Mitch just stared out the window.

"Oh Mitch," Danni said, "I forgot to tell you. The Michelin guy's wife called. She wants you to go on Maury with her."

"You... ARE THE FATHER!" Chance continued her thought for her.

"Exactly!" Danni screamed. "Nice catch, Hun!"

Mitch just shook his still-oversized head. "Can we just please stop somewhere and get me some fucking Benadryl?" Mitch pleaded.

"Come on, guys," Ellie announced, trying to be serious through the smile that owned her face. "Leave him alone."

"Okay, okay," Chance said. "Sure dude, next exit with a gas station, we'll pull off."

The car was quiet for a minute or so.

"It's okay, Mitch," Ellie said in a motherly tone. "When we stop, do you want me to get your Blues jersey out of the trunk?"

"What?" Mitch asked. "No. What's that going to do?"

"Well," Ellie said, "You always said you wanted a Blues bobble head in your car, so I just thought you'd..."

Chance started howling with laughter and pounding the steering wheel before Ellie could finish.

"I just thought you wouldn't want to miss the opportunity!" Ellie yelled over her own laughter as Chance and Danni joined in loudly.

Mitch just rolled his eyes, and then couldn't help but laugh a little as well. Yeah, he was still pissed off at Ellie, but that was pretty funny.

"Seriously though, Ellie," Danni spoke up. "You probably don't want to have kids with this guy?"

"Why?" Mitch asked sarcastically. "Because I told you guys I'm allergic to camping?"

"Uh, nooo, Mr. Sensitive," she said with feigned condescension, "I was more concerned about Ellie and the size of the skull she'd have to push out."

"Oh dear God," Ellie said as her eyes widened at the thought.

Mitch just sighed loudly.

"I mean," Danni continued. "If you did have his kid, at least you'd know to name him Jack."

"*Jack*?" Chance asked confusedly.

"Yeah, after the fast-food guy," Danni smiled. "Heck Ellie, *you* may have to go on Maury to find out who's the father."

Everyone laughed more loudly. Mitch wasn't smiling anymore. The joke was old, and he was once again tired of being the butt of the jokes. He just stared blankly out the car window... as best he could through his swollen eyelids, anyway.

"That reminds me," Ellie added. "I'm hungry."

CHAPTER 27

IF YOU LAY YOUR CARDS ON THE TABLE,
I'LL LAY MY LOVE ON THE LINE

Monday morning came too soon for Mitch. Even though his face had finally deflated a few hours after they'd gotten home, he was still a little out-of-sorts from the weekend and the fifteen Benadryl it took to get his head back to regulation size.

When he'd dropped Ellie off, she had tried to talk to him, but he made up a lame excuse about not feeling well and just wanting to go home. Even though Ellie knew inside that he was lying, that he was still angry, she'd acquiesced and gave him his space.

Mitch was only partially paying attention to the work he was churning out. He was mostly debating within himself about whether he wanted to proceed with Ellie as he typed away feverishly. He knew he didn't want to lose her, and maybe she wasn't *completely* wrong about him getting started on the novel, but he wasn't going to let what happened just slide, either. There was no way she was going to think she could pull that again with him. As he slugged it out with his keyboard, his desk phone rang. Without looking at the number, he answered.

"Mitch Paulson."

"Hi sweetie, it's Ellie."

"Hi," Mitch replied as indifferently as he could say it. For a moment, he was mad at himself for not checking the caller ID first. If he had, and had seen it was Ellie, he wouldn't have answered.

"Listen Mitch, I'm really sorry about this weekend," Ellie began. "I was just in a really bad place, and I was pissed off about a lot of things, and I got drunk, and then I took them all out on you."

"OK," Mitch replied flippantly.

"Besides," Ellie justified, "that was the wrong time to mention my butt and the play in the same sentence."

"And that makes locking me out of my car to sleep in the woods OK?" Mitch snapped back.

"No, but..."

"This apology is sounding more like a justification," Mitch deadpanned.

"Aw, come on," Ellie pleaded. "Give me another chance."

"OH!" Mitch replied. "OK, then. Please hold," he said coldly.

Ellie then heard a series of clicks followed by muzak from The Carpenters.

"This is Chance," Chance answered.

"Chance?" Ellie asked. "I was trying to talk to Mitch."

"Oh," Chance replied, "OK."

Ellie then heard another series of clicks, followed by the muzak for Muskrat Love.

"Mitch Paulson," Mitch answered.

"Very funny," Ellie deadpanned. "Can we finish our conversation?"

"Sure," Mitch replied. "I think you were somewhere in the middle of groveling, then took a left turn into 'I'm-not-totally-wrongsville'."

"OK look, I'm a bitch, OK?" Ellie confessed. "Lemme take you out to dinner and make it up to you."

This out-of-the-blue offer, coupled with Ellie's obvious urgency to make it up to him, made Mitch pause and think.

With everything that happened over the weekend - a camping trip which he didn't even want to do in the first place, the fight, the tent, and his face inflating to the point that it looked like he'd been raped by a bicycle pump - he wanted to stay mad at this woman, at least for a little while. But he couldn't. He couldn't even fake irritation anymore. Maybe it was the fact that she was so worried about him being angry with her that made him realize it, or maybe it was the fact that even though his mind was telling him to dump her, his heart wouldn't even consider it. Regardless of the reason, it suddenly hit him like a ton of bricks. He was in love with her.

"OK," Mitch replied, his growl slowly changing into a smile. "Should I pick you up at eight?"

"No, it's gotta be an early night," Ellie pleaded. "Can we make it six? I've got another audition tomorrow that just came up. And I've got to practice my lines."

"OK, I'll see you at six." Mitch agreed.

"Thanks, honey." Ellie sighed.

They both walked in to the Broadway Blues bar, the site of their first date. But as Mitch walked in, he felt like that he was fielding hateful stares from the bar's faithful patrons. He tried to keep his head down as they walked to the table. Ironically, it was also the same table where Mitch and Ellie had sat for their first date. They smiled at the waitress as she delivered the menus. Mitch leaned back, ran his hand through his hair and sighed.

"What's wrong?" Ellie asked.

"Nothing," Mitch replied, "just a long day, that's all. I'm actually just happy to see you."

"Me too," Ellie replied. "Hey, I just wanted a little time with you. I'm really sorry about the whole camping trip fiasco."

Mitch shrugged in forgiveness.

"By the way, you know Claire is getting married next month, right?"

"Yeah."

"Well, she needs ushers, at least Mother says she does," Ellie explained. "Would you and Chance be interested in being ushers for my sister's wedding?"

Mitch mulled it over in his head wondering about being in a wedding involving Ellie's family.

"Yeah, no problem" he answered.

"Great! It would be a big help to her and I would *love* to see you in a tuxedo," she said smiling.

As the waitress approached with an expressionless face, Mitch thought she was the waitress from the last visit but wasn't positive.

"The manager said if you plan to go anywhere near the stage you need to let us know, so we can unplug the black lights," she said indifferently.

Mitch suddenly recognized her as their first waitress. "I don't know wha..." he replied, opting for denial.

"It's nothing personal sir," she continued, "It's just that, well, the bassist just got his cast off a few weeks ago and can finally play again. And Smokey, the lead singer has also just..."

"The blind guy?" Mitch interrupted.

"Yeah, that's him," the waitress nodded.

"Come on, how could I have hurt him? He's blind!" Mitch pleaded.

"Yeah, well, he's been blind since birth, but that night he swore he saw something, and he was so convinced he could see that he tried driving himself home. He was lost for two days."

"Nu-uh! Are you serious?" Ellie asked. "Where was he?"

"Oh, it's OK, *now,*" she answered. "We found him three blocks over in a warehouse truck lot with the rear wheels propped up on a fence post he'd driven over. So, just let us know first if you're going to go see the band, okay?"

"Uh, OK," Mitch agreed as Ellie, who had just noticed the same hate-filled glares, slowly lowered her head as well.

"Um, could I get a beer and Chablis for her?" he asked.

"No, Mitch," Ellie answered, "I have about thirty lines I have to memorize tonight and I really need this job."

"OK, suit yourself," Mitch sighed. "I just thought you might like to have a drink while you read this," Mitch said as he pulled out a folder.

"What is this?" she asked.

"Well, it's a promise," Mitch offered.

"What kind of promise?"

"A promise to give you the other chapters as soon as they're written."

"The novel?!"

"Well, the first two chapters. Talking to your dad at Christmas really got me thinking, and after what happened this weekend, well... I realized that I need to get going on this. So, today, at work, I popped out the first two chapters. I want you to read them and tell me what you think."

"I'll read them, you know that, but I don't know what my opinion will be worth. I'm probably not going to be much help."

"That's not what your dad said," Mitch said as he handed her the folder, smiled and took a long drink from his beer. "So, can I get you that Chablis?" he offered again with a smile.

"Okay, but just one."

He watched Ellie read it with apprehension as the waitress dropped off their drinks. He watched her eyes, her facial expressions, her sighs and laughs, waiting on any cue to get an inside track on what part of the story she was at and what she was thinking. He was pretty sure that he could guess which sentence she was reading by her reaction, still...it wasn't enough. Her opinion meant everything to him. He struggled with his patience as she read.

Ellie finished, handed it back to Mitch, and smiled.

"You're such a good writer," she gushed. "When are you going to finish the next chapter?"

Mitch was a little confused by the question.

"Are you asking me because you're excited to read more, or are you just trying to 'inspire' me again?"

"Of course I want to read more, and since you put these two chapters together so quickly today, you could have the whole *novel* done in just a few weeks, right?"

"Hey," Mitch replied, a little annoyed by her comment, "it's not like I just started thinking about the story this morning and popped out the first two chapters after lunch. This has been formulating in my head for a few years now. I have a general outline of the story, but the details still have to be created. It's not simply a matter of typing it out."

"Hey, I'm not saying it's just data entry," Ellie replied. "But, just imagine if you had started this a few years ago. You would probably already be published *and* living the dream. I just wish I was as in control of my destiny the way that you do. I have to wait to be picked as best out of a hundred other women who are reading the exact same lines. I have to do it perfectly, according to this particular director's criteria, and somehow have to stand out from the rest."

"Ya know, it's not nearly as easy as you make it sound," Mitch scorned. "I have to actually create something from nothing. Do you realize how difficult that *is*? Do you know how many Sci-Fi books there are on the market right now? Well, of course you do, your old man has nine of them in publication himself!

"So, somehow, mine has to be different from all of them. It has to be something original. I mean, since it's sci-fi, it helps that I can make up the names and the places, but then I have to track all that stuff throughout the book! I know it sounds trivial, but it's a pain in the ass - especially when you don't want to lose the message by simply trying to blow your readers' minds with outrageous tales of the fantastic."

"Mitch, I know," Ellie nodded. "I grew up with my dad, you know."

Mitch took the last drink of beer.

"Then you should know you can't knock one of these out in a few weeks like you just said, not even a few months! Hell, I *wish* writing a novel was as easy as going in, regurgitating a few lines I memorized on the way to the audition, giggling, and maybe shaking my stuff a little for the director."

Two guys at a nearby table laughed as they overheard Mitch, but most people – including Ellie – just glared at him for being just another asshole treating his date badly. When he looked back from laughing with the college boys at the next table, the smile left his face immediately.

Ellie had simply put some money on the table and was quickly putting on her coat.

"Hey, I was just exaggerating, babe." he said with as much contrition he could muster. "Just tryin' to get my point across, ya know?"

Ellie looked at him very hard.

"Mitch, I was not at all trying to diminish what you're trying to create, and I hope you know that," she sneered. "If this is payback for yesterday – and, God, I truly hope it is - then let's call it even and leave it at that. But if what you said to me is how you truly feel about me and my dream, then I don't see any reason for us to continue."

Her words made reality crash back in onto Mitch like a meteor - and the knot in his gut reinforced the realization that he'd gone too far.

Ellie turned and began to walk away.

Mitch sat there for a second – unsure if he should pursue her or let her walk out and cool off. He then leapt up.

"Okay, okay," he said as he grabbed her arm. "Come on, sit back down."

She just stared at him blankly.

"Please," he begged.

As they started walking back to the table, Mitch continued.

"I'm sorry, it's just... I don't know. I wanted you to read it, hopefully like it, and just, I don't know, be happy for me."

"And I am!" Ellie said emphatically.

"Then please," Mitch begged again, "please just ease up on the pressuring. I just wanted to enjoy a victory lap tonight after I finished the first two chapters. But I felt like you thought this was easy, that anybody can do it. All I wanted was to celebrate finally starting on it for real... ya know, talk about the characters and story? Then I got offended and I took it too far. Believe me when I tell you I won't ever try to diminish what you do ever again."

"Okay," Ellie half-smiled. "So, we agree that neither of our dreams are easy or stupid, deal?'

"Deal," Mitch agreed enthusiastically.

"Alright then, let's just pretend these past two days never happened." Ellie offered.

"But... not *everything* in the past two days was bad," Mitch snickered.

"Well, no, I guess not," Ellie smiled.

"You know, Ellie," Mitch continued. "These little conflicts we've had, it's been kind of good, in a way."

"What?" Ellie scoffed.

"It's made me realize how much you mean to me," Mitch continued. "I know it sounds crazy, but these little battles we've had made me think about what my life might be like without you, and... well, I didn't like seeing a future where we didn't work. If things work out the way I think they're going to... well, let's just say that I gotta have you around."

Ellie felt her cheeks flush as she silently smiled.

"A man can't live without his muse," Mitch continued. "And I'm not about to lose mine."

"No, you're not," Ellie replied

CHAPTER 28

WHAT IS THE NAME TO CALL
FOR A DIFFERENT KIND OF GIRL

At Hair Solutions, the Pet Shop Boys were playing over the speakers. Ellie was at the front desk reading a six-month-old issue of Cosmo and trying to block out the mundane conversations around her that she normally conducted with every customer.

She thought that she had done well in the auditions earlier this morning, but even through the dialogues, she still heard Mitch's words about her dream. She'd had no clients all morning, so it gave her more time to ponder what Mitch had said last night. And even though he had apologized, for some reason, it still bothered her.

The phone rang, and she rolled her eyes, sighed, and tossed the magazine on the glass case in front of her.

"Hair Solutions," she answered tersely.

"Hi, may I speak to Ellie, please?" Mitch asked.

"Speaking."

"Hi," Mitch replied with a smile.

"Hello. What's up?" she said, matter-of-factly.

"OK, what's wrong?" Mitch asked, immediately feeling the cold verbal shoulder she was giving him.

"Nothing," Ellie deadpanned. "How are you?"

"Um, fine," Mitch replied, not believing a word of it, "Hey, can you come over tonight?"

"No," she replied.

"Um, OK," Mitch again, proceeding cautiously. "Why not?"

"Are you sure you don't think us actors are all stupid ditzes?"

"Ellie, we discussed this," Mitch pleaded.

"I know, but that really hurt. I'm just wondering if you really do care about my dreams. I mean, you haven't even asked about the auditions this morning!"

Mitch, stunned, just started chuckling.

"Babe, I've been on the phone with you for, what, thirty seconds? I was going to ask you about..."

"Well, if you'd had, you'd know that I got a callback for tomorrow," Ellie replied with a pout.

"Aw, see? That's great, babe!"

"And *that's* why I can't come over tonight."

"Well then, I'll come to you," Mitch replied.

"No Mitch, I need to concentrate."

"I'll help," Mitch smiled. "C'mon – you need someone to read the other lines, don't you?"

"Fine. Six P.M.," she ordered. "Sharp."

"See ya then," Mitch chuckled.

Later that evening, Ellie sat at her kitchen table reading the script for her audition. She read a line and said it to herself numerous times, each time placing emphasis on a different word until it sounded natural. She then stood up in her kitchen, trying to visualize the staging and the camera's location, and then incorporated her body into the delivery.

Somewhat satisfied, she went to the next line and repeated the drill.

As six P.M.-*ish* arrived, there was a knock at the door. She pulled the curtains back, and Mitch's giddy face was nearly pressed against the window.

"Hi honey," he said as she opened the door. "Guess what? I've got something I need you to see."

"Mitch, I..." she began as she pulled the papers from the folder. "Is this..."

"Well," Mitch said, trying to act humble, "just chapters *three through five*, but yeah!" his words quickened. "I sat down today and told myself I needed to keep going. Before I knew it, I had the next three chapters written."

"OK, but Mitch," Ellie pleaded. "I know I've been pressuring you about this, but I've got to be ready for the audition tomorrow."

"I know," Mitch smiled widely. "Can you at least read chapter three for me really quick?"

"What, right now?"

"Um, yeah..." Mitch nodded eagerly.

Ellie looked into Mitch's eyes and realized how important this was to him.

"Alright," she sighed as she rolled her eyes and sat down.

Mitch sat there quietly as she read. He studied her features, and thought to himself how much he loved everything about her – her hair, her nose, the way she moved her lips while she read. This woman had gotten into his life like no other woman had, and her opinion meant everything to him.

As Ellie read, Mitch patiently waited for her to finish. To his surprise, she didn't stop at Chapter Three. She kept reading until there were no more pages left to read.

"Mitch," Ellie quivered. "Oh my God."

"Yeah?" Mitch asked, hoping she liked it.

"You named a character after me?" Ellie sighed.

"Well, yeah... a *minor* character," Mitch teased. "I'm kidding, she's going to have an important role in Jacob's future."

"It's... incredible," she replied. "It's so vivid, the characters... and... and I hate the fact that there's nothing more to read right now. Wow, Mitch. Just wow."

"Awesome!" Mitch yelled. Yeah, I can't wait to finish it."

"I'm happy for you Mitch," Ellie smiled as she leaned in and kissed him.

"Thanks!" Mitch smiled. "Now, your turn. Let me help you practice your lines."

"OK," Ellie agreed. "Here, you read the part of 'Man'."

Mitch turned his copy of the script to face him. Ellie stood up from the table and instantly flashed her "happy spokeswoman" smile.

"You know," Ellie began reading, "My husband and I have been together for fifteen years now."

"Yep," Mitch read along, "We have four beautiful kids and are very active in the church."

"We couldn't have asked for more," Ellie continued. "We pretty much have the perfect life together. So you can imagine how relieved I was to discover that there's now just one pill that relieves both of my conditions."

"We *both* were," Mitch answered, following the script. "And that's why we're thrilled about this new drug... aw, *hell no*." Mitch said as his eyes instantly widened.

"Mitch!" Ellie yelled, dropping out of character.

"You *can't* read for this part," Mitch stated.

"Why not???" Ellie insisted.

"Because!"

"Read it!" Ellie insisted, pointing at the script.

"Babe, have you considered..."

"READ THE *DAMN LINE!*"

Mitch cringed and let out a loud sigh, then resumed reading.

"And that's why we're thrilled about this new drug..." he cringed, "...*Herpadone*,"

"That's right, honey," Ellie said as she resumed character without missing a beat. "Just one tablet a day both shortens the duration of my herpes flair ups while also controlling my urges for heroin."

"I can't do this..." Mitch muttered, falling out of character again.

"YOU SAID YOU'D HELP!"

"Ugh," Mitch sighed. "Great, I'm going to be seen in public with the spokeswoman for herpes-infested heroin-addicts."

"JUST READ!"

"Fine!" Mitch acquiesced as he sank further into his chair with each word. "Without Herpadone, I might have never met her. But now we can share a *wonderful life* together while managing the mistakes of her past."

"Hey, no one's perfect," Ellie shrugged as she again returned to character, smiling like Vanna White. "But with Herpadone, you don't have to pay for your mistakes for the rest of your life. Herpadone is not right for all people. People using Herpadone should not use heroin within twenty-four hours of taking Herpadone. Most side effects include headache, nausea, and dry mouth. In rare instances, people taking Herpadone reported bloody discharge, uncontrollable flatulence, oily stool, and feelings of depression. If you begin to feel suicidal or experience sudden urges for random acts of violence towards those in your immediate vicinity, stop taking Herpadone and seek medical attention immediately."

Ellie then stood up taller and smiled.

"Ask your doctor if Herpadone is right for you. I know I did."

"No, honey... *I* did." Mitch mockingly smiled like a bad actor.

"That's not in the script!" Ellie scolded.

"It should be..." Mitch commented. "Where'd this church-going father of four find this tramp? An outreach program?"

"Are you going to help me with this or not?"

"No." Mitch said plainly as he started to pace back and forth in her kitchen.

"Why not?"

"Because I don't want to be seen dating a disease-carrying smack whore from TV."

"Mitch," Ellie pleaded. "It's just a commercial! And this stuff probably really helps people."

"Tide helps people!" Mitch countered. "Couldn't you find a detergent commercial? I bet NASCAR forbids open-sore-riddled-opium-queens from being spokespeople!"

"Mitch," she insisted, all the while trying not to laugh at Mitch's absurd tirade, "if I were the Tide spokeswoman..."

"How about condoms? Didn't Trojan need a Magnum spokeswoman? Now that's a woman I'd be proud to be seen with in public. Or, weren't there at least any *curable* VD drug ads available? Come on – *you've* met my friends! I'll - no, *you'll* never live it down. *Please* don't be the heroin herpes girl."

"Mitch," she laughed. "I think you're overreacting."

"How many people are actually competing for this role, anyway?" Mitch continued undaunted. "I mean, shouldn't you get the part for just showing up and being willing to have your face tied to *smack* and *herpes*?"

Still laughing, Ellie tried to explain.

"Look Mitch, I need to enhance my portfolio with some work."

"Yeah, but..." Mitch insisted.

"And it pays $4000.00 for a day's work."

Mitch shot a blank stare at her.

"OK," he suddenly replied, "from the top, then?"

CHAPTER 29

SO SPEND SOME TIME
AND SHOW YOU CARE

Over the next month, Mitch and Ellie seemed to
fluctuate between growing closer and fading away. Some
days seemed to be better than others for both of them, but
most of the arguments came from Ellie's newfound general
irritability. Mitch merely chalked it up to "that time of the
month," but he'd become so engrossed in working on the
novel that he didn't notice that her "time of the month" had
stretched into the entire month.

Mitch had re-doubled his efforts on the novel, sneaking
time away from his manuals at work to write it. And while
maintaining his rabid lifestyle of going out with Ellie, or
the boys – or both – to happy hours, Blues games, or local
plays (Ellie's idea), and trying to keep up with deadlines at
work, well... his life had gotten more hectic, but in a good
way. Mitch started to feel like he was in more control of his
life than ever. Even though he had recently discovered the
horror and necessity of "re-writing", he still had the woman

of his dreams, he was still working towards the career of his dreams, and he was still able keep his old lifestyle and circle of friends. His confidence was never higher.

Ellie, on the other hand, was feeling like her dreams were slipping away. Yes, she was finding semi-steady work in local commercials while keeping her day job, but with all the time and money she was spending with Mitch, she began to wonder if she was ever going to save enough money to go to New York. And even if she ever was able to save enough money, she also began to wonder if Mitch would be willing to move there with her when that time came – especially considering Mitch seemed pretty happy in St. Louis with his friends. And that thought began to weigh on her, because while one side of her didn't want to lose Mitch, the other side didn't want her to lose *herself*.

And that was the true source of her sudden irritability, even though she may not have been fully aware of it. To make matters worse, since Ellie wasn't leaving for New York any time soon, she didn't really feel the need to resolve what was bothering her just yet.

The other reason she'd been blowing off her concerns was because any free time she did have was being consumed by helping her sister Claire with her wedding. And since it was approaching fast, any New York plans – or any other worries - weren't even going to be considered until Claire was happily off on her honeymoon.

On the eve of Claire's wedding, Ellie was nearly as stressed as Claire, with numerous last-minute arrangements that still needed attention. She knew that she didn't have much to worry about when it came to Mitch, but she often wondered why she'd even asked Chance to be an usher in the first place. And being the human wild card that Chance was, Ellie was taking no chances.

Claire was already spending the night with Ellie so she could help her get ready in the morning. But just to make sure Chance didn't show up smelling like a bottle of whiskey (or worse, *didn't show up at all*), she also had asked Mitch and Chance to spend the night at her place.

On the drive over to Ellie's, Chance was giving Mitch an earful about having to spend the night at Ellie's house. Mitch wasn't exactly enamored with the idea, either – considering it was first game of the first round of the playoffs that very night, and the Blues were going up against the Blackhawks. But considering how everything had been going between he and Ellie over the last few weeks, he decided it was a good idea to appease her.

As they pulled onto her street, the usual row of neighbor's cars lined the street in front of her house. With Ellie's father's Bentley in the driveway, Mitch had to park on the street as well - directly behind Lawrence's Hummer.

As they grabbed their bags and began walking up to the house, Chance was still complaining relentlessly. Suddenly, his voice trailed off.

"Whoa!" he said. "Who's fuckin' Bentley?"

"Oh," Mitch answered. "That's Chris's car. He's letting Claire use it for the wedding."

"Who the fuck is Chris?" Chance demanded.

"Ellie's Dad, remember? I told you about him after Christmas."

"Dude, you have *got* to marry this girl." Chance said as he gawked at the car.

"I'll do my best," Mitch sighed.

As they got to the front door of Ellie's house with duffle bags in hand, Ellie opened the door. Once Chance saw Ellie, he resumed his tirade.

"Ya know, Ellie, you really don't... trust..." Chance began stuttering uncomfortably as he walked into Ellie's family room. As Mitch caught up to Chance, they both stood silently for a second, absorbing the implications of the fold-out bed that she had prepared for both of them.

"Aw", hell no," Chance instantly dismissed.

"What?" Ellie asked.

"No way am I sleeping in the same bed as *him*," Chance seethed while glaring at Mitch.

"No shit," Mitch sneered back.

"Boys, c'mon!" Ellie pleaded as she stepped in between them. "What's the problem?"

"Are you serious?" Mitch asked.

"You guys are roommates, I thought... " Ellie began.

"No, obviously you didn't," Mitch interrupted.

"You two are the biggest homophobes I know," Ellie sneered.

"We're NOT homophobes!" Chance barked. "We're dudes. And dudes don't sleep together!"

"Guys," Ellie pleaded. "It's just one night."

"What, you think is Fear Factor?" Chance continued. "I am NOT spooning Mitch!"

"Damn right you're not!" Mitch added. "If anyone's getting spooned, it's you, bitch."

"GUYS!" Ellie yelled. "Knock it off!"

"Babe," Mitch asked, "why can't we just sleep in your room, and Danni and Chance sleep in here?"

"Hush!" Ellie whispered strongly. "Claire's in the back room, Mitch. You know how she is about her 'values'. She's been with Jack for the past 2 years and she doesn't believe in pre-marital activity. I want to respect that."

"But her God is OK with me spooning Mitch for eight hours?" Chance scoffed.

"Try to spoon me, and we'll see exactly how that'll turn out." Mitch threatened.

"ALRIGHT, ALRIGHT, FINE!" Ellie screamed as she stormed to the bed, flung the blankets across the room, and slung the fold-away back into the couch. "Make your own damn beds! You two figure out who gets the loveseat."

"DIBS ON THE SOFA!" they both announced simultaneously, then turned and glared at each other.

Chance then turned to Ellie.

"Look, what's up with this 'making us sleep here tonight' crap, anyway? You *really* don't trust us, do you...?"

"Um, hello?" Ellie replied. "This is my sister's wedding tomorrow, Chance. You volunteered to help set up chairs and be ushers."

"Um, correction," Chance interrupted. "*Mitch* volunteered us."

"Regardless," Ellie continued. "The rental people will be here at 7:30 in the morning, and you boys have to be ready to go. We've got 300 chairs to set up and only a half an hour to do it."

"What's this 'we' shit?" Chance sneered.

"Uuuuugh," Ellie groaned in frustration. "*You two* will only have about an hour to get them set up, then *you've* got to shower, get in your tuxes, and be ready to seat people by 10:30. Mother says the guests should start arriving by then, so we won't have a lot of time."

"Yeah, but we still could've been here on our own by 7:30," Chance said, shaking his head back and forth with wide eyes.

Ellie just glared at him incredulously.

"Chance, the only place you've ever been - except your bed - at 7:30 in the morning is at one of those all-night bars."

Chance pointed right at Mitch while Mitch was getting his blankets laid out on the couch.

"Dude, OK, first? Stop it. I get the couch! STOP IT!" he pounded on the back of the couch. "Second," he growled under his breath at Mitch, "you gotta stop talking about the fuckin' strip clubs, *I mean it*!"

"Dude!" Mitch retorted. "*She* said 'bar', not strip club! You just tipped your own hand there."

Danni walked through the room in the middle of the conversation.

"Not listening!" she announced as she kept her head down and walked into Ellie's room, never breaking her gait.

"Boys, PLEASE!" Ellie pleaded, putting her hands in a prayer position and briefly bending her knees. "My sister is my best friend and this is her big day! You two can't screw this up for her! Just PLEASE do what I'm asking, just this once."

"Fine," Chance sighed and slung his pillow onto the loveseat.

Mitch walked up to Ellie and put his hands around her waist.

"Look babe," he comforted. "We're here, OK? We're here, on the couches, just on the other side of the door. We'll be right here if you need us for anything. If we need to start earlier, to load the car, run to the store - *anything*. We're here, it's under control - nothing's gonna go wrong now, OK?"

"Mitch, look," she began, "you don't understand. I'm just..."

"*OK?*" Mitch insisted.

Ellie sighed and agreed.

"OK," she smiled as she kissed him. "Thank you for helping me. I'm glad you're here."

"I am too, I just wish I was in *there*," Mitch replied, pointing his eyes at Ellie's bedroom door.

"Oh, honey, I do too. We just can't tonight with Claire here, OK?"

"OK," Mitch growled.

She kissed him on his nose.

"OK then. I'm going to... oops! Better hang daddy's keys up!" she announced as she walked to the kitchen door and hung the keys on the hook. "OK, *now* I'm going to bed. It's going to be a looong day tomorrow, so don't stay up all night, alright boys?"

"Sure, mom," Chance groaned.

Mitch just shook his head.

"At least keep the TV down for me, will you, honey?"

"Absolutely, babe," Mitch replied and pecked her on the lips. "Goodnight."

"Goodnight."

Mitch walked back around the couch and saw his blankets and pillows on the floor next to the loveseat. Chance was situating his blankets on the couch.

"Hey!" Mitch protested. "What the fuck?"

"What?" Chance said indifferently as he continued to prepare the couch. "You volunteered me, you got me stuck in your girlfriend's house against my will – ON A FRIDAY NIGHT WHEN THE BLUES ARE PLAYING GAME ONE OF THE PLAYOFFS – and *now* you expect me to sleep on the loveseat? Nuh-uh."

"It's *my* girlfriend's house," Mitch insisted.

"It's *my* back that's gonna be setting up chairs for Saint Claire's little ceremony so she can finally get laid with a clean conscience," Chance countered. "You wanna mess that up?"

Mitch, knowing he needed Chance's help more than he needed the big couch, gave in.

"Fine," he growled.

They both prepped their makeshift beds, giving each other the silent treatment the entire time. Chance turned to Mitch after setting up the couch.

"Gimme your keys."

"Why?" Mitch asked, still angry about losing the couch.

"I got a surprise for you, bud."

Mitch slung the keys at Chance, who grabbed them in mid-stride and walked out of Ellie's front door. As Mitch finished setting up the loveseat, Chance re-emerged through the door, carrying a cooler, a bag of chips, and Blues jerseys. He laughed wickedly as he put the cooler down and slung a jersey at Mitch.

"Who's your boy?" he smiled proudly.

"ALRIGHT!" Mitch replied as he slipped the jersey over his head. "You da MAN!"

"That's right," Chance nodded, "and that's why I'd be spooning you, bitch!"

As Chance circled around the couch, he admired the large armoire with its massive doors standing in front of the couches. He knew Ellie came from money and just envisioned the majestic flat screen television that must be waiting behind those rich oak doors.

"Rich just called while I was outside," Chance said. "He said the pre-game festivities just ended and the game's about to start. Open those doors and 'Game On'!" he proclaimed.

Mitch grabbed a beer from the cooler, walked to the armoire, and opened the doors, revealing a 13-inch RCA tube television that looked like something Goodwill wouldn't accept.

Chance's face just sunk at the immense cavern that housed the tiny television. The whole thing screamed "travesty" to his sensibilities.

"What the fuck is *that*?" he asked.

"What?" Mitch replied. "It's a TV."

"I hate you more right now than I've ever hated anyone in my entire life," Chance replied numbly.

"C'mon dude," Mitch said. "We can pull the couches closer."

The first period wore on, and Chance and Mitch screamed and howled at each close play. As the period came to a close, the boys suddenly erupted as the Blues tied the game with less than a minute to go.

"Can you two *possibly keep it down*?" Danni yelled from behind Ellie's bedroom door.

"Sorry baby," Chance replied meekly. "Wait, are you in bed with Ellie?"

"Um... yeah..." Danni replied softly, with the seductive uncertainty of a porn star. "But don't come in, we're both naked."

Chance and Mitch turned and looked at each other for about a half-second with eyes wider than the English Channel, then simultaneously leapt over their respective sofas like Olympic hurdlers and sprinted to the bedroom door.

As Chance reached for the doorknob, the door slung open. In the doorway stood Danni and Ellie – both fully dressed in coverall silk pajamas and glaring harshly at the boys with their arms crossed.

Chance and Mitch's smiles sank instantly. Danni reached out and lightly smacked Chance's face.

"Seriously?" she said, rolling her eyes in disgust. "You thought we were in here on top of each other? This is how bright my boyfriend is? I can't believe I let you sleep with me!"

Chance kept his little-boy-caught-being-bad face and giving her his "I'm sorry" puppy eyes.

Mitch then pointed at Chance's face and openly mocked him.

"AHAHAHAHAHA!"

Danni reached out and smacked Mitch's face, instantly silencing his mocking laugh and causing him to immediately switch to *his* best sorry-puppy-dog face as well.

"That's for thinking you could join Chance in his orgy..." she continued her scolding. "What, do you think Ellie is some porn-star-in-waiting? I can't believe Ellie lets you sleep with her, either."

Ellie tried to disguise her laugh by coughing and turning away. She then turned back to admire the view of these two grown men being reduced to "I'm sorry, Mommy" expressions.

"GO............TO..............BED," Danni ordered.

The boys turned obediently toward the couches and walked away.

As Danni closed the door, she and Ellie stifled their laughter as best they could and hugged.

"That was awesome," Ellie whispered.

"I told you," Danni whispered, "I grew up with three older brothers, I know how to handle boys."

'You're gonna make a great mom someday," Ellie quipped.

"So long as I only have boys," Danni added.

As Mitch and Chance slowly trudged back to the couches, they both flipped themselves over the back of them and plopped onto the cushions.

"That was uncool," Chance pouted.

"Totally," Mitch agreed.

The second period came and went without either team scoring, and both Chance and Mitch kept their voices down... as best they could. The TV commercials and intermission reports took what seemed an eternity, but they both remained sprawled out and motionless like any other common form of vegetation. Finally, as the third period was about to begin, they both sat up. As the camera zoomed in on the center ice dot, the TV picture suddenly went black, quickly followed by "Technical Difficulties" emblazoned across the screen.

"Holy shit!" Mitch exclaimed. "What the fuck???"

"You got the game?" Chance said into his phone as Mitch turned to look at him. Chance had always had Budgie's on speed dial, and he was already talking to Renee.

"Who are you talking to?" Mitch asked.

"Cool," Chance replied as he hung up.

Chance turned to Mitch and whispered urgently. "Renee says they still have the game. We should run to Budgie's really quick to catch the third period."

"Okay. Wait. What? No!" Mitch exclaimed. "You're crazy!"

"C'mon Mitch – it's the first game of the playoffs," Chance whispered more loudly. "The girls are obviously asleep – they were exhausted when we got here from doing wedding stuff all day. We're just five minutes away from Budgie's!"

"And what if we get caught?" Mitch countered.

"*And what if we get caaaaught...*" Chance mocked. "Grow a pair, you *wuss!* So what if we get caught? If we get caught, it'll be when we're sneaking back in here after the game. Ellie and Danni are totally asleep now. If they find out, they'll be a little pissed, but they'll get over it because we'll still be here in the morning so they can work us to death. In the end, nothing will go wrong with Claire's wedding - so there's no harm, no foul."

"Chance, dude, Ellie's kind of a light sleeper," Mitch countered with uncertainty.

"And your car is parked five cars down the road! Behind Lawrence's *fuckin'* HUMMER! She'll never know whose car is being started."

"I don't know," Mitch hedged. "This wedding thing is really important to her. She insisted that we spend the night if we're gonna do this."

"And we ARE spending the NIGHT!" Chance whispered angrily. "Or didn't you notice your feet hanging off the loveseat? Look, we've waited four years for the Blues to even get back into the playoffs! We're grown men. We can handle this – hell, we *deserve* this!"

Mitch sat there in the darkness of the "Technical Difficulties" image on the screen.

He glared at Chance.

Chance just glared back waiting for a response, even though he already knew Mitch was going to give in. He was just waiting for Mitch to convince himself enough to say "OK."

"Hmmm... no harm, no foul?" Mitch asked.

Chance just smiled.

"No harm, no foul," he restated. "But if we wuss out and not catch this third period – buddy, that's a match penalty, a game misconduct, and we should expect a stiff fine from the league!"

Mitch lifted his head over the back of his loveseat and looked at Ellie's bedroom door as it reflected the flickering light from the TV. He stared at the door intently, as if by doing so he'd be able to tell if Ellie and Danni were truly asleep. Thinking he was going to regret this, he sat up and began sliding his jeans on.

"Yeah?" Chance popped up and whispered. "Really? Alright Mitch! I knew there was a man in there *somewhere*!"

As Mitch stood up to grab his wallet, he leaned over.

Do you think you could possibly shut your fuckin' pie hole long enough for us to get out of this house without getting caught?" he whispered forcefully.

Chance, realizing Mitch's point, changed his expression from excited teenager to serious businessman.

"Oh, yeah, sure dude," he whispered. "Done."

CHAPTER 30

THIS IS MY ESCAPE,
YES I'M ON MY WAY

Mitch gently closed the side door of Ellie's house, and, hearing the click of the latch, they swallowed their laughter, and scurried down the driveway. Once at the street, they switched to a full-on sprint towards Mitch's car.

Mitch quickly unlocked his car, leaned over and unlocked the other side as Chance slid in. Mitch then heard the ding of his car as he inserted the key.

"And we're off," Chance proudly announced.

But as Mitch turned the key, the ding fell silent and all the interior lights faded to black.

Mitch released his twist on the key and the dinging and lights returned.

"Oh no," Mitch pleaded. "Not now, baby. Please don't – not now!'"

"No no no no NOOOO!!!" Chance pleaded.

"Come on, girl!" Mitch begged as he turned the key again, only to have the dinging vanish and the lights dim again.

"C'mon, baby. Don't do this to me now!" he again pleaded as he turned the key repeatedly. "You know I love you!"

But the car was apparently indifferent to Mitch's pleas. Mitch then slammed his hand on the steering wheel.

"DAMMIT!" Mitch yelled.

"Well, Mitch," Chance replied calmly. "Guess there's only one thing left to do."

"I know, bud. I'm sorry my car's acting up. We'll just have to catch the next game."

"Oh no," Chance countered as he stepped out of the car. "I didn't say anything about giving up."

Mitch got out of his car and rested his arms on the roof of his dead vehicle.

"Well, we won't make it to Budgie's in time if we walk," he said, "unless you've got a battery charger up your ass..."

"Mitch," Chance replied calmly as he gazed at car in the driveway. "We'll take the Bentley."

Mitch's eyes nearly popped out of his head at the sheer absurdity of Chance's suggestion.

"WHAT? NO! No way, forget it!""

Chance just sneered at Mitch.

"Mitch, the keys are hanging right by the kitchen door."

"No – no – no," Mitch continued. "Look, we're beaten. Let's just call it a night and cut our losses."

"We're not beaten, Mitch," Chance implored. "Do you think the Blues are giving up because they're tied right now in the other team's building? They're not quitting – they're adapting! Right now! They're figuring out a way to win! That's all we have to do."

"I'd rather take Ellie's car and take my chances with her."

"Oh yeah," Chance dismissed. "That's brilliant. You'd rather open the back door again, open Ellie's bedroom door, *try* to remove her keys from her purse - after grabbing the keys to the Bentley, of course - *THEN*, after opening Ellie's *FUCKING GARAGE DOOR*, you want to back the Bentley into the street, back her car out, put the FUCKING BENTLEY *BACK IN THE FUCKING DRIVEWAY*, close the garage door, and *then* head off to Budgie's? *That's your fucking plan???!!!*

"No, that won't make any noise at all..." Chance sniffed. "Are you *totally fucking insane*? Especially when we could just crack open the side door, reach in, grab the Bentley's keys off the hook, close the door, and leave?"

"Even if I did agree to grab the keys to the Bentley," Mitch rebuked. "Ellie's dad's car is parked right outside her window. There's no way we can get that thing started without her hearing it."

"No problem," Chance replied. "We'll put her in neutral, push her up the block a little ways, start her there, and we're off."

Mitch glared at Chance.

"Look, between the two of us, we can push it up this hill," Chance continued. "It's not that steep."

Mitch just continued to stare at Chance in disbelief.

"Mitch, the third period has already started. We don't have time for this! Now either grow some cojones, or go back and just accept the fact that you're going to be Ellie's little bitch for the rest of your life."

Mitch blew a hard breath through puckered lips and thought for a second. He then turned and headed back to Ellie's house.

Chance stood on the street as Mitch disappeared into the shadows of Ellie's house. As Chance stood there, a tricked-out Honda sports car zoomed past him. Chance spun around to see the car as it clipped a metal horse about 50 feet up the hill - sending the barricade and it's flashing orange light flying off to the right side of the road. The car stopped briefly, then sped away.

"You idiots," Chance mumbled to himself. "How did you bozos not see that thing?"

Mitch then reappeared from the shadows of Ellie's house with the key to the Bentley in hand.

Chance just smiled.

"Alright," he whispered pumping his fist down, "Way to go, *Mitchster*!"

The stress Mitch was feeling was written all over his face as he unlocked the car and stood in the open door.

"Dude," Chance whispered excitedly, "it was fuckin' hilarious! You should've seen it! This car just came by and..."

Mitch turned and just glared at Chance.

"Shut the fuck up!" he mouthed silently.

Chance nodded in apology and positioned his hands against the trunk of the car, giving his body to the weight of the car.

"OK," Mitch barely whispered, standing on the ground with one hand on the open door and the other on the wheel. "We're gonna walk this back, I'll turn the wheel once we get her on the street, straighten her out, and then I'll join you back there to push this up the hill. Then, once we're far enough away, you hold it, I'll get in and start her while I step on the brakes. Then you can run up and jump in. Got it?"

"Hey," Chance whispered back, "why don't I do the steering and you do all the heavy pushing?"

Mitch stepped out from within the open door and started to stomp towards Chance thinking he should kick his ass right then and there. He then stepped out of the door and began walking towards the house, threatening to abort the entire mission.

Chance threw his hands up apologetically.

"OK, OK," he whispered. "We'll do it your way."

Mitch climbed in and put the key in the ignition. The car responded with its dutiful dinging as Mitch dropped the car into neutral. He got out and they began slowly walking the car out of the driveway. Chance began stepping backwards with the car as Mitch manned the steering wheel. As it reached the street, Mitch turned the wheel until the car was facing straight up the hill. He straightened the wheel, closed the door, and ran back to help Chance push it up the hill.

"Damn," Mitch said. "This thing is heavier than I thought it'd be."

"Yeah," Chance grunted, "twelve-cylinder engines are huge, but with both of us pushing, we got it."

As the car slowly crept uphill, Chance smiled at Mitch.

"Ya know," Chance offered, "this is gonna be a great story for the fellas once we get to Budgie's."

Mitch laughed and agreed as they pushed. But unbeknownst to them, the inside of the right front tire narrowly missed an open manhole previously protected by the metal horse that had been knocked away by that sports car.

"Yeah," Mitch agreed. "This is the kind of story we're gonna tell our grandkids about."

As the car passed over the open manhole, Mitch continued rambling.

"Maybe this wasn't such a bad idea," he commented, looking up the road.

Suddenly there was a sound like rubber ball being sucked into a vacuum hose, but Mitch just continued looking up the road and pushing.

"Man I hope we don't miss too much of... the..." his voice began to break as the car suddenly began to push back on him. He shot a look over to the space previously occupied by Chance.

"Chance?" he asked in a panic.

"Mitch!" Chance growled from below the road. "My ankle – Shit! Dude, I'm in the manhole!!!"

"Chaaance!!!" Mitch began to whisper more forcefully as the car began pushing him back downhill. "Oh God! Chance!!!" he started whisper-screaming, leaning his entire body on the car while his shoes slid helplessly along the pavement. "Get up here and help me!!!" he fake-whispered so loudly it was nearly a normal speaking voice.

"I think my ankle's broken!" Chance yelled back.

As the right front tire grazed the edge of the manhole again on its way back downhill, it caused the wheel to turn slightly, making the car begin to roll towards the row of cars parked bumper-to-bumper along the right side of the street.

Mitch, realizing the slight change in the car's direction, turned his head to see the cars lined up along the curb, as if waiting in line to be side-swiped. Mitch redoubled his fight with the car, shoving with everything he had, to no avail. His feet slid frantically with each leg thrust, as if he was sprint-skating - albeit backwards.

"No, no-no, no, no..." Mitch muttered as he shoved against the trunk.

His pleas went unanswered as the Bentley began scraping the first car. The screeching of metal was drowned out only by the sound of both cars' anti-theft devices erupting into the night. Through the rear window, Mitch saw the Bentley's airbags suddenly deploy.

"CHAAAANNNCE!!!" Mitch was yelling full-throated now. "Oh Jesus Christ, please... STOP!!! Oh God!!! CHAAAANCE, WHERE ARE YOU!!!!!"

As the Bentley gained momentum and started scraping the second car, setting off its alarm, Mitch turned around to try to push the car using his back. But his shoes continued to slide out from under him as he shoved his feet outwards in futility.

Chance's hand appeared from the manhole as he pulled himself up. Upon seeing what was happening, the words "Oh shit" fell from his lips.

Sparks flew as the Bentley tore into a third car and set off its alarm, with Mitch desperately slapping his hands all over the trunk of the Bentley in a vain attempt to find a way to get the car to stop. One part of Mitch's mind freaked out even harder as he realized Ellie's dad's car was scraping and screeching right in front of Ellie's front door.

"CHANCE!!!" he screamed. "WHAT THE FUCK ARE YOU DOING??? GET OVER HERE!!!"

Chance was now on his feet, limping somewhat quickly towards the metallic growls and screeches.

"Coming bud!" he yelled half-heartedly, but not really trying to get there. Chance had already conceded that it was too late, so he saw no reason to hurry.

The Bentley then began to scar a fourth car, setting off its alarm as well.

"CHANCE, FOR GOD'S SAKE!!!" Mitch continued to scream while now shoving on the Bentley like a football player hits a tackling dummy. "GET...THE FUCK...DOWN... HERE!!!"

With all five cars' alarms now blaring, Mitch again looked behind him and saw Lawrence's Hummer was next. His heart raced with terror of the thought of what Lawrence would do to him. He then remembered Lawrence's obnoxious anti-theft system and he simply quivered. Yet in that instant, Mitch had an idea.

"Drive it in to this car before it hits the Hummer!" he thought.

He stopped pushing on the car and quickly opened the door. He batted recklessly at the already-deflated airbag as he shoved himself into the driver's seat.

However, he misjudged the speed of the Bentley as he turned the wheel. The now grappling-hook-shaped corner of the Bentley eagerly gouged itself into the Hummer's driver side door and began carving into it.

On impact, the Hummer's custom car alarm erupted. Metal and paint curled off the Hummer like pencil shavings as the Bentley shredded the length of the SUV. The Bentley finally came to rest by catching the corner of the Hummer's oversized bumper.

Mitch sighed for a second, relieved the Bentley had finally stopped. He looked behind him to see his piece-of-shit car, which had been spared from the carnage.

"Isn't it ironic, don'tcha think..." he half-sung dejectedly.

As Ellie and Danni came running out, they both stopped in the middle of her front lawn – completely stunned by the amount of damage before them. Ellie put her hands on her head in disbelief.

Then suddenly, Claire stumbled out from the shadows of the house while rubbing her eyes. She then just stopped in the yard, absorbing what she was seeing. Her jaw slacked open wider than her eyes. She then simply dropped to her knees and began bawling openly.

"BWAH HAW HAW HAW HAW!!! BWAH HAW HAW HAW HAW HAW!!!"

The cacophony of lights, sirens, and voices swirled around Mitch, and he suddenly felt lower than he'd ever felt in his life. He saw Chance limping towards him, and for the first time in his life, he truly and fully hated Chance for his relentlessness. But he knew it didn't matter, anyway.

Chance continued his limp towards the wreckage.

"I thought he said he wanted to do this *quietly...*" Chance muttered.

Mitch opened the door and tried to get out, but he realized that his shoelaces were caught on the brake pedal. Defeated, he slunk back into the seat.

"There's no way I'll ever feel worse than I do right now," he thought.

And then, a door from another house flew open violently, and out walked Lawrence.

"OK, I was wrong..." he cringed, realizing an impending ass-kicking on the way.

Lawrence was apparently very unhappy, and he was apparently walking towards Mitch. He was also apparently coming over to pummel Mitch. Lawrence's shirtless form approached as he lowered his head and began walking faster, his large muscular frame rippling in the light of the street lamps. His stomps seemed unstoppable. For a moment, Mitch – for some reason – thought of Pamplona.

"Hi Lawrence," Mitch waved meekly with wide, innocent eyes. He then raised both hands innocently and flashed his 'Bud, you're not going to believe this...' smile. But that did absolutely nothing to slow Lawrence's forward progression.

Chance, noticing Lawrence and the direction he was heading, again mumbled, "Oh shit," and began to limp more quickly.

"Hey Lawrence!" Chance called cheerfully while waving his arms, "Hey, bud - look at it this way! Your Hummer saved Mitch's car! You should feel good about that!"

Lawrence completely ignored him and continued his stalking pace toward Mitch.

Mitch, now frantically shaking his tethered leg like a cat with tape on its paw, was still trying to get his laces free. As Lawrence came within striking distance, Mitch thought,

"*Okay, just like I did at the hockey game.*"

"Look!" Mitch glared very deliberately while pointing right at Lawrence, "I have *insurance!*"

"By that, I hope you mean health insurance," Lawrence sneered as he slugged Mitch with everything he had.

Mitch's head bounced off the headrest and came to rest on the steering wheel. As Mitch faded into unconsciousness, he thought to himself, "*Wow, that didn't even really hurt that m....*"

CHAPTER 31

TELL ME WHAT TO DO,
WHY CAN'T I MAKE IT RIGHT

Mitch slowly regained consciousness as the beep from the ECG machine stirred him. He looked around and concluded he was in a hospital somewhere. As his eyes cleared, he noticed his vision being impeded by the tape and stint attached to the bridge of his nose. Yet he could still see Chance lying in the bed next to him, his ankle wrapped in ice and his nose buried in a copy of Maxim.

Suddenly, Mitch's memories of what had just happened came flooding back to him, and he inhaled in deep horror.

Chance suddenly looked up from his magazine when he heard Mitch breathe.

"Hey, Mitch," Chance smiled. "You alright?"

"Oh my God," Mitch whined, lifting his hand to his head, which pulled the IV tube with it.

"Dude, you took Lawrence's shot to the noggin like a champ!"

"Oh my God!" Mitch repeated much more desperately. "Chance, I've totally fucked everything up! I've... no, WE'VE totally fucked everything up!"

"A *knocked out* champ... but a champ, nonetheless," Chance continued, ignoring Mitch's comments.

"I can't believe we did that!" Mitch continued as well, equally ignoring Chance. "What was I thinking???"

"I know," Chance agreed. "We totally should have backed the car *down* the hill instead. I mean, think about it... how much easier it would have been if we'd just used gravity to our advantage???"

Mitch turned and looked at Chance with utter incredulity. He then saw a metal bedpan within reach. He grabbed it, clinched his teeth, and began slugging Chance in the chest with it.

"OW!!! Dude!!!!" Chance protested. "What are you...? OW! OW, FUCKER! That hurts!!!! Watch the head!"

Mitch stopped for a second and looked at Chance lying there. Spying the wrapped ankle, Mitch leaned forward and began slamming the damaged foot instead.

Chance screamed in agony as Mitch slugged away at the injured ankle. Desperate to make Mitch stop, Chance reached up and hooked his fingers into Mitch's injured nostrils and twisted.

Mitch screamed as well while still slamming Chance's ankle. They both fought and screamed while straining against the numerous wires and tubes attached to them. The bouncing, lunging and straining looked uncannily like two tangled marionettes being held up by someone in grips of a grand mal seizure.

Two large orderlies ran into the room and separated them. But by now, Mitch was in a full rage.

"YOU STUPID MOTHER FUCKER!" Mitch screamed. "YOU'VE RUINED EVERYTHING FOR

ME!!! ELLIE'S NEVER GOING TO SPEAK TO ME AGAIN!!!"

"Like this is *my* fault???!!!" Chance shot back. "All you had to say was 'NO'!"

Mitch suddenly stopped struggling with the orderly and slunk back into his bed. Even though he had said 'no' numerous times, even though he knew Chance would have never stopped hounding him if he had refused – in the end, he was just as responsible because he didn't stand up to Chance, because he didn't refuse, but mostly because he *did* go along with it.

Mitch grabbed his cell phone off the nearby table.

"JEM limo service please," he said into the phone.

"Cool! Are you getting a limo to take us home? Chance asked.

While Mitch waited for the operator, he shot a despondent glare at Chance.

"Never talk to me again," he warned.

"Dude, trust me," Chance reasoned. "We'll look back and laugh about this one day."

Mitch turned his attention back to his phone. "Is this JEM Limousine?" he said. "I need a limo for 7:30 a.m. Yes, 7:30 today. Yes, I realize it's only six hours away. Make it your nicest one available. *How* much? Ugh, yeah... that's fine. Fine. Send it to this address, please..."

CHAPTER 32

I LOOK AT YOU
WITH SUCH DISDAIN

A few days had passed and Mitch had not heard from Ellie, despite the countless messages of apology he had left on her home phone, her cell phone, and with the receptionist at her salon.

Mitch was trying to bury himself in his work and ignore the gnawing in his stomach. He couldn't work on the novel anymore, it reminded him too much of Ellie. He simply sat in his cube, a mere shell of the excited and confident man that occupied that very same cube just a week ago - when his desk phone suddenly rang.

"Mitch Paulson," he mumbled.

"Hi," Ellie replied tersely.

"Ellie!" Mitch exclaimed. "Babe, listen..."

"You need to come get your stuff," Ellie interrupted, completely void of emotion.

"Wait, babe, we..."

"I'm not your *babe*," Ellie sneered. "You need to come get your things."

"But I can explain..."

"No, Mitch. Not this time. You can't explain. And if you try, it'll only piss me off more."

Mitch felt the air leave his lungs again. It was the exact same sensation he felt when he first saw Ellie, only much darker.

"Just throw it all out," Mitch replied. "There's nothing over there I care about besides you."

"Yeah, that's real poetic. Come get your shit."

"OK," Mitch sighed. "When?"

"As soon as you get off work."

Mitch pulled up to Ellie's house with a heavy heart and a chest that felt like it was full of cotton. Even his eyeballs began to quiver in their sockets, and his steps towards her front door reflected it. He sighed, knocked on the door, and looked down.

Ellie opened the door and stepped back into the house. Sitting on her kitchen table were Mitch's things. His clothes were neatly folded, his CDs were neatly stacked beside them, and Chance's cooler sat behind them all. All of this was hard enough to witness, but what really broke Mitch's heart sat atop the clothes. It was the folder he'd given Ellie, the folder that contained the first five chapters of his novel. It didn't matter that he had the story saved on his computer. To see it sitting with the rest of his things was the ultimate message. It truly was over, and she wanted nothing left behind to remind her of him.

He stood there for a second, just inside her kitchen door. Ellie stayed against the far wall, not making eye contact.

"Don't I get a chance to apologize?" he asked.

"You've already apologized 46 times in all the messages you've left. I get it. You're sorry."

"Ellie, listen..."

"Mitch, just grab your things and leave, OK?" she ordered, never looking up from the floor.

"But..."

"But nothing," Ellie replied calmly yet deliberately. "You want to live like you never left college. Hey, it's your life. Go live it."

Mitch felt the sting of her indifference and looked away. He then saw the cardboard boxes scattered throughout her living room and his eyes sank.

"You're leaving?" he asked.

"Yes."

"Where are you going?"

"New York, like I always said I would. You've begun to follow your dreams. It's time I started following mine."

"I always thought we'd follow our dreams together..."

"Yeah right," Ellie scoffed. "Let's go hang out again at Budgie's, have a few drinks, hang all over each other and talk about our *big* dreams – all the while *pretending* that we're working towards them. Ya know, in college, you can get away with all that bullshit. But college is FUCKING OVER, Mitch - yet somehow though, you just never actually left. You, and all your buddies," she laughed in disbelief. "You're all still living that life. And that's... that's just not the life I ever wanted."

"I'm not just *talking* about my dreams anymore, babe," Mitch said as he grabbed the folder. "I'm finally working on it, and now you're leaving? Do you know how hard it was for me just to get this started? It was like jumping out of an airplane..."

"And I still need to jump out of my airplane!" Ellie countered. "But I can't do that in St. Louis, Mitch! And even if I could do it here, I don't want to with you."

"But, I accomplished all this because of you... because with you, I believed I could do it."

"You did all this just to impress me, Mitch?" Ellie yelled as her anger grew. "Some *dreamer you are!!!* I thought you wanted to *affect* people, *remember?* Not just one person, but civilizations? Have an influence on people for years to come? All of that bullshit?"

Mitch sank both physically and emotionally as she said those words.

"Yeah, well..." he tried to explain.

"Well what?" she snipped.

"Well," he sighed, "you changed my priorities."

Ellie suddenly felt less sure of herself as she looked at the man she'd convinced herself she no longer loved.

"Look Mitch," she sighed, feeling a tear welling in her eyes, "you did impress me with your writing. And I'm sure if you ever do finish your novel, you will impress other people as well. But that's just not enough. I need to grow up. And... and you need to grow up, too."

Mitch nodded and felt his own tears beginning to well. In order to save face, he grabbed everything and headed for the door.

As he opened the door, he looked her right in the eye.

"Good luck in New York," he said.

The screen door bounced once and settled into its frame. Ellie watched as Mitch's silhouette paused for a second just outside the door, then moved away.

CHAPTER 33

PICKUP STOMPDOWN

As Mitch sat at Budgie's, he tried to man-up and put on a brave face. He shoved the pain down until only arrogance and bitterness came from his lips – at least, it did whenever anyone tried talking to him.

Rich walked up behind Mitch and slapped his shoulder.

"No luck trolling for guppies tonight, Mitch?" he asked.

Mitch just sneered at Rich's bravado.

"Rich, if my fish were in a 'barrel' like your married ass is, I wouldn't be giving advice on baiting. Just... just go spear the starfish a few more times for us single guys, OK?"

Rich rolled his eyes, unwilling to let Mitch sulk.

"Look, Mitch, Danni dumped Chance, too... you don't see him crying in his beer."

Mitch looked over at Chance, who was sitting in a booth with two young ladies, and an arm around each of them. They both looked young enough to be products of his youthful conquests, if any of those stories were actually true. Regardless, they were all laughing and smiling as if nothing was wrong in the world.

"Trust me, Rich – he's crying on the inside," Mitch replied, even though he really only said it to convince himself it might be true.

"Wow," Rich commented. "You writers really *are* pussies."

"Really, Rich?" Mitch turned to confront him. "How I should find my true love? How should I find the woman I want to spend the rest of my life with, have children with? Should I try to land my soul mate with some lame attempt at wit by using a pick-up line that you took off the internet? I mean, *seriously*?"

"No, dumbass!" Tom yelled from the table they were all crowding around. "How about you just find a chick that'll make you feel better *tonight*? Hey, ya think Chance is looking for a *soul mate* tonight?" he continued, pointing his beer bottle towards Chance. "He's looking for jail bait."

"Look Mitch," Rich added, "all you need is a good pickup line."

Chance had been charming the two young ladies, but still had an ear on the conversation that Mitch was involved in and an eye on his roommate and best friend – who he knew was not getting over Ellie as quickly as he should be.

"So, what are you saying?" Mitch continued as he stepped into Rich's face. "You have some secret mojo charm line that never fails?"

Rich stood there slightly dumbfounded, not sure if Mitch was angry enough to take a swing, or just depressed enough to take a moment of pleasure from publicly disarming him.

Chance recognized the impending confrontation, excused himself from the table, and walked up to Mitch.

"Hey bud," Chance said calmly as he put an arm around Mitch's shoulder. "We're all friends here. Settle down."

"Fuck off, Chance," Mitch scoffed. "I've been trying to find someone else – even something superficial for the night. But it's no good. I don't have a polished pick-up line like the rest of you do."

"Dude, it's not what you say – it's all in *how* you say it." Chance explained. "Tell ya what - remember the story you told me about what you saw in Amsterdam – with the ping pong balls and the cow glove?"

"Yeah," Mitch asked.

"See that little wallflower over there that I've been talkin' to all night?" Chance pointed across the room, "I'm gonna go over there and pick her up using that exact story."

Mitch looked across the room to see a very reserved-looking young woman sitting against the wall with a friend. His instinct to spare this woman from Chance was overridden by the glee he'd get from seeing her threaten legal proceedings against him.

"This I gotta see," Mitch replied. "I'll bet half of your rent next month that she smacks you across the face as soon as you start that story."

"Mitch," Chance sighed, "women are like watchdogs. Once they sense fear, it's over. They lose all respect for you immediately."

Mitch shot Chance a suspicious glare.

"Hey I can even make it more lucrative for ya," Chance added. "Come sit behind me so you'll know I told her the whole story. Then if I leave with her, you pay my *entire* share of the rent for this month. If not, I'll pay yours."

"You're completely fucking nuts, you know that?" Mitch stated. "But, you're on! Let's go."

"Okay," Chance quickly smiled assuredly. "I like your spirit, my friend. Follow me."

"This, I gotta see," Mitch said confidently – even though, in the back of his mind, he was already a little worried that Chance could win this bet.

Mitch sat behind the girls at a nearby table as Chance walked up. Chance introduced himself to the girls and immediately started in about his recent trip to Amsterdam. Chance proceeded to go in to every graphic detail about the unbelievable things that Mitch had seen – even though he told it as if he'd witnessed it himself - complete with hand gyrations, vivid descriptions, and even a few sound effects. At one point, Chance actually put one foot up on the table to complete the visual.

Mitch's jaw went slack as Chance turned to the wallflower.

"So," Chance asked, "you wanna get outta here?"

She just stared blankly at Chance and, while still in a mild level of shock, blushed and tilted her head. She then grabbed her drink and slammed it.

"Lemme grab my keys," she smiled.

Chance then put a $20 on the table and offered his arm to her. She grabbed her purse and keys, wrapped her arm around Chance's

"Don't wait up for me," she whispered back to her friend.

As they left Budgie's, Mitch slowly got up and slung his legs back to the bar in disgust. He couldn't believe that Chance just hijacked his most disgusting sex story they'd both ever heard, and turned it around to use it as a story to charm a woman. He sat down in front of Renee and ordered another beer.

As he was sitting there still trying to figure out what just happened, he noticed a woman, dressed very provocatively, walk into the bar. She walked across the room, sat right next to Mitch and smiled. Mitch smiled back and evaluated her "tolerability quotient." Based on her clothing and her obvious comfort level with her own sexuality, (along with the jilted, illogical arrogance that he could do anything Chance could do), he introduced himself and proceeded to tell her the same story about his recent trip to Amsterdam.

Mitch, however, stumbled over a few of the details and became visibly uncomfortable as he relayed the same details that Chance sailed through by simply flashing his knowing smile. Not to be outdone, though, Mitch trudged on through the tale, mimicking – yet minimizing – the gyrations and conveying a hint of shame as he finished the story.

Overall, he thought he pulled it off pretty well for a first try. And he told himself that he'd told the story exactly the same way that Chance had.

"So," Mitch smiled, albeit horribly uncertain, "do you wanna get outta here?"

The woman stared at him, void of expression.

"Lemme grab my keys," she said.

Mitch turned and looked away with widened eyes and mouthed the words *"No fucking way."* As he turned back to her and smiled, she raised her keychain to his face and depressed the button that released pepper spray directly into his eyes.

"Aaarrrggghhh!" Mitch screamed as he fell backwards off his stool and onto the floor. "What the FUCK???" he screamed.

"YOU!" she yelled as she stomped on his balls, causing all four limbs to jut out like a squeeze toy's eye balls. "FUCKIN'!" she stomped again, with Mitch's limbs responding identically. "PERVERT!" she screamed and stomped one final time. Again, Mitch's nervous system reacted the same way.

She then turned and stormed out of the bar. Mitch rolled to his side immediately and whimpered in fetal position. He remained on the floor, being reduced to a moaning and writhing lump of humanity.

"Hospital..." he muttered meekly.

Renee leaned over her bar and asked, "What'd you say, Mitch?"

"Hospital," he whispered again.

"Somebody call 911," she sighed as she shook her head at him with pity.

One of the same orderlies that broke up Mitch and Chance's bedside war from earlier in the week wheeled Mitch out of the hospital

"Alright, Mitch," he sighed. "Here's your cab. Good seeing you again. Don't be a stranger!"

"What about the pain?" Mitch asked.

"Just remember to keep frozen peas on it."

"Oh which, my eyes or my balls?" Mitch asked

"Uh... both, actually," the orderly answered.

Mitch's taxi pulled up to the apartment just as Chance's taxi was dropping him off as well. Chance stumbled out of his cab, aching and sore with beet-red eyes from all-night sex. Mitch stumbled out of his cab, aching and sore with beet-red eyes from the mace and ball-stomping. They both walked towards the door to their place in the same disheveled manner.

Chance then noticed Mitch's appearance and how similar it was to his own.

"AH HA HA!" Chance gloated. "See bud??? I TOLD YOU!!! It works *every* time!"

Mitch just grunted, holding the bag of peas on his crotch as he opened the door and began trudging up the stairs, all the while ignoring Chance.

"Hey dude, no thanks necessary," Chance said proudly with his hands raised. "Wait, what are you holding against your balls?"

"Frozen peas," Mitch mumbled.

"Great idea, Mitchster!" Chance praised. "I should have grabbed some peas from her freezer, too! My boys are killing me!"

Mitch, without looking, slung the bag backwards at Chance, hitting him square in the face. The bag exploded as semi-frozen peas bounced everywhere and scattered down the staircase.

"Dude, what the fuck?" Chance asked. "Those things were, like, on your balls! Freakin' *gross*."

CHAPTER 34

THE BROKEN LIGHTS ON THE FREEWAY
LEFT ME HERE ALONE

Chance and Mitch were back at Budgie's again the very next night, albeit at Chance's urging. Chance seemed completely unfazed by his newfound freedom, moving effortlessly as he hopped from table to table and hitting on anything in a skirt. He almost seemed to relish being set free – even though anyone else on the planet would call it "getting dumped."

Mitch wasn't doing nearly as well. He tried to convince himself that Chance was right, that he shouldn't be missing Ellie, and that he should just try to find another woman. But neither the pep talks nor the "what a selfish bitch" reassurances made a difference, no matter how much Mitch wished they did. He just ached, and he kept aching just a little too much to be able to dismiss the pain with macho bravado.

Still, he sat at his bar and watched countless people flirting back and forth, smiling and laughing, just enjoying life – and he envied every one of them. He then looked around and became angered that every corner of his bar now reminded him of Ellie. He looked at the dartboard and remembered the time she beat him. He looked at the jukebox and remembered the countless fun arguments over which songs to play. He even looked out the window to distract himself, but the bright evening sunset told him that summer was on its way – which made him remember all the summertime plans he and Ellie had made.

The more Mitch sat there, the more he became trapped within his own thoughts. One side of him was sounding a lot like Chance, calling himself a pussy about how he was handling this whole thing. Then there was the other side of him, metaphorically curled up and wounded in a dark corner of his mind - indifferently telling the first side to fuck off.

He wanted to scream. He wanted to punch something. He wanted... dammit, he just wanted Ellie back. But since that wasn't going to happen, he felt even more enraged as he looked around the digs of his "second home." He just couldn't believe that his favorite hangout was now nothing more than a giant monument to the woman who'd dumped him. And that thought alone made him nauseated.

He let out a big sigh and took another drink of his beer.

In his blur of flipping between memories and present time, he didn't even notice the two young ladies taking seats right next to him at the bar. As they sat down chatting, the one sitting closest to Mitch asked him if the seats were taken.

Mitch looked at the ladies indifferently.

"What?" Mitch said. "Uh, no."

"Good," the one girl said as she and her friend sat down.

Mitch looked at her and was impressed by her beauty. And, since she'd chosen to sit right next to him, he half-smiled as he evaluated this newly-arrived lady. With wide eyes, a dark complexion, and an air of bubbly fun about her, Mitch momentarily thought she may be the cure for the state in which Ellie had him.

She looked down a little, flattered by Mitch's attention, and then looked up at him and saw the hint of sadness in his eyes.

"Hey," she smiled, "if you're going to hang out with us, you're going to have to smile like you mean it. We're having a five-year reunion here."

Mitch, accepting the invitation, smiled a little more.

"OK, then," he laughed. "My name's Mitch, and for the rest of the night, I'll smile from ear-to-ear for you ladies."

"That's better," the first girl smiled.

"So what's your name?"

"I'm Tanya," she replied and extended her hand. "And this is my long lost friend, Abagael."

"Nice to meet both of you," Mitch smiled. "So, what's up with the reunion, anyway?" Mitch asked. "What kept you two apart?"

"Well, I just moved back from Flagstaff," Tanya said. "So, that's one reason."

"That," Abagael added, "and she finally dumped her asshole, loser, deadbeat, goin' nowhere ex-boyfriend."

"Really," Mitch said, feeling the double-barreled irony of both answers.

"Yeah well, when I figured out that he wasn't going to do anything with his life, I figured it was time I moved back here to be closer to family," Tanya explained. "So, here I am. What are you doing here?"

"Well, this is my hangout when I'm not working."

"What do you do?"

"I'm a writer," Mitch said proudly. "I'm finally getting through my first novel, but in the meantime I work for a software company."

"Well, at least you have your life together," she said. "Ya know, I've always thought about writing a book myself. You and I should go out sometime," she said, half-jokingly.

"Sure," he replied as he handed her his business card. "Wow, your boyfriend must've been a real piece of work for you to flee the state. What'd he do to you?"

"Aw, nothing, and that was the problem. He just wasn't going anywhere. I decided it was best to just leave."

"Just leave?" Mitch echoed as he shook his head, feeling a little angrier. "Whaddaya mean?"

"Well, you know, rather than waiting for him to get his life together, I decided it was time to move on."

"And what do *you* do?" Mitch replied.

"Me?" Tanya replied. "Well, I'm a receptionist, but like I said, I hope to be a writer someday."

"There seems to be a lot of that going around, lately," Mitch chuckled.

"What do you mean by that?"

"Nothing. Lemme buy you and your friend a drink."

"Aw, that's so sweet," Tanya agreed in a kind voice. "Finally, a *nice* guy."

Mitch handed Renee a $20 and told her to give Tanya and Abagael another round. Renee flashed him a sideways smile as she took his money and went to the wine cooler.

As Renee delivered the drinks to the ladies, Mitch smiled a little more to himself, thinking Tanya might be *just what he needed* to get over Ellie. All he had to do was, as Chance would say, "close the deal."

"You're right, we do need to go out sometime," he smiled confidently as he pointed to his business card sitting in front of Tanya. "Maybe we can talk about writing over dinner? I know this great little Italian place that I think you'd like."

"Well, thank you, *Mark*," Tanya said, already forgetting his name. She then rolled her eyes at Abagael, letting her friend know exactly how *uninterested* she was.

Mitch recoiled a little as he caught a glimpse of her eye roll. He suddenly realized that they were merely manipulating him for free drinks, and he suddenly hated her a little more because never, in his entire life, had he felt so exploited by someone he *didn't even know*.

Mitch pushed himself back from the bar and slowly shook his head in disgust, even losing the desire to correct her about his name.

"Have a nice reunion, ladies," he shrugged as he started to walk away.

But then Mitch stopped dead in his tracks as he heard a celebratory "clink" of the two wine glasses he'd just paid for, followed quickly by Tanya and Abagael's adolescent giggling. From a dark corner of the wounded side of Mitch's mind came a simple phrase.

"Aw, hell no. Not this time."

"What *is* it with you chicks???" Mitch asked as he spun back around to confront the girls. "You'll fall for guys that treat you like shit, but when someone tries to be nice to you and treat you as an equal, you pull *this bullshit???"*

"Did you just call us *'chicks'*?!" Tanya asked indignantly.

"Shut up Tina." Mitch said smoothly, purposely renaming her.

Tanya and Abagael suddenly lost their smiles as Mitch stared off into space, ignoring them for just a second.

In that brief disconnected pause, Mitch experienced what some refer to as "a moment of clarity."

Instantly, all of the background noise from the bar-- the television, the jukebox, the chatter, the sound of Renee washing glasses, *everything* – it all fell silent in his head.

And as he stared off into nothing in particular, it all seemed to make sense.

"Wait," he realized as his eyes suddenly glazed over with epiphany. "I *get* it. I think I finally understand you women. You spend the early years your of life seeking daddy's approval, but when you messed up *like we all did* growing up, daddy broke your heart when he got mad at you. Then you *all* made the same critical mistake - you began to believe that daddy's love was conditional, that you had to somehow 'do' or 'be' something more to ensure he'd always love you.

"And this situation just kept replaying itself throughout your life. Got in trouble, Dad got mad. It happened over and over again until it got to the point that you could only recognize 'true love' as something that could only be given by someone who completely looked down on you. If a man respected you, then *that* man must be stupid - because you determined long ago that you are *waaay too fucking flawed* to ever be *truly* respected."

The bar quieted as Mitch's tirade got louder, slowly drawing everyone's attention on him. And, as usual at Budgie's, most of the "everyone's" were guys.

"And so it goes," he continued ranting, "throughout your life you buy in too heavily to the 'Perfect Angel Princess' title with which daddy anointed you. But when you *did* mess up and he got angry, the thought never occurred to you that all you did was *just... simply... mess... up*, nothing more! All you saw was that, somehow, at that moment, you were no longer worthy of daddy's love. You were somehow blemished, imperfect, *STAINED*. No longer a princess, but wanting nothing more than to get back into being worthy of that title."

In that moment, Budgie's – sonically, at least – went from a bar to a funeral home.

"See, I get it now," Mitch seethed. "You all complain about wanting to be treated as equals, yet you lose respect for any man who actually *does* treat you as an equal. You use words like 'nice guy' when one of us comes along – hell, guys like me may as well be gay, because you like having us as friends, but you'd never consider falling for one of us. You're all completely incapable of actually loving a man like that because he doesn't treat you with that *conditional* love that you've learned from daddy.

"A man gives you security, and you mock him. He gives you loyalty, and suddenly he's 'crowding' you. A guy like me accepts your faults like he accepts his own, and he's a chump. My God! If he does all that for you, then he can't possibly *really* love you... because, in your twisted perceptions, he kisses your ass too much and, after all, you're not *really that good... and anyone with a fucking brain can see that!*

"So then, if some guy does show you unconditional love, he must be weaker and dumber than you, right???"

"Mitch," Chance said as he suddenly cut through the gathering crowd and grabbed Mitch's arm. "Hey, um..."

"Fuck you, Chance," Mitch growled as he wriggled his arm free. "This needs to be said."

He then turned back to Tanya.

"So, here's the *real* score. If you really want a woman to love you, you have to only show her love occasionally – because that's all she's capable of understanding. And, honestly, that's *fucking pathetic*. We have to treat you like the dumb carrot-chasers that you are? Really? 'Here horsey, here's the carrot,'" he mocked as he held out his arm. "I promise you'll get love if you keep working for it! Ugh, how short-sighted and insecure! Pavlov would be so fuckin' *proud!*

"Now it's become a chicken or the egg thing. Are nice girls truly only attracted to assholes, or have guys figured out that women are only attracted to assholes and they willingly play the part? Either way *Trixie*," he taunted, again intentionally using the wrong name, "that's a fuckin' baaad plan – 'cause, either way, you ladies *lose!*

"Ya know, your gender's greatest failure is your inability to recognize the difference between kindness and weakness. The fairer sex, my ass. There's not a *God-damned* thing about any one of you that's fair!'"

Chance again grabbed Mitch's arm and spun him around.

"Dude, look!" Chance pleaded. "Dr. Phil just called. He wants his shtick back, OK? Reel it in!"

"Why?" Mitch sniffed dejectedly as he shoved Chance away. "Dude, we've *all* been played... *all* of us, *all* along! We were all told, 'If you want to keep her, respect her, treat her as an equal, honor her...' HA! You want a woman to love you? You'd better demoralize her just as often as you enable her, if not more."

Mitch then refocused his rant on Tanya.

"But because you're all soo fucked in the head, it ends up being that good guys like *me* get dismissed *only* because we can't justify *shitting* all over the women we love in order to keep them! Then, that female idiocy only allows the asshole dudes to inherit the Earth. And then you idiots mate with those assholes and – guess what – you end up having *mutant-idiot-asshole-children!!!*

"And later in life you cry because your kids are all acting like idiots and assholes, and you have the nerve to cry, 'Why me???!!!'

"Poetic justice, if you ask me," he smiled wickedly as he shrugged at Tanya. "Well, I'm not playing that game anymore. I'd rather die alone than play that. Fuck a bunch of you if you can't get past your daddy issues. Y'all fuckin' *disappoint* me. My equal? *My ass.*"

Mitch turned and stormed out of the bar as the crowd watched with the kind of silence normally reserved for a wake. The door bounced a few times and then came to rest in its frame, and the bar continued to remain silent.

There were a few laughs and smiles from the men in the bar as the crowd suddenly went back to their previous conversations. Chance just stood there flashing his trademark smile and nodded as he crossed his arms and stared at the door that was still settling back into its frame. Even if he wasn't sure what to make of Mitch's diatribe, but he was suddenly damn proud of his friend.

Tanya was still sitting there like a wide-eyed victim of a random assault. Dumbfounded, shell-shocked, and unsure of what had just happened, she tried to regain her bearings. Then Abagael leaned over to her.

"Are you gonna call him?" she asked Tanya as she placed a finger on Mitch's business card and slowly dragged it towards herself. "Because if you're not, I am. He's *totally* hot."

CHAPTER 35

IT'S A FEUD TOO FAR
THAT'S GONE ON TOO LONG

Mitch sat quietly in front of SportsCenter, shaking his head introspectively. In the background, he heard Chance stomping up the stairs towards the apartment, and he sighed heavily at the thought of his roommate's arrival.

"MITCH!" Chance nearly squealed as he slung the door wide open. "THAT WAS *AWESOME!!!*"

Mitch didn't smile or even flinch. He just kept staring at the TV.

Chance noticed that Mitch hadn't moved, so he flipped on the light.

Annoyed by the sudden brightness, Mitch turned and gave Chance a *"What do you want?"* look.

"See, that's what I've been talkin' about all along!" Chance continued. "You finally see how to work women! Bud, I see *many a lady coming your way* in your future now," he sung.

"I thought I'd found my lady," Mitch deadpanned as he turned back to face the TV.

"Well, you got past that tonight," Chance laughed. "Nice work! Those chicks are *so* gonna call you."

Mitch continued to sit there, unresponsive.

"Hey, Mitch," Chance clapped his hands in front of Mitch's face. "Welcome to the real world. Those chicks, they're never who you *think* they are. They all eventually expose their flaws. I was about done with Danni and her bullshit about me checking out other chicks, anyway. Hey, it's not like I was *acting on* my impulses... sheesh! They're all dumb bitches, anyway. At least you finally get it."

"*That* was your big sacrifice?" Mitch asked mockingly. "You gave up plowing other women?"

"Well, *yeah*," Chance shrugged. "How many other guys are willing to do that?"

"In reality?" Mitch countered. "Or in Maxim?"

"Whatever, dude," Chance dismissed. "As if there's a difference."

"Chance, I didn't even mean any-fucking-thing I said! I lost it for a second, I pigeon-holed every woman on the planet as a victim of their daddies, and I blasted that girl with it! I just pasted my rage on those two, and... yet... somehow... *you're happy about it????*"

"Well duh," Chance countered. "You finally got it. You *understand*."

"Seriously?" Mitch pursued. "Dude, how was *I* right? I mean, did you see anything in Danni other than a piece of ass?"

"Yeah... strategic warfare tips," Chance said. "Now we're *so* gonna kick their asses next year in the online tourney. That, and she had a good job, so it was nice not having to spend *my* money all the time to keep her happy."

"Holy shit," Mitch shook his head. "You had such a good thing there, bud. You just don't get it."

"Look dude," Chance sniffed, "when I'm ready to run the clock out, I'll find the right one. Don't worry."

"Ya know what just absolutely kills me?" Mitch shuddered. "Somewhere, along some tragically honest timeline, I know you're probably right. Someday, some woman that you absolutely do not deserve to have will come along and decide that you're the guy for her. Believe me when I say that I will be truly happy for you when that day comes, but I'll never understand it."

"Yeah you will," Chance insisted. "You get it, *now*. Mitch, love is nothing more than a competition where the person that cares the least holds the most power. I mean, you totally captured it when you laid into that chick tonight!"

"I DON'T BELIEVE IN ONE FUCKING WORD OF WHAT I SAID!!!"

"No," Chance argued, "*remember exactly* what you said! You totally nailed it!"

"Chance, as easy as it is for you to find women, it's equally that hard for me," Mitch pleaded. "I lay my heart on the line and get nothing. You piss up and down their legs and get whatever you want. I mean, seriously... it's not like you built a better hut than me. Is that what it really all comes down to? I don't get it. I swear, I don't understand, but this shit has got to stop right *fucking* now!"

"Amen, brother!" Chance agreed. "Fuck Ellie! Fuck Danni! They're all just bitches who expect you to be everything that *they're* not. You're driven, you have goals... they have, I don't know, *hopes*. You've finally proven yourself as an independent man."

"Yeah," Mitch agreed. "That much, you're right about."

"And by that, you're finally free of anyone's judgment," Chance continued.

"Yeah."

"You're finally free to be yourself."

"Yeah."

"Then dude, BE YOUR OWN MAN!" Chance ordered, as if he were Mitch's drill sergeant. "Stop worrying about what other people think and – for once - live own your life!"

A glimmer suddenly crossed Mitch's eye.

"You're right."

"You know I am," Chance smiled arrogantly.

"I need to be my own man," Mitch agreed.

"Absolutely."

"Free from others' expectations and demands."

"You know this..."

"I need to claim my own destiny."

"FINALLY!" Chance proclaimed to the heavens.

"I need to rely on myself for once."

"Yep, definitely."

Mitch stopped for a second, trying to pick his words carefully. Chance, still relishing in the revelations that he thought he'd helped Mitch realize, waited for Mitch to continue.

"Chance," Mitch said as he turned to his friend, "you need to go."

"OK, where?" he asked excitedly.

"No, Chance. You need to move," Mitch rephrased. "You need to find your own place."

"Alright bud, I'm right there for..." Chance paused, suddenly realizing what Mitch was saying. "Wait, what? What are you talking about?"

"Chance, you're right. I need to be my own man."

"Hey Mitch, maybe you should take the whole 'independence' thing a little more slowly. Maybe with some baby steps, ya know?" Chance pled.

"You know Chance, you've been pushing me around and exploiting me since we were in college," Mitch chuckled to himself. "You've played me and manipulated me more times than I care to count, but I put up with it because I always believed that you were my friend."

"Um, yeah," Chance agreed. "I am your friend. That's why we both need to stay here while..."

"While what? While I let you cheat in everything... like video games and paying the bills?" Mitch continued laughing, almost in a tone of disbelief. "While I sit back as you talk all your shit, watch you make more money than I do? While you ride in – *hell* – DRIVE my car? While you skate on anything that resembles responsibility? And, oh yeah, while I sit back watching you steamroll women and wipe them off your heels as you move to the next one? All the while telling me that I'm the one who sucks because I don't shit on them?"

Chance stood there, unsure of what to say next.

"Chance, you gotta get your own place, bud," Mitch restated. "Now."

"Hey, this place is half mine, remember?" Chance protested.

"No, it's actually all mine," Mitch shrugged. "Remember, they wouldn't let you sign the lease because of those credit cards you never paid off from college?"

"You *mother fucker*!!! Who the FUCK DO YOU THINK YOU..."

"Chance, dude," Mitch stated calmly yet assertively. "I'm sorry, but I have to do this for me - just like you were just saying."

Chance stood there silently. Some part of him realized that he had no other manipulations with which to influence Mitch.

Chance suddenly slunk in defeat.

"So, are we *at least* still 'buds'?" Chance asked plainly.

"Oh yeah," Mitch reassured. "We'll always be buds. But right now, I gotta make good with me. Just now, you gotta go.

"Vaya con Dios and all that bullshit, ya know?" Mitch said with a shrug.

Chance looked at Mitch and gave him a look that Mitch had never seen before. For the first time since they'd become friends, Chance wasn't sure what to do next.

Mitch continued to stare at him with a smile of absolute assuredness.

Chance, having never seen Mitch with this level of clarity, simply turned and walked out the door.

As he let the door of his soon-to-be former home close behind him, he sighed.

"Fuckin' Mexico," he mumbled. "NOW he listens..."

CHAPTER 36

WORKIN' AND PRACTICIN'

Monday rolled around, and Mitch took the stairs again. This time, his eyes were clear, his skin looked alive, and his expression was one of confident determination. He turned down the hallway towards his cube more quickly than normal. The breeze created by his pace and the energy coming off him caused a few of his co-workers to peek over the walls of their cubes like curious prairie dogs.

The determination in his gait was obvious. But as he got to his cube entrance, he didn't turn in to it. He just kept walking – straight to his boss' office. He quickly rapped on his boss' door.

"Gotta minute?" Mitch asked.

As Mitch sat down before his boss could answer, he began explaining that he needed to take some time off – all three-plus weeks of his accrued vacation time.

After a brief discussion, Mitch got up and walked out with a wide smile. His co-workers stared in bewilderment as his boss stood in his office doorway, chuckling and shaking his head. The smile on his boss' face displayed a realization that maybe all the hope he'd had for Mitch was going to be realized.

Mitch walked into his cube, grabbed a small stack of Manila folders, and dropped them on a nearby co-worker's desk. He then turned back to look at his boss.

"Reallocated," Mitch smiled.

His co-worker's eyes widened with horror as he opened his mouth to protest the sudden increased work load.

"You're lucky I like you, Mitch," his boss laughed. "Get outta here – we'll manage until you come back."

Mitch spent the next three and a half weeks sitting on his couch, pounding away on his laptop. Over the next few days, Chance popped in and out, slowly moving things out of the apartment.

But in between stretching, scribbling on his white board, writing - and *re-writing* - chapters, Mitch would only take "thought breaks" to scrub hot sauce off the walls or engage Chance in brief arguments that included phrases like, "Nooo, that's *my* pint glass."

Remarkably, Mitch finished his first novel in his three and a half weeks of vacation time. He thought that it was ready, that *he* was ready.

But even if he was ready, no one else was.

Mitch went back to work at Razor, and months passed as Mitch juggled his meetings and deadlines with relentless submissions of his novel to countless publishers and agents. He sought advice from other published writers, and even went through three complete re-writes.

One day, Mitch looked up and it had gone from May to September in the blink of an eye. But Mitch was never better. He'd lost about 20 pounds since he'd stopped hanging out at Budgie's so much. He didn't miss all the drinking - and he certainly didn't miss the morning hangovers, either. For the first time in his life, he felt like he was somewhat in control of his destiny.

He laughed as he looked at the calendar - awed by how quickly the past months had disappeared. He also wondered how long it would be before he got a response, or if he even *would* get a response. As he perused the upcoming Blues home games schedule, he quietly wondered how long he could keep this pace up before he'd simply have to be happy with the fact that he'd finished the novel - and stop forcing these publishing houses to send him their unending rejection letters.

He looked at his current work load, and shrugged as he began planning his days off around the impending Blues training camp schedule.

"*After all*," he thought as he smiled, "*it's a new season.*"

Then, unexpectedly, the phone rang.

CHAPTER 37

SHE'S COMING OUT INTO
A WORLD SO WONT OF LIGHT

Two months later, Mitch was walking through a New York City borough with his new book contract in hand. After making a few phone calls and following the trade papers, he found out where Ellie was living.

As he compared the address on the building to his scribblings, his heart felt heavy. For a moment, he debated if he should even try to talk to her. But he told himself that he'd come this far, and he wasn't about to let her go without one last try.

He began walking up the concrete steps to the front door of the flat. Just then, the door opened and emerging from a dark hallway was Ellie. Mitch stopped dead in his tracks and, once again, felt every ounce of air leave his lungs.

Ellie looked at Mitch and smiled, until she realized it was him. Her smile immediately sank.

"Mitch, what are you doing here?" Ellie asked uncertainly. "What do you want?"

"Well, I... I miss my best friend."

"Where is Chance? Is he alright?"

"No, not Chance," Mitch shook his head. "You."

She looked at him confusedly, then just gazed at the floor.

"You need to go, you shouldn't be here."

"Look, I'm here because I'm doing a book tour and I just wanted to stop by and see how things were going."

Ellie just looked up at the sky, unable to look Mitch in the eye or even say anything. She was too surprised by all the feelings that had reappeared without warning.

"I heard you got the role, by the way," Mitch offered. "Congratulations! Broadway, finally! Hey, I don't know if you heard, but I sold my novel. That's what the book tour is about. Hey, maybe one day they'll turn it into a movie and I'll be as big as George Lucas. At least there's no more user manuals in this writer's future."

She remained standing there unresponsive.

"I've stopped going to the bar, too. And, check it out, I've lost a little weight! So now, I'm closer to actually *being* good-looking, right?" Mitch begged, just trying to get her to crack a smile. "And I've got my finances in order. You'd be surprised how much easier it is to keep track of your money when you no longer have a bar tab, ya know?"

Ellie felt her heart tearing as she wanted so badly to run up and hold him, but she wouldn't let herself do it.

"Ellie, please," Mitch continued. "My life was crazy before you came into it. You showed me how good it can be when you just try to get what you want. Dammit Ellie, we were good together. We just *fit*. I know that I had a lot of growing up to do, and I think I've done it."

"If you did all that for me..." she whined.

"No, Ellie, I didn't do it for you," Mitch replied. "*I did it for me*. When you left, at first I thought that if I met anyone who was even one-tenth the person that you are, I would NOT ever lose them from still living like an idiot. So I made all these changes because I realized that I was a mess, and that you were the best thing that's ever happened to me, and... because I *knew* that I blew it."

Ellie just stood there listening as she again switched her stare to the ground.

"But even after I made all those changes, it wasn't enough," he continued. "I *still* didn't feel complete. So I had to try to get you back. That's why I'm here now.

"I'm here now because I was initially terrified that I'd never feel this way about another woman, but then I realized that I simply don't ever *want* to feel this way about another woman – *only you*. I can't stand the thought of not having you to share the rest of my life with."

Ellie quivered and bit her lip – wanting to order Mitch to leave, and also wanting to hear the rest of what he had to say.

"Ya know, after you left, as the months went by, it kept getting harder and harder just to fuckin' breathe," Mitch said. "That's not *supposed* to happen... unless you're meant to be together.

"Even with all the changes and good things that have happened to me, it hasn't been good enough. Accomplishing all these things has felt great, but it's also felt ... incomplete. I've been wanting so badly to tell you everything that's been happening to me. I've been missing so badly everything about you – the stories of your day, hearing your voice, smelling your scent... hell, just *seeing* your smile. And I've been going crazy because I want to share with you everything that's been going on with me.

"When I kicked Chance out, you were the first person I wanted to call. When I got the book deal, the only person I wanted to celebrate with was you. When I finally bought a decent car, all I thought about was our arguments about the name I chose for her. You were completely *engrained* in my life, and it feels so empty without your voice in my ear.

"And, just a few days ago, I realized that I can't love anyone as completely as I love you. So, *that's* why I'm here. I *have* to try to save us."

Ellie stood there as Mitch left that last statement dangling between them. For a moment, neither of them said a word.

"Mitch," she finally began, while choking on tears.

"Look, just give me another chance," Mitch interrupted. "We can do this – we can be even better than before."

"Look Mitch, this isn't one of your stories, OK?" she said with gritted teeth and newly moistened cheeks. "The hero doesn't always get the girl in real life."

"WHY NOT?" Mitch demanded. "What is art if you can't find pieces of your own life within it? Art, movies, books, music... they're all completely valueless unless there's something in it that you can relate to.

"Babe," Mitch sighed as he eased his pleas, "I'm willing to write the happy ending for us, but I need you to play the role of my muse."

Her eyes began to moisten as he continued.

"We *worked* before, hell – we were GREAT before. I *know* it. You can't tell me you don't feel anything for me anymore, can you?"

Ellie could suddenly no longer breathe. She paced back and forth across her doorstep as if there was no place left on Earth where she could stand that would make the aching stop.

"It doesn't matter, Mitch," she stammered, trying to be strong. "This isn't a movie. This is reality. And in *reality*, sometimes... sometimes people don't live happily ever after," she choked. "Sometimes the story doesn't have a happy ending. Sometimes...it just *ends*. No fairy tale, no resolution. Sometimes, in life, things just end."

Mitch saw how conflicted Ellie was becoming.

"OK, look," he said, "I'll make this easy. If you're willing to give us another try, just say 'yes'. If you want me to leave and never bother you again, just say 'no', and I'll go."

As she found it increasingly harder to hide her tears, she simply covered her lips with a finger.

"Aw, Mitch... *dammit*."

Mitch moved towards her with his arms extended, sensing she was about to give him the chance he so desperately wanted.

"I can't lose you," he smiled. "I just..."

"No," she said suddenly, still choking on her tightened throat. "No, Mitch."

Mitch stood there confused, unsure of what she meant.

"Mitch. *No*." her voice shook. "OK? *No*."

Mitch stopped and slowly dropped his arms, realizing the gravity of her words. He let his head fall as he turned and began to walk away. He got about thirty feet from her door when he turned back to see her still standing in the doorway, wiping away tears and quivering.

"I couldn't move on without trying one last time," he called out to her. "I just had to take one last shot at getting you back, 'cause we were just *too* right."

He then turned around again and continued to walk away. Ellie continued to sit at her door, tears streaming down her cheek as she watched him go.

Mitch got about a hundred feet from Ellie's doorstep when he pumped both fists at the heavens and screamed, "LONG LIVE THE DREAMERS!!!"

Upon hearing his cry, Ellie began crying even harder. She watched as Mitch walked to the end of the street, turned the corner, and was gone.

CHAPTER 38

HOW LONG DOES IT TAKE SOMEBODY
BEFORE THEY CAN BE SOMEONE

Mitch was back in his apartment, which only housed indiscriminately scattered moving boxes. He followed his landlord as she inspected every room with her checklist. As she made her way out of the bedroom area and began examining the living room, she noticed a few nicks on the living room wall and shrugged. Mitch just smiled and shook his head. She then proceeded to a large box in the middle of the floor and stopped, looking at it suspiciously.

With a shove of her hip, she moved the box to reveal a black stain hidden by the box. She shook her head and laughed.

"There went the deposit," she smiled.

"OK, OK, I understand," Mitch laughed.

As the movers came back in to grab more boxes, Mitch told them to go ahead and take the big box that the landlady had just shoved. They smiled and nodded as they grabbed the box and carried it out.

As the landlady finished, she turned to Mitch.

"OK, well, everything else seems to be in order," she said as she handed Mitch the checklist. As he quickly signed the paper, she added, "Good luck in L.A."

"Thanks!" he replied.

At that moment, Chance bounded into the apartment with his usual energy.

"You ready?" he asked.

"Yeah," Mitch nodded as he took one last nostalgic look at the place that had been his home for the past ten years.

"OK," he sighed, "let's go."

Chance and Mitch ran down the stairs as if they were college freshmen again, chasing each other and slapping the walls of the hallway while howling as they thundered down the stairs. One more time of disturbing the peace in the complex seemed not only appropriate, but necessary.

As they exited the main door, Chance charged to the driver's side of Mitch's car. Mitch stopped and stood up taller for a second.

"Aw," he mocked. "Chance finally has a car."

"Yeah, fuck off," Chance smiled back. "The title's been transferred and I got the new plates, so don't worry. Now get in before you piss her off."

As Chance pulled up to the airport, he put the car in park and turned to Mitch.

"So, you're still gonna keep in touch, right?" Chance asked. "I mean, you're not going to forget all of us non-celebrities back here, are ya?"

"Chance," Mitch chuckled. "Dude, you're my bud. You always will be. And I'm always gonna need you as my bud – that's not going to change."

"Good!" Chance nodded. "Right back at ya."

Mitch got out of the car and slung his backpack over his shoulder.

Chance reached into the back seat and grabbed a few firecrackers. He rubbed them together in his hands until the gunpowder began falling onto his shoes. He then popped out the drivers' side door.

"Hey, hold up!" Chance called.

"What?" Mitch asked, turning around.

"I'm seeing you off," Chance shrugged, as if it should have been obvious.

"Chance, they won't let you past security without a ticket," Mitch explained.

"I know." Chance said. "I bought one."

"Where are you going?" Mitch asked.

"Through security," he smiled.

Mitch walked up to the security checkpoint, put his bag on the x-ray machine's belt, walked through the sniffer sensor, grabbed his bag on the other side, and started walking to his gate.

Chance followed right behind, walking through the same sniffer sensor. Suddenly alarms erupted and lights flashed. Chance lifted his hands to the heavens and smiled blissfully as the security guards tackled him from behind.

Mitch suddenly spun around to see Chance at the bottom of the pile. He felt a twinge of panic and began to head back to help his friend, but Chance shot him a knowing smile and gave him two thumbs up. They picked him up off the floor and carried him into the security wing of the airport.

Mitch just smiled back and nodded.

"*Good luck with Carrie and Terri, bud,*" he mumbled to himself as he turned back towards his departure gate.

CHAPTER 39

...AS IT SHOULD

One year later, in a small conference room in the Los Angeles Full Service Marriott, the casting for the movie based on Mitch's book had begun. The hanging partitions made the room threateningly deep and narrow for all who entered. At the end of the room, the movie director, the casting director, the producer, a studio executive, and Mitch sat in front of a heavily curtained window that let in just a enough light to give off a soft white glow across the floor.

As actresses came and went from the room, the group briefly discussed everything they'd perceived from each of their cold readings, and made their notes atop the plastic white table. After another actress finished her reading and the group finished their debating, the casting director picked up her walkie-talkie.

"Send the next one in," she ordered.

The door slowly opened and in walked Ellie. Her head was up as she greeted each face - until her eyes came to Mitch, who was seated at the far right of the table. Suddenly, her eyes sank as she tried to keep smiling, even though the smile came off like that of a beauty pageant runner-up.

Mitch froze for a second, unsure that it was Ellie. He quickly looked at the roster and realized that the actor listed as 'Ellie Alexander' was *Ellie*. He suddenly realized that she'd adopted her father's pen name as her new stage name.

Ellie's steps slowed as she got closer to the table, her heart racing harder with each stride. Mitch looked back up at her and squinted with disbelief as she got closer. There was a palpable silence as she came to a stop at the mark on the floor.

"Ms. Alexander," the casting director said, wasting no time. "Please read from the top."

Ellie stared at Mitch with a mix of desperation and confusion. She didn't even respond to the casting director's commands.

Mitch stared back at her, flush with every kind of emotion. But the mixture of all those feelings merely manifested itself as a blank stare across his face.

"Ms. Alexander?" the casting director restated with obvious annoyance. "We don't have all day."

"Oh, of course," Ellie stammered as she shook off Mitch's stare and re-focused.

"Oh God," she began, panicked as she fell into the role. "Should've thought this whole 'escape' thing through a little better."

"Open the door, fivers!" the casting director replied, while trying – and failing – to accurately capture the moment while reading from the script.

"*Downstairs!*" Ellie commanded as she was now fully engrossed in the character. She shuffled her feet as she pretended to run down a non-existent stairwell.

"Sarah?" the casting director said.

"Yeah?" Ellie replied.

"Duck," the casting director said.

Ellie threw herself onto the floor, bouncing in a way that was both painful and, honestly, comical.

"OK," the director interrupted. "That was good. Now read the highlighted lines from scene 21."

Ellie read for all the sections from which they asked her and, honestly, spent more than a fair amount of time showing what she would bring to the role.

After Ellie finished delivering another line, the group sat in silence for a moment. Ellie wasn't sure if they were impressed or horrified, but Ellie knew she'd made an impression.

"Well done," the casting director replied. "We'll let you know. Thank you."

Ellie nodded and smiled, fully aware of the routine. She then thanked them, turned, and walked out of the room.

As the door settled, a fierce debate ensued. Mitch only stared at the door as the producer and casting director, who were sold on Ellie, wanted to send the rest of the actresses home. The studio executive and movie director, however, vehemently insisted that the auditions continue. But Mitch never heard a word as they argued back and forth. His eyes had still not left the doorway.

The casting director suddenly turned to Mitch.

"Mitch, what do you think?" she asked.

Mitch didn't flinch.

"Mitch!" the studio executive yelled. "What did you think?"

Mitch just sighed and slowly turned to them with a look that was one thousand miles away.

"You, um..." he replied uncertainly, "you guys need to excuse me for a second."

The other four moaned and called after him as he jogged for the door, ignoring their protests.

He bolted into the lobby and frantically looked side to side, trying to find Ellie. He suddenly saw her walking towards the revolving door at the front of the hotel. He turned and ran after her.

Before she could reach the door, Mitch grabbed her arm and pulled her back into the lobby. Ellie was talking on her cell phone when her eyes met Mitch. She looked at him with uncertainty.

"Hi," Mitch said.

"Let me call you back," Ellie said into her phone.

Mitch guided her to a column in the lobby and leaned against it as if to provide some semblance of privacy.

"What are you doing here?" Mitch asked.

"My agent got me some auditions in between plays," she explained. "I didn't think this was your novel... the names aren't..."

"Focus groups," Mitch smiled. "The character names didn't fit the demographics."

Ellie smiled, knowing Mitch was finally fully aware of 'the business.'

"Well then," she asked with a smile of justification, "how much of the book is yours?

"The book?" Mitch smiled back and nodded. About 70%. The screenplay? Even less."

Ellie laughed at her little victory, even though it had taken this long to realize it.

"So," Mitch asked, "are you doing OK?"

"Yeah," Ellie sighed. "My career seems to be taking off. I've got a few TV shows that I'll be guest-starring in, and, you know... overall, things are good."

"Well, good to hear," Mitch sighed.

They both leaned against the column silently for a moment and pressed their foreheads against each other, not saying a word.

Mitch then suddenly straightened up.

"Hey," he said, "I gotta get back."

"Yeah," Ellie half smiled as she adjusted her hair. "I gotta get going, too. More auditions, ya know. This agent of mine keeps me movin'. Besides, I'm sure you've got a lot of other aspiring actresses to audition."

"Yeah, I do," Mitch admitted. "But hey, I'm still good with as much time as you've got to give."

Ellie felt her belly pull in a little tighter when she heard that phrase again.

"Hey," Mitch smiled kindly. "Good luck... with *everything*."

"Yeah Mitch," Ellie smiled back and nodded knowingly, "you too."

As she turned away, Mitch called out, "Take care of yourself, babe!!!"

Ellie paused, suddenly remembering how much she loved it when he called her 'babe'. But she then resumed her gait and passed through the revolving door.

Mitch watched her leave the lobby and turn to her right, walking along the 10-foot high plate windows that ran along the sidewalk of the front of the hotel.

As he watched her walking away, he whispered to himself, "Look back at me, look back, look back, *c'mon babe...*"

As Ellie neared the edge of the last window, she peeked back at Mitch through the corner of her eye and smiled softly, all the while tucking her hair behind her ear like he'd seen her do one hundred times before.

As soon as he saw his wish granted, Mitch just smiled. He then turned back and returned to the conference room.

As he re-entered the room and saw the melee at the table, the studio executive looked up at Mitch.

"Well?" he seethed. "We're *waiting...*"

Mitch sighed with a little bit of melancholy. He also stood there and scrutinized the stare from each one of them, then waited for a moment before responding. The little hellion inside of him enjoyed making them sit silently through an intentionally dramatic pause.

They all glared at him with baited breath.

"Let's get the next one in here," he finally replied.

"THANK YOU!" the studio executive announced as she high-fived the director, while the producer and casting director looked to the ceiling and moaned.

The sun was setting on the roof of the parking garage as Mitch walked to his car. His eyes weren't even watching his steps and his thoughts weren't on any of the other actresses – "*or 'actors'*," he thought. He reminisced about Ellie as he approached the car and slung his satchel into the back of his convertible.

He sat in his car, let out a deep sigh, and smiled - feeling a small piece of happiness from knowing that Ellie was truly living her dream, too.

As he turned the key, his phone rang. Mitch looked down, and his caller ID displayed the word "Asshole".

"Chance!" Mitch called out gleefully as he answered the call. "What's up, my brother?"

"How's it goin, my man?" Chance yelled.

"Great! I'm working my ass off, but the movie's coming together. We're breaking for the next two days so we can attend the GLAAD parade tomorrow and then celebrate with Brian and Dave's when they get married tomorrow night."

"Those two guys you've been working on the screenplay with?" Chance asked. "They're a ... *couple?*"

"Chance, I told you that."

"No, I think I'd have remembered that. But, whatever. So you're going to the GLAAD parade tomorrow, too?"

"Oh yeah! Times are a-changing, Chance," Mitch smiled. "This is one of those times I think it's for the better. Brian and Dave are really happy together, and I'm grateful they asked me to attend the wedding. And when have you ever known me to turn down a giant pre-party, right?"

"No shit," Chance replied through the phone as Mitch backed the car out of its parking spot. "That's very cool. Well, enjoy it! But dude, lemme tell you about the game last night!"

"Chance, I've got NHL Center Ice... don't worry. I watched it - in HD on the 70-inch I told you about last week."

"OK dude, stop rubbing it in!"

"Hey, I've offered to fly you out here how many times now?" he corrected as he put the car in drive.

"I know, I know," Chance replied.

"Look, the Blues are playing the Kings here in two weeks," Mitch interrupted. "Lemme take care of you – c'mon out and we can party with some starlets."

"Whatever dude," Chance sneered. "You're not *that* big."

"Well, not *yet*, no. But I'll fake it until I make it," Mitch said as he drove his car out of the garage. "Hey, by the way, you'll never guess who I saw today."

"Don't care, Mitch," Chance said. "The name-dropping is getting a little old. So, I took your advice and mapped out the idea for the novel. Here's the deal."

"Don't tell me you *listened* to me for once," Mitch laughed.

"Shut up for a second," Chance interrupted. "OK, so we got two buddies who... OK, fuck it. This is the *last time though, dude*. Who'd you meet today?"

"Ellie Alexander."

"Um, *OK...*" Chance replied confusedly, not recognizing the name at all.

"Well, that's her stage name – *now*," Mitch said. "It was Ellie, dude! She auditioned today for the role of Sarah. Apparently, she took her dad's pen name as her stage name."

"*'Ellie'* Ellie?" Chance asked in a high pitched voice. "Aw, you pussy! You already gave her the role, didn't ya?"

"Nope," Mitch chuckled. "No, I didn't."

"But you're *going* to," Chance persisted. "You big pussy. You're going to take her back, *just like that*."

"No, dude – we didn't give her the role."

"Well," Chance paused, unsure of how to respond. "Good, then. OK, so here's the story idea. We got two buddies who are broke, and one of them is trying to get published in Penthouse forum..."

"Nice," Mitch said. "So we're not selling this to Disney, are we...?"

"Shut up and let me finish, '*Hollywood*,'" Chance mocked. "So anyway, they go to this yard sale and find a word processor, but it's not *just* a..."

Chance suddenly couldn't let go of what Mitch had just told him, though.

"Are you *really* not going to give her the part?" he asked incredulously.

Mitch merely laughed again.

"Well, we'll see," Mitch admitted. "She's getting a callback tomorrow."

"I KNEW IT!" Chance laughed.

"Fuck off and tell me the rest of your story idea," Mitch insisted.

The light from the sunset glinted off the rear bumper and the Aston Martin logo on the trunk, with the license plate that read "LVD1UWT".

As he listened to the rest of Chance's idea, he began to think it just might work as a great tale. Mitch laughed and nodded along to Chance's ideas as he drove into the Los Angeles sunset.

THE END